also by melissa grace

The Midnight in Dallas Series

Home Is Where You Are

Home Again

Long Way Home

Feels Like Home

Coming Home

praise for marjorie & me

"I laughed, cried, and couldn't put it down." —Abby Jimenez, *New York Times* bestselling author

"I blew through *Marjorie & Me*! Melissa Grace writes a big beautiful story about the power of female friendship and never giving up on the love we deserve. May we all be so lucky to have a ghostly mentor like Marjorie in our lives. A spooky delight of a book!" —Katie Garaby, Parnassus Books in Nashville, TN

"Melissa Grace has crafted one of the sweetest, most endearing stories of love, unfinished business, and almost-lost opportunities. This is one you'll want to hold close to your heart." —Thomas Wallace, Reading Rock Books in Dickson, TN

"A poignant and whimsical journey of unlikely friendship, and fighting for true love. *Marjorie and Me* will warm your heart, charm your soul, and have you remembering what it feels like to fall in love." —Leah Brunner, author of the *DC Eagles* series

"A beautiful story about finding friends, family, and love in unexpected places, *Marjorie & Me* is one of those truly special books that leave you wishing you could read it again for the very first time." —Jen Davis, author of *For Eva*

"*Marjorie and Me* is the story of how magical the friendship bonds between women can be, often crossing generations, and in the case of Marj and Kat, even planes of existence!" — Lauren H. Mae, author of *The Fate Factor*

Marjorie & Me

Marjorie & Me

MELISSA GRACE

This book belongs to those who've lost someone they love.
May you find pieces of them within these pages.
May you find yourself too.

chapter one

"WAIT, SO HE TOOK YOU TO KAYNE PRIME LAST NIGHT?"
Becca Flores plunks her freshly-refilled water bottle on the
table and takes her seat beside me in the studio during the last
break of the eight o'clock hour. "But you don't eat red meat."

I stare ahead at the KWSL logo emblazoned on the wall
across from us. It's surrounded by awards won well before my
time as a cast member of the top-ranking morning radio
program in the country.

"I don't usually," I admit. "I didn't want to mention it or
make it a thing, though, you know? It's not a big deal." I don't
mention that my date, Ethan, felt compelled to sit beside me
in the booth instead of across. Same-side sitters freak me out
because I hate hearing people chew, and I don't need to be in
such close proximity to anyone's onion breath. But it was just
one dinner. Not an offense worth writing someone off over.

Becca lifts her brows at me and sips through her straw.
With the genes of her Italian-model mother and her ridiculously good-looking Mexican father, she's one of those effort-
lessly beautiful women who can come in wearing yoga pants
every morning without so much as a dot of concealer and still

manage to look like she's doing a shoot for *Vogue*. Not to mention that she graduated from Berkeley and plays drums in a popular cover band. She doesn't have to worry about impressing the people she dates because her mere existence is spectacular. It would be annoying if she wasn't also one of the kindest people on the planet and my best friend of five years.

"When are you seeing him again?" she asks.

"We were supposed to get together tonight, but he's got to be Dungeon Master for his friends."

She heaves a dramatic sigh. "Please tell me that's code for something kinky."

"Har, har," I say. "It's something to do with a role-playing game. Anyway, I'm going to go watch him at his recreational soccer match on Saturday instead."

"But you hate sports."

"I don't *hate* sports," I say. "I like David Beckham?"

"Because he looks good in a suit." She pins me with an accusatory glare.

"What?"

"It's just that, from what I can tell, you have nothing in common with this guy," she answers. "On your second date, he took you on a five-mile hike."

"It was a scenic view."

"No offense, but you're more of an indoor cat. And what about your first date?"

I run my fingers through my long dark hair. "We met for a drink."

"He took you to a wine bar. You don't even drink wine, Kat."

"You make me sound like I'm boring and hate everything."

"That's not what I'm saying. You like thrifting and

karaoke in dive bars. You somehow suffer through yoga classes when they make me want to namaste my ass in bed," she ticks off. "You read, and you know the words to every nineties pop song ever written. But do any of these guys you date know that? Do they know that you, Kathryn Simon, are the funniest person to play Cards Against Humanity with or that you actually like bourbon? Do they know a single thing about you?"

"Of course they do," I insist, but even as the words come out of my mouth, I wonder if they're true. I never even give the guys I date my nickname on the off chance they're listeners of *Eddie in the Morning*.

"You not being able to get past a third date would suggest otherwise."

Before I can argue, our cohosts, Eddie and Jude, return to the studio and take their seats, signaling the end of our break. The four of us are tucked around a circular black table, one that could easily hold a family of four chatting about their days over lumpy mashed potatoes and dry meatloaf. Not that I've had any experience in that area in twenty-two years.

"Last hour. Let's do this." Eddie slips his headphones back on, and we do the same.

"You're listening to Eddie in the Morning *with Eddie, Becca, Kat, and Jude, and we're paging Dr. Love."*

The music of the prerecorded lead-in ends, leaving Eddie's silky voice to fill our ears and the airwaves. "We're ten minutes into the nine o'clock hour, which hopefully means the kiddos are out of the car because we're about to get into some of our adult content. Every Friday we do a segment called 'Paging Dr. Love' where we help you get your love life back on track. So if you need advice on dating, sex, or relationships, you can call us up right now, and we'll give you our completely unbiased and unprofessional thoughts on what you should do."

"Hey, you've been married for what? Twenty years?" Becca asks Eddie, her long dark hair and the gray hood of her sweatshirt framing her face.

"Nineteen," he answers. He smooths a hand over his bald head. Eddie Englund is the namesake of our show and my mentor. I started as his intern when I was twenty-one, back when he was the only Black radio personality employed by KWSL Nashville—before he became the industry powerhouse he is today.

"At least one of us knows what we're doing," Becca adds.

"And it's definitely not me." It's a known fact amongst my friends and listeners alike that I haven't made it past a third date in three years.

Not since Nick.

But that's all changing with Ethan. This weekend, I'll break my streak.

"Do as she says, not as she does, folks." Eddie chuckles as our producer, Cassie, sends us the information about our first caller via Teams, which we can see on our laptops. "It amazes me every week that you fine people want our advice, but it seems Megan here is hoping for exactly that. Good morning, Megan."

"Hi," she drawls. "I'm such a big fan of the show. Eddie, I've been listening to you since back when you did the top five at five."

"Then we've been together a long time, haven't we? That was—what? Twenty-five years ago?" The joy on Eddie's face is evident in his voice. "I think I still had hair the last time I did afternoons."

"And Kat, I just want to tell you I love you so much,"

Megan says. "I'm a few years older than you, but I relate to your dating struggles a lot."

"Aw, thanks, friend. I appreciate that." Hearing things like this never gets old. "So, our producer tells us you're having some dating trouble. What's going on?"

"Okay, so there's this guy," she begins.

Jude speaks up. "And that's your first problem." It's easy to forget sometimes that Jude Keller grew up in Georgia when he looks like the love child of the ocean and the California shoreline.

"Took the words right out of my mouth," I tease. "Doesn't every problem start with some guy?"

"To be fair, I date both men and women," Becca interjects, "and there are plenty of problematic people of all kinds out there."

"What's going on with this guy, Megan?" Eddie asks, bringing us back to focus.

She sighs. "Well, my coworker set us up, and he seemed great. He's got a good job, he's nice looking. He actually calls instead of texts."

"That's considered a good thing?" Becca asks. "I don't use my phone for that. Anyway, continue. I sense a 'but' coming on."

Megan gives a nervous laugh. "We met for dinner last night, and things were amazing at first. He pulled my chair out for me and ordered us a bottle of wine. The conversation and drinks were flowing, and then…something weird happened. And I'm trying to decide whether it's a deal-breaker or not."

"What happened?" Eddie nudges.

"I was telling him about my new puppy," Megan explains.

"He got really sad and told me his dog passed away from cancer."

Becca frowns. "That's terrible."

"It is," Megan agrees, then hesitates. "It's just what he said afterward that kind of freaked me out."

"Don't leave us in suspense," Jude prods. "What did he say?"

"He told me she's always with him," she continues, and my fellow cast members and I exchange sympathetic glances. "And I said of course she is—that she'll always be in his heart."

"That's sweet," Eddie says. "What's wrong with th—"

She cuts him off. "But he said no. That she's in his trunk."

Audible gasps fill the studio.

"What?" the four of us cry.

My stomach churns. "What does that mean, exactly?"

"Yeah, did he maybe have the dog's ashes in his car?" Jude asks. "Because I get that, especially if it happened recently."

"It was three years ago," Megan clarifies.

"Well, grief knows no timeline, right?" Leave it to empathetic Jude to give this guy the benefit of the doubt.

Then Megan delivers the final blow. "It's taxidermied."

Eddie explodes into raucous laughter and has to back away from the mic, while Becca looks as though she's going to hurl.

"Nope," I say. "Absolutely not."

"Now hang on a minute," Jude begins, but I hold out a hand to stop him.

"Let's say she overlooks this, they get married, and live happily ever after," I say. "What happens if she dies first? Is he gonna be driving around with *her* taxidermied corpse riding shotgun? This is totally a deal-breaker."

"Yeah, Megan," Becca adds. "You better run, girl."

"I mean, yeah, the taxidermy thing is a little weird," Jude concedes.

My flabber is ghasted. "A *little*?"

"Would it be any different if it was just the ashes?" he asks.

"No," I deadpan.

"But—"

"No," Becca and I say together.

"I'm with the girls on this one," Eddie chimes in. "I could give the guy a pass if it was the dog's ashes, but even then, three years seems like a long time to be riding around with them in your car. I don't think you can come back from this, Megan."

"Oh, come on. Give the guy a chance. At least you know he's sentimental," Jude offers with a smirk. "I mean, a lot of guys can't even remember an anniversary."

"The bar really is on the floor, isn't it?" Becca asks.

"The bar is in hell," I say.

"That's for sure," Megan agrees. "Yeah, I think you guys are right. I can't go out with this guy again. It's too weird for me."

"But don't give up the good fight, all right? Your person is out there. I feel it in my bones." Eddie says this with such confidence that I almost believe it could be true for me too.

A message from Cassie containing the info for our next caller pops up on my laptop screen as we end our chat with Megan.

"Next we have E on the line, and our producer tells me

you need help letting someone down easy," Eddie says. "Tell us what's going on, E."

The caller blows out a breath before his deep voice fills my ears. "I've been seeing this girl. We went out a few times, and I'm supposed to see her again this weekend, but…I don't know, guys. It's just not gonna work."

Goose bumps spread over my arms. God, this guy sounds familiar. His gravelly tone does remind me of the narrator of the book I was listening to on the drive to work this morning. That's got to be it.

"Did something happen?" Becca asks. "Was the chemistry off?"

"She has no personality," E explains. "Every time I ask her about herself, she changes the subject back to me. I don't even know what she does for a living."

I swallow hard, Becca's words from moments ago piercing my thoughts.

Jude cocks his head. "Wow, really? In our career-obsessed society, that seems almost impossible."

"Maybe she's just trying to show she likes you," Becca reasons. "I've been on a lot of dates where the other person won't shut up about themselves. Someone asking questions and showing some interest doesn't sound so bad."

"We've been out three times, and I don't know a single thing about her," he says.

I bite down on the inside of my cheek, a pit forming in my stomach. Why does this feel personal? I don't normally get so…triggered by a caller, but every word he says lands like a direct hit. I attempt to shove the thoughts down. Becca just got in my head. There's no way this is Ethan. Besides, if it was, why wouldn't he say that instead of calling himself E?

"Anyway, she wants to see me this weekend, and I need to

let her know I'm not interested," E continues. "I don't want to ghost because I'm not a jerk, you know? So, I was hoping you guys could help me craft a text to send to her."

Jude nods. "You've come to the right place."

"Hold on a sec," Becca says. "Are you sure you don't want to give this another shot or at least have a conversation? I feel bad for this girl because what if she was just nervous?"

E hesitates. "Look, if she was a ten, maybe, but this chick is a six at best."

Becca's eyes roll so far back in her head, I fear they'll get stuck.

There's no way he's talking about me…right? I'm at least an eight. Okay, maybe a seven and a half. I'm suddenly self-conscious of the oversized sweatshirt and jeans I put on this morning. Picking out the perfect outfit at 4:30 in the morning isn't at the top of my priority list, but no matter what I dress my midsize body in, I like to think I'm pretty cute.

What are the odds Ethan would call in to *my* show, anyway? Sure, it's popular, but that doesn't mean he listens.

"Dude, seriously?" Jude asks, rubbing his hand over the back of his neck. "That's not nice."

Eddie lifts his brows in my direction, as though he's telepathically asking if I'm going to stare a hole into the wall or actually participate in my job.

"You must be an eleven," I say, but my usual spunk is gone, and the words just come out sad.

"Oh, I am," E says with a confidence he does not deserve. "And she has these tattoos all over her arms. Tattoos are fine, I guess, but hers are just so basic. I mean, flowers? How creative."

His sardonic tone makes my cheeks flame as I tug the sleeves of my black sweatshirt over my fingertips, covering the grayscale magnolia sleeves inked on my pale skin. The blooms represent my grandmother's favorite flower and the middle name she gave my mother—the very same one passed down to me.

"What's your problem, man? Tattoos are cool." Jude's gaze snags on me. "A lot of tattoos have some sort of meaning behind them. What you see as 'basic' might symbolize something meaningful to her."

"Don't bother, Jude," Becca says. "Let's just send this poor woman a text and put her out of her misery."

"Obviously, you need to type her name first," Eddie begins. "Surely you at least know that much about her."

"And maybe something like 'I've really enjoyed hanging out with you, but I think we're looking for different things,'" Becca offers. "'I wish you all the best in finding what you're searching for.'"

"Yep," E replies. "Okay. Hey, Kathryn..." He says it slowly, then repeats the message Becca crafted for him word for word as the blood drains from my face.

"That's good," Jude says. "Send that."

I'm cold and hot at the same time. My throat feels like it's three times its normal size. It can't be me. Kathryn is a common name. And as E has so astutely pointed out, floral tattoos aren't exactly unique. There's no way. There's no—

A text pops up on my laptop. The words blur in front of me, but that's okay. I don't need to read the message because I already know what it says.

"Ethan?" I ask. The air is sucked from the room, taking all sound with it except for that of my heart pounding in my ears.

Becca gasps, her hands covering her mouth.

"Wait, how do you know my name?" he asks.

"Because it's me. I'm Kathryn." My eyes burn. "You

know, the *six at best*." For a moment, I'm eleven years old again in Coach Cantrell's gym class, wetting my pants because he refused to give me the hall pass.

Becca reaches for my arm, and Jude clenches his jaw.

Before any of us can say anything, a dial tone fills our headphones.

Eddie, the consummate professional he is, swoops in to pull me from the rubble of my broken dating dreams.

"Coming up next we have your chance to win two tickets to the KWSL birthday bash, right here on *Eddie in the Morning*. We'll be right back."

chapter two

I SPEND THE REST OF THE NINE O'CLOCK HOUR HIDING IN THE break room of the marketing office downstairs, but not before doing the walk of shame to the elevator, passing the pitying gazes of interns and producers as I flee the scene. I'm used to my personal life being content for the show. But the stories I share on the radio are carefully curated anecdotes. It's one thing to put out a three-minute segment about my dating woes but having someone say I'm a solid six who's blander than a piece of dry toast—on a show that broadcasts all across the country, no less—is entirely different.

Most people at least get the courtesy of being ghosted or rejected in private, but it happened to me with over a million tuning in. As much as I wanted to go straight home and pull the covers over my head, I still had another hour to go.

After downing a cup of coffee, I stand tall and take the elevator back up for our weekly staff meeting, catching a glimpse of my reflection in the mirrored doors. *Ugh. Maybe I am a six.*

The meeting begins with our usual check-ins and content pitches for the following week. We spend the majority of the hour ignoring the elephant-sized rebuff heard round the world, but I know there's no way I'm walking out of here unscathed.

"Finally, I think we need to address what happened," Eddie says, casting a sympathetic smile in my direction.

"Can we not?" I ask, running my finger over the rim of my coffee mug. "If we could pretend it never happened, that'd be great, thanks."

Becca rests her forearms on the table. "Kat, that guy is a jackass. Everyone who listens knows you have one of the best personalities. You're witty and kind. You're always looking for ways to give back to the community and make our lives better."

"Our annual back-to-school supply drive wouldn't exist without you," Jude reminds me, pushing a hand through his golden hair.

"And I can always count on you to scream-sing Britney Spears songs in the car with me when I'm sad." Becca reaches across the table to squeeze my hand. "I love you. That guy doesn't know what he's talking about."

"They're right," Eddie says. "And I think you're in a unique situation here."

I look at him with pleading eyes. "No. I don't want to turn this into a bit. All I want is to forget about it."

"And we will if that's what you want," he continues. "But hear me out first, okay?"

I sigh and manage a reluctant nod.

"After you left the studio, we got dozens of calls in support of you," Eddie explains. "And the social media team has already been bombarded with messages."

"I don't want people's sympathy," I start, but Eddie holds up a hand to cut me off.

"That's not what we're getting. Yes, there are a lot of folks who empathize with what happened, but it was more than that. People were proud of you for not taking it lying down. You could have acted like you didn't know him, but instead you called him on his mean comment toward you. Listeners have always gravitated to your dating stories, but this...*this* has made them invested in seeing you get your happy ending."

I choke out a dry laugh. "Yeah, well, as you can see, I'm closer to walking on the moon than that ever happening."

"Except that we're already hearing from dozens of men who want to take you out, to show you not all guys are eggheads like Ethan," Eddie says. "By the time this segment hits the podcast later, I'm guessing that number could be in the hundreds."

I groan. I hadn't even allowed myself to think about the online listeners, the ones who find us through social media clips or the daily podcast we put out for those not in our syndicated markets. Now my humiliation will live on for days, maybe even weeks to come, as people discover it through these other channels.

That's just perfect.

"I'm not sure I like where this is going." I sit back and fold my arms over my chest. "You want me to use the show as my own personal ad?"

"What if we screen everyone and pick your dates for you?" Becca asks. "Because no offense, but you kind of suck at it. I think your picker might be broken."

My mouth falls open. "You're supposed to be on my side."

"I am," she says. "Of course I am. But what if we can actually find the right guy for you or at the very least, end this three-date streak once and for all. Maybe you're looking in the wrong places. Maybe you're trying too hard and not letting these guys see how amazing you are. Or maybe the entire male population has lost their ever-loving minds, but we can't know for sure until we give this a real shot."

I narrow my eyes. "What exactly are you suggesting?"

"Like Becca said, we would screen everyone ourselves and pick who we think would be your best matches. We'll set up the dates for you, and after each one, we'll get feedback—from you *and* the other person. It'll be a prerecorded segment, so we can avoid a repeat of what happened today. It'll be a dating report card of sorts, but it's also bigger than that. This isn't just about finding the right person. It's about overcoming —brushing yourself off and trying again."

I take a sip of my coffee. "Y'all were *busy* the last hour, huh?"

"It's just an idea," Eddie says. "One that won't happen without your consent."

Becca nods her agreement. "But I think you should consider it, and not just because it'll make for great radio. Kat, you deserve something *good*. You deserve to get past the three-date mark with somebody—somebody who not only knows you're a ten but who loves everything about you."

I press my fingertips to my temples and blow out a breath before turning to Jude.

"You've been awfully quiet," I say. "What do you think of all this?"

Jude and I rose in the ranks together with him being two years ahead of me. He was a phone screener while I was an intern, but unlike some of the others that came up with me, he never acted like we were competition. He only ever treated me as a friend.

He drags his teeth over his bottom lip. "I think what that

guy did back there sucked and I…we all just want you to be happy."

I raise my brows. "That's a cop-out answer if I ever heard one."

He shakes his head and chuckles softly. "It *would* be *great* radio, but I don't think that's a reason to do it. It has to be something you want."

"How many dates are we talking?" I ask, causing Becca and Eddie's faces to light up. "*Not* that I'm agreeing to anything yet."

"As many as it takes to find the right guy," Eddie answers. "But of course, we'll do whatever you're comfortable with."

I tap a raisin-colored nail against my mug. "Look, I need some time to process what happened today. Can I have the weekend to mull it over?"

"Of course," Eddie says. "If we're going to run with this idea, I think we should start rolling it out first of the week. But I mean it, Kat, it's okay to say no."

I nod. "I'll think about it."

Eddie claps his hands together. "All right. Meeting adjourned. Y'all have a good weekend."

I start to stand, but Eddie holds out a hand. "Do you mind sticking around for a sec?"

"Okay." I sink back into my chair as Becca rounds the table, bending down to hug me and kiss me on the cheek.

"I've got my passport ready, and I'm fully prepared to make the trip out to Jingo tonight," she teases.

Everyone always gives me shit about choosing to live in a small town forty-five minutes from downtown Nashville where our studio is, but I don't care. Nothing beats the charm of a city with only three stoplights and not having to hear your next-door neighbor sneeze through paper-thin walls.

"Thanks, babe," I say as she heads for the door. "I'll let you know."

Jude squeezes my shoulder. "For the record, you've never been a six."

"Not even when I lost that bet last year and had to wear my makeup like the Joker the entire week of Halloween?" I ask.

A smile tugs at the corner of his mouth. "Not even then."

Jude holds his hand up in a wave and shuts the door on his way out, leaving Eddie and me alone.

He regards me with the sincerity of a concerned father whose daughter just got her heart broken for the first time.

"You okay?" he asks.

"Yeah, of course. I'm fine."

"None of what that loser said was true. You know that, right?"

"What if it is, though?"

"Kathryn Simon," he chides. "Don't you dare give that asshat a second thought."

"I just mean there *is* a common denominator in all these failed relationships, and it's me," I say. "You can't deny that."

"I can, and I will," he insists. "You're too good for all these fools. For every single man who didn't see what he had right in front of him."

A lump forms in my throat because I know he's no longer just referring to the men I've dated. When I started as an intern at KWSL, Eddie didn't just become my mentor. He became the father I never had.

Or had, then lost.

Eddie went above and beyond the scope of a professional guide. Under his steadfast leadership, I worked my way up from intern to assistant producer, to full-fledged producer, to gaining a coveted spot as a cast member seven years ago. But over the years, he's done much more than help me find my voice. He delivered groceries to my door when I got Covid during the height of the pandemic and once picked me up on the side of I-65 when my car broke down in the middle of the night. When my beloved grandmother passed away my second year at the station, he sat beside me at the funeral, right where my dad should have been, and he's been sitting beside me ever since.

He leans forward, fixing his dark brown eyes on me. "You've been dealt some difficult hands over the years, kid, but you've never folded. You go all in every time. Don't let this time be any different."

"I won't," I promise.

He studies me, as though looking for any hint of doubt before he finally nods.

"Kat, there's another reason I asked you to stay behind. I need to tell you something." His voice is serious, stoic. "And it's big."

"Way to bury the lede, man," I tease, though my stomach is a clenched fist. What could it be? In a matter of half a second, my mind leaps from the station going bankrupt to life-threatening illness.

"I've been waiting to tell you until I knew for certain," he says. "And I'm sorry to do it today after—"

"You're freaking me out, Eddie. Just spill it."

"I'm retiring at the end of next year."

I exhale a sigh of relief. "Geez, I thought you were dying or something."

He grins. "But if I did die, would you taxidermy my body and keep it in your car?"

"You know, it would let me use the HOV lane, which would come in handy. So, it's not a no."

We both laugh, but the respite I feel is short-lived. Eddie is leaving. He's the heartbeat of the program, of the entire station.

I can barely swallow. "What does this mean for the show? It's *Eddie in the Morning*. There's no show without you."

"Don't know yet," he admits. "There are still a lot of discussions to be had. But it's time, Kat. The kids are grown and out of the house. Tai wants to travel more, and God knows neither of us are getting any younger."

I can't deny he deserves this. He's earned the right to ride off into the sunset and enjoy sleeping past 4 a.m. But selfishly, I don't want him to go. Not just because his retirement potentially puts my job in jeopardy. What happens when we no longer see each other at work every day? Will I lose him the way I've lost everyone else?

"Can we keep this between us for now?" he asks. "Until I know more about next steps, I'd prefer not to tell Becca and Jude."

"Of course," I say, though my own voice sounds far away. "I won't say a word."

"Thanks." He gives me a soft smile, rising from his seat. "Well, get on outta here and try to enjoy your weekend, all right? Don't let what that guy said get to you."

I stand and move toward the door, but Eddie stops me one last time, enveloping me in his arms. It's not until then that I feel the corners of my eyes begin to sting.

"I just want you to know that whatever happens next, I'm always gonna be a part of your life, kid," he says, his voice low. "No matter what changes, this remains."

My words get lodged in my throat, and all I manage is a weak nod before pulling out of his embrace, all but sprinting for the exit.

I don't look back.

chapter three

The bell above the old batten door chimes, and the scuffed wood floor creaks beneath the weight of my boots. A soothing cocktail of lavender, patchouli, and Earl Grey tea wrap me in a dreamy warmth, like one of those fancy, over-priced throw blankets that line store shelves this time of year in anticipation of holiday gift exchanges, chilly evenings, and the desire to hibernate the second it starts getting dark at 4 p.m. With only two weeks left in October, the latter is imminent, and I'm soaking up every last ray of sunshine my pale behind can get.

"Kat, I was hoping I'd see you today." The owner of Whimsy and Wu gives me an empathetic smile from behind the counter, tipping his to-go cup with a tea tag hanging off the side toward me in greeting. A sense of peace washes over me, taking some of the stress from the morning with it. This is my happy place, and it's exactly where I need to be after the whole Ethan debacle and my talk with Eddie.

The sign above the register could have easily been purchased from a pixie in a woodland forest, with scripted letters comprised of colorful blooms and expertly carved oak.

Considering that well over half of the contents of my house came from this magical shop, it feels like home.

"Hey," I call, stepping farther inside with the black coffee I picked up on my way over, blowing my espresso-colored bangs out of my eyes.

Dennis Wu's olive skin is swathed in a cream turtleneck and a cashmere blanket scarf that would look ridiculous on anyone but him and Lenny Kravitz. The man possesses more style and charisma in his perfectly-polished pinkie nail than I have in my entire body.

"So," he says in his velvety baritone, dragging out the *o* while peering at me over the rim of his round tortoiseshell frames. "I'm sorry to hear about what happened with the boy."

Being a personality on the top syndicated morning show means everyone already knows my business before I ever have to tell them, which I suppose has its benefits. At least I don't have to relive the pain from incidents like the one that happened this morning over and over again.

"At thirty-five, are they still boys?" I ask.

He takes a sip of his tea. "The fact that you're asking tells me all I need to know about why you're still single. Of course they are."

"Even you?" I ask as I approach the counter, resting my forearms over the smooth reclaimed wood.

"Especially me. I'm a forty-year-old teenager. Honestly, I don't know how Thomas has put up with me these last thirteen years. Must be because I'm devilishly handsome and debonair. Anyway, enough about me." He boops my nose with his finger. "How are *you*?"

I force a smile. "I'm fine. It's not like I thought we had

some great love connection. I *did* think I was gonna finally make it to date four, but I guess it wasn't meant to be."

He comes around the counter and wraps me in a hug.

"That doesn't make it hurt any less," he says. "That guy is a loser who doesn't deserve to breathe the same air as you, all right? All that nonsense about being an eleven. I bet he looks like a hemorrhoid."

I snort. "Thanks. I guess if I want to know what a stable romantic relationship looks like, I'm going to have to keep living vicariously through you."

"I'm a married man, Kathryn. Romance is dead," he whines. "Do you know what Thomas and I did on our last date night? We drove forty-five minutes into Nashville to buy toilet paper in bulk from Costco."

"That sounds pretty incredible to me. All those free samples on the little toothpicks? It's like getting a mystery charcuterie board."

He rolls his chestnut eyes. "Yes, I love putting fresh dog food next to the prosciutto. Really adds an unexpected pop of flavor."

I scrunch my nose. "Ew."

"Exactly. So, what's next? Maybe we should revamp your dating profile. Last I saw all you had on there besides your photos was some quirky tagline about how much coffee you drink. They should probably know more about you than your caffeine intake, which should be studied, by the way," he quips. "As far as I know, you've never even told any of these guys about your job, and that's one of the things you love most. Plus, it's a really interesting fact about you."

I groan, trying on an old spoon ring from the display on the counter. "I don't even want to think about my stupid profile. Or dating."

"Do we need a sip and swipe date? I'll bring the bourbon and we can reject every man on Bumble."

I laugh as I begin to move through the shop, weaving around the pre-loved objects: knickknacks that once rested on mantles, paintings that watched as families caught up about their days over dinner, and clocks that judged people for decades over their lack of punctuality.

"I don't think so, but Eddie did talk to me about possibly turning this whole situation into a segment," I say, unable to keep the annoyance from my voice. "Like I'm some *Bachelorette* science project gone wrong."

Dennis follows close on my heels, straightening a worn copy of *Wuthering Heights* on a shelf next to a 1960s-era typewriter.

"Oh?" he asks. "What did he say?"

I fill him in on the meeting, telling him everything Becca and Eddie said.

"You have to do it," Dennis insists once I'm finished. "This is too good an opportunity to pass up."

"And you're basing this on…what?" I pause, my finger lingering on an old rolltop desk.

"Well, I wasn't going to say anything because I knew you were probably in a delicate place, but since Eddie mentioned it first…" he begins, tidying a few ceramic bowls that line an arched rattan shelf beside me. "I did take a gander at the station's social media pages after all this went down. Eddie's right. You have so much support behind you, and there are guys in these comments who want to take you out."

I haven't been able to so much as open Instagram for fear of what might be waiting for me. Even when the court of public opinion is on my side, I don't like how much it gets in my head.

"What makes you think these guys are any better than Ethan?" I ask.

"I'm not saying they are, but with the rest of the cast vetting them, I think you have a better shot at finding someone who could be a potential match."

"I don't know. This just seems like another way for me to be humiliated."

"What you've been doing isn't working," he says. "Not since…well, you know."

"Nick," I finish for him. "You can say his name. You're not summoning a demon."

"And I know you don't want to hear it, but I think your friend Becca had it right. What if there's something you're doing to keep people from getting close to you? Or maybe you're attracting unserious and emotionally unavailable men because you yourself are emotionally unavailable."

"You're a lot less fun since you started listening to those self-help podcasts," I tease. "Can we go back to the time in our friendship when you automatically assumed I did no wrong?"

"Can't." A sly grin creeps over his mouth. "I know too much. I've seen where the bodies are buried."

I take a sip of my coffee. "Because you helped me hide them. So do I have to pay extra for the therapy or is that free?"

"Consider it a special for friends and family," he says with a smirk as he starts back toward the counter. "I just want you to find someone worthy of you, but you can't do that if you won't let people get to know you. And I happen to think you're something special. You're one of my favorite people, and that's saying something. Because I hate everyone."

I laugh as I follow him to the front and set my cup down. "Which is fair."

Dennis's smile settles into something more serious as he studies me.

"Is anything else going on?" he asks. "Besides this Ethan stuff?"

"What do you mean?" I school my expression, keeping it as neutral as I can.

"You just seem…off. Sad. Your energy feels different."

"Well, I did get embarrassed on national radio this morning, so I'm sure that has something to do with it." *Or the fact that I haven't made it past a third date in three years. Take your pick.*

He hums in response. I'm fairly certain he doesn't believe me, but he lets it go anyway, and I'm grateful.

I drop my gaze to the ground, and something shimmery catches my eye. A faded cardboard box rests on the floor next to the checkout, filled with various items: a table lamp with no shade, some sort of floral painting in shades of pink, and mismatched candlesticks. But what catches my eye is a sparkling vessel, a vase that appears as though it's been encased in champagne bubbles.

I rescue it from the pile. Something so beautiful should never be tucked away in a dusty old box.

"Where did this come from?" I ask, turning it in my hands, mesmerized as the light dances over the surface.

Dennis takes a sip of his tea. "Burton came by today with some of the rejects from his latest storage unit purchase."

"*This* was a reject?"

He shrugs. "He said it was a fake. Nothing valuable."

"But it's gorgeous." My chest tightened as dozens of broken reflections gazed back at me. How could someone cast something so lovely aside, regardless of what it's worth? "How much?"

Dennis cocks his head to the side. "For you? Ten dollars."

"Sold," I say, digging into my bag for my wallet as the bell above the door chimes.

"Welcome in." Dennis swipes my card as he greets the customer who replies with a polite nod. "So, brunch on Sunday?"

"Dawn's Diner?"

"Cinnamon roll tower and bottomless mimosas?" He waggles his brows as he reaches for the twinkling urn, stopping abruptly once it's in his grasp. He brings it to his ear and gives it a gentle shake. "Oh my God. Is someone in here?"

I choke on a laugh. "Well, for ten dollars, they're coming home with me."

"Suit yourself," he says before wrapping it in a sheet of brown paper and placing it into a bag. "See you Sunday."

"See you." I loop the handle over my arm and grab my coffee, stepping back out into the brisk autumn air.

chapter four

I SLEEP IN TILL 11 A.M. SATURDAY AND SPEND THE afternoon running errands, starring in my own melodramatic music video set to my favorite sad girl autumn playlist. The rain splattering against the windshield and the leaves blowing in the wind are unpaid supporting actors. I only pause my performance long enough for the clerk at the grocery pickup to load my things in the trunk.

The gravel crunches beneath the tires of my SUV as I pull into the drive and park to the side of the cottage I call home. It's white brick with hot pink shutters and a full-length covered porch perfect for sunset watching. If Barbie were looking for real estate in Tennessee, this would be it.

With the hood of my sweatshirt pulled over my head, I scurry around back to grab my food when the bag I'd left in my car from Whimsy and Wu yesterday catches my eye. I manage to haul everything inside in a single trip, including the vase, placing it on the butcher-block countertop with a thud.

A soft meow greets me as my seven-year-old Ragamuffin cat, Delilah, circles my feet. She was named after my favorite radio personality, the host of *Delilah After Dark*. It was her words that comforted me when I had a hard time falling asleep after I lost my mom at thirteen, which was most nights. Her voice became a beacon of hope, one I wanted to become for others someday.

"Delilah," I sing, stooping to scratch the top of her head, but instead of soaking up the pets as she normally does, she bolts across the open space and dives under the couch.

"Nice to see you too," I mutter, beginning to put away the groceries, pausing long enough to pop open a cold beer. With the food stashed away, I unpack the glittering vase, setting it on top of the bar for now, resolving to find it a more permanent home later.

I pad into the bedroom and kick my shoes off before unhooking my bra from beneath my sweatshirt, slingshotting it onto the dresser. After swapping out the jeans I'd thrown on from yesterday for sweatpants and fuzzy socks, I head to the en suite and push up my sleeves. Just as I'm about to run water in the sink to wash my face, a yowling noise causes me to freeze with my hand on the faucet.

What the hell was that? I poke my head out of the bathroom and wait. Another deep, bellowing wail that sounds like something you'd hear in one of those horror movies about demonic possessions echoes throughout the house. I'd only heard it one other time, when Delilah came toe to toe with the neighbor's escaped Chihuahua on the back patio. She didn't go outside for a month after that.

"Delilah?" I call, waiting as though she might answer. *Never mind. All good here. Just saw a weird shadow on the wall. Going to the litter box—you need anything?*

A low growl pierces the air, and I panic. She's never done that before. I'm convinced there's an intruder, and I've left my damn phone in the kitchen, rendering me unable to call for help. Someone is here to burgle me or kill me. Possibly both. With trembling fingers, I reach for the closest thing resembling a weapon I can find—a curling iron. My breath shakes as I tiptoe from the room, mentally running through my options of what to do when I come face-to-face with my attacker. Bludgeon them with the barrel or strangle them with the cord?

So, basically, I'm about to die. What a fantastic ending to an already craptastic week.

I hold my breath as I creep down the hall, back toward the kitchen, where Delilah's snarls are getting louder, coming to a stop when I hear a woman's voice.

"Stop that, you vile beast." Assertive and southern, it sounds like old money. Not like someone intent on making my death the next true crime documentary.

My heart pounds against my ribs when I round the corner, curling iron poised to strike.

Delilah's gray and white fur is standing straight up, her eyes focused on a woman who looks to be in her sixties with shoulder-length auburn hair, wearing a peach skirt set. The top button of her sweater is open, revealing a classic strand of pearls.

What the hell kind of burglar is this?

"Hey!" I shout. "Who are you, and what are you doing in my house?"

She has the audacity to look at me like I'm an inconvenience.

"What do you suppose you'll do with that, hmm?" she asks. "Curl me to death? I survived the eighties without getting a perm, and I'll survive you too."

My mouth drops open as my gaze falls to her feet, clad in nude pumps.

"Who wears heels to rob someone?" I fire back.

"Rob you?" She barks out an unamused laugh. "Of what? A pair of sweatpants with a week-old coffee stain on the thigh? Perhaps you have another shirt that resembles a Hefty bag I could take. That'd be a real treasure." Her sharp green eyes regard me with disgust. "The only thing of any significant value in this insipid heap is my urn."

Excuse the hell out of me. I did *not* live through getting humiliated on-air yesterday only to be shamed by an intruder.

"Your what?" I ask as she struts over to the bar where the shiny vessel sits on the counter.

"My urn," she says louder, as though the problem is that I can't hear her, not that this entire situation makes no sense.

"Listen, lady, I don't know whose urn that is, but I bought it from my friend's store. Did Dennis tell you where I live?"

"That strange man you were speaking with yesterday? No. I never made his acquaintance."

I don't put the curling iron down. This broad is off her rocker.

"What did you do then?" I question. "Follow me here?" Was she at Whimsy and Wu when I was there? If so, that meant she'd been following me for the past twenty-four hours.

The woman scoffs and stalks toward me, but her heels against my wood floors make no sound.

That's not normal.

"*Follow* you? You have some nerve accusing me of that after putting me in your trunk and leaving me there for hours. For heaven's sake, what do you do in your vehicle that makes it smell like feet?" She holds up a hand. "Actually, I don't want to know."

"What? It doesn't smell like..." I trail off, the words

disappearing from my tongue. Not only did this woman follow me, but she got in my car and spent enough time there to comment on its scent.

I blink, my mouth going dry. Am I having a breakdown? Do I need to call the police? And what exactly would I tell them? That a southern biddy has broken into my house to insult me?

She folds her slender arms over her chest. "Will you put the curling iron down? And call off that depraved animal."

Delilah hisses as though she resents the insult.

My brain is spinning, trying to make sense of what my eyes are seeing.

"Whose urn is that?" I ask.

"Mine."

I swipe my hand over my now sweaty forehead. "Yes, I know it's yours, but…who's in it? Is it your husband or something?"

She rolls her eyes. "He wishes he had the ability to pick out something so exquisite. The last time he picked out anything of value was when he asked me to marry him. No, I told you. It's mine."

"Ma'am, are you lost?" I ask, pinching the bridge of my nose. "Do you maybe have a caregiver or someone I can call?"

She glowers at me. "Are you suggesting I'm not in charge of my faculties? Because, young lady, I assure you I am."

I place the curling iron on the counter, no longer concerned this woman is a threat, but annoyed that I still have no idea how she got here.

"Okay, enough of the bullshit, all right?" I snap. "Who are you, and how the hell did you get into my house?"

"Don't you take that tone with me, missy," she scolds.

"And watch your language. That's very unbecoming of a young woman."

I press my lips together, barely holding in the stream of curse words piling up behind my teeth.

She huffs out a breath, extending one hand to me. "My name is Marjorie Lockwood, and *that*" —she points to the sparkling cinerarium with the other— "is my urn."

I give her a blank stare, blinking rapidly as though that would somehow make her disappear and I'd discover I'm having a real doozy of a dream. Or is it a nightmare?

"Well, are you going to shake my hand or not, Kathryn?"

Wait. How does she know my name? I almost respond with another snarky remark, but curiosity outweighs my annoyance.

Slowly, I reach for her dainty fingers, but when I should be making contact, my flesh passes right through her hand.

The last thing I hear as my knees turn to mushy noodles and my vision goes dark is the sound of Marjorie's voice.

"Oh, for crying out loud, Kathryn."

chapter five

"WAKE UP, KATHRYN." MARJORIE'S SHARP TONE ORDERS AS my eyelids flutter open. "Can you hear me?"

Can I hear the dead woman standing over me in my kitchen? Yes, I can.

I start to sit up, but she holds out a perfectly-manicured hand to stop me.

"Now, wait a moment," she says. "Take deep breaths and go slow. You hit the ground pretty hard."

I do as she says because taking advice from a ghost makes about as much sense as anything else happening right now. My lungs expand with air, and I blow it out as I do a mental check of my body, stretching out my fingers and wiggling my toes. Nothing appears to be broken.

"How's your head?" she asks, regarding me with her piercing jade eyes.

I move my fingers to my forehead, then all the way around my skull until I've touched the entire surface without pain.

"I—it's fine," I answer.

"It's a wonder you didn't give yourself a concussion," she says with a huff. "Do you think you can stand?"

I nod and ease to my feet, placing one hand on the counter to steady myself.

"Pour yourself some water. You look green, Kathryn."

My mind desperately attempts to draw some sort of logical conclusion about what's happening as I pull a tumbler from the cabinet and fill it straight from the tap. Lucid dreams, a bad batch of beer—though I'd barely managed two sips before I left it in my bedroom. Have I been drugged? What about carbon monoxide poisoning?

"How do you know my name?" I turn to face her before guzzling the metallic-tasting liquid.

"Yesterday, I heard your friend call you that at his quaint little shop where he sold you my urn for ten dollars when it's worth over five grand. It's an Andre Vieux."

"A what?"

She rolls her eyes. "An Andre Vieux. He's a world-renowned artist from France." She soundlessly strolls the few steps into my living room, regarding the space with disdain. "Not that you have the faintest understanding of fine art."

I choose to ignore her dig. "An artist who makes urns?"

"No. I was an avid collector of Andre's work, and when I discovered I'd be in need of an urn, I knew I didn't want just any old tin box. So, I commissioned him to make me something unique. A luxurious final resting place."

The urn glitters in the low light of the kitchen as Marjorie gazes at it with a wistful smile. It's elegant and beautiful, not unlike Marjorie herself. But it also seems too small to contain her larger-than-life personality. And her five-foot-five frame that's standing in front of me.

"That's a tiny place to spend an eternity," I say, the shock of what just happened beginning to wear off. "Don't you wish you'd gotten something bigger? Maybe something with, I dunno…a walk-in closet and a sunroom?"

"Hilarious," she replies in a tone that indicates she finds me anything but. "I didn't exactly foresee being chained to the damned thing for all of eternity, nor did I expect to find myself stuck with a tattooed miscreant and her flea-ridden cat, but here we are."

"There has to be some rational explanation for this," I say, leaving the glass on the counter before moving to the living room and sinking onto the worn corner of my old floral couch. "One that explains why I think I'm communicating with a spirit."

"You're not having a breakdown—at least not as it pertains to me." Her gaze flicks around the room as she sits on the armchair near the sofa, crossing her feet at the ankles as she looks down her narrow nose at me. "Though from the looks of you, I wouldn't be surprised if you're experiencing some sort of personal catastrophe. Or do you always look like…*this*?" She gestures at me with the demure flourish I would expect from a queen or deity, not the ghost of a judgmental southern woman.

"Like what?" I ask, pressing my tongue to the roof of my mouth.

"All disheveled and sad."

"I had a crappy week, okay?"

"Still, one mustn't let their outward appearance reflect their internal turmoil, lest they signal to everyone that they're in crisis."

"Considering you're a *literal ghost*, I'm not sure I'm the

one having a crisis here." Though, I am talking to a dead woman, so maybe we're *both* having one.

"You should try wearing your hair down," she suggests, as though we were two old frenemies shooting the breeze. "Maybe a little makeup."

"I *am* wearing makeup." *Tinted moisturizer and mascara counts, right?*

"Perhaps a little more rouge would—"

"Nope." I bolt to my feet and begin to pace the small room. "Listen, Marjorie, I'm sympathetic to your" —I pause and wave my hands in her general direction— "*situation*, but I can assure you, I'm not the one you want to haunt, all right? So, you should go into the light now or whatever it is you…you know…*do*."

"Don't you think if it were that simple I'd have done it already?" she snaps.

"Can't you go haunt someone else?" I plead. "Don't you have some family or friends?"

She huffs a bitter laugh. "No. I don't."

"What about Dennis, my friend at the shop? He really vibes with this kind of stuff. He's very into astrology and chakras. I'm pretty sure he's dabbled in witchcraft. He would be much better suited to your ghosty needs."

Her voice is monotone when she speaks again. "While that all sounds endlessly fascinating, I'm not sure he'd be of much use."

"Why not?" I ask. No one is better prepared for a spirit invasion than Dennis Wu. In fact, I'm pretty sure being haunted *Ghost Whisperer* style is on his bucket list, right up there with befriending a murder of crows.

"Because you're the only person who's ever been able to see me."

An icy chill passes through my body. "In how long? When did you…when did you pass?"

"In October," she says, and I'm met with momentary relief. It's October now. Hasn't Dennis said something about the veil being thin this time of year? Whatever that means.

"Of 2016," she finishes, and my heart plummets to my stomach.

"Holy shit."

"Language," Marjorie warns.

"Lady, you are nine years dead, and you're worried about curse words?"

"There's no need to get hysterical, Kathryn."

I press my fingers to my temples. "No. *No.* This is not my problem."

"What isn't?" she asks.

"The mean dead lady sitting in my living room," I shout, and for the first time I see a chink in Marjorie's armor. I feel like an Ethan-level asshole.

Her face falls, and she's silent for a moment before her fire returns.

She rises and faces me. "I didn't exactly choose you either, missy, but right now, you're the only option I've got."

I hold my hand up like a white flag. "I've had a tough couple of days, Marjorie. I didn't mean to…I'm sorry." *And now I'm apologizing to a ghost.*

She holds me in her stern gaze, and I start to wonder if her eyes will turn red or if she's going to erupt into flames. But then, she softens ever so slightly.

"Fine," she says.

I blow out a breath and head back toward the kitchen, nearly tripping over Delilah who has finally come out of hiding after watching me hit the deck.

"What are you doing?" Marjorie asks as I dig through my purse, extracting wads of receipts, dollar bills, and God knows how many ChapSticks.

Finally, I pull out my phone and hold it up. "Calling reinforcements."

chapter six

"I came as fast as I could. I all but kicked my last customers out of the shop." Dennis is wearing a woven hooded poncho with a bottle of bourbon tucked under his arm when I open my front door an hour later and usher him inside. "How are you holding up? Are you ready for that sip and swipe?"

"I'm…fine." It's not the truth, but it's what I'm going with for now. There are more pressing issues at hand. "Actually, I didn't call you here to judge guys on Bumble with me. I'm having a bit of a problem."

"Oh? What's going on?" His voice is filled with concern as he breezes into my kitchen, immediately pulling down two glasses and pouring us each two fingers of the amber liquid.

Marjorie is seated on the armchair, and much to her dismay, Delilah hasn't allowed her out of her sight.

"Kathryn, can you please lock this…this *thing* in a bedroom or something?" Marjorie asks, wrinkling her nose.

I release a slow and steady breath, nodding toward where Marjorie is judging me.

"*That*," I say, "is my problem."

Dennis's gaze follows the direction I'm indicating as he pushes one of the tumblers into my hand.

He furrows his brow. "What?"

I feel like I'm losing it. "You don't see?"

His eyes snag on something as he strides toward the den, and I'm filled with relief. He stops, tapping a finger to his chin.

"Now that you mention it, that lamp really isn't doing anything for the vibe of the room, but I have to admit, when you said you had an emergency, I didn't think it was of the home decor variety."

I let out a groan of frustration, storming past him and into the living room. "It isn't. Forget the lamp. I'm talking about her." I jab a finger in Marjorie's direction.

Dennis's eyebrows furrow. "The chair? I don't see anything wrong with it. I mean, it's a little granny for my style, but—"

"Not the chair," I cry. "The woman *in* the chair."

Marjorie smirks. "Perhaps I misjudged your friend. He really does seem to have impeccable taste."

"What woman?" Dennis asks, his head tilted.

"The dead woman sitting in my chair right now," I answer, and Dennis immediately pulls me to sit on the couch and takes my glass, setting it on the coffee table.

"You know what—maybe you should sit this one out," he says.

"I'm being haunted by a woman named Marjorie. She was inside the urn I bought from you yesterday."

Dennis massages one of his temples, glancing from me to the chair and back to me again.

"Kat, this has been a tough week for you," he begins. "Stress can affect people in strange ways."

"I know how this sounds." I bury my head in my hands. "But this isn't some manifestation of me cracking under pressure. I'm telling you, she's sitting right there. I can see her just as clearly as I see you."

"Seeing people who aren't there can be indicative of something more serious," he reasons. "Have you scheduled an appointment with your doctor?"

"No. I know what I'm seeing, Dennis. She's real." *She is, isn't she?* I'm beginning to doubt everything I know to be true. Could this be some sort of vivid stress dream?

"That's exactly what I've been trying to say," Marjorie adds, unhelpfully.

"Please believe me." Though, I'm questioning whether *I* believe me. If I managed to get things so wrong with Ethan, who's to say I'm not wrong now?

Dennis studies me for a moment, then nods. "Okay. If this Marjorie is real, when did she die?"

"October of 2016," Marjorie and I answer in unison.

He pulls his phone from his pocket and begins tapping over the screen.

"Does Marjorie have a last name?"

"Lockwood," we answer, and I turn to Marjorie.

"You do know he can't hear you, right?"

Dennis casts a quick glance at me but says nothing.

Marjorie folds her arms over her chest. "You can't expect me to just sit by while the two of you talk about me like I'm not here, Kathryn."

"And where did Marjorie live?" Dennis questions.

"Marjorie Lockwood of Nashville, Tennessee, passed away October 10th, 2016, at age sixty-five from complications with colon cancer," she replies. "Marjorie graduated from Vanderbilt University in 1972 with a degree in fine arts, and she maintained her passion for creative expression throughout her life, serving on the board of directors for the Nashville Culture Club for more than twenty-five years. She is preceded in death by her parents, Lucille and Richard Grant and survived by her husband, Conrad Lockwood. That was my obituary. Tell him that word for word."

I do as I'm told, repeating each line as she feeds them to me.

Dennis's mouth opens then closes as he presses a palm to his chest. He must have found a record of Marjorie's obit online, and based on his reaction, I'm assuming everything I've said matches up.

"Oh my God, you're being haunted," he shouts, bounding from his seat. "What's it like living my dream?"

"Well, for starters, I didn't know ghosts were so judgmental," I say with a shrug.

"I'm not being judgmental," Marjorie insists. "I'm offering advice."

"*Unsolicited* advice," I correct her.

"She's talking to you now, isn't she?" Dennis asks, sitting back down, leaning closer to where Marjorie is perched on the wingback chair.

"Yep," I answer.

He's giddy as though we're in high school, and he just discovered his crush wants to take him to prom.

"Ask her what she thinks of me."

"So not the point," I say. "What do I do?"

"Besides enjoy every last second of this absolute miracle you're experiencing right now?"

"At least someone around here has the good sense to recognize my value," Marjorie hisses.

I groan. "I am *not* Jennifer Love Hewitt, okay? How do I

get rid of" —I stop midsentence as Marjorie glares a hole in the side of my head— "I mean, how do I *help* Marjorie… *move on*?"

Dennis removes his glasses, cleaning them with the edge of his poncho as he considers my question.

"You're into a lot of spiritual stuff, right?" I ask. "Have you ever read anything about this? Is there some kind of *Going Into the Light for Dummies* book I can check out from the library?"

He continues watching the armchair, as though he thinks if he waits long enough, Marjorie might appear to him too.

"Since she's been here so long, I'm guessing she has some sort of unfinished business," he says.

"Like what?" Marjorie and I ask.

"Some sort of loose ends she needs to tie up. Maybe there's an answer she never got or a score she never quite settled," he explains. "Or perhaps there's a lesson she didn't learn during her time on earth, and she's stuck here until she figures it out. But once she does, she'll cross over."

He says it like it's a simple math equation. If we can find out what's keeping her here, she'll disappear from my living room and into that bright light. *No problem.*

"Oh for heaven's sake," Marjorie mutters.

I shake my head. "But how do we know what her unfinished business is?"

"*That* I can't help you with," he says. "You need to talk to her, learn more about her life and the people in it. Who did she love? Who did she despise? Does she have any regrets?"

Marjorie scoffs, then storms from the room, leaving an icy breeze in her wake that causes Dennis and me to shiver.

"So, she's stuck here?" I ask, panic coating my voice. "With me?" I've had some bad roommates before, like the girl

I shared a dorm with my freshman year at college who used to have sex to death metal until three in the morning, but at least she was *living*. And according to the sounds I heard on the other side of the wall, she was living quite well.

Dennis takes a sip of his bourbon. "Since you're the only one who can see her…yeah. Looks that way."

"But why me?" I whine. "I'm not spiritually gifted or sensitive or whatever."

"I don't know." Dennis sighs, lifting his shoulders to his ears, then dropping them. "Maybe there's a lesson in this for you too."

"This is absurd," Marjorie snaps as she paces in the kitchen. "Is the burden of a woman on earth not bad enough? Must she spend eternity figuring out some ridiculous puzzle? I have learned all I wish to learn. Why can't I just rest in peace?"

I drop my head against the cushion and stare at the ceiling. "I hope you're planning to leave the bourbon. I have a feeling I'm gonna need it."

chapter seven

Dennis leaves after realizing Marjorie has no interest in entertaining his questions about life on the other side. Though I have to admit, I'm curious too. Do ghosts have the ability to see *everything*? Is the outfit you die in what you're stuck with for all of eternity? Do you learn the world's most sought after secrets when you cross over? If I kick the bucket before my favorite show's next season comes out, will I still be able to find out what happens from the afterlife?

"I think I know what my unfinished business is." Marjorie's announcement slices through my thoughts.

"Lay it on me." I take a slow pull of my bourbon, curling my legs beneath me on the couch. The sooner we figure this out, the sooner Marjorie spends her eternity doing something besides getting on my damn nerves.

"My husband," she begins, pacing the living room floor as Delilah watches with rapt attention. "Conrad had his new plaything moved in not even six months after I died. She's the ex-wife of a friend of ours."

Oof. Seriously? What a colossal jerk.

"Got her a ring the size of a small continent," she says, her face wrinkled in disgust. "Anyway, I knew all about his little affair with Annabelle. He thought he was so stealthy with his tawdry, clandestine meetings, sneaking around, saying he was playing pickleball with the Crabapples when the man couldn't so much as cough without pulling a hamstring. But I knew. I just didn't care because at least that got him out of my house."

I tilt my head, my lips twisted to one side. "I don't know, Marjorie. If you were as…disconnected from him as it sounds like you were, I'm not sure confronting him about his infidelity is big enough cause to warrant keeping you earthbound indefinitely."

"That's not the part that's keeping me here," she insists. "He gave that horrible woman my mother's diamond earrings, the ones I asked to be cremated in. They were passed down to my mother from my grandmother, and they were supposed to go with me. If I can get them back, I'm sure I'll go into the light."

My mouth falls open. "He *gave* them to her? What an ass." It's bad enough he cheated on her, but to give his mistress Marjorie's heirloom earrings? "Geez. I thought *my* picker was broken."

"Oh, it is," she says with a pointed stare. "I heard what happened on your radio program yesterday while your friend Dennis was listening. And I was there for your entire conversation with him afterward. He's right, you know. You need to take this Eddie fellow's advice. He seems to have your best interests at heart. He sounds so handsome, by the way. Shame he's married."

I blink. "A shame for who, exactly? Because last time I checked, you're dead."

"Yes, well, no matter." She waves me off as she perches on the edge of the armchair. "Because this time tomorrow, I'll have gone into the light, and this entire ordeal will be behind us."

"Hang on," I say, holding up my hand. "So, if no one else can see you, how are you planning to get these earrings back?"

"You, of course. You're going to go there tomorrow and get them for me."

A bark of laughter escapes my mouth. "I don't think so, Marjorie. I am not going into some stranger's house and stealing a pair of diamond earrings. What are you trying to do? Get me arrested?"

She sighs heavily. "Stop being so dramatic, Kathryn. Nobody said anything about theft."

"Then how exactly do you propose I do this?"

"You knock on the door like any other civilized human being and speak with Conrad," she says, as though the answer is obvious.

"But he doesn't know me," I cry. "He's not going to hand over these earrings to some random chick that shows up on his doorstep."

"Of course, you'll need to put on something more presentable than...*this*." She gestures over my comfy ensemble with displeasure.

I snort. "I could be wearing a ball gown, and I assure you I'm not going to walk away with anything but a harassment charge. Are you going to pay my bail? Oh, right. No, you're not because you're *a ghost*."

She leans forward, her stern eyes fixed on me. "He will give them to you because I'm going to tell you *exactly* what to say. By the time we're finished, he'll know I'm standing right there beside you."

"Absolutely not," I protest. "Look, I'm sympathetic to

what you're going through, and what he did *really* sucks, but I can't go to this dude's house and—"

"It's *my* house," she fires back. "The one he wouldn't have if it weren't for me."

"This is not happening."

"Do you know what Conrad did after I died?" she asks. "He put me in the attic. Couldn't even let me rest on the mantel of my own home. The one my family paid for. And after that gold digger Annabelle moved in, they put me in a dusty storage unit next to some of my favorite things and boxes of Conrad's old baseball cards. Like I was some old rubbish that didn't deserve to take up space any longer."

I squeeze my eyes shut, her words burrowing themselves under my skin.

"You don't know what it's like, Kathryn. To be cast aside like you're nothing." Her voice breaks, taking my heart along with it.

"Actually, I do," I admit, meeting her gaze. And for a moment, she's not just the really judgmental ghost harassing me. She's a woman in pain, having been forgotten by the one person who was supposed to love her most. We may have a lifetime of time and space between us, but we are the same.

"You're the only one who can help me," she says. "Please."

I exhale slowly and nod. "Okay."

Her eyes glitter with hope. "Okay?"

"Yeah."

She rises with a renewed sense of focus. "We should start picking out your outfit for tomorrow. Do you even own a dress?"

I pin her with a withering glare. "Don't push it."

<h1 style="text-align:right">chapter eight</h1>

"This is a bad idea," I say, climbing out of my SUV with Marjorie's urn swaddled in a crocheted throw blanket my grandmother made for me and stuffed into a brown paper shopping bag.

"You need to relax, Kathryn." Marjorie walks next to me, but only the heels of my boots click against the natural stone driveway. I pull my jacket tighter around me. Something I've learned about spending time with my new ghost friend is that there's a temperature shift when I'm this close to her. It's like standing next to an ice sculpture.

After spending the morning arguing about what I'd wear to carry out our mission, we finally left the house just after noon.

"And you should have gone with that brown skirt," Marjorie scolds. "You look like you belong to a motorcycle club or the mob."

I side-eye her. "I'm sure you're well acquainted with both."

She was distraught when I walked out in my outfit choice: comfy black jeans, a band tee, and my leather jacket. But on the off chance this whole ordeal were to end with Mr. Lockwood killing me, I wanted my ghost outfit to be on point. Marjorie quickly realized arguing was useless if she wanted to get this done right away because Annabelle always had brunch followed by bridge with the girls on Sundays—something Marjorie and Annabelle used to do together. Going today was the only guaranteed way to avoid Annabelle, Marjorie's "friend" who married her husband six months after she died.

Geez. With friends like that, who needs enemies?

"I have full range of motion in these pants," I say, giving Marjorie a demonstration by taking excessively long strides. "In case I need to make a quick escape or drop-kick somebody."

She releases an exasperated sigh. "There'll be no need to resort to violence. He'll give you the earrings. You just tell him what I say, word for word."

"Right." I blow out a breath as we ascend the expansive front staircase.

Marjorie's former home is exactly what I imagined. The white Victorian mansion looks as though it was ripped right out of a magazine spread. It's too beautiful to be real. The front door is crafted from wrought iron and tempered glass and money and probably worth at least two of my mortgage payments.

"Go on. Ring the bell," Marjorie orders. "What are you waiting for?"

"Give me a minute," I hiss, shaking out some nervous energy. "Be patient. It's not like you can get more dead."

"The sooner you speak to Conrad, the sooner this will all be over, and I'll be out of your hair. Isn't that what you want?"

Point taken. I ring the bell, and the chime is so loud it reverberates outside. Through the glass, I can make out the outline of a spiral staircase and a chandelier. I squint, looking for any signs of life, tapping my toe against the concrete.

"Would you stand still?" Marjorie hisses. "You're worse than a toddler who's had too much sugar."

"You know, I don't think he's home," I say, beginning to back away from the door. "We should go." I could probably just Google *how to banish a ghost.* I'm sure there's a Reddit thread somewhere full of advice.

"Kathryn," she scolds me, and I groan.

"Fine."

The sound of footsteps over marble, then the snap of the deadbolt, makes me freeze in place. My heart thuds in my ears as the heavy door creaks open in a slow, horror-movie-like fashion, revealing Conrad Lockwood.

Even if Marjorie hadn't told me what he looks like, I'd know it was him. He appears to be in his late seventies or early eighties, but he's still handsome in an old movie star kind of way. He's wearing slacks and a navy sweater that brings out the blue in his eyes. It's easy to get an idea of what Marjorie saw in him all those years ago.

"Hello." Conrad greets me with a tight smile. "How can I help you?"

I open my mouth, but no words come out.

"Say something," Marjorie commands. "Don't just stand there."

"Uh—hi," I say. "My name is Kat. Kat Simon. And I was hoping I could have a moment of your time." *I'd like to talk to you about your internet service provider. Also, your dead wife.*

"Whatever it is you're selling, Ms. Simon, I can assure

you, I'm not interested." He starts to close the door but I hold out my hand.

"I'm not selling anything, Mr. Lockwood. I'm a friend of Marjorie's." *Under duress,* I add silently. "Was a friend. We know—knew each other."

Marjorie steps toward him, and he shivers slightly before folding his arms over his broad chest.

"You were?"

I nod, and he gives me the once-over, his gaze settling on the bag looped over my arm.

He opens his mouth, closes it, then opens it again.

"I apologize, Ms. Simon. I'm just a bit puzzled. If I may say so, you look very young, which would mean you were even younger when my wife passed away. And you don't look…like the company she usually kept."

"Our relationship is…*was* unconventional." Well, it's not a lie. "I have something for you."

"Your comeuppance," Marjorie mutters.

He studies me a moment more before stepping aside. "Do come in."

"Thank you," I say, crossing the threshold.

Conrad shuts the door and ushers me farther inside.

"Can I get you anything to drink?" he asks, leading me into a lavish sitting room.

"I'm okay, thanks," I answer. "This won't take long."

The space is filled with rich tapestries and textures in beautiful gemstone shades and floor-to-ceiling windows. There's an oil painting mounted over the fireplace that's the size of a TV and a mahogany grandfather clock Dennis would love to get his hands on. And—

"Is that a flamingo?" Marjorie snaps, and I realize that *yes*. Yes, it is. There's *several* of them, in fact. Pink figurines, framed watercolors, and statues are littered throughout, like some live-action game of "One of These Things is Not Like the Others." Only it's dozens, not just one.

Conrad gestures toward the couch. "Please, have a seat."

I oblige as Marjorie stalks around the room, her face distorted with disgust.

"Focus," I mutter through gritted teeth.

"I beg your pardon?" Conrad asks as he sits across from me on the matching loveseat.

"Gorgeous," I say with a plastered-on smile. "Your home. It's gorgeous."

"No thanks to him," Marjorie retorts.

Conrad hums in agreement. "Now, Ms. Simon, what is it you wanted to give me?"

"A piece of my mind," Marjorie snarls as she moves to my side.

I clear my throat. "Mr. Lockwood, what I'm about to tell you is going to seem…strange."

He tilts his head, crossing one leg over the other. "Go on."

"I have a message for you from Marjorie."

"She left a letter for me?" he asks. "And she left it with you?" His confusion is obvious. Why would someone like her have even associated with the likes of me?

"Not exactly," I answer. "The truth is, I didn't know your wife when she was alive. Her urn was sold to my friend's thrift store, and I bought it a couple days ago, and Marjorie is still attached to it. She's been…speaking to me."

To prove myself, I pull the urn from the bag.

A small gasp escapes his mouth as he leans forward to inspect it closer.

He presses his lips together and studies me for a full

minute, and I start to wonder if I should worry about him having a gun.

"Do you think this is funny?" he asks. "To come into my home and tell me you've been chatting with my dead wife?"

"I promise you, nothing about this is fun. Or funny."

His voice gets louder. "What on earth would possess someone to do such a thing?"

"Trust me, I don't really want to be here, but Marjorie thinks you hold the key to the unfinished business keeping her here."

He huffs out a sarcastic laugh. "Oh, so she's here now."

"Yes," Marjorie and I say.

"Since you're already wasting my time, I'll bite and prove your little scam wrong before I have you arrested."

I cast a worried glance at Marjorie who stares straight ahead, piercing Conrad with invisible daggers.

"What are my parents' names?" he asks.

"Theodore and Rose," I reply once Marjorie gives me the answer.

This shakes his confidence but only slightly.

"You could have found that information somewhere." He sounds like he's trying to convince himself. "On Google or something."

"Ask me something personal. Something only Marjorie would know."

"Fine. Where did Marjorie and I consummate our marriage on our wedding night?"

"Ew. Please. Anything else," I beg.

"It's a trick question," Marjorie says. "Because we didn't consummate anything. Conrad had a little trouble *performing.*"

I tell him this, and the color drains from his face.

"Don't worry," I add with a patronizing smile. "I hear it happens to lots of guys."

He doesn't so much as blink, sitting so still I fear his soul has left his body and he's now a ghost himself.

"Mr. Lockwood?" I ask.

He drags a hand over his mouth. "What does she want?" His eyes dart to the space beside me, the one he sees as empty but actually contains Marjorie's angry form.

"Her mother's diamond earrings," I answer. "The ones you gave Annabelle. She said she was supposed to have taken them with her."

He shakes his head. "I can't give you those earrings. They're some of my Anna's favorites. She'll notice they're missing."

"Tell him if he doesn't give them to you, you'll be forced to show Annabelle his love letters from Patricia," Marjorie says.

I don't know who Patricia is but based on Conrad's reaction when I tell him this, I'm guessing if Annabelle found out about her, his marriage would be over.

He nods, rising to his feet. "I'll be right back."

When he leaves the room, I turn to Marjorie, who is wearing a satisfied smirk.

"Who's Patricia?" I ask.

"The wife of one of his colleagues," she answers. "Annabelle wasn't the only person he was having an affair with."

"And do you actually have these letters stuffed in your urn or something?"

"Of course not," she says with a dismissive flick of her wrist. "I burned those ages ago. But he doesn't know that.

And if you could get your hands on my urn, why couldn't you have those letters too?"

A grin spreads across my face. "You're kind of diabolical."

"I'm choosing to take that as a compliment."

I wish I could have even a fraction of the confidence Marjorie has. She has moxie oozing out of her pore-free skin.

"It is," I say. "Believe me, it is."

chapter nine

An hour later, I'm standing next to Marjorie, both of us hovering over her urn, which is now placed at the center of my coffee table. The earrings we coerced from Conrad are clutched in my hand.

I look up at Marjorie. "So, should I just take the top off and drop 'em in? Are you gonna shimmy inside like a genie?"

"There will be no *shimmying*," she insists. "But I suppose you should put the diamonds in there. I can't exactly put them on, can I?"

I shrug and carefully unscrew the lid before letting the glittering stones fall into the darkness.

Marjorie pushes her shoulders back and holds her head high.

"Now what?" I ask.

"We wait for the light." She releases a deep breath as though she's exhaling all the troubles that plagued her here on earth.

A moment passes, then two.

"Is anything happening?" Will I be able to see the light

when it comes? What if the paperwork got filed wrong and it tries to take me instead?

"No," she answers flatly.

"Not even a little light? Like a flashlight? A pen light?"

She shakes her head.

"Are you sure?"

"I think I'd recognize a bright light! Where is the damn thing?" she snaps.

"Maybe it's running behind?"

"It's not a Greyhound, Kathryn. It doesn't run on a bus schedule."

I throw up my hands. "I don't know, okay? I've never died before. How do you know the light doesn't arrive on a bus?"

She rolls her eyes.

"A Jesus bus. You know, like, we ride for Jesus." I manage a weak pump of my fist. "No?"

"Have you ever considered thinking before opening your mouth?" She stamps her foot, and it might have startled me if it actually made a sound. "Why isn't it working? *This* is my unfinished business. I'm certain it is."

I sink onto the couch and look up at her. "What if it isn't?" I was dead certain Ethan was going to be the guy to break my third-date streak, and we saw how *that* turned out.

"It *has* to be."

My eyes follow her as she paces the living room floor, while Delilah observes from her perch on the back of the sofa.

"Let's think about this," I reason. "There has to be something you're missing."

She collapses onto the armchair, her fingers pressed to her forehead like a woman on one of those nineteenth-century fainting couches.

"It's no use," she whines. "I'm stuck here, Kathryn. Forever."

"Try to calm down. Let's—"

"I'm going to be all alone. I was alone when I was alive, and I'm going to spend eternity the same way."

Marjorie weeps, her head buried in her hands, and my chest tightens. In the twenty-four hours I've known this woman, she's proven herself to be tough as nails. But even those made of steel have a breaking point.

"Hey," I say, the intensity in my voice surprising even me. "Look at me."

She lifts her tearful gaze to meet mine, and I lean forward.

"You're not alone, okay?" I say. "You've got me."

"Oh please." She sniffles. "You don't want me here. You think I'm a judgmental shrew."

"Well," I begin, "You've had your moments."

Her sobs start back up again, and I redirect.

"But you're also one of the strongest, most powerful women that ever lived. Or died." Yes, having her around has been an…*adjustment*, but it's not been *all* bad. I have to admit, it's kind of nice having someone around besides Delilah.

She swipes her fingertips beneath her lashes. "You don't mean that."

"Of course I do," I say. "I wish I had your confidence— your poise. You're a force, Marjorie. You're a goddamn hurricane."

"Language," she warns through the faintest hint of a smile.

"We'll figure this unfinished business thing out," I promise, realizing that Marjorie's mission has become mine too. I couldn't walk away even if I wanted to—and I *don't* want to

—because I know what it's like to be pushed aside and left behind. To feel like you have no one.

"How?" she asks.

"I'm not sure," I admit. "It'll take time, but we won't give up. *I* won't give up."

She nods and blows out a breath, straightening her spine. "Thank you."

"You're welcome."

"I'd like to do something for you in return," she says. "To repay you for what you're doing for me. I believe I can help with your dating troubles."

Oh no. No, no, no, no.

"There's really no need to—"

She cuts me off with a wave of her hand. "I insist. You said you wish you had some of my confidence. Well, I can help you with that."

I gulp, my mind already spinning with thoughts of how she plans to deliver this *help*.

Maybe it won't be so bad. I might have to put on a dress and walk across the room while balancing a book on my head.

"You're going to say yes to Eddie's proposition," she continues. "And then I'll go on the dates with you so I can tell you what you're doing wrong."

I choke on my own spit. "You don't have to do that."

"It's already settled," she says. "You'll firm up the details at work tomorrow."

It wasn't a question, and as much as I want to protest, I can't make the words come out. She looks so damn happy to have a project to focus on. I'll let her have one date before I tell her thanks, but no thanks.

How bad can one date be?

Then I remember Ethan.

"The truth is, I think I need to take a break from this whole dating thing," I say. "Maybe I should just stay single for a while."

"Nonsense," she argues. "You're young and successful. Your fashion sense leaves much to be desired, but we can work on that."

I hesitate. "I…I don't know."

"I'm not taking no for an answer."

"Okay, then." I run my tongue over my teeth. "I guess we're doing this."

"Perhaps we should start thinking about what you'll wear when you meet your next suitor."

"Actually, I'm pretty tired," I say, stifling a yawn. "The last few days have been…a lot."

Her mouth falls into a momentary frown. "Yes, well, I should let you get some rest."

Sleep sounds better than just about anything in the world, but I can't stand the look of disappointment on Marjorie's face, so I suggest a new plan.

"What if we have a girls' night?"

She arches her brow. "A girls' night?"

"We can watch some movies. You pick a favorite, and then I'll pick one," I offer. "And we can just hang out…talk."

"Hang out," she repeats as though the concept is foreign to her.

I chuckle. "You know, like friends."

Her green eyes light up, and she bites back a smile.

"I'd be delighted, Kathryn."

chapter ten

"So, did you give some thought to what we discussed on Friday?" Eddie asks when I take my seat in the studio twenty minutes before our 6 a.m. segment on Monday morning. Becca steals a hopeful glance in my direction, and Jude lifts his gaze from his laptop, awaiting my answer.

"Good to see you, Eddie," I say, taking a swig of my coffee. "I had a great weekend circling the drain. Thanks for asking."

"Nice to see you, Kat. How was your weekend." It comes out as a statement, not a question. "Have you made a decision?"

I sigh and drop my head back, staring up at the ceiling. "I have."

The agreement I made with Marjorie the day before replays in my mind. While I'm not necessarily thrilled with the idea of being on the receiving end of all of her *feedback*, I have to admit, it might be helpful to have an unbiased opinion on what I can do to improve my dating life.

"And?" Eddie and Becca prompt as Jude continues to wait quietly.

"I'll do it," I answer. "Under one condition. I can back out at any time if things get weird."

"Weirder than letting your friends set you up with strangers who listen to our show?" Becca asks.

"If you want to stop for *any* reason, we'll pull the plug," Eddie assures me. "You have my word."

"Fine," I say. "These dudes have to be better than the ones I've dated lately."

Becca snorts. "Never underestimate a man's ability to be mediocre."

"I had the social media team get started on some graphics over the weekend." Eddie taps a few keys on his laptop before turning it so I can see the screen. One of my headshots has been placed on a colorful background with the words *Are You Kat's Purrfect Match?* in bold print at the top.

I nearly choke. "Whoever came up with that needs to be fired."

Eddie cocks his head. "I came up with it."

"I said what I said."

Becca grins. "It's cheesy and fun and exactly what we need to grab people's attention."

"Were there any other possibilities to choose from?" I ask.

"It was either that or *Are You the Kat's Meow*," Eddie answers.

"So no." I roll my eyes. "Please don't turn me into a joke."

"We won't," Eddie says. "The titles are just to catch people's attention. I worked on the application your potential dates will have to fill out this weekend, and it's thorough."

"Literally, there's, like, fifty questions on it." Becca winds her hair into a bun on top of her head, fastening it in place with the elastic on her wrist. "I've already seen it. Trust me, anyone who applies is doing so because they *really* want to go out with you."

"I hope you kept the puns to a minimum," I quip.

"No puns were harmed in the making of this form," Eddie says.

"Should I be concerned with how much work you put into this before I ever agreed to do it?" Do they think I'm such a disaster that they've been dying for the opportunity to save me from myself? "What would you have done if I'd said no?"

"Simple," Eddie replies. "I would have deleted it all. But I told you last week, if we're doing this, we've got to strike while the iron is hot. I wasn't sure you'd say yes, but I wanted to be prepared in case you did."

"I want final approval of the application," I say.

Eddie nods. "Of course."

"Are you sure about this?" Jude finally speaks, shifting his chair so he's facing me. "Do you really want to open up your love life to so much scrutiny?"

Eddie raises his brows as Becca pins Jude with an annoyed glare.

"It's the same thing I do now with my dating diaries," I answer with a shrug.

"Sharing our personal lives is part of the gig," Becca adds.

"But this is different." Jude's focus is entirely on me. "Your segments are just that—*yours*. They're your perspective, and you only share what you want to. If you go through with this, you're inviting in the perspective of these guys who'll be forming opinions and making snap judgments about you from a two-hour date."

"That's why we'll be prerecording the segments," Eddie says.

"But that just prevents the listeners from hearing it."

Jude's brown eyes never leave mine. "It doesn't stop *you* from *experiencing* it."

My shoulders tense, and there's a gnawing sensation in my stomach. What exactly is he getting at here? I'm not sure, but it feels reminiscent of the gut punch I received from Ethan the other day. It sounds like yet another person saying I'm somehow not good enough.

"And?" I ask, swallowing hard.

"I just don't want to see you get hurt again," he says. "That's all."

"Is my first impression really so offensive that there's no way these guys will possibly have anything nice to say?" It certainly hasn't been positive enough to get anyone to consider dating me seriously, and the last person who *did*… ugh. I can't even think about it.

"God, no. Of course not. That's not what I meant," he insists. "Kat, you know you're one of my favorite people, okay? But what happened the other day was brutal, and you didn't deserve it. I'm just looking out for you."

"I'm a big girl, Jude. I can handle it." I deliver the words with a confidence I don't feel. If the next guy's feedback is anything like Ethan's, I may never go on another date ever again.

It's easy for Jude, though. He's gorgeous and kind and charismatic and perfect—the kind of guy who owns any room he's in.

"I'm sorry, Kat." Jude's eyes are so soft when he looks at me, I almost forget he thinks I'm a disaster who's bound to botch these dates.

"Don't worry about it," I say.

"Seriously, I'm really—" he begins, but I cut him off.

"I said it's fine." I rise to my feet and grab my coffee cup, desperate to get out of this room, to have five blessed seconds of not being perceived. "I'm gonna go get a refill. Anyone need anything?"

My three cohosts shake their heads.

Eddie holds up a hand to stop me. "But hey, you *are* sure, right? If you have any doubts at all, we don't have to—"

"I don't," I say, my voice firm as I linger in the doorway. "Announce it today. I'm ready."

chapter eleven

MARJORIE REGARDS MY OUTFIT THROUGH SLITS, LIKE A CAT trying to decide whether my lap is worth sitting on before determining it most definitely isn't. It's Thursday evening, and she's in my bedroom helping me decide what to wear for my *Purrfect Match* date tomorrow—the first of two scheduled this weekend. Clothes are scattered across my bed, the quilt on top slightly askew.

"It's a bit short," she remarks, sizing up the black mini I've paired with a chunky turtleneck and tall boots. She stands beside me, though her reflection is nowhere to be found in my full-length mirror. "And where are your pantyhose? It's chilly out. You'll get hypothermia if you don't have something covering your legs."

"Something covering my legs?" I echo. "You mean like the pants I had on two outfits ago that you said made me look like a lumberjack?"

"You can't wear denim," she insists. "You're going on a date, not changing the oil on your pickup truck."

"Fine," I say, wobbling on one foot while pulling my shoe off the other. I nearly fall over as I yank the remaining boot down my leg. "But I draw the line at pantyhose. It's like a nylon straightjacket for your toes."

"What about a black cocktail dress?" she suggests as I stumble back inside my walk-in closet. "You can't go wrong with one of those."

"Yeah, but it's too fancy for where we're going," I say. "He's taking me to dinner at this new farm-to-table place that just opened up. It's casual."

A cardigan falls off a hanger as I fumble through the disaster area that is my closet.

"The sweater you had on was nice," she concedes. "That dark green really accentuates your features. Do you have something else you could try with it?"

I sigh, rocking back on my heels as I consider my options. "I'm thinking."

Finally, my eyes land on the perfect thing. I trade the mini skirt for a long silky one in a bold leopard print before stepping out of the closet with a twirl.

"What about this?" I ask.

Her nose wrinkles. "It's leopard."

"And? Leopard is a neutral."

She pins me with her dubious gaze. "I suppose animal print is appropriate for a date on a farm."

I choke on a laugh. "We aren't having dinner *on* a farm. It's a type of restaurant. It just means they serve food that comes from local farms."

"Interesting," she says, pursing her lips as she circles me, continuing to analyze my frame. "It's growing on me. But you'll need accessories. Keep the bag simple—black so it matches your shoes—and some gold earrings, perhaps?"

I pad to my dresser and open my wooden jewelry box, digging through it for a pair of hoops.

A chill runs through me as she peers over my shoulder. "Yes, those will do just fine."

"Great." I disappear back inside the closet to strip out of the ensemble.

"What do we know about this young man?" she asks as I come back out, plopping the clothes atop the chair across the room so they'll be ready for tomorrow.

"He's actually a reporter for one of the local news stations," I answer, diving onto the mattress. "Which I like because that means he at least understands my career on some level. Not that I'm a journalist, but we're both in the public eye."

"What's his name?" she asks, taking a seat at the foot of my bed.

I stifle a yawn. "Todd Summers."

"Sounds like he should be the weatherman," she says. "Do you have a photo?"

I pull up one of his social media pages on my phone, turning the screen to face her. Her eyes widen as she takes in his perfect swoop of dark hair, thick eyebrows, and angular jaw.

She nods in approval. "He's quite handsome, isn't he?"

I drop the phone onto the bed and slip under the covers, my head propped against the pillows. "He's been voted most eligible bachelor in the *Nashville Scene* three years in a row."

"I look forward to seeing him in person tomorrow. Which reminds me, how is this going to work since we discovered this week that I can't go more than a few feet away from the urn?"

On Wednesday afternoon, I'd tried to take Marjorie to Whimsy and Wu with me, only for her to evaporate into thin air before my SUV reached the end of the driveway. I went back inside to find her in the kitchen, shaken and more than a little confused as to how she got there. The second time, I buckled the urn into the passenger seat and the venture went off without a hitch.

"I'll bring the shopping bag I took you in the other day. Just say I had to make a stop on the way to the restaurant and the locks on my car are broken, so I don't want to leave anything valuable in there."

"I can't wait to get out of here tomorrow and enjoy a night on the town," she says. "I appreciate you leaving me with some form of entertainment, but there's only so much reality television one can endure."

"How about I find something else for you to watch tomorrow?" I ask.

"That would be much appreciated," she says. "Well, I suppose I should let you get some rest. You have a big day ahead tomorrow."

She rises, but I hold out a hand to stop her.

"Marjorie?"

"Yes, Kathryn?"

I study her, the corners of my mouth turned down. "I'm sorry you've been stuck here all this time. I can't imagine how lonely it's been for you." Actually, I can. I may not be a ghost, but that doesn't stop me from feeling invisible sometimes.

She gives me a faint smile. "You get used to it after a while."

"But for *years*?"

"Time passes differently for me than it does for you."

"How so?" I ask.

She sinks back onto the bed. "I don't know how to explain it. It's almost as though I'm living with the remote stuck on Fast Forward. Or at least it was that way until I found you."

"I'm not sure if that's a good thing."

"I like having the company," she admits. "And it's given me time to try and figure out what my unfinished business could be."

I frown. "I'm guessing there haven't been any developments on that."

She shakes her head, disappointment shrouding her gaze. "Not yet."

"It'll come," I promise. "I know it will."

"I hope so." Her tone is soft, yearning. "You should get some sleep."

"I feel bad because I know you don't sleep, and you're spending all these hours alone."

"Don't. I find ways to keep busy."

"How?"

"I revisit some of my happiest memories," she answers.

"With Conrad?"

"No." She huffs out a laugh. "My happiest memories happened before he did."

Her answer shocks and saddens me. I knew her marriage with Conrad had been tumultuous at times, but was it always that way? Did she spend her entire life feeling miserable?

The grim expression on her face makes me choose not to question her on it further—at least for now. Instead, I sit up, my legs crossed in front of me.

"Hey, can I ask you…a weird question?"

She smirks. "I would expect nothing less from you."

"Are you stuck in that one outfit for all of eternity?" I know it's silly, but Marjorie is kind of my own personal guide to the afterlife. If I can better understand what it's like for her, maybe I can also get an idea of what it was like for my mom and grandmother.

A grin tugs at her lips. "I wouldn't have suspected you'd be interested in my fashion choices."

I shrug. "But aren't *you*?"

"I'm not sure, to be honest," she says, glancing down at her peach skirt suit. "I've never tried to change my outfit. I wouldn't know how, even if I wanted to."

"But do you? Want to?"

"Of course I do. I loved my clothes," she replies with a dreamy sigh. "I had a closet full of beautiful designer pieces and—oh! The shoes." Her eyes are filled with such joy it makes me want to hear more.

"Tell me about one of your favorite things to wear."

"Only one?" she asks, resting a finger against her chin. "I had a beaded navy gown I loved that I wore to a charity gala. It had long sheer sleeves and made me feel like royalty. The only caveat was that I had to wear heels about an inch taller than I usually preferred because the seamstress forgot to hem it. My feet have never hurt more than they did that night, but it was worth it."

My mouth falls open as Marjorie speaks. As she describes the dress and the way it made her feel, the suit on her body transforms into an intricately beaded masterpiece.

"M-Marjorie," I say, blinking slowly as I lean forward. "Your…you…look down."

She gasps when she does, immediately standing to twirl in her gown.

"This is…this is my dress," she cries, her eyes filled with wonder. "Just look at it. Isn't it beautiful?"

"It sure is," I say. "It's stunning."

The realization of what she accomplished washes over her. "I did that."

"Try it again."

"How?"

"Think of something you used to wear and how it made you feel."

"Yes. Right." She squeezes her eyes shut and presses her lips together, fists clenched at her sides. And once again, her outfit morphs right in front of me. This time it fades into a cream shift dress with blush-colored heels.

She nearly squeals when she opens her eyes. "I did it again."

"Yes." I chuckle. "Yes, you did."

She beams at me. "You go on to bed. Don't worry about me. I'll just be trying on everything I ever owned."

"Hang on," I say with a laugh. "I think I've got at least another couple outfits in me."

The sparkle in her eyes is worth any missed sleep.

chapter twelve

MARJORIE WRINKLES HER NOSE AS WE APPROACH THE restaurant the next evening, smoothing her hands over the tweed skirt suit she decided to wear because it matched the color of my sweater.

"Are you sure this is the place?" she asks.

"Yeah," I say with a laugh, the heels of my boots clicking against the pavement. "It's inside a converted shipping container."

Evo's exterior is simple, all black-and-white with sleek lines, and the entrance is illuminated by a row of iron sconces. There's a small vacant patio off to one side surrounded by soft globe lights.

"It's so…industrial."

I stop just outside the door and blow out a breath, tightening my grip on the shopping bag containing Marjorie's urn. "Okay, you remember the rules?"

"Yes," she answers with an eye roll. "I'm to observe only."

"Quietly. That's the most important part."

"Quietly," she repeats. "But what if—"

"No. No *what-ifs*. You cannot have me in there looking like I'm talking to myself on this date. We'll debrief in the car, and you can give me all the feedback you want." And I'm sure she'll have *plenty*.

"Yes, fine," she says, and I narrow my eyes at her.

"I mean it, okay? No funny business."

She huffs. "I already agreed, Kathryn. What do you want? A blood oath?"

Actually, yes, but that would be impossible considering the circumstances.

I reach for the handle and pull it open, revealing an interior that's the exact opposite of the outside—cozy and warm with the scent of garlic and fresh-baked bread filling the air.

"Well, this is lovely," Marjorie says, taking in the space. "I just adore those little chandeliers."

"Hi, can I help you?" the hostess asks when she spots me looking around.

"Yes, I'm meeting someone," I reply just as Todd catches my eye from a booth in the back and waves. "Oh, that's him. Thanks."

Wow. He's even more handsome in person than he is on TV.

"My word," Marjorie says from behind me as we weave through the dining room. "He's *gorgeous*. Would you look at that hair?"

"Kat." Todd greets me with a smile that makes my heart leap into my throat as his six-foot frame rises to hug me. "I'm so glad we could do this."

"Me too," I say, sliding into the seat across from him, placing the bag next to me.

"What you got there?" he asks as Marjorie sits on my other side.

Since I can't tell him about the dead lady who accompanied me to judge my every move, I give him the cover story about shopping before I came and my car locks being broken. Before he can think to ask what I bought, the server arrives to take my drink order.

"Only one," Marjorie insists. "You don't want him thinking you're a lush."

I cough and begin perusing the menu. "So, have you been here before?"

"Yeah, it's one of my favorites," he answers, taking a sip of the amber-colored liquid in his glass. "The hot chicken is great."

"Don't get that," Marjorie warns. "You don't want dragon breath."

I rest my head on my left hand, physically blocking her out.

"So, Todd," I say. "I'm excited to hear more about you."

"You've seen my social media, right?" he asks, his eyes not lifting from the menu.

"Um, yeah, of course. I've seen you on the news and all that, but I want to know more about, well, *you*. The things people may not know just from following you online."

"Well, I'm up for a position with one of the major networks. I actually just returned from my third interview." He sits back, resting his arm over the top of the booth. "It would be an in-the-field reporter gig, but my agent thinks I could easily work my way up to being an anchor."

"That sounds prestigious," Marjorie comments.

"Wow, congratulations." I set my menu aside. "I'm guessing a job like that will require you to relocate."

He nods. "Nothing is set in stone yet, but I'm starting to look for places in New York City."

Marjorie turns toward me with a grin. "I always loved New York."

I ignore her and tilt my head. This clearly isn't brand-new information, so why did Todd want to go out with me knowing he has one foot out the door?

"That's great," I say. "And a big shift from living in Nashville. How are you feeling about it?"

He gives a noncommittal shrug. "I've always known Nashville wasn't a permanent home for me. I try not to stay anywhere longer than five years. I like to keep my options open, you know?"

Actually, no, I don't. I've worked in the same place for more than a decade and lived in the same town my entire adult life.

"Ah, so you're no stranger to change," I say instead as the server returns with my beer.

"Change might do you some good too, you know," Marjorie mutters. "Especially if it means going home to someone besides your cat."

I grit my teeth and mentally shove an elbow into her side.

"Not at all," he replies, his gaze following a pretty server who makes her way past us. "I thrive on it."

"Did he just—" Marjorie cranes her neck in the direction of his stare and gasps. "He was looking at that girl's behind. Did you see that?"

I didn't, but that's probably not even what he was doing. Maybe he just recognized her from somewhere.

Todd leans forward. "Enough about me. I want to hear more about you."

Normally, I'd find a way to redirect the conversation back to him. I'd be on a fact-finding mission to discover what kind of woman he wants so I would know exactly what boxes I needed to check. But not this time. I want Todd to get to know the real me.

I open my mouth to speak, but Todd continues.

"I mean, how did you manage to amass a social media following of almost a hundred thousand people?" he asks. "I've been stuck at 20k fans for over a year."

Marjorie's emerald eyes are locked on him like a cat hunting its prey. "He wants to talk to you about your *fan base*?"

"No offense, but you're not even in television." Once again, Todd keeps going before I can say anything. "Radio is dying out, but somehow you're thriving. What's your secret?"

My brow furrows. Why did that sound like a backhanded compliment?

"I don't like this, Kathryn." The air surrounding Marjorie gets colder. "I don't like it one bit."

I attempt to put her words out of my mind. It's not like talking shop on a date is abnormal, especially considering that my show is the reason we're on this date to begin with.

"No secret," I answer with an awkward laugh. "We have a successful show, and people love Eddie. I'm just lucky listeners love the rest of us too."

"Do not downplay your accomplishments, young lady," Marjorie scolds. "That's not luck. That's hard work."

Once again, Todd's line of sight follows the same pretty young server. And this time I don't miss the way he watches her bend over.

"Well, my agent thinks we could help each other," he says, returning his gaze to me. "And I agree."

"He thinks he can *help* you?" Marjorie scoffs. "With what? What could this man possibly offer besides his teeth-whitening routine?"

"I'm sorry," I begin. "I don't think I understand."

"My agent thinks we could spin this dating thing into a publicity grab."

His words are like fingers curling into a fist around my stomach.

"Everyone loves a love story, right?" He takes a sip of his drink. "And we're both well-known public figures. People will eat this up."

I don't know about the people, but the pit that's growing inside me feels like it could swallow me whole.

Marjorie is fuming. "This Tom Brokaw wannabe sure has a lot of nerve."

"We can post enough stuff on our social media to make it look believable," he continues. "We'll take a couple days to shoot some photos and videos together and batch some content to release over the next few weeks. By the time I'm on the national news, we'll have a human interest story of our own. Just think how good this will be for us."

"Us?" I echo.

"Let's go." Marjorie rises to her feet beside the booth. "Don't you dare waste another moment on this clout-chasing cling-on."

"Yeah, *us*." Todd leans forward. "Radio isn't gonna be lucrative forever, and besides, once Eddie decides to go, the rest of you are kind of screwed, don't you think? You should be considering other avenues to keep people interested. This could really open doors for you."

It's a painful reminder of Eddie's impending retirement, but not quite as painful as looking at Todd's stupid face. "So you'd be doing me a favor, is that it?"

He's either too stupid to detect the sarcasm in my voice or he simply doesn't care.

"Exactly," he says with a grin.

"How kind of you." My voice is flatter than his tire would be if I could only figure out which car in the parking lot belongs to him.

"This man is unbelievable," Marjorie sneers. "Come on. Get your things."

Todd gives me a smile that can only be described as condescending.

"Don't mention it. Really," he says. "You seem cool, Kat. I'm happy to help."

And I'd be happy rearranging his face.

I huff out a dry laugh. "You know what? I'm actually all set. In fact, I think I'm gonna leave."

Marjorie is muttering her frustration as I start to gather my things and slide out of the booth.

"Now wait a minute." Todd's hand darts out to grab my wrist. "Don't get emotional. Let's talk about this."

Beside me, Marjorie's nostrils flare, and she jabs her finger in his annoying face.

"You unhand her this instant," Marjorie snaps, and Todd's tumbler shatters, sending liquid splattering across his suit.

The sound of breaking glass startles us both enough that he lets me go.

Curious patrons glance our way, their conversations fading to faint murmurs.

Todd releases a shaky breath. "Holy shit."

I look at Marjorie with wide eyes as the lights of the fixture above the table flicker. *Holy shit, indeed.*

Marjorie blinks, her rage softening. "Was that…me?"

The color drains from Todd's face. "How did…how did you do that?"

I press my palms to the table and lean close to his ear.

"Here's what's gonna happen tomorrow, *Todd*," I say. "When Eddie calls you for the segment, you're gonna say that our date went *great*—that you were *so* into me. But I'm gonna say that while you seem like a nice guy, I just didn't feel that spark. I'll leave out the part about how Nashville's most eligible bachelor is also a complete asshole, but only if you promise I'll never hear from you again."

"I promise," he squeaks.

"Let's go, Kathryn." Marjorie folds her arms over her chest, her nose stuck in the air as she heads for the door. I start after her, but spin on my heel and return to the table.

Todd cowers as I reach for what's left of my beer and chug it down before plunking the glass back on the table.

I smirk and call over my shoulder, "Thanks for the drink."

chapter thirteen

Marjorie and I hit the nearest fast-food drive-through where I order enough for both of us, despite the fact that she doesn't actually eat anything. I barely park the car in the rear of the lot before I chomp into my double cheeseburger, ketchup dribbling down my chin. Not only am I annoyed that my night turned to shit, but now I'm sitting here eating something I don't even really like.

She recoils as though I just bit the head off a pigeon. "For heaven's sake, it's already dead. There's no need to attack it with such gusto."

"I'm starving," I garble around a mouthful of fries. "This whole thing was a big mistake. I'm canceling the date for tomorrow and this whole stupid segment while I'm at it. I don't know what I was thinking, agreeing to this."

Marjorie regards me with unyielding eyes. "Now you listen to me. You can't just give up because one man was a fool. If women did that, they'd stay single forever."

I snort. "You say that like it's a bad thing."

"It's *not* a bad thing at all if that's what you truly want, but it isn't, is it?"

I take a pull off the extra-large soda I ordered. "All I know is, I'm tired of feeling like this."

"Feeling like what?"

"A six at best," I blurt out, Ethan's criticisms from a few days ago haunting me. "Not good enough. Like no one will ever want me."

Like no one will ever love *me.*

"You mustn't let what that Todd fellow did get to you. There are plenty more fish in the sea, and they probably use less hair gel too."

"This is ridiculous." I flop my head against the seat. "I don't need anyone, anyway. It's not like I have a bad life. I'm fine on my own." There's enough truth in my words to almost convince me they're not a lie.

"But you *want* someone, and there's no shame in that," she says softly, "it's okay to want more."

I bark out an unamused laugh. "Yeah, well, that's gotten me nowhere, so I think it's time I let that go."

"What is this about, Kathryn?" Marjorie asks. "Because it clearly has to do with more than Todd, so what is it?"

I sigh and take another bite of my burger, chewing through my thoughts. She's right. Beyond being nice to look at, Todd isn't exactly a catch. This sense of hopelessness follows me everywhere because it's *in* me—embedded within my soul like a splinter I can never quite reach.

"There was someone in my life a while back," I say, shoving my food back in the paper sack. "Nick. We were together for two years. He was the first guy I let into my life since..." I trail off and clear my throat. Since my dad—the one man I thought would never abandon me—left. "Well, in a really long time."

"I see," she says with a nod. "What happened?"

"I loved him," I answer, my voice barely above a whisper. "Maybe the problem was that I loved him too much. He was…my world."

"He didn't feel the same?"

I hesitate for a moment. This isn't something I tell most people. It's hard to admit to myself, let alone another person. But I suppose if I'm going to talk to anyone, it may as well be Marjorie. She has to take it to the grave since, well, she's already dead, and I'm the only one who can see her. Besides, what's she gonna do? Judge me? She can't possibly hurt me anymore than Nick did.

"He did until he didn't. There was no big fight. He didn't cheat or lie." In a way, it was worse. "It started with little things. He stopped asking about my day. Even on the few nights we didn't spend together, we always talked about what was going on in our lives. The silly mundane stuff nobody but the person you love even cares about. But one day, he just… stopped asking."

Marjorie's face softens as she waits for me to continue.

"We settled into the whole couple thing early on, curling up on the couch and binging old sitcoms after dinner. I loved it because his commentary was always better than whatever we were watching. But Fridays were the one night a week we went out," I say. "Until one day when he had to work late. I didn't think it was a big deal. I thought we'd pick up where we left off the next week. And we did, but then things started coming up more often than not—a friend was in town or he was just too tired."

"Oh, Kathryn." Marjorie frowns, her sympathetic gaze fixed on me.

"I thought that was just how relationships were, you know? You get comfortable and things start to change." I was just so thankful to *have* someone that I didn't mind. "Then he stopped kissing me goodnight. That's when I finally realized we were in trouble. I tried to talk to him, to do something—anything to make it better—but it was too late. He'd already fallen out of love with me."

"I'm so sorry."

"Sometimes I wish there had been some big conflict, a deal-breaker we couldn't get past because I think that might hurt less than the truth." I release a shaky breath. "He was the first man I was truly myself with, but that wasn't enough to keep him. *I* wasn't enough."

"You have to know it wasn't because you were lacking in any way. Sometimes that's just the way things are. Sometimes loving someone isn't enough," she says, a melancholic expression passing over her like a dark cloud.

"Ever since then…I haven't been able to get past a third date with anyone. Sometimes the guys are jerks like Todd, but really…I think the bigger problem is me because I'm afraid to let anyone in." I squeeze my eyes shut, letting the tears slip down my cheeks. I've never admitted this to anyone, but there's something about Marjorie that makes me feel like I can. "I try so hard to be whoever I think the other person wants me to be that they never know *me*."

"And by keeping everyone at arm's length, there's no real risk of getting hurt. Because they aren't rejecting you. They're rejecting who you've allowed them to believe you are," she says. "It's almost like you're playing a character. There's the woman these men see, and then there's the one sitting here beside me."

"Yeah, but apparently neither are worth sticking around for, so—"

She cuts me off, her voice firm but not admonishing.

"Young lady, you stop that this instant. There'll be no more of this feeling sorry for yourself. I won't tolerate it, especially when it doesn't sound as though you've given anyone a real chance since your last relationship. And no, Todd doesn't count."

I sniff, swiping my fingertips beneath my lashes. She isn't wrong.

"You said you wished you had my confidence. What was it you called me the other day?" she asked. "A hurricane? Well, let me tell you something about hurricanes. They're a force of nature, and they sure don't cry in parking lots while drowning their sorrows in food that could outlast a nuclear war. You know why? Because they're too busy tearing shit up."

I clutch my invisible pearls. "Marjorie. Language."

She rolls her eyes and bites back a grin. "Sometimes it's warranted."

"Like shattering glasses and flickering lights?" I ask. "How did you do that, anyway?"

"I don't know," she admits. "I was so provoked by that boy's behavior toward you that I was seeing red, and it just… happened."

"It was badass."

"*Language.*"

I raise my brow at her. "You broke Todd's drink and sent it flying all over him. It's warranted."

She squares her shoulders and fluffs the ends of her auburn hair with her palm.

"It *was* pretty badass, wasn't it?" she asks, her eyes sparkling in the soft glow of the street light.

I sigh. "At least I know that if tomorrow's date goes as poorly as tonight's, you can intervene."

"Does this mean you're not canceling after all?"

"I mean, I can't very well tear shit up locked inside my house, can I?" I pop a fry into my mouth. "And I'm finishing every bit of this food. If it can survive the elements, imagine how well it could preserve me."

"Have you considered the possibility of eating a vegetable?"

"Have you considered that I can just leave you and your judgments about my food choices at the house tomorrow?"

She smirks. "Noted."

"So, why do you think what Todd did set you off?" I ask. "Not that he wasn't a first-class jerk, but I'm just surprised it was enough to unlock these powers."

Her mouth settles into a hard line. "He reminded me of someone I used to know."

"Who?"

"My best friend." The words come out like she tasted something sour. "At least I *thought* we were best friends. Frances and I met when we were students at Vanderbilt. We did everything together. She even knew about…" She trails off and drops her gaze. "She just knew me in ways no one else did."

"What happened?"

"Frances came from a well-to-do family, but not in the way I did," she explains. "My father was something of a mogul. He was the CEO of a major media conglomerate called Garnet Press, and a career there was guaranteed success. Conrad joined the company after we were married, and then Frances wanted her husband to work there too."

"So, what was the problem?"

"The problem was that I knew her husband Teddy. He'd embezzled from his previous company and been let go. He was lucky he wasn't arrested," she says. "I told her I couldn't in good conscience refer him to work at Garnet. When I refused, she stopped speaking to me."

"She had to know you couldn't put your father's business in jeopardy."

"I don't think she cared much about that. When I thought back on our friendship, I realized so much of it had surrounded what I could do for her: put in a good word for her so she could get into the best sorority, help her and Teddy become members of the country club we belonged to. She wanted the benefit of my status without any of the responsibility or sacrifices it required."

"She was using you," I say. "The way Todd wanted to use me."

She nods. "It broke my heart because she was the one person I considered a friend. The one person who really knew me. For so long, I thought she was the only person who understood me."

I frown. "Did you ever tell her that?"

"No," she replies. "Because when I wouldn't help Teddy, she wrote me off completely. We never spoke again."

It hits me like a thunderclap. "What if that's your unfinished business? What if you're supposed to tell Frances how much that hurt you? Make peace with her?"

Her hand covers her mouth. "Oh my. You could be right."

A slow smile spreads over my mouth. "Only one way to find out."

chapter fourteen

Marjorie and I spend much of Saturday online trying to hunt down Frances Beaufort. Or more accurately, *I* spend most of the day online while Marjorie huffs at me for not typing fast enough. While Frances doesn't appear to have any social media accounts herself, we do manage to find a man by the name of Michael whom we believe could be her son, so I send him a message under the guise of being related to Marjorie, looking to reconnect the two of them. Now, all we can do is wait.

"I can't believe Michael hasn't responded yet," Marjorie says as we head down the sidewalk toward the brewery where I'm meeting *Purrfect Match* number two, Hudson Lowe. "Can you look again?"

"I just checked before we got out of the car," I reply, shifting the urn's nondescript paper shopping bag to my other hand. "I only reached out a couple hours ago. Give him time."

"You're right," she says, and I wish ghosts could hold pens because I'd love to get that in writing. "Okay, remind me what this Hudson fellow does again."

I drop my voice so other passersby can't hear, lest they

think I'm talking to myself. "He's a session musician—a guitar player. And he does this because he *doesn't* want the attention, so at least I know he's not using me for clout. From what I know, he likes craft beer and nineties music, so he can't be too bad."

But I made sure to schedule this as a drinks-only date, just in case.

"He's handsome too," she remarks. "Todd's nice looking in the way movie stars are, but Hudson's photos make him appear more approachable."

While Todd was gorgeous, he was almost too pretty to be real, which isn't my usual type. But Hudson has soulful eyes, golden hair, and the kind of smile that makes you feel like everything's gonna be okay. He reminds me a lot of Jude, actually.

"I'm excited to meet him. Thanks for convincing me not to bail."

She flashes a pleased grin. "I'm glad you decided to give this another go. Wouldn't it be something if this man ends up being exactly what you're looking for?"

"That would be great, and hey, maybe we'll have a message waiting from Michael by the time we get back to my house. I'm manifesting it."

"Manifesting?" she asks as the cool autumn breeze rustles the leaves of the trees lining the street, but not her perfectly-styled hair.

"You know, when you put a goal or wish or whatever out into the universe to attract it."

"That's absurd."

I shrug. "Dennis swears by it. He says that's how he found his husband."

"Don't you suppose if that were possible the whole world would be filled with billionaires?"

"That's assuming everyone would only try to manifest money. Why not success or happiness?"

"Sounds like money to me," she says with an ironic laugh as we approach the vibrant exterior of Rainbow Brews and Taproom.

"Some people might want to manifest love, or in your case, closure."

"Mine is an extenuating circumstance. If I was alive and believed in this nonsense, I'd be trying to attract wealth."

"Right. Because it appears your wealth made you *so* happy." I shoot her a knowing glare, and she harumphs as I swing open the door to the bar.

The energy inside matches the outside—lively and bright. Each wall is decked out in vivid murals painted to represent the diversity of Nashville that locals and tourists alike love to photograph. I've been here a few times before and was thrilled when Hudson suggested it.

Marjorie glances around, studying the quirky interior, and I'm bracing myself for some sort of criticism when she surprises me.

"This is adorable. How did they make the lights look like clouds?" She gazes up at the high ceilings lit by puffy fixtures in shades of purple, blue, and pink.

Hudson catches my eye from the bar and waves.

"He's cute, Kathryn," Marjorie says as we make our way toward him.

"Kat." Hudson's smile lights up the room as he rises from his stool and pulls me into a hug. "Here, let me take your bag for you."

"Don't let him drop me," Marjorie warns.

"Oh no, I'm fine," I say. "I stopped at an antique store on the way here, and I can't seem to go in those places without finding something."

"What do you like to drink?" he asks. "I'll order and you can grab us a table so you have somewhere to set your stuff."

"Oh, *and* he's a gentleman," Marjorie purrs.

I tell him what I want before Marjorie and I set off in search of a table. We settle at one by the window, and I place my bag and purse on the floor while Marjorie sits diagonally from me.

"What are you doing?" I ask through gritted teeth.

"After what happened with Todd, I want to keep a close eye on this one."

"No drink explosions unless he's a creep."

"I won't. But perhaps I could assist him in spilling yours on those ripped-up jeans you're wearing. Really, you look like one of those rock and roll delinquents from the eighties."

"And that's bad because?"

She doesn't get a chance to answer because Hudson takes his seat beside her, immediately shivering.

"Bit of a draft over here," he says, sliding my drink over to me. "You cold? I'll give you my jacket."

Marjorie nods in approval. "Already off to a much better start."

"I'm okay," I answer. "Thank you, though."

"I have to be honest," Hudson begins, a hint of a flush on his cheeks. "I'm a little nervous."

"What? Why?" I ask.

"I've never done anything like this before—writing into a radio station to go out with someone," he admits.

I chuckle. "Having my coworkers pick out my dates is new for me too."

"Well then, here's to new experiences." He holds his beer out toward me and smiles.

"I'll drink to that," I say, clinking my glass to his.

"So, what did you get at the antique place?" he asks.

"Show him," Marjorie encourages. "Let's find out if he has good taste."

I lean down to grab the glittering vessel and place it between us.

He furrows his brow. "Uh…that kinda looks like—"

"An urn?" I finish for him. "Yeah, I know."

His fingertips graze the reflective surface.

"Watch those hands, mister," Marjorie scolds.

"It's definitely unique," he says. "What are you gonna do with it?"

"I don't know," I answer honestly. Because what *am* I gonna do with this thing, even after Marjorie goes into the light? "But it's cool, right?"

He nods. "I have to admit, I'm not really an antiquing kind of guy. Not that there's anything wrong with those places, but I guess I've seen enough horror movies that I always worry some of this stuff will have an angry old spirit attached to it."

I nearly choke on my beer but manage to disguise it with a laugh.

Marjorie folds her arms over her chest. "Some of us are quite pleasant."

"That is certainly a risk," I say with a grin. "There are few places I love more than an antique shop, though. Actually, one of my friends owns a store like that out where I live."

He gives me a confused look. "You don't live in Nashville?"

I shake my head. "I live west of here, a county over, in Jingo."

"Yikes," he says. "Jingo. That's…kinda out there, isn't it?"

"I don't mind," I answer. "I like the small-town vibe. It's a slower pace, you know? Peaceful. I feel like I live more intentionally out there. I can't just have anything I want delivered at any hour, but what it lacks in convenience, it makes up for in charm."

He takes a sip of his lager. "No Instacart?"

I chuckle. "Nope."

"Uber Eats?"

"Afraid not," I say. "But there is this cute café near me that serves cinnamon roll towers for brunch, and really, what else does one need?"

He pushes his hand through his hair. "I don't know. My entire life kind of exists within a ten-to-fifteen-minute drive, so it's hard to imagine being that far away from everything. Do you ever think about moving to the city?"

My heart sinks when I imagine how small his world must be.

"No, but even if I were to move, I wouldn't want to live in the middle of everything. I love Nashville—don't get me wrong—but being in a small town feels like my own personal escape from the world." I hesitate for a few seconds. "Maybe I can show you around sometime?"

"Yeah, um, maybe." His response is half-hearted. He smiles again, but I already know this will be our one and only date. He's not interested in trying to understand one of the things that means the most to me.

I clear my throat and stand. "Excuse me. I'm just gonna find the restroom real quick. I'll be right back."

"Take your time," Hudson says, shivering as Marjorie rises to follow me.

"Are you all right?" she demands, trailing behind me. "Are you feeling ill? You need to know I can't handle throw up, Kathryn. I'm a sympathetic vomiter."

I don't respond until we're locked inside one of the single-use stalls.

"I'm fine," I promise. "But can ghosts even puke?"

She groans, and her fair complexion pales to an even more ghostly white. "Don't say puke."

"You're the one that brought it up."

"Why are we in here instead of out there with Hudson?" she asks, taking in the multicolored tiles. "I like him. He seems nice."

"He's perfectly fine," I say. "But he isn't for me. Did you see his face when I suggested showing him around where I live?"

She bobs her head from side to side. "I suppose he didn't seem thrilled with the idea."

"To put it mildly."

"Is that really a deal-breaker for you? You wouldn't consider living in a proper city if you met the right person?"

"No," I reply. "I moved back to Jingo after college because that's where I lived with my grandmother when I was a teenager. She loved it there because she knew everybody, and everybody knew her. They loved her."

A lump forms in my throat, just as it does anytime I think of my grandmother, which is the main reason I avoid it.

"Your town is special to you." Her face softens. "Perhaps if this young man knew—"

"I don't want to give him the whole sob story about why living there is so important to me." I lean against the wall and cross my arms. "Besides, he shouldn't have to change something about himself that he's happy with."

"And neither should you," she says matter-of-factly. "The right person won't dismiss something that's clearly meaningful to you."

I drop my gaze to the toe of my boot drawing invisible circles onto the floor.

"Maybe there is no right person for me." The realization doesn't feel like a gut punch so much as a resigned acceptance, as though being alone is something as inevitable as paying taxes or dying.

"Look at me," Marjorie commands, though her tone is gentle.

I do so with a sigh.

"You were right earlier. About the money not making me happy. I was a wealthy woman, but I was not rich. Not in the ways that mattered."

I frown. "Marjorie, I didn't say that to hurt you."

"You didn't. But when you're right, you're right. I know we don't see eye to eye on everything. We've led very different lives, but there's something you have the chance to do that I'll never get again. You have the chance to find love." There's a sadness in her green eyes that tells me she's speaking from experience. "Promise me you won't give that up."

I don't want to, but what if the best I can hope for is a string of Conrads or Todds? "I know things between you and Conrad weren't exactly a fairy tale, but did you really never feel like you found love?"

As quickly as her vulnerability appeared, it's replaced with a tight smile.

"That's a story for another day," she says. "Now, what would you like to do? Do you want to leave?"

"No," I answer. "It's just a drink, and who knows? Maybe he could end up being a friend."

"Friends are good."

There's a sincerity in her expression that makes me wonder if she considers me one.

"Yeah," I say. "Yeah, they are."

chapter fifteen

We don't hear back from Michael Saturday, much to Marjorie's disappointment, and after my failed date with Hudson, we both need a distraction. So we're grateful when Dennis suggests grabbing a cinnamon roll tower from Dawn's Diner to go and bringing it to my place for brunch on Sunday. Despite Dennis not being able to see or hear Marjorie, I suspect she still appreciates having someone else around who knows she exists.

"Marjorie Lockwood, everyone. The woman, the myth, the legend." Dennis raises his coffee cup in her honor. I'd just finished recounting my date with Todd and how she'd made his drink explode, causing the lights to flicker like we were in a haunted house.

"Oh, it was nothing." Marjorie's hand flutters in a dismissive wave but her smile betrays her nonchalance.

"Your modesty is no good here," I say as Delilah slinks over to her bowl for a midmorning snack. "We already know you're a badass. Did I tell you she can change her outfits at will too?"

Dennis presses his hand to his heart. "Gives me something to look forward to when I leave this earthly plane."

"*That*'s what you're excited for?" I tease. "I thought it would be eavesdropping on people to see what they have to say about you."

He leans in. "I love gossip, but only when it involves someone else. What folks have to say about me is none of my business. If they're talking about me, at least they're on a fascinating subject."

"That's a good attitude," Marjorie says. "One I wish I'd adopted when I was younger."

"Have you tested to find out what else Marjorie can do?" Dennis asks.

I lick the icing off my fork. "She's not a science experiment, Dennis."

"I know that," he chides. "But we've been given an open line to the spirit world, Kat. Aren't you both at least a little curious?" He looks toward the chair at the head of the table Marjorie is seated in. "Marjorie, if you can break glass and flicker lights when some blowhard makes you mad, imagine what else you could do if you focus all your energy on it."

She lifts her brows and tilts her head. "Hmm."

"We could just try a couple of things," he continues. "Consider it research."

"You don't have to do anything you're not comfortable with," I tell her, shooting Dennis a look.

"Of course not," he insists, his eyes still on Marjorie. "But don't you want to know?"

She bites back an excited grin and turns to me. "It could be kind of fun, don't you think?"

"I'm in if you are."

Dennis pushes the jarred candle at the center of the table toward her. "Here, see if you can light this."

I immediately pull it away. "How about we try something that doesn't involve fire and a possible 911 call?"

"You're no fun," Dennis teases. "Okay, then. Try to move this spoon back toward me." He sends the utensil closer to her and sits back, folding his arms over his chest.

"How on earth do I do that?" she asks.

"No clue," I answer. "Dennis, you're the spiritual expert here. How do you suppose that would work exactly?"

He taps a finger against his mug. "I can't know for sure, but if I had to guess, I would say you need to start by clearing your mind. Begin with deep, cleansing breaths."

"Tell the dead woman to breathe," I chide, and Marjorie stifles a laugh. "Got it."

"Oh, whatever." He huffs. "You know what I mean. Close your eyes. Do whatever it is you would do to bring yourself back to center."

"Yes. Right," she says, straightening her spine. Her eyes close and she sits quietly for a moment.

"Now what?" we both ask.

"Think of a time where you felt strongly about something," he suggests. "We know anger works, so try that. Think of a time when you were pissed off. Allow that feeling to flood your body so it's as though it's happening in real time, then channel that into moving the spoon."

She opens her eyes and scoffs. "And how does one channel a feeling into moving an object?"

I repeat her question for Dennis, and he pauses a moment.

"Imagine the emotion as a gust of wind. Visualize it. Give it a color inside your mind. Red, perhaps," he explains. "Then,

I want you to use that air to slide the spoon toward me." He mimes the motion with his hands.

"Visualize the feeling," she says to herself.

I shrug. "Sounds like as good an idea as any."

She closes her eyes once more and goes still. The room is silent except for the ticking of the clock that echoes from the living room. A full minute passes, and I'm thinking there's no way this is going to work when all of a sudden, the spoon flies from the table with such force that it skims over Dennis's head before clanging to the floor.

Delilah screeches and scatters toward the living room, diving under the couch as Marjorie gasps. My hands fly to my mouth.

"My God, woman," Dennis says, touching his palm to his scalp. "I said slide the spoon, not slice my head off with it."

She winces. "Sorry about that."

"That must have been a doozy of a memory," I say.

"I was remembering when that awful woman Annabelle moved my urn to the attic like I was nothing but an old box of out of style clothes to be forgotten," she replies, bitterness dripping from her voice.

I nod. "That'll do it."

Dennis blows out a long breath. "Maybe we should see if you can harness other emotions. Less violent ones, perhaps?"

"Like what?" Marjorie asks.

"Think about a time you felt really, truly happy," I say. "Pure joy."

"And let's *not* move an object this time. How about you try to make this light flicker?" Dennis points to the fixture over our heads.

"Okay. Yes. I can do that. Think of something joyful." She squares her shoulders once again and squeezes her eyes shut.

Dennis and I exchange a glance, and I wonder if I should grab the fire extinguisher just in case this goes horribly awry.

The faintest smile passes over Marjorie's face, and the light above us flashes brightly before burning out completely, causing us to jump.

Dennis bites back a grin. "Well, that was an improvement."

Marjorie looks up at the now dead bulb. "Sorry."

I chuckle. "You know what? I think that's enough practice for now. I only have so many light bulbs." I rise from my seat and head to the counter to refill my mug. "More coffee, Den?"

He shakes his head. "I've hit my limit. I don't know how you can drink so much. What is that? Your third cup?"

"Fifth," I correct as I reach for the carafe.

"My IBS could never," he jokes.

The screen on my phone flashes, catching my eye from its spot on the bar as I start back toward the table. I reach for it, and my heart jumps into my throat when I see the notification that Michael has returned my message.

Marjorie doesn't miss my surprised expression. "What is it, Kathryn? Did you get something back from Michael?"

"Yes," I say as I swipe to open the app.

"Time for more unfinished business with Marj?" Dennis asks. "That's a great name for a podcast, by the way."

Marjorie shoots him a look that I'm glad he can't see before jumping to her feet and rushing to my side. "What does it say?"

I swat her off as I open the thread. "Give me a second." I squint and begin to read, my excitement quickly fading to disappointment.

"Well?" Marjorie presses. "Is that her son or not?"

"Yes," I answer.

"Then why do you look like that?" she asks. "That's wonderful news. We'll find out where she lives and go as soon as possible."

I sigh. "We can't."

"And why not?" she counters.

I turn the screen so she can read the words for herself. "Because she's dead."

chapter sixteen

Dennis leaves in a hurry once all my lights begin flickering at the same time, a couple of them bursting and going dark as Marjorie paces through the house. The second I told her what Michael said about his mother, the theatrics began.

"This is just like Frances," Marjorie hisses. "One month! You mean to tell me she couldn't have waited to drop dead for *one more month*? She wasn't there when I needed her before. I don't know why on earth I expected her to be here now." She throws her hands up in frustration as she stomps soundlessly across the hardwood, causing a couple of framed art prints on the kitchen wall to crash to the floor.

I flinch and nearly tell her to watch her step when I remember she has no flesh.

"I could be wrong, but I think dying constitutes a pretty good reason for her not being here," I say, my eyes following her path of rage as I silently pray she doesn't send my house crumbling down to a pile of rubble.

She scowls. "This is not funny, Kathryn."

"Of course it isn't," I reply, leaning against the counter. "But I don't think she died just to spite you or anything."

"Well, what else am I supposed to think?" she snaps.

"Oh, I don't know. Maybe that the woman was seventy-six years old and had a massive coronary?" I cross my arms and give her a *are-you-freakin-serious* stare.

She huffs, her fists clenched at her sides. "What about my unfinished business? What if talking to Frances was the only hope I had for crossing over?"

"She isn't."

"How can you know that?"

"I guess I don't," I admit. "Not for certain, anyway. But I find it hard to believe that God, the universe, whatever entity is in charge here would send Frances on to the afterlife without having her check in with you if your eternities were somehow connected."

This elicits another groan from Marjorie, but I can tell my words are starting to get through because she's finally standing in one spot.

"Look, I know figuring out your unfinished business is important," I continue, keeping my voice calm and even. "But don't you think you're being a little…selfish?"

Her lip twitches, and she won't make eye contact.

"Her son seemed pretty broken up about it," I say. "Maybe you and Frances never got to hash things out, but it sounds like you might have still had a lasting impact. Doesn't that count for something?"

Michael had sent back a long, thought-out reply about how Frances had spoken a lot of Marjorie over the years, that she'd mentioned having regrets about their falling out. He went on to say that after being used by his father one too many times, they *both* had stepped away from him for good about fifteen years prior. Frances never remarried, but she'd found joy in working part time at a daycare and watching her two grandchildren grow up.

"What you told her all those years ago might have stuck with her," I say. "She may not have been able to quite see it then, but you probably planted a seed that grew over time until she finally had the strength to leave her marriage."

Marjorie's expression deflates. "I suppose you're right."

"I know she bailed on you when you wouldn't cave to what she wanted," I say. "But you cared about her. Doesn't it give you a little comfort to know she made the right choice, even if it was much later?"

"Yes, all right," she relents. "It does. But I don't understand how she didn't end up trapped here, and I did."

"Maybe she didn't have any unfinished business. And perhaps that's at least in some roundabout way thanks to you."

She sighs and drops her gaze, steepling her fingers together. "What if we can't figure out what my unfinished business is?"

"We will," I promise. "I won't give up until we do, but you've got to be patient."

"That's never been my strong suit."

"Sure could have fooled me." I don't realize I've said this out loud until I'm met with a glare. "What if patience is part of whatever lesson that's keeping you here?"

"Then I suppose I'm doomed," she says, emphasizing every word.

"I'm serious. What if that's your lesson?" I ask. "What if you're supposed to learn patience?"

She tilts her head, tapping a finger to her chin. "You could be onto something."

"We shouldn't rule out anything at this point." I rack my

brain, trying to think of ways she can exercise patience. "What if you try to visualize patience the way you were doing with your emotions? Let it wash over you."

Hope flickers in her green eyes. "You really think that could work?"

"I have no idea," I say with a shrug. "But it can't hurt to try, and besides, patience seems less…destructive than other things."

I gesture toward the broken shards on the floor, and she winces.

"I'm sorry," she says. "I didn't mean to break your pictures."

"It's oka—"

"They were ugly, though, so I may have done you a favor."

I stare at her, unblinking.

She clears her throat, then closes her eyes. "I'm channeling patience."

That makes two of us.

She stands straighter, touching her ring fingers to her thumbs, her face beginning to relax. Nothing happens—not so much as a flicker of a bulb. I don't know whether to be glad or annoyed.

"I'm being patient," she says like a mantra.

"Clearly."

Her eyes snap open, and she stomps her foot, causing the mug on the counter between us to rattle. "This is ridiculous. Nothing is happening."

"It was worth a shot," I say. "Don't get discouraged. It'll just take some time to figure it out. I'm back at work tomorrow, which means you'll have plenty of uninterrupted time to think."

"I can't spend another day alone here," she insists. "I'll lose my mind."

"So, to be clear, that's not what you're doing right now?" Because it feels like we're both one minor inconvenience away from a full downward spiral.

"I mean it. I want to go to work with you in the morning."

"That's not happening."

"And why not?"

"First of all, you've killed half my lights. Do you know how much electrical equipment is at the radio station?" I ask. "A *lot*. You could wipe Nashville off the grid if something pisses you off."

"I'll be on my best behavior," she assures me.

I narrow my eyes. "Why don't I believe that?"

"Please, Kathryn."

"No."

"Please."

"Still no."

"I said please."

"It's not happening."

Her nostrils flare as she puts her hands on her hips. "So help me God, if you leave me here tomorrow, I will knock every ugly painting off your walls, I will flip tables and figure out how to start a fire in the hearth just so I can throw that pathetic excuse of a couch into it."

I grit my teeth and release a long breath through my nose. Part of me thinks she's bluffing, but I'm too broke to find out for sure.

"Fine," I mutter. "We leave at five."

chapter seventeen

I ARRIVE AT THE STATION THE NEXT MORNING WITH MARJORIE'S urn in the paper shopping bag I've been using, and I stuff it under the table, between my spot and Jude's. However, it doesn't occur to me until I take my seat in the studio that my usual antique shop ruse isn't going to cut it because there are no shops open at 5 a.m.

Eddie is the only one already there, but thankfully, he's on a phone call with his back to me, which gives me a little time to consider what I'm going to say.

"Oh my," Marjorie practically purrs. "He's handsome, isn't he?"

I shoot her a glare.

"Best behavior, I know," she says, holding her hands up in mock surrender.

Think, Kat.

Why would I bring a random urn to work as though it's show-and-tell? No one else here has a passion for antiques the way I do, and I've never brought in any of my thrifted treasures before, except for the Magic 8 Ball I found in a Goodwill bin a couple years ago, but that was just for fun. Can I even come up with a believable reason as to why I have an urn under the desk?

Outlook not so good. Very doubtful. My sources say no.

"Morning," Becca says as she comes in, plopping her bag on the floor.

"Mornin'," I answer, but there's no feeling in it. I'm too distracted by what the hell I'm going to say when someone asks about my urn—and they will because we're always in each other's business. It's kind of part of the job.

"She's a lovely girl," Marjorie says. "My goodness, she's stunning. Isn't she stunning?"

I clear my throat, and Becca shivers, pulling the sleeves of her sweatshirt over her hands. "It's freezing in here. Are you cold?"

"Uh, what?" I ask, nearly choking on my coffee midsip.

Becca studies me for a moment. "Are you okay? You seem weird."

"She's right," Marjorie informs me. "You're acting stranger than usual."

So not helping.

"I'm fine," I reply, but my voice comes out all high-pitched and wrong.

"You don't seem fine," Becca says, her gaze filled with concern.

"You really don't," Marjorie adds, and if she wasn't already dead I would strangle her.

"I said I'm fine." Said every not-fine person ever. Eddie glances over his shoulder, plugging one ear as he takes his conversation out into the hallway.

"Hey." Jude's greeting slices through the tension as he comes in to take his seat. "How's everyone doing?"

"Now, who is this gorgeous man?" Marjorie murmurs, and I wish the floor would open up and swallow us both.

"Kat's being weird," Becca announces, and I busy myself with turning on my laptop.

"I am not," I insist as my fingers tap along the keys. I'm so nervous I accidentally type the wrong password three times before I get logged in.

"Oh yeah?" Jude flips open his own computer. "Why's that?"

"I don't know," Becca says. "She's all jumpy."

"I'm not jumpy," I reply, but it takes every bit of effort I possess to keep from shouting the words.

"You do seem a little jumpy," Jude says, his brown eyes boring into me.

"You do," Marjorie agrees, and it's then I know telepathy does not exist because she doesn't receive my mental *would-you-kindly-shut-the-heck-up* memo.

Jude lifts his brows before returning his attention to his screen. "Shit. This thing's about to die. I forgot to plug it in this weekend."

Oh no. Oh no, no, no, no, no.

He's going to go for the outlet under the table.

The very one that is just inches away from the bag in which Marjorie's remains are contained.

"I'll get it," I volunteer, though it comes out almost frantic.

But the offer is useless, because Jude is already leaning down. "I've got it."

He plugs his charger in, and his gaze snags on the bag. "What's that?"

"What's what?"

Maybe I should claim ignorance and act like it's not mine.

Oh my God. What is that? Definitely not a dead lady whose spirit is in this very room because that would be crazy!

"Oh dear. We should have discussed how you were going to explain my urn," Marjorie says.

You think?!

Jude gestures toward the bag. "That sparkling thing."

My throat tightens, and my mouth feels dry and gummed up, like I just swallowed a giant spoonful of honey.

"Um..." I stall as Becca rises to check out what he's talking about, and *oh my God, why did I think this was a good idea*?

"Oh wow," she says. "What *is* that?"

"Uh..."

"Are you having a spell?" Marjorie asks. "Cough if you need me to create a diversion."

Absolutely not.

Jude cocks his head as he lifts the urn from the bag. "It looks like—"

"It's my cat," I blurt out.

Becca gasps, and Jude's eyes widen as he eases the urn back into the sack.

"Honestly, Kathryn," Marjorie mutters. "My Andre Vieux has been reduced to a cat coffin."

"What?" Becca cries, wrapping me in her arms. "Did it happen this weekend? I'm so sorry. Why didn't you call me?"

"I'm still...reeling from it all," I manage and plead with the karmic gods to not actually take my cat. "It doesn't seem real, you know?"

Probably because it isn't.

"I'm so sorry, Kat," Jude says, reaching out to squeeze my arm. "I didn't mean to—"

His touch sends a ripple of warmth through my body, and

I feel guilty for relishing his comfort. "It's okay. You didn't know."

"Sweetie," Becca begins, taking her seat beside me and rolling it closer. "I know you love Delilah, but I'm not sure if bringing her to the office is what's best for you. You might need space to…you know…heal."

Not to mention that it was only a few days ago when I advised a woman to head for the hills after discovering her date's taxidermied dog had been chilling in his trunk for a few years. This isn't worse, but it isn't better, either.

"I just…" I can't argue because if this *was* real I never would have brought my cat's ashes to work. But I have to pretend this isn't out of character for me. "I…"

"No, hey, look at me," Jude says, and when I do, a tiny jolt of electricity zings through me. "You do whatever you need to do to cope right now."

"I'm sorry," Becca adds. "Jude's right. I know this just happened, and I get how much she meant to you."

Guilt gnaws at my stomach because they're being so understanding, and I'm lying to their faces. But I can't tell them the truth—that I'm seeing dead people, or more accurately, one really determined, judgy, super sassy dead lady.

"Is there anything I can do?" Jude asks, rubbing his fingers along my arm.

"No," I answer quickly. "No, I'll be fine."

"I mean it, Kat," Jude says. "Anything you need, I'm here."

Marjorie stands between us, watching Jude intently. "This young man…he cares about you."

"Me too," Becca says. "Seriously."

"Did you know this?" Marjorie questions, and I feel my cheeks burn.

Yeah. As a friend.

"Kathryn?" She moves so she's in my face, and I nearly jump out of my skin.

Right. That whole telepathy thing doesn't work.

I squeeze my eyes shut, willing her to disappear, but she doesn't, as evidenced by the shiver that vibrates through my body.

"It's chilly in here," Jude says, removing his hand and rising to shrug off his olive green jacket. "Here, take my coat."

"Oh, I'm oka—"

"Take the man's coat," Marjorie orders, and the overhead light flickers.

I jump to my feet. "Actually, now that you mention it, I am a little cold."

Jude holds the jacket open so I can slide my arms inside, and Marjorie looks pleased as punch. And admittedly, I don't hate being swathed in Jude's scent. God, has he always smelled this good? Like spiced rum with a hint of cinnamon.

"Thanks," I say, giving Jude a soft smile before dropping my voice low so there's no chance of our boss hearing us in the hall. "Can we...not tell Eddie? You guys know how he worries, and it's just...hard to talk about."

He nods. "Of course."

"Yeah," Becca agrees. "It stays between us until you decide to tell him."

"I appreciate it," I say, returning my focus to my laptop screen, but even as I do, I feel Jude's eyes lingering on me.

Marjorie leans down and speaks directly into my ear. "You know, your friend was right when she said your picker was broken because I think the right guy has been under your nose all along."

chapter eighteen

MARJORIE IS ON HER BEST BEHAVIOR THROUGHOUT THE morning broadcast, meaning that while she insists on giving me her two cents on *everything*, at least she stops flickering the lights. She's by my side as we record some ads and a couple of segments that will air later in the week, ending with my part of Todd's *Purrfect Match* update. Luckily, I don't have to be present when they talk to him.

I keep things tactful when we're recording, but as soon as the mics are off, I tell them everything while Marjorie provides color commentary only I can hear.

"That boy was a weasel." Marjorie paces the small room with her hands on her hips.

Jude shakes his head. "I can't believe you guys picked him. He's always given me the creeps on TV."

Becca frowns. "Damn. He seemed so nice."

I snort. "I'm sure he's plenty nice as long as he's getting something out of it."

"We'll keep his spot extra short," Eddie says. "I don't want to give him any more time than he's already been given."

"Did you go on your other date?" Becca asks, her voice soft. "Were you up to it?"

"Why wouldn't she be up to it?" Eddie questions. "You okay, Kat?"

Panic flashes through me, but Becca quickly swoops in with a save.

"I just meant because her first one was so rough," Becca explains. "I wouldn't blame her for wanting to postpone the second one."

I clear my throat. "Um, yeah, I went. Hudson was cool. Just not for me."

Jude casts pointed glances at Eddie and Becca. "I thought you two were screening these guys."

Becca is taken aback. "We are."

"Nothing is going to be foolproof," Eddie says with a wave of his hand. "The application process is in-depth, but there's still a lot that can't be accounted for on a form. Chemistry, for starters."

"Or if they're clout-chasing liars," Becca adds.

Marjorie leans down in Jude's space, regarding him closely. "What I want to know is why Jude didn't fill out this application when he clearly likes you?"

Jude shrugs. "All I'm saying is that maybe you need to inspect these things a little more carefully."

Becca gives him an incredulous look. "We have Cassie checking them out too, and we *would* have you, but you told me you didn't want to be a part of it."

I furrow my brows. He *isn't* a part of it? I was never told explicitly that he *wasn't*, so I just assumed he was also weighing in on who he thought would be my best matches.

"Did you hear that?" Marjorie's eyes glitter with excitement. "I'm telling you, Kathryn. I think this Jude fellow has feelings for you."

"Why didn't you want to do it?" I don't just *want* to know. I *need* to know.

"Because he's in love with you," Marjorie practically sings.

Not now, Marj.

Jude runs his hand along the back of his neck. "I think the idea's a little ridiculous is all. It feels like we're…I don't know…auctioning you off or something. I just think you deserve better than that."

"Him! You deserve *him*," Marjorie cries, her hands fluttering like manic butterflies. In her overzealous enthusiasm, she accidentally brushes her fingers against Jude's shoulder, and I catch him shudder.

My jaw clenches as I glare at her.

"You know if you're not comfortable continuing we can call the whole thing off," Eddie reminds me.

The room and my heart seem to have been knocked askew. *Do* I still want this?

"I really think we have some good matches lined up for you this weekend. Wait till I send you their pics. They're hotties."

Marjorie smirks. "I'll be the judge of that."

"What do you think, Kat?" Eddie asks.

Jude fixes his gentle eyes on me, and for a moment, I think he's mentally telling me not to do it. But that's silly. First of all, as we've established, telepathy isn't real. And second, Jude is my friend and nothing more. While I know all of that to be true, I can't shake the way he's looking at me— like there are a million unsaid thoughts swirling inside his brown irises.

"Kathryn," Marjorie says. "You're staring."

"Let's keep going," I answer, though my heart isn't in it.

Eddie nods. "Good. We'll get these next two dates set up for this Friday and Saturday night, as long as that still works for you."

"Yeah," I reply. "That's fine."

When I glance back at Jude, I find he's returned his focus to his computer screen.

I push my fingers through my hair. Marjorie is just getting in my head, and it's causing me to see things that aren't there.

Eddie snaps his laptop shut. "All right, team. I've got to head out for a meeting. See y'all in the morning."

"Bye," I call as he heads out the door.

Once he's out of earshot, Becca leans over to touch my arm. "I have band rehearsal this afternoon, but I'm all yours afterward if you need me."

"Thanks, Bec," I say. "But I'm okay. Really."

She rises to her feet and squeezes my shoulder. "If you change your mind…"

"I promise I'll let you know."

She nods and tosses a wave over her shoulder as she strides out.

"How exactly are you going to keep up this ruse about your cat?" Marjorie asks. "Surely someone will come to your house eventually and realize she's very much alive."

I rest my elbows on the table and press the heels of my palms into my eye sockets. That sounds like a problem for future me.

Jude stands at the same time I do, but instead of saying his goodbyes, he lingers while I reach for my bags.

"What do you have going on the rest of the day?" he asks.

"I'm just going home." *I have a very busy afternoon*

ahead, attempting to figure out why looking at you is making my insides go all squishy.

He taps his fingers along the back of his chair. "Why don't we hang out, take your mind off things for a bit? We can go to Billy's and do some day drinking. Get those chicken nachos you like."

I raise my brows. Billy's is my favorite little pub near the station, and it's always the place I request to go on those rare occasions our schedules align for after-work drinks. It's no secret I love the place, but I never would have thought Jude would remember what I like to order there.

I tuck my hair behind my ear. "Oh, um, actually, I should probably get ho—"

"Have you lost your mind?" Marjorie asks, stepping between us to face me.

He runs his hand over the stubble on his chin. "Right. Yeah. Of course."

"Kathryn." Marjorie's voice is a warning bell. "We're going. Tell him we're going."

Jude gives me a sad smile. "Okay, well, if you need anything, I'm here."

I realize I'm still wearing his coat. "Oh, I should give you back your—"

"Tell him," Marjorie practically roars, causing the lights to flicker wildly.

Jude's eyes widen. "That was weird. Must be a power surge."

"And there'll be another one if you don't go with him," Marjorie hisses. "Perhaps I'll even manage to drain the batteries in both your cars, so you're stuck here together."

"You know, on second thought, day drinking sounds great."

chapter nineteen

It's midafternoon, so Billy's is mostly dead minus a few patrons sipping pints at two tops watching ESPN on one of the giant televisions. Jude doesn't even blink when I grab the bag containing the urn from the passenger seat. Instead, he takes it from me and carries it inside.

We sit at the bar sipping our beers while we wait for our nachos to arrive, and Marjorie glances around with her nose wrinkled in disgust.

"I don't suppose you have some sanitizer for this stool," she says, eyeing the vacant spot next to me where the bag containing her urn rests on the floor. "Some bleach, perhaps."

I have neither. Never mind that she's a ghost and therefore cannot catch any germs.

"This Billy person certainly spared no expense on the decor." She glances around at the stickers, posters, and polaroids stuck to every square inch of wall space. Some of them are so old they've begun to yellow around the edges. There's a Pac-Man machine that's been out of order since we started coming here and an old jukebox in the back corner streaked with so many fingerprints, it probably needs its own hazmat label.

"So, you mentioned earlier that the second date didn't go well either," Jude begins. "What happened?"

"He was nice enough, but his entire life is basically within a ten-mile radius, and he had no desire to change that," I explain. "You know how much I love living in Jingo, and to be fair, I don't plan on giving that up, either."

"And why would you? It's a nice place," he says. "I've actually looked online at houses out there from time to time."

Marjorie's ears perk up, and she lifts one perfectly arched brow. "Well, isn't that interesting?"

Interesting, peculiar…exciting—all words that come to mind. "You have? How did I not know this?"

"Probably because I never mentioned it." He takes a swig of his drink and shrugs. "It was just something I've considered. I enjoyed the times I've been out to visit your place. And that store you took me to was pretty cool. What was it called? Wu and Whimsy or something?"

I smile. "Whimsy and Wu."

"That's it," he says with a nod. "Plus, I love the small-town feel, you know? The slower pace. Being able to see the stars at night. Besides, real estate is a lot more affordable the farther you get from the city, and I'm at the point that I'm ready to lay down some roots, get out of condo living. Also, my neighbor's a tool."

I chuckle at that.

"I think the biggest reason is sitting right beside him," Marjorie remarks. "There are a lot of small towns outside of Nashville he could choose from, but he just so happens to want to live in yours?"

"And you're there," Jude adds. "Maybe we could even

carpool to work sometimes. Saves on gas, *and* it's good for the environment."

"I hate to say I told you so." Marjorie is bubbling over like an uncorked bottle of champagne. "Actually, what am I saying? No, I don't. *I told you so.*"

I bite back a grin. "I had no idea you were so passionate about the environment."

"Hey, I recycle." His lips curve upward, framing his eyes with the most adorable crinkles. "But the company wouldn't be too bad, either."

"I agree," I say. "Well, I still have the name of the realtor I used. One of only two in town."

"Send it to me," he replies. "Maybe it's time I start looking into it more seriously."

"Sure." I find the contact in my phone and AirDrop it to him.

He thanks me as the middle-aged bartender with a long blond braid returns with our nachos and two shot glasses of what smells like tequila.

"Wait, we didn't order these," I say, gesturing to the clear liquid.

"It's from that guy in the corner," she replies. "Said he's a big fan of the show."

We turn to see a guy in the corner, flipping through the pages of a newspaper, who raises his pint glass to us.

"You guys are the best," he calls out. "Been listening to *Eddie in the Morning* forever. Just wanted to show my appreciation."

"Thanks, man," Jude replies, and I wave as the bartender leaves us alone with our food and shots.

"That's the good stuff too," I say, gesturing toward the tequila.

"Then we best not let it go to waste." He picks up one of the glasses and holds it out toward me, waiting for me to grab the other.

I reach for the remaining shot and take a whiff. "Wow, I don't know. It's been years since I've done one of these."

"One won't hurt," Marjorie says. "Just drink plenty of water before we leave."

Jude nudges me with his elbow. "Come on. You've had a hell of a few days. We said we were gonna day drink. Let's commit."

"What the hell." I clink my glass to his. "Cheers."

The liquid burns as it slides down my throat, making my limbs feel like warm, buttery noodles.

"That *is* the good stuff," Jude says. "Even my toes are tingling."

I laugh. "I think that's just what happens when you try to drink shots in your thirties."

Marjorie points to the plate of steaming nachos. "Now you both need to eat before that tequila goes straight to your heads."

As if he heard her, Jude stuffs a loaded chip into his mouth. "So, you're really going forward with this *Purrfect Match* thing."

"I mean, why not?" I ask, though the laissez-faire optimism I began the experiment with is fading. "I don't exactly have guys beating down my door over here."

"That's because a lot of guys are idiots and wouldn't know a good thing if it bit them in the ass," he says.

Marjorie holds out a hand, inspecting her nails. "I would have to agree."

"While I would love to place blame on the stupidity of others, I highly doubt that applies to *every* man I've ever been out with," I say. "I figure I have nothing to lose by trying. And who knows—maybe this is how I meet the right guy."

"Maybe." Jude takes a sip of his beer. "But I doubt it."

I narrow my eyes as I turn toward him, the alcohol causing all filters to fly out the window. "Okay, what gives? You've been against this from the jump. Why?"

"No, I haven't," he argues.

"Oh yes, you have." And it's starting to get in my head. "But what I don't understand is *why*. Is it so unfathomable that someone could actually be interested in me?"

Marjorie immediately rises to his defense. "That's not what he's saying."

My brain knows that, but my heart is on a roll, all my insecurities spilling out before I can shove them back inside.

Jude opens his mouth to speak, but I cut him off.

"You've been cagey about this since Eddie brought it up. Is it really so unbelievable that I could find someone? That I could be happy?"

"What? Of course not." He touches my hand, a spark of electricity pulsing through my veins, before I snatch my arm away like a petulant child.

Now I remember why I stopped drinking tequila in my thirties. Besides the fact that it takes me two to seven business days to recover from a hangover, it makes me hypersensitive and emotional.

"You need to calm down," Marjorie warns. "You're being unreasonable."

"*You're* being unreasonable," I shoot back before I remember that Jude has no clue we're actually a party of three.

Marjorie sighs. "Oh dear."

Jude pushes a hand through his hair. "I'm not being unreasonable. I just don't want to see you waste your time on some loser."

What am I doing?! Stop talking.

But my mouth doesn't get the message.

"Yeah, well, it sounds to me like you think no one is good enough. But really it's just me who isn't good enough, right? Why don't you just say what you mean, Jude?"

Shut up, shut up, SHUT UP.

He looks at me as though he's been slapped. "What the hell, Kat? You *know* that's not what I'm saying, and I damn sure don't think that. But you're right about one thing. I haven't been telling you how I really feel."

"Oh yeah?" I ask, my initial fire beginning to smolder. "And what's that?"

He pins me with his gaze, unwilling to let me go. "That I don't understand why you keep going out with these jackasses that don't deserve you when I'm right here. When I've always been *right here*."

Marjorie and the rest of the bar fade away, leaving Jude and I floating, suspended in this moment.

Jesus, what was in that tequila?

I release a shaky breath. "What?"

His hand slides along my jaw and into my hair. "You heard me."

He's so close I can make out the different shades of brown in his eyes, each one my new favorite color. Or maybe they'd always been my favorite, and I somehow forgot. But before I can decide, he leans forward and presses his lips to mine. They're soft but firm in all the right ways, their sweetness causing stars to burst behind my eyes in technicolor.

Then as quickly as the kiss started, it stops, and I immediately crave his warmth.

"I...I'm sorry," Jude murmurs. "I shouldn't have done that. Not that I haven't wanted to because God, have I wanted to, but—"

"Shut up." I don't want words or explanations. I don't want to pretend for a second this wasn't the best kiss of my life. All I want is him.

"What?"

"I said shut up," I answer before I take his face in my hands and make him.

Then, the lights in the bar go dark.

chapter twenty

JUDE BREAKS OUR KISS, HIS BROWS FURROWED AS THE LIGHTS come back on. "What's with all the electrical issues today?"

Marjorie lets out a girlish squeal, causing the lights to flicker once more.

"Transformers," I blurt before second-guessing if that's a real word or a sci-fi movie. Either way, it seems reasonable. "The electric company must be testing them."

He cocks his head like a golden retriever. "Is that a thing?"

How the hell would I know?

"Yeah. Totally." I take a long pull of my beer as I twist to face Marjorie, shooting her a *could-you-chill-on-the-light-show* glare.

She clears her throat and straightens her blouse, her usual demure demeanor returning. "You know what? I'm going to give you two some privacy."

My eyes widen. *Really?*

She smirks. "This has clearly turned into a date—one I don't think you need my expertise on. So you take your time.

I'm going to just…" She gestures toward the opposite corner of the bar. "I'll be over there."

I grin as I slide my beer back on the counter.

"Good luck," she whispers as she sweeps past us, pretending to be riveted by the conversation happening between the couple in the corner.

Jude's eyes are soft when I turn back to him, and I've never felt more cherished than I do here in his gaze.

"That was…" He touches my cheek, his thumb swiping gently over my bottom lip. "Do you have any idea how long I've wanted to do that?" My face must convey the shock I feel because he adds, "You look surprised."

A breathless chuckle rises from my throat. "Because I am."

He smiles. "Oh, come on."

"What?"

"You really didn't know about my big fat crush on you?"

My entire sense of reality tilts on its axis. I feel like I'm being told the sky is yellow after a lifetime of knowing beyond a shadow of a doubt that it's blue.

"No, I didn't," I say. "How would I?"

"I guess I just thought it was obvious," he answers. "Every time we discuss one of your dating segments, it's all I can do not to tear my hair out because it kills me. I always wished it was me you were going out with."

I blink. "But you never asked."

"I know."

"Why didn't you say something?"

"I almost did," he says. "Twice."

"When?"

"The first was when you got promoted to producer. We

were working side by side, and everything felt right. But then Lexi, that cohost who trashed the dude on-air that she'd been seeing from upper management, got fired, and I was offered a spot in the cast. The station freaked out and implemented the no interoffice dating policy. Of course, they've relaxed on that a bit over the years, since Cassie almost left just so she could keep seeing Doug from marketing."

"Okay, that's fair," I concede. "When was the second time?"

"Right before you started dating that guy. *Nick.*" The name sounds bitter coming off his tongue. "I'd finally worked up the courage to talk to you, and I was gonna do it the night of the company Christmas party the year Eddie booked it at Opryland Hotel. I had this whole thing planned in my head. I was gonna steal you away for a walk outside to look at the lights, but then you came in with him. You looked so…happy. I couldn't bring myself to tell you and mess that up."

I can't stop myself from imagining what might've happened if he'd told me or the sense of loss I feel knowing that he didn't. "But even after Nick and I broke up, you never said anything. If memory serves, you started seeing someone soon after that. It got pretty serious too."

"Yeah," he says with a nod. "I remember feeling so… heartbroken that I'd missed my chance with you. While I licked my wounds, I let my mother, of all people, set me up with a resident at Vanderbilt—the hospital where she works—and that's how I met Lauren."

"You were with her for a while, weren't you? Even after Nick and I split up. My memory is kind of fuzzy on that because it seemed like we heard about her more than we saw her. I thought you two might end up getting married."

"I did too," he admits.

"What happened?"

He shifts on his stool and tugs at the hem of his shirt. "I got a job offer in Dallas to host my own morning show."

"What?" I feel as though he's thrown his beer in my face. "You were gonna leave?"

"I thought about it."

"Why?"

He blows out a breath. "I thought I was ready for a change. To make my own mark on the world of radio."

Once again, I find myself picturing a different outcome. Jude *leaving*. Not seeing him every day. Never having this moment. "But you didn't go."

"No, but I was there for a good part of my holiday break that year and came really close to signing the contract."

"Why didn't you?"

"Because Lauren didn't want me to," he answers. "I'd spent the better part of three years supporting her during her residency, going to every event she asked me to attend, but when I wanted her to do the same for me, she couldn't do it." He pauses for a beat and swallows before adding, "Or wouldn't."

I reach out and touch his arm. "I'm sorry, Jude."

"I'm not," he says. "It was the final straw that made me realize she was never going to show up for me the way I did for her. Everything she ever asked of me, I did because I knew it was important to her. You mentioned how you didn't see her much, but that wasn't for a lack of trying to get her to come to things at the station. She always had an excuse, always prioritized everything over me—her job, her family, and friends. I was always at the bottom of her list."

"Do you regret your decision?" I ask, though I'm not entirely sure I want the answer. It's hard to imagine the show or my life without Jude.

"No. Staying was the right choice," he replies. "I ended up telling Eddie everything, and he helped me figure out what I was missing in the job since becoming a cast member. That's when he put me in charge of the interns. I wanted to make my mark in the industry, but I didn't need my own show in order to do that. What I *did* need was to pour my energy into mentoring people who have the same passion for radio that I do." He pauses, his gaze holding mine. "And to tell the truth, I didn't want to be away from you."

He lifts his shoulders and drops them with a sigh.

"So, why didn't you ever ask me out after all this? We were both single. In fact, I couldn't even get past a third date."

He runs his hands down his face. "What if I had and you didn't feel the same? That would change the chemistry of the show forever, and we've got a good thing going there. Not to mention, if I did anything that caused you to leave, Eddie would murder me."

I wince. "Yeah, he probably would."

"You're my friend, Kat, and I was afraid of losing that. Of losing *you*. I'm still scared, to be honest."

My chest tightens, and I swallow hard.

"Ultimately, I decided not to tell you because I'd rather have you in my life as a friend than not have you at all."

His admission squeezes the air from my lungs. It's a fear I know all too well—those I love walking away from me. My fingers reach for his of their own accord, twining together as though they'd been in on the secret all along.

"How long have you felt this way?" I ask.

"Honestly?" A faint flush appears on his cheeks. "Since your first day as an intern."

"No way."

"Way."

It seems impossible because Jude is gorgeous, kind, funny…he's everything a girl could want, but I never allowed myself to consider the possibility beyond the occasional daydream.

"Seriously?" I was so certain he didn't feel anything beyond friendship for me, and even if he did, the not-enough-ness that's haunted the walls of my heart far more than Marjorie ever has would follow me into the relationship, waiting to jump out and send him running.

"Why's that so hard to believe?"

I snort. "First of all, because I remember what my hair looked like then. That short bob was not it."

"You were so damn cute." He pushes an unruly strand of hair out of my eyes. "You used to wear those little sparkly clip things behind your ears."

"Yeah, I had to pin my bangs back while I was growing them out because I looked like Lord Farquaad." The memory makes me cringe a little, but it takes on a slightly different hue as I recall us working a promo event at a nightclub when one of those bobby pins fell out. I'd been so self-conscious over how I looked that he helped me hunt down a paperclip and wove it into my hair to fix it in place.

"I loved it."

"I'm glad you find joy in my hair trauma," I say.

"I don't know about the hair trauma, but I've always found a lot of joy in you." He takes my hand, his thumb passing over my knuckles, sending tiny goose bumps trailing up my arm.

"Really?"

"Do you really not see how amazing you are?"

If I'm so extraordinary, why am I still alone? "I can honestly say I've considered myself many things, but amazing isn't one of them."

Now Jude is the one left stunned. "Why?"

"Because people always leave." The answer escapes before I can catch it, like a cat barreling out of the house, longing for a freedom it's not actually ready for. "I let them in, they realize I'm not good enough or not what they wanted, and they bail."

"Not everyone." He squeezes my hand. "Eddie's still here…Becca…*me*."

"Eddie and Becca are different," I say.

"How so?"

"They've seen me at my worst. In ways you haven't." Eddie has spent years mending the pieces of a heart he didn't break, while Becca's talked me down from the proverbial ledge every time I've considered giving up the idea of finding someone. When hope felt like a luxury I couldn't afford, they always had some to spare.

"Yet," he adds. "But I want to."

I take a deep breath and shift in my seat. "Jude—"

"Look, I know this isn't quite the same thing," he says. "Eddie is your mentor, and Becca is your best friend. They know you differently than I do, but I want to know you like that, Kat. I want to know you in every way you'll let me."

My heart flutters, buzzing like a ladybug caught in the globe of a ceiling fan, just longing to fly.

"Give me the chance to stay," he whispers.

I search his face, studying every perfect line time has carved into his skin since I've known him. Each one reminds me of the life we've shared, two parallel paths inching closer and closer together.

"Okay," I say with a smile.

His lips stretch into a wide grin. "Yeah?"

"Mm-hmm," I reply. "But there is one thing we need to think about."

"Besides how good you taste?"

Correction: two things. "While that's certainly worth discussing, it's not what I had in mind."

"Let me guess. Eddie and Becca. The show."

"Exactly."

The hand that isn't holding mine rubs over the back of his neck.

"I think we need to keep this to ourselves," I say. "We need time to figure out what this is and telling them just adds unnecessary pressure."

"You're right. We don't tell them. At least, not right now."

I hesitate. "But then there's the issue of the *Purrfect Match* thing."

"Yeah…that," he says with a grimace. "I think you have to continue going on those dates for now. If you pull the plug, Eddie and Becca could get suspicious."

I squeeze his fingers. "But are you okay with me doing this?"

"Are these dates just for the sake of the segment or are you still considering other options?" he asks. "Not that you aren't entitled to keep your options open, but—"

"No," I answer, cutting him off. "This is just for the show. I want to see where this can go, Jude. With you."

He nods. "Then I'm okay with it, but you have to promise me something."

"Sure. Anything."

He leans closer, the warmth of his breath tickling my skin. "Your kisses are reserved for me."

"Deal," I say, as he closes the distance between us, his lips colliding with mine.

The world narrows to just the two of us and a distant shriek of delight that plunges the bar into darkness once again.

chapter twenty-one

"I told you Jude had feelings for you, Kathryn," Marjorie chirps as we head home down I-40 West. "Didn't I tell you?"

"Yes," I reply, glancing over my shoulder as I change lanes. "Yes, you did."

She presses a hand to her chest. "I just knew it."

"You know, you're pretty in tune with people for a woman who has no pulse," I tease.

Marjorie beams, ignoring my remark. "So, how was it?"

"What?"

"The fine cuisine at Billy's." She fixes me with a sardonic stare. "*The kiss.* How was the kiss?"

I bite back a grin. "Which one?"

She squeals and steeples her fingers in front of her mouth. "So?"

I sigh. His scent is still wrapped around me, clinging to my clothes from wearing his jacket all afternoon. I can almost feel his lips on mine, tasting of tequila and dreams I never want to wake up from.

"It was the best kiss I've ever had," I admit, my cheeks burning hot.

"For heaven's sake, tell me everything," she says with a girlish giggle. "I need details."

"Who even are you right now?" I ask with a laugh.

"Were his lips soft? He didn't use too much tongue, did he? Some men get a little…overzealous and it's like kissing a drooly Saint Bernard."

My brows shoot to my hairline. "You want to know how much tongue he used?"

"What?" She feigns innocence. "Come on, Kathryn. Let me live vicariously through you. Do you know how long it's been since I was kissed?"

"How long?"

Only the sound of rubber rolling on asphalt fills the space between us, and I wonder if she heard me. When I glance over, she has a wistful expression on her face.

"Marjorie?" I ask.

She smiles, but it doesn't quite reach her eyes. "Yes, sorry."

"You okay? Where'd you go?"

"I just realized I don't remember when my last kiss was," she confesses. "Gosh, it's been a long time. Conrad and I weren't exactly in love, as you know." Just as quickly as the crack in her veneer appears, it's patched over. "But that's all the more reason for you to tell me about yours. Come on, now. Out with it. What was it like?"

My heart hurts for her when I imagine how alone she must have felt all these years—how unloved. It's a feeling I've worn ragged like an old pair of sneakers, walking down a busy street, desperately begging people for directions, but they don't respond. They don't even look, leaving me aimless and wandering. But when Jude kissed me, it was as though someone heard me, finally *saw* me, and handed me a map and the key to the city.

"It was…perfect," I answer finally. "It was soft and sweet, but it was confident too. Like he knew exactly what he wanted, and what he wanted was me."

This elicits a genuine smile. "And I believe he does. The way that boy looks at you, it…" Her voice fades, that far-off, melancholic expression returning.

"It what?"

"It's just really lovely." Her face is sincere, but her eyes are sad. "And you deserve it."

I get the distinct feeling there's more she isn't saying, but I don't push.

"If it hadn't been for you, I'm not sure I would've given this a shot." I blow out a breath, my fingers gripping the steering wheel. "In fact, I probably would have kept convincing myself there was no way Jude could feel anything for me other than friendship."

"You've been sabotaging yourself by always preparing for the worst possible outcome. You're constantly waiting for the other shoe to drop," she explains. "And in doing that, you've been unable to see what's right in front of you."

The truth in her words stares back at me, unblinking. "You're right. I guess I have."

"But you see it now, and that's what matters," she says. "Just keep yourself open to it, and don't try to convince yourself you don't deserve this. Because you do."

Again, I get the feeling there's more to her words, something lingering just beneath the surface, but she doesn't divulge it, and I don't pry.

"So, I suppose this means you get to avoid going on any more of those *Purrfect Match* dates?" she asks.

"Not exactly," I reply, explaining what Jude and I agreed upon.

She nods. "That makes sense."

"It's going to be strange, because I don't really want to go on these dates. I just want to spend time seeing what Jude and I could be."

"But you're right to continue because Eddie finding out could add a layer of complication you don't need. Outside pressure will only make your self-sabotaging tendencies worse."

She's absolutely correct, of course, but perhaps there could be some additional benefits to not backing out of this whole *Purrfect Match* thing. "Maybe we can use these dates as test runs for the ones I have with Jude."

She arches her brow. "*We?*"

I grin. "Well, yeah. Unless you're too busy haunting someone else."

"No." She chuckles. "No, I'm not. I guess I just figured you wouldn't want me to go with you anymore now that you have Jude."

"I mean, I might ask you to stay at home when I go out with him, but I still need you, Marjorie," I say and realize it's true. "I want you to help me build some confidence and become a badass like you so I don't wind up crashing this plane before I even get it off the ground."

Her face softens. "I suppose I *do* need something to keep me busy while we try to figure out what my unfinished business is."

"So, you'll help me?"

She nods, and her eyes crinkle with excitement. "Of course. We're a team."

"Hell yeah, we are," I agree. "Speaking of, I've been thinking about your unfinished business, and I'm wondering if we've been going about this all wrong."

"What do you mean?"

"So far, every thread we've tugged on has been attached to some sort of hard feelings. Conrad being a manwhore and giving Annabelle your mother's earrings, Frances using you," I explain. "What if your unfinished business has more to do with someone who made a positive impact on your life?"

She purses her lips and taps a finger to her chin. "You might be onto something."

"Is there someone from your past who helped you?" I ask. "Someone you never told how much they meant to you."

She gasps so hard I nearly slam on the breaks. "What the hell was that? I thought you saw a deer or something."

"How did I not see this before?" she cries, completely ignoring me. "I know exactly what my unfinished business is."

"What?"

She throws her hands in the air. "It's so clear. I can't believe I didn't—"

I cut her off. "You wanna fill me in here?"

"Natalie," Marjorie says. "She was my caretaker when I got sick. I wasn't...well, let's just say I wasn't the easiest person to be around."

"You? Not easy to be around?" I ask, flattening my palm against my chest. "Never."

She narrows her eyes at me. "You think you're so funny."

"I *know* I am," I tease. "Tell me more about Natalie."

"I hired her after the cancer spread, and it became clear I

needed more assistance than my worthless husband was willing to offer," she says. "He couldn't be bothered to change his tee time, let alone sit with me through chemotherapy."

I grip the steering wheel, the thought of Marjorie sitting alone in a treatment room with needles in her arms enough to make me want to mow down Conrad with my car and turn *him* into a ghost.

"I was so bitter about my circumstances and feeling sorry for myself," Marjorie continues. "I didn't make it easy on Natalie when all she did was try to make my life better. She was more than my nurse. She was my friend. Maybe the only one I ever really had till now."

My mouth goes dry. It took Marjorie getting sick and dying to feel like she had someone who cared. As alone as I've felt, there have always been people I could count on to be a safe haven. First, my beloved grandmother. And now Eddie, Becca, and Dennis who are always there even when my stock is down.

"Natalie went above and beyond what was asked of her," she says. "Beyond what I paid her to do. There were many evenings she stayed with me long after her shift was over. Sometimes we just sat in the silence of each other's company. Other times she would ask questions about whatever ridiculous program she'd found on television or about my life in general."

Her description of Natalie makes me think of the way Becca always seems to know when I need her. She can tell if I need to talk or just rot on the couch together while some dumpster fire of a reality show plays in the background.

"I snapped at her a lot." She drops her gaze to her hands, twisted on her lap. "It wasn't due to any fault of her own. I was just so…angry. My entire upbringing revolved around status, influence, and power. Then I spent my adult life consumed by these influential circles, being important. But when I got sick, none of that mattered. Not one of those people was there for me. They were quick to show up at my funeral, pretending to be sad, all while picking over my legacy like buzzards."

My heart sinks, and I frown. "I'm so sorry."

"Not as sorry as I am for ever trusting those two-faced bimbos to begin with," she counters. "And for not thanking Natalie for everything she did. For never telling her how much she meant to me."

Her voice breaks, and when I glance over at her, her eyes are misty.

"We'll find her," I promise. "And you can tell her."

"What if it's another situation like Frances?" she asks. "What if we can't find her or she's already gone?"

"Let's not borrow trouble," I reply, repeating the advice my grandmother used to give when I found myself ruminating over made-up scenarios that hadn't even happened yet.

She stares out the window, her head resting against the seat.

"Hey," I say, snapping her out of her reverie. "I mean it. We'll find her, okay? We'll find her, and we'll figure out what your unfinished business is no matter what. You know why? Because we're a team."

She swallows hard and drops her gaze. "Thank you."

"If you really want to thank me, you'll help me figure out what to wear on my date with Jude tomorrow." My lips curl upward. "He's taking me to dinner."

Her enthusiasm returns with a grin. "Sounds like we're in need of a girls' night."

chapter twenty-two

After I send out some initial feelers online in an effort to find Natalie, Marjorie and I spend the first half of the evening tearing apart my closet in search of the perfect outfit for my date tomorrow and arguing once again about whether or not leopard print is a neutral, which it is.

Once we decide on a floral dress in a deep plum shade with sheer sleeves, I return to the kitchen with my empty mug and Marjorie and Delilah on my heels.

Marjorie eyes me as I pour myself another cup of coffee. "Are you trying to stay awake for all of eternity?"

"All the better to hang out with you, my dear," I tease, taking a big gulp.

She chuckles and shakes her head as Delilah slinks past us to get to her food bowl, meowing in disgust when she realizes it's empty and I've dared not to feed her a second dinner.

"So, what should we do with the rest of our girls' night?" I ask.

Marjorie's face turns serious as she rounds the bar where her urn is currently displayed.

"Actually, there's something I'd like to discuss with you," she says.

I tilt my head to one side and join her, placing my drink on the counter. "Okay, sure."

"It's about your date with Jude tomorrow."

I regard her through slits. "We've talked about this. I need to do this one alone."

"No, no. It's not that." Her expression softens. "I'd like you to wear my diamond earrings."

I gasp. "Really?"

She nods. "They deserve a night on the town, and *you* deserve something special to wear for this occasion."

I press my hands to my chest to keep my heart from bursting right out of me.

"But Marjorie, those are family heirlooms. I know how important they are to you."

"And a lot of good they're doing, hiding in the depths of my urn." Her gaze falls to the shimmering cinerarium. "Besides, you said you wanted me to help you find your confidence, didn't you? Well, every woman needs a piece of jewelry that makes her feel beautiful."

My nose burns and my eyes sting with the effort it takes to stop myself from turning into a blubbering mess. "But what if I lose one?"

She waves me off. "The clasps on those things are like iron fists. You'll be lucky if you can get them off."

Warmth spreads through my limbs, the sincerity of her request not lost on me.

"I don't know what to say," I admit.

"Say you'll wear them."

I meet her smile with one of my own. "I'd be honored."

"Wonderful," she says. "It's settled. Now all that's left to do is get them out of there."

I freeze. That means I have to break back into the urn and fish them out.

I shake my head emphatically. "Oh no. No, no, no. Absolutely not."

"How else are you going to wear them?" she asks.

I hold up my hands. "Marjorie, I appreciate the gesture, but there's no way I'm grave robbing you to wear your earrings."

"Oh, don't be ridiculous," she chides. "You're not robbing anyone. I'm offering them to you."

"You don't understand. I'll have to" —I pause and drop my voice to a whisper— "open you up to get them out."

She scoffs. "I'm asking you to reach inside an urn, Kathryn, not perform open-heart surgery."

"But they're in there with your ashes," I counter. "There's got to be some karmic law against disturbing people's remains."

"For heaven's sake, just open the thing up, reach in there, and get them out," she argues.

"What if your body dust gets *on* the earrings?" I shudder just thinking about it.

"Then you rinse them off like any sane person would do. It's not that difficult."

"Rinse them off? What if it's, like, your leg or a finger or a vital organ?"

She crosses her arms over her chest and fixes me with a glare.

"Fine," I whine, wringing my hands and trying to shake off the creepy vibes this gives me.

"Hurry up."

I approach the urn as if it might bite me before unscrewing the top, positioning one eye over the opening. The inside is so dark I can't see anything.

Delilah meows up at me as though she thinks *this* is where her second dinner is hiding.

I start to reach my hand inside but freak out and withdraw my fingers with a screech.

"I can't," I insist.

Marjorie releases an exasperated sigh as I scoop up the vase and slide open a drawer to retrieve a slotted spoon.

"My God," Marjorie mutters.

I'm steeling myself to ladle these diamonds like dumplings out of a pot when the chime of the doorbell echoes through the house, making me yelp.

"Are you expecting someone?" Marjorie asks, her brows furrowed.

"Besides the grim reaper coming to punish me for messing with the ashes of a dead person?" I hiss.

She shoots me an unamused glance as I pad toward the foyer, urn and spoon still in hand.

I swing open the door, expecting to find a kid passing out missing dog flyers or even Dennis waiting to spill some sort of tea. But when my eyes land on the person standing on my front stoop, I nearly choke on my own spit.

"Becca," I say. "What are you doing here?"

She's holding a floral arrangement and a pink cardboard box that I recognize from one of our favorite cookie shops, staring at me with wide eyes.

"I just wanted to come check on you." Each word is bubble wrapped as though one wrong sentence could cause me to shatter.

Fragile. Handle with care.

That's when I realize that from her vantage point, I just answered the door with my dead cat's ashes *and a spoon*.

"Oh dear," Marjorie says. "Keep her here as long as you can. I'll deal with Delilah."

How? How are you going to do that when you are a ghost?

But I can't ask any questions. All I can do is stall and hope this interaction doesn't end with Becca coaxing me out of the house to drive me to the nearest hospital.

"You didn't have to come all the way out here," I say, not moving an inch.

She studies me as though trying to decide the best way to tell me it's clear I need all the help I can get.

"Shoo!" Marjorie shouts at Delilah from the other room. "Get! Move!"

"I wanted to," she settles on instead. "Can I come in?"

"Right. Yes." I step aside and blow out a shaky breath.

A loud crash echoes from the kitchen, and I don't know who is more surprised—me or Becca.

"What was that?" she asks, pushing past me, starting for the kitchen.

"I'm sure it was nothing." I brace for impact, knowing Becca is going to have a *lot* of questions when she discovers my supposedly dead cat is very much alive.

"That was *not* nothing," she argues as I follow her to where the noise came from and find that both Delilah and Marjorie are nowhere to be seen. Instead, we find the utility closet open and the broom laid across the floor.

"Broom," I say. "It was the broom."

Becca surveys the room, her gaze snagging on Delilah's empty food dish. "Doing some cleaning?"

I nod. "I figured it was time. To put away Delilah's things, I mean."

"Now you be quiet," Marjorie hisses from a distance. "Don't make me come back in there."

A door slams from the other side of the house, causing Becca and me to jump.

"The heat must have kicked on and sucked my bedroom door shut." The excuse comes rushing out of my mouth. "Old house and all."

Whatever the sound was or wasn't seems to be the least of Becca's concern, her focus squarely on the urn in my hands as she places the flowers and bakery box on the counter.

"Kat, what are you doing?" she asks as Marjorie rounds the corner.

"Delilah is locked in your room," Marjorie whispers.

"I already told you," I answer Becca. "I was cleaning."

"That's not what I mean," she replies. "Why are you answering the door with Delilah's ashes and…a spoon?"

My eyes flash to Marjorie, desperate for an answer that doesn't make me sound like I've lost my marbles.

"Don't look at me," she mutters. "If you'd just pulled the damn things out of there like I told you, you wouldn't even be in this mess."

"I dropped my earrings—I mean, my friend's earrings in there," I say and immediately regret it.

"You what?" Becca asks as Marjorie's eyes widen. "How did you do that?"

Heat rushes up my neck, sweat breaking out along my hairline.

"Well, I didn't drop them so much as I put them in there," I add as though that makes this any better.

Becca opens her mouth, then closes it again. "Why?"

I press my lips together, trying to trap whatever unhinged thing I'm about to say inside.

"You see, my friend Dennis…he asked me to hide these earrings for him," I explain. "They're an heirloom he, uh, recently inherited from his grandmother. Everyone in his family wanted them. Dennis's second cousin even tried to break into his house to find them. It was a whole thing."

Marjorie rubs her temples as the skin in the middle of Becca's forehead creases.

"And you thought the best place to hide them was in your cat's urn?" Becca asks.

"Well, I figured it was a place no one would think to look," I say, toeing the line between quirky and deranged. "I wasn't thinking clearly when I made that choice, and I was about to try to fish them out when you showed up."

Becca cocks her head. "But…what's the spoon for? Why can't you put your hand in there and grab 'em?"

"Thank you." Marjorie throws her hands in the air. "That's what I said."

"Because her ashes are just…*in there*," I say.

Becca stifles a laugh. "Babe, no. They put the remains in a sealed plastic bag."

"How can you be sure?"

"We had our family dog cremated when I was a teenager," she answers. "Seriously, it's fine. Give it here."

Before I can stop her, she grabs the spoon and tosses it in the sink before plucking the urn from my grasp.

My throat goes dry. "Wait. No. You don't have to do that."

What if that's just for animals?! What if Becca is about to give Marjorie a postmortem pat down?

"It's fine," she insists, already elbow deep in the vase.

My hands fly to my mouth, and I shoot Marjorie a panicked glance.

"At least buy me dinner first," Marjorie quips as Becca scrunches her nose, her fingers digging inside the urn. "Hey! That tickles!"

Marjorie giggles, clearly pleased with herself, and I'd kill her if she wasn't already dead.

"Got 'em," Becca says, and sure enough, she pulls out the sparkling diamonds—ash-free—and examines them. "Wow. These are gorgeous."

"These friends of yours have good taste," Marjorie remarks.

"No wonder the whole family is fighting over them." Becca places the earrings in my palm.

I close my fist around them as she sets the urn on the counter. "Thanks."

"No problem," she says, returning her focus to me, searching my face. "You know I'm here for you, right?"

"Of course I do," I answer.

"I mean it," she replies. "Anything you need, I'm here."

"I know." And I *do* know. But how do I tell her a truth this complicated?

"I just…I wanted to say I'm sorry. I wasn't as sensitive as I should have been earlier. When you came into work with Delilah's urn, I was…concerned," she continues. "But I understand you're grieving, and I just want you to know that I love you and I'm here to support you in any way I can."

"Thank you," I say, hugging her. "I love you too." For a moment, I consider spilling my guts—telling her about Marjorie, Delilah, and even Jude. The idea of unburdening myself of all these secrets has me opening my mouth to speak, but the words die in my throat.

When she pulls away, she glances at the broom and Delilah's empty dish.

"Do you want me to help you clean up?" she asks. "Put some of Delilah's things away?"

"No," I answer quickly. "I mean, I think it's something I need to do myself."

Marjorie gives a nod of approval. "Nice save."

"Okay." Becca squeezes my arm. "I'll leave you to it, then."

I walk her to the door as we say our goodbyes when I hear a distant *meow*. I hold my breath and pray she doesn't hear it, but no such luck.

"What was that?"

"TV," I answer. "In my room. Must've left it on."

Becca scrunches her brows. "That sounded like a cat."

"I was watching one of those channels you leave on for your pets," I say, unable to believe the words coming out of my mouth. "You know, with the birds and kittens and puppies and stuff. Delilah loved it."

Becca gives me a sympathetic smile and embraces me again. "I just know wherever she is, she's watching it with you."

"Yeah," I squeak. "She is."

"Okay, I'm gonna go, but call me if you need anything," she says. "I mean it."

"I will," I promise as she steps into the night.

I make sure she's in her car and backing out of the driveway before shutting the door, leaning my back against it.

"That was a close one," Marjorie says.

I drag my hands down my face. "How am I supposed to keep this up? Eventually, someone is going to realize Delilah is very much alive."

"For what it's worth, I think you could tell Becca the truth."

No. No way. I can't. "She'll think I've lost my mind." Hell, there are some days I still wonder if I have.

"At first, perhaps," she admits. "But look at Dennis. It took him a minute to wrap his head around the idea, but he did."

"But Dennis and Becca aren't the same," I counter. "Dennis lives for chakras and spirits and ghost hunts. Becca is pragmatic. She needs hardcore evidence."

"All I'm saying is that she loves you, and while she might struggle to understand at first, I think she would believe you."

I shake my head. "I can't take that chance." Becca is one of the few people in this world I can count on, and I can't risk losing her—I won't.

"All right," Marjorie concedes. "I understand."

I open my palm, the teardrop diamond earrings shimmering back at me, and smile.

"They really are beautiful," I say, my chest filled with so much gratitude, I fear it might all come pouring out.

When I lift my gaze to meet hers, her green eyes are glittering with excitement.

"Come now, Kathryn," she says, gesturing for me to follow her down the hall. "I want you to try them on."

chapter twenty-three

"HAVE I TOLD YOU HOW BEAUTIFUL YOU LOOK TONIGHT?" Jude asks after the server drops off our drinks and leaves us to peruse the menu.

My cheeks burn, and I laugh softly. "Only about twenty-seven times."

His mouth stretches into a wide grin. "Then let's make it twenty-eight. You're just…you're gorgeous. You always are, and it feels good to finally be able to tell you that."

The atmosphere at Silk & Ivory is dreamy. Greenery climbs the walls, giving way to a dark ceiling, lit by constellations of chandeliers. The luminaries at the centers of the tables with crisp white linens give the illusion of dining on a cloud floating in a starry sky.

"This place is stunning. You're setting the bar impossibly high for these *Purrfect Match* dates," I say with a wink.

"You're onto me," he replies, taking a sip of his bourbon.

Not only had Jude selected this gorgeous restaurant himself, but he'd also insisted on driving out to Jingo to pick me up. Marjorie came in with the assist when he arrived, keeping Delilah corralled in the bedroom while I answered the door. She sent me off with a gentle reminder to not try too hard, to simply let this evening unfold as it's meant to, and be myself because Jude likes me exactly as I am.

My fingers reflexively go to one of the diamonds adorning my ear as though doing so might summon Marjorie herself or even an ounce of her poise.

"Those are nice," Jude remarks, nodding toward me.

"Hmm?" I ask before I realize what he's referring to. "Oh thanks. Mar—" I cut myself off. "My friend let me borrow them. They're a family heirloom."

"Wow, that's a good friend."

"Yeah," I say. "Yeah, she is."

Jude rolls up his sleeves, and the sight of his tanned, muscular forearms nearly stops my heart. He's always been handsome, but I haven't fully allowed myself to appreciate just *how* handsome he is till now. He got dressed up for our date, wearing gray slacks and a white button-down. His hair looks touchable in that messy-on-purpose way, and his five-o'clock shadow only serves to make his jaw look even more defined.

"Kat?" He tilts his head, catching my eye, and that's when I realize he'd been speaking.

"Sorry, what were you saying?" It was next to impossible to hear him over the sound of my heartbeat thudding in my ears.

"I was just asking how you're feeling," he says. "We didn't get a chance to talk much at work today. I was worried about you."

I shake my head in confusion. "What? Why?"

He narrows his eyes. "Because of Delilah."

I'm lucky Jude's forearms haven't made me forget my

own name, let alone the lie I told him about my very not-dead cat.

"Right," I answer, taking a long pull off my old-fashioned. "I'm just…trying not to think about it."

"I get it. Grief is…it's hard," he says, glancing down for a second. "Do you remember when my grandpa got put in hospice?"

My chest tightens. "Yeah, I do."

Jude had been a wreck. His grandfather, whom he lovingly called Pop, was his best friend—the person he aspired to be. Up until his COPD worsened, he'd even come with Jude to some of the show's charity events like our school supply drive and the fashion show to raise money for a local domestic violence shelter.

"You covered for me so many times during those three months after the doctors told us there was nothing else they could do," he says. "All my scheduled appearances on top of your own, researching for the entertainment news, helping me run interference with the interns just to allow me to be with him as much as possible." He pauses and clears his throat. "I don't know if I ever told you how much that meant to me."

"I was happy to do it," I say. "My grandmother was the most important person in my life, and I would have given anything to have had more moments with her."

Jude gives me a wistful smile. "Pop liked you. Every time I saw him, he asked about you."

I can't hide my surprise. "He did?"

He nods. "Remember the concert we hosted? The one where Becca's band performed?"

"Of course." It was a benefit show for unhoused youth that brought folks out in droves.

"You asked him to—"

"Dance," I finish for him, the memory sharp in my mind. "They played that punked out version of an old Sinatra song, and he looked so cute groovin' off to the side by himself. I couldn't very well leave Pop hanging."

Jude laughs fondly, his eyes nearly disappearing as he does. "He talked about that for weeks. It meant a lot to him. Said he hadn't danced with anyone since my grandma died."

"Your pop was sweet. Light on his feet too. He had me *working* that dance floor." It was my favorite moment of the entire evening. Maybe it's because of the close relationship I had with my grandmother, but I've always felt grandparents were special people. He may not have been mine, but for that moment in time, he was.

"I know," he says with a light chuckle. "I have a photo of you two from that night. It actually lives on my mantle."

"Wait. The one from our website?" I ask, recalling it instantly. Our social media manager took pictures that night and happened to catch one of Pop twirling me. It was the top photo in our gallery from the evening.

"I asked the marketing department for a copy," he admits. "It was the last event he got to attend with me. We didn't get a photo together, but having one of the two of you felt like the next best thing."

I inhale a shaky breath as his gaze holds mine.

There've been instances in my life where time slowed, and I could almost feel the earth spin—when I was acutely aware there was more happening than what I could see with my own eyes. Moments that forever split my days into a before and an after. As I find myself tracing every line of Jude's perfect face in my mind, I realize this is one of those moments, and I want to memorize the second I feel my world start to shift.

"Pop said you were a great dance partner," he says.

"Is that so?"

"Mm-hmm." Jude reaches across the table and takes my hand in his. "He also told me to stop being such a chicken shit and tell you how I felt about you."

I grin. "That Pop sure knew what he was talking about, huh?"

"What can I say?" He squeezes my fingers, his brown eyes shimmering gold in the soft light. "He was a wise man."

chapter twenty-four

"So, I know you have a couple of *Purrfect Match* dates this weekend, but do you think I could steal you away for a while on Sunday?" Jude asks on the drive back to my house, the passing streetlamps casting shadows over us.

"Those are Friday and Saturday, and they're just drinks," I answer. "Sunday I'm all yours."

He hums his approval and reaches across the console, threading his fingers through mine. It's a gesture that feels both surreal and completely natural. After dinner, we lingered at the restaurant, finally ordering dessert because we weren't ready for the evening to end, but we felt guilty for holding up the table. Even after knowing each other all these years, we never seemed to run out of things to say or learn about each other.

"Have something particular in mind?" I stroke the back of his hand with my thumb.

He nods. "There's a ghost tour in Franklin, and I thought we—"

"A what?" I blurt. There's no way he said what I thought he did. *Ghost?* He must have said something else. Boat, maybe? We're landlocked, so probably not that. Goat? Right. Because *that* makes sense.

"You know," he says. "A ghost tour. It's where a guide takes you to different places in the city and tells you all the haunted lore. I've been to a couple of them before, and they're fun."

You want a ghost tour? Boy, do I have the ticket for you. I can get you a front-row seat.

I clear my throat. "I had no idea you were into the whole paranormal thing."

He shrugs. "I mean, I'm no ghosthunter or anything, but I do find it all sort of fascinating."

"How so?"

He glances my way. "It's just the whole mystery of the unknown. What happens when we die? *Does* anything happen? Where do we go?"

The things I could tell you, Jude.

"And what do you think?" I ask, feigning nonchalance.

"I'd like to believe this isn't all there is, that we live on in some way," he says. "And not to get overly nerdy about it, but if energy cannot be created or destroyed, then it's likely there *is* some sort of existence after death."

Up until Marjorie came into my life, I hadn't given much thought to this, at least not since my mother passed away. I'd spent many nights as a teenager lying awake talking to her just in case she was still there. I've heard people say they can feel the presence of their loved ones after they leave this earth, but I never did. It didn't happen after my grandmother passed, either.

"Kat?" Jude squeezes my fingers. "You okay?"

"Yeah, of course. Sorry." I force a smile, pushing the memories from my mind.

"I didn't freak you out with all this ghost talk, did I?"

"Definitely not," I reply. "I was just wondering if you ever felt your pop after he passed away."

"A few times."

I blink. "Really? How? When? Did you *see* him?" A pang of jealousy needles at my heart. I've always envied those who sensed the spirit or energy of their deceased friends or family and wondered why I couldn't. If I let myself think about it too much, it makes me sad because I wonder if maybe I wasn't worth sticking around for—in life *or* in death.

He shakes his head and chuckles softly. "No, nothing as concrete as that. It's more of a…feeling. It usually happens when I'm doing something that connected us when he was alive—like listening to old records or doing the crossword in the Sunday paper. Or when I'm having a hard day and wish I could talk to him."

"So, how do you know it's him?" I can't help but wonder if it's really him or if it's wishful thinking, and even if it is, does it matter so long as it makes Jude feel better?

"I suppose I don't," he admits. "Not for sure, anyway. But I feel the same way I did anytime I was with him. Peaceful, safe…loved."

My chest constricts. Perhaps my mom and grandma were still around, but I've just been too closed off, too hurt to feel them?

"I didn't mean to get all sentimental on you," he says with another squeeze of my hand. "I promise to leave all that at home on Sunday. Besides, I don't even know any of these ghosts on the tour. I have no attachments to them whatsoever."

My mouth quirks as he turns into my driveway. "You

never know. Maybe one will hitch a ride and go home with you."

He barks out a laugh. "Wouldn't that be something?"

I clamp my teeth over my bottom lip as I unbuckle my seatbelt.

You have no idea.

"Hey, if rent prices keep going up, I might need a roommate. Think I could get them to split the cost?" he teases.

I grin. "I'm guessing their financial contributions are limited, but they might be able to haunt the place enough that people start moving, forcing them to bring prices down."

He nods, scrunching his nose like he's mulling it over. "Now the question is, how do I get a ghost to follow me home?"

I have one you can borrow, I think as he comes around to the passenger side to open the door. *Sounds like a lucrative business model, actually. Rent-a-Ghost, for all your haunting needs. We kill the competition (then hire them).*

"So, is that a *yes* on the ghost tour?" he asks, offering me his hand.

"Absolutely," I answer as we start toward my porch. "How else will we find a spirit to move into your building?" *Besides accidentally purchasing an occupied urn from a thrift store.*

"Good," he says as we climb the front steps. "Then it's a date."

"Yes, it is."

He gazes at me under the glow of the porch light above the door. There's a softness in his expression, a warmth that makes me want to invite him in and tell him about all my ghosts—the one that haunts my house and those that haunt my mind, but I know it's far too soon for that. For now, I'm just happy the veil has been lifted, allowing us to see each other like this.

"I had a good time tonight." Though *good* feels like a major understatement.

"Those *Purrfect Match* dates don't know what they're up against," he says with a wink as he steps closer, lifting a hand to my cheek.

I bite back a grin as his thumb traces the line of my jaw. "They don't stand a chance."

"That's what I like to hear," he whispers before leaning in and bringing his lips to mine. This kiss starts off slow and tentative as his other hand finds mine, twining our fingers together. Then our tongues collide, making my knees weak and my heart pound. It's perfect and effortless and I want it to last forever.

"Now *that* is a kiss." Marjorie's voice causes me to jump with a sharp yelp, and I narrowly avoid headbutting Jude in the nose.

When I open my eyes, Marjorie is standing off to the side and Jude's brow is creased.

"You okay?"

"Sorry." I quickly swipe my hands over my head and arms. "I thought I felt a spider."

"I didn't mean to startle you," Marjorie says with a sheepish smile. "I heard the car pull in, and I suppose I got a little too excited to hear about your date." She moves closer to Jude, scanning over him with a nod of approval. "He really is something special, Kathryn. I was never one for blond men, but this Jude fellow might have converted me."

Her proximity causes Jude to shiver.

"It's chilly," he says, reaching out to touch my arm. "You should get inside."

I nod. "Right. I'll see you at work in the morning."

He presses one final kiss to my lips before backing down the steps, pausing at the bottom of the stoop with a Cheshire cat grin on his face. "I won't lie, it's gonna be hard to sit next to you tomorrow and not be able to kiss you."

Marjorie fans herself with her hand. "My word, he *is* charming, isn't he?"

A smile spreads across my face. "Yeah, it will."

"Night," he calls over his shoulder.

"Good night," I say, pulling my keys from my purse and heading inside with Marjorie on my heels.

Delilah is there to greet me as I lock the door, meowing wildly as though reading me the riot act for daring to stay out past her bedtime.

"You must tell me everything," Marjorie insists as she ushers me toward the living room. "Come now. Sit."

I float behind her and flop onto the couch with a dreamy sigh. "It was perfect."

"I knew it would be," she says, taking a seat beside me.

"Everything was…" I trail off and grab a throw pillow, hugging it against my chest with a squeal. "It was the best night I've had since, well, *ever.*"

"I can't wait to hear all about it."

I drop my head against the cushion, then turn to face Marjorie. A wistful smile plays on her lips.

"What?" I ask. "What's that look for?"

Her expression is tender, almost proud. "You just…you seem happy."

For so long, I've been coasting through life, not happy, not sad…just numb. The joy coursing through my veins feels almost foreign. "I am."

"I hope my earrings brought you some luck tonight."

"You know, something did bring me luck, but I don't think it was the diamonds," I admit. "It was you."

Her eyes glisten, and I want to reach out and squeeze her hand, but I can't, so I settle for the next best thing.

"So, where should we start?" I ask.

Her face lights up and she leans closer. "From the beginning, and don't leave anything out."

chapter twenty-five

"I GOT SOMETHING," I SHOUT, BOLTING UPRIGHT WHERE I'M sprawled on the couch watching TV with Marjorie, phone in hand early Thursday evening.

She jumps from her spot beside me with a gasp. "For heaven's sake, you scared me to death."

I lift my brows. "Interesting choice of words."

"You know what I mean," she says, swatting at me like I'm a pesky fruit fly. "Anyway, what did you get?"

"A lead on Natalie," I answer. "The manager at the company she worked for previously wrote back. He sent me the last email he had on record for her." When I contacted the home health agency she was employed at previously, I did so under the pretense that I was the family member of a former patient.

Marjorie's eyes widen. "You think we might actually find her?"

"All we can do is try," I say, already typing out a message to the address I was given, explaining that I'm a friend of Marjorie Lockwood's, hoping to get in touch with her. A couple of moments later, I hit send and toss my phone onto the cushion. "Now we wait."

I rise and head to the kitchen to feed Delilah, then refill my coffee, but before I can even reach the pot, my phone chimes, alerting me I've received an email.

"Kathryn, your phone," Marjorie announces. "It dinged. Is it her? Do you think it's Natalie?"

"I doubt it," I reply, filling my mug. "It's barely been two minutes."

"Could you at least check?" she asks as I pad back to the sofa.

"Geez, give me a second." I grab the device and open my email account. Sure enough, there's a reply waiting from Natalie Colter.

I read the message out loud.

"'A friend of Marjorie Lockwood's? I remember Ms. Lockwood well, but I don't recall her ever having visits from friends.'"

Marjorie grimaces. "Well, she's not wrong about that. Write her back."

I do, explaining that I didn't get to visit Marjorie when she was ill, but that I'd stumbled across something intended for her. Once again, her reply is almost instant.

"'The woman I knew wouldn't have left anything for me except for a pile of dirty dishes and an unsolicited opinion about my hair. I'm fairly certain I don't want anything she left for me.'"

I shoot Marjorie a look.

"What?" she asks. "She used to wear it in a knot on top of her head. The thing could have housed an entire family of birds."

I pinch the bridge of my nose. "I don't think reminding

her of that is gonna convince her to meet up with us, so what should I tell her?"

Marjorie huffs. "Tell her you were going through an old box of my things and you found a letter I wrote to her."

"And that it says how amazing her hair looked?"

"She'd come closer to believing I left her a one-way ticket to the moon."

I hold my phone at the ready, thumbs poised over the screen. "You're gonna have to give me a little more to work with here."

She tilts her head, thinking. "Tell her it mentions that reality program she used to insist we watch—you know, the one where people are sent off to a deserted island where they're forced to carry torches and forage for food."

"*American Idol*," I quip. "No, wait. *Dancing with the Stars?*"

She rolls her eyes. "Here we go."

"*Survivor?*" I offer, more seriously this time.

"That's the one," she says. "It was fascinating, all the things those contestants did. They were so clever. I think I could have made it on that show."

"In what world?"

"What? You don't think I could rough it?" She folds her arms over her chest. "I'll have you know I once spent two weeks at the beginning of June without air conditioning. Times like that teach you to be resourceful."

"Uh-huh." I lift my brows. "And what exactly did you do? Go stay at the Holiday Inn?"

She scrunches her nose. "Of course not. We stayed at The Hermitage."

"That's a five-star hotel," I say. "In what way is that resourceful?"

She looks at me as though I've lost my mind. "This was back in the days of Fan Fest, Kathryn. Do you have any idea how hard it was to get a room within fifty miles of the city that didn't smell like day-old bacon? Do you understand the negotiating skills that required?"

I blink. "Right. Anyway." I begin typing my message. "*Survivor* fan. What else does this nonexistent letter say?"

"That she used to polish my nails," she says, her eyes on her lap. "Toward the end, I wasn't able to keep up my beauty appointments, so Natalie started doing them for me. She learned how to roll my hair too. God knows I used to fuss about it, but it wasn't because of her. She was actually quite good at it. I was just having a hard time accepting the loss of my independence." She pauses, a pained expression on her face. "The loss of…well, everything."

The air is heavy for a moment as I imagine what it felt like for Marjorie to receive her death sentence. My mother and grandmother both passed unexpectedly. There was no warning, no slow decline or last words. One second they were here, and the next they weren't. As painful as it was to lose them, I'm thankful they didn't go through what Marjorie did. They died all at once instead of a little at a time.

I put my thoughts together in an email, hopefully giving Natalie enough details to understand this isn't some sort of elaborate hoax and send it off with a request to meet in person at her convenience.

Marjorie's shoulders drop, and she shrinks into herself.

"Hey," I say, placing the phone between us. "You okay?"

Her cheeks are red, her mouth turned down. "She may not want to agree to this. I was awful to the girl, so I can't exactly blame her."

"We'll figure this out," I insist, though I have no plans for what to do if Natalie blows me off or tells me to go kick rocks. "I'm not giving up."

We both stare at the phone, seconds becoming minutes before we return our eyes to the television. But neither of us are really focused on it, our gazes constantly shifting to the rectangle on the cushion, waiting for the inevitable *ping*.

But it doesn't come.

chapter twenty-six

By the time Sunday evening arrives, I still haven't heard a word from Natalie, and my hope that she'll meet with me is waning. Meanwhile, Marjorie is distraught.

"She's not going to give me the time of day, and I'll never be able to complete my unfinished business," Marjorie cries before I leave for my date with Jude. "I'll be stuck here in limbo for all of eternity."

"That's not going to happen," I assure her, though I'm growing less and less confident by the hour. "Maybe I just caught her off guard and she needs a few days to think. You have to remember, this came out of nowhere for her and was probably pretty strange considering...well, that she didn't think you liked her very much." This does little to assuage her fears, but I try to redirect her focus. "You don't even know for sure if Natalie is your unfinished business, and if she won't talk to us, then it has to be something else."

I have no idea if this is true, but I have to stop her from spiraling. She puts on a brave face, but I can tell she's still worried when I leave to meet Jude.

"You okay?" Jude asks, looping an arm around my shoulders as we start down the sidewalk toward the bookstore where our ghost tour is to begin. "You seem quiet."

"I'm fine," I say because I can't exactly tell him I'm worried my dead friend might be stuck here on earth, causing me to be on my own permanent ghost tour. I also can't mention how bad I feel about lying to him about my not-dead cat.

"You're not scared, are you?"

"If I am, will you hold me close and never let me go?" I tease.

He grins, squeezing me tighter. "I'll do that anyway."

We reach our destination a few minutes early and give our info to the guide before standing aside to wait for our tour to begin.

Downtown Franklin is filled with people taking advantage of the final weekend of October. Some are in cozy sweaters, while others are in costume, likely headed to Halloween parties or trunk-or-treats. There's a chill and thrill of excitement in the air.

"So," I say, beaming up at him. "What would you do if you saw a real live ghost?"

His hands slide around my waist. "*That* is an oxymoron."

I shoot him a playful glare. "You know what I mean."

He cocks his head. "What kind of ghost are we talking about here? One with empty black voids for eyes and rattling chains or more of the *Casper* variety?"

"Neither. What if you could see a spirit and they appeared exactly as they did in real life, but they're not visible to anyone but you?"

It's a specific question, but not completely out of left field, considering what we're doing. He's proven he's not totally creeped out by the paranormal, but how would he feel if he found out I have a ghost living at home?

"First, I think I might shit myself," he answers. "But once the shock wears off, that could be kinda cool. I guess it depends. What does this hypothetical ghost do? Do they try to scare me and watch me sleep like a weirdo, or do they understand healthy boundaries?"

I snort. "For the sake of this conversation, let's say they have boundaries." *If he's open to the idea of this whole ghost thing, we can deal with the rest later.*

"So, they'd be invisible to everyone but me." He scratches the back of his head. "As long as we get along and they're not trying to freak me out all the time, I don't see a downside. I appreciate friends who have different life experiences than I do, and well, that's about as different as it gets." He pauses a beat. "What about you? What would you do?"

"Pass out, probably," I answer as though that isn't *exactly* what I did when I realized my sassy pearl-wearing home intruder was actually a ghost. "But like you, once I got past the shock, I think it could be fun."

I don't bring up the extra benefits—having your own personal guardian who can shatter a glass or flicker the lights when you need her to (and even when you don't), offer unsolicited style and life advice, and be a friend who's always game for a girls' night.

"Good to know," he says with a nod. "In case we happen upon any unattended spirits with impeccable boundaries tonight."

I rise on my toes to give him a quick kiss, then he clears his throat.

"Speaking of things that have the potential to be scary,

how were your *Purrfect Match* dates?" he asks, running his fingers through his hair.

"Not bad," I say. "It seems like Eddie and Becca are being more careful with their selections."

Jude lifts his brows. "Are they now?"

I briefly catch him up on my weekend, leaving out the part about how Marjorie stayed next to me the whole time, pointing out when I subconsciously steered the conversation back to them and encouraged me to share things about myself.

"Don't worry. I'm not running off with Andrew."

He narrows his eyes. "Andrew, huh?"

"What would you prefer I call him? Bachelor number one?"

He smirks. "I would prefer you didn't call him at all."

"And I won't," I say. "But we both know if I pull the plug on the segment too soon after agreeing to continue, they're gonna be suspicious."

"I know, I know. You're right," he assures me. "I'm just messing with you. I guess this means I don't get to stop wooing you just yet."

"Is there supposed to be wooing happening right now?" I tease, glancing around as though there should be visible signs of said wooing. "Where's this woo you're referring to?"

He feigns offense. "Are you not feeling wooed? I'm wounded." He drags out the *ooo,* and I laugh.

I gesture toward where the other attendees are beginning to gather. "Nothing says romance like a little death."

"Hey now," he says, tightening his arms around me, enveloping me in his warm scent. "I'll have you know, this tour is plenty romantic."

"Oh?"

"Mm-hmm," he answers. "Plenty of opportunities to pull you close if you get scared."

"What if I don't get scared?"

"Plenty of opportunities for *you* to pull *me* close if I get scared," he replies, leaning down so his mouth is dangerously close to mine. "More than a few dark corners to disappear into and steal some kisses."

"Are the kisses being stolen from me or the ghosts?"

His mouth twitches into a smile. "I'm done with you."

I close the distance and press my lips to his. "No, you're not."

He folds me in his arms and rests his head on top of mine.

"No," he says, "I'm definitely not."

chapter twenty-seven

Neither Jude nor I walk away with any new spirits, but by the time I return home that night, there's a message waiting for me in my inbox from Natalie that reads:

Okay. I'll meet with you.

I exhale a sigh of relief and relay the information to Marjorie, who is ecstatic.

"Do you think she's available now?" she asks, following on my heels as I pad to my room to get ready for bed.

"First of all, it's eleven thirty," I say. "And actually, that's enough of an explanation. So, no. I'll find out what days she's available and set something up."

"*Set something up?*" Her tone is sharp. "No, you need to tell her to meet you tomorrow morning."

I step into the closet to change. "You *do* know I have a job, right? And I'm betting she does too."

"But this is important," she whines, muffled by the wall separating us as I pull a sweatshirt over my head and switch into a pair of cotton shorts.

"I'm not denying that," I reply, striding over to the bed and flopping down next to where Delilah is already lying. She lifts her head and regards me through narrowed eyes as though she's silently telling me off for being out past her bedtime. "But Marjorie, the world can't always bow to your every command."

"And why not?" She folds her arms over her chest.

I blink and roll my lips inward. "Do I really need to answer that?"

She huffs. "But my unfinished business!"

I point to the digital clock on the nightstand. "*But it's eleven thirty.* I already stayed out way later than I should have, and I've got to be up in five hours to get to the studio. Have some patience."

"We already determined that learning patience isn't my unfinished business," she argues.

"That may be, but you *do* have to learn that the world can't revolve around you all the time." I stifle a yawn, already dreading the incessant beep of my alarm. "Not because it's your unfinished business, but for my own sanity."

She releases a frustrated groan and stomps her foot, which might have more of an impact if it made a sound.

"Will you at least email her back tonight?" she asks.

"Fine," I concede. "Then you're going to let me sleep."

"But you still have to tell me about your date," she says, sitting at the foot of my bed.

"Three questions, and then you let me rest."

We stare at each other, our gazes locked in a stalemate.

"Yes, all right," she agrees. "Email first, then three questions."

I tap out a message to Natalie before plugging in my phone and placing it face down on the nightstand.

"Fire away," I say, nestling deeper beneath the covers and switching off the lamp.

"Okay, tell me everything."

"That's not a question."

"Semantics."

"Three *specific* questions."

"What's the fun in that?" she asks.

"And now it's two."

"Oh fine," she pouts. I can't make out her form in the darkness, but I can practically hear her eyes roll. "Did you have a good time?"

"I did." Every moment spent with him is somehow better than the last. He's the kind of dream I never want to wake up from. "He's…he's really special."

"Good. I'm glad." Her words are softer now. "You deserve that. You deserve someone who treats you like the treasure you are."

My throat grows thick. "Treasure? And here I thought I was a tattooed miscreant," I tease. "With no fashion sense."

"Yes, well, you are nothing if not multifaceted," she quips.

I chuckle. "What else do you want to know?"

She hesitates. "Tonight, when you were on that tour…did you see any others?"

My brow furrows. "It was a pretty full tour. About fifteen of us."

"No," she says quickly. "I meant…people like me. You know…in case I wind up stuck here. It would be nice to know there are others out there."

My heart sinks through the mattress and into the floor.

"I didn't," I admit. "But I doubt any of those places are haunted, anyway. I mean, who knows if the stories they told us were even real?" I try to make my next words sound extra convincing. "You're not going to be stuck here. I promise."

It's not a promise I can make, and we both know it, but

she doesn't point that out. In fact, she doesn't say anything at all. A moment passes, and she sniffles, which feels like a punch to my gut.

"Marjorie?"

"Get some sleep, Kathryn," she answers. "I'll see you in the morning."

A cold spot touches my covered leg, then she's gone.

chapter twenty-eight

Much to Marjorie's dismay, Natalie is out of the country on vacation and won't be available for another week. After putting the kibosh on Marjorie's suggestion that we hop the next plane to France, I redirect her focus to helping me through the early days of dating Jude. We analyze texts together and giggle like school girls far past my bedtime for nearly seven days before we shift our attention to my next set of *Purrfect Match* dates—drinks on Friday night and brunch Saturday morning.

The guys are fine, but the best parts of the outings are having Marjorie there reminding me of my worth. She says it so many times I start to believe her.

I take Marjorie back to my house before heading over to Jude's Saturday evening, where he cooks me the most delicious penne alla vodka. After dinner, he puts on an old record before we settle on the couch together with cups of coffee.

"How did I not know you can cook like that?" I ask, sinking into the overstuffed cushions, curling my legs beneath me.

"Just think what you could have had all this time," he teases.

Jude's condo is cozy, filled with dark neutrals and navy walls. A couple of standing lamps cast a soft glow over the living room.

"Now this is a Jude cup of coffee." I take a whiff of the warm, nutty aroma and sigh before taking a sip. "I always know when you make the coffee in the break room because you make it better than anyone."

His eyes widen. "You can tell when it's me?"

I nod. "There's something different about it. I don't know why. What do you do? Bring in your own special beans? Keep a coffee grinder in your car?"

"Not quite," he says with a chuckle. "But I do add a pinch of cinnamon and nutmeg and a dash of salt."

I blink. "We *have* those things in the break room?"

"We do. In the cabinet above the fridge."

"Wait, there's a cabinet above the fridge?" I've been in that break room hundreds of times over the years, and somehow I cannot recall.

"And that's exactly why I keep it there. Nobody pays attention to it, which means the interns won't use my stuff on their oatmeal in the mornings."

I bite back a grin.

"What?" he asks.

"I think it's cute you have a secret stash of nutmeg." It also feels warm and cozy and distinctly Jude. "And now I only want coffee the way you make it."

He smiles. "I'm glad somebody appreciates it."

"How could they *not*?"

"You'd be surprised," he says, taking a long pull from his cup. "Lauren actually hated the smell of coffee."

"Ah, so you two were doomed from the start," I joke.

"Pretty much," he replies. "She was more of a tea girl."

"Hey, I can get behind a tea latte on occasion," I say. "And what about the other girls you've dated since then?" I shoot for nonchalance, but land somewhere between nosy and inquisitive.

He leans closer. "Is that your way of finding out if I've been with anyone since Lauren?"

"*Maybe*," I say, drawing the word out.

"There was no one else," he confirms. "Only a couple of dates. No one serious enough to be around for morning coffee."

"So Lauren was your last relationship?"

He nods.

"You mentioned your mother was the one who set y'all up, right?"

"Mm-hmm."

My throat tightens. "How did she take it when you two split?"

"Not great." His jaw ticks ever so slightly. "My mom loved Lauren. They're a lot alike—driven and focused. My mom has kind of been her mentor because Lauren wants to be a cardiothoracic surgeon like she is."

"Oh wow. I bet that's been tough." It's also something I can't compete with unless his mom decides on a massive career change and wants to pursue radio.

"Yeah," he admits. "Still is. They work at the same hospital, so it's been…challenging."

A pit forms in my stomach, heavy like lead. What will Jude's mother think about him being with someone new? And is there even a small part of Jude that misses his ex?

Before my thought train can veer off track, Marjorie's voice enters my mind.

He's here with you, Kathryn. That's what matters. He likes you.

"Has that been weird for you?" I ask. "Them working together?"

He runs a hand along the back of his neck. "My mother *does* feel the need to tell me every life update Lauren gives her, which I could do without."

I wince. Is she hoping Jude and Lauren will reconcile?

Once again, Marjorie appears in my head.

You're self-sabotaging. Remember your worth.

"I think my mom got set on the idea that Lauren was my person," he says. "And in her mind, I'm running out of time to find love because I'm thirty-seven. She doesn't get that not everyone finds their soulmate at twenty-two."

"Twenty-two?" I echo. I could barely manage to find *myself* at that age, let alone a life partner. "How did your parents meet?"

He places his mug on the coffee table and leans back, turning toward me.

"They were both in college at the University of Tennessee," he answers. "My mom had been working herself to death because she'd taken on such an insane course load. Anyway, she was walking to a lecture one day when she started feeling funny, and she passed out right there on the sidewalk. My dad saw it happen and rushed over to help. She says that when she opened her eyes, he was all she could see. He brought her to the clinic to get checked over. Her blood sugar had bottomed out because she'd forgotten to eat that day and had been running on fumes. So, my dad insisted on taking her to lunch, and they've been inseparable ever since."

"That's so romantic." The story itself is sweet, but the admiration on Jude's face is what makes me melt.

"The way she tells it, he all but carried her to that clinic, effectively sweeping her off her feet. And he says an angel fell out of the sky that day and into his arms." He gives me a faint smile and gently pushes a piece of hair from my eyes. "But love doesn't always happen like an epic fairy tale. Sometimes it happens one page at a time."

His warm brown gaze holds mine, and my mouth goes dry as I think of the ways my relationship with Jude has grown over the years. From colleagues to friends, then friends to… more. It didn't happen overnight, but in thousands of sentences written between the years.

"I know she means well," he adds. "She just wants me to have it all like she did."

"And what do *you* want?" I ask, hoping it's me.

"I think we all have our own version of what having everything means. For her, it was settling down, having a kid and a career she can be proud of. I'd like to get married someday, but I'm not on a timetable." He reaches out and touches my shoulder. "The fact that we're sitting here together now shows I'm nothing if not patient. I'm willing to wait for what I want."

"And what do you want?"

"In the future or right now?"

"Let's start with right now," I answer.

"So many things," he says, his voice a low rasp. "But right now, all I can think about is kissing you."

I lean forward, my words a whisper on his lips. "Funny, because that's all I can think about too."

chapter twenty-nine

MARJORIE AND I MEET NATALIE LATE AFTERNOON ON MONDAY at a small coffee shop near her home in Columbia. It's a chilly, rainy day, and the place is empty minus a couple of patrons working on their laptops with headphones on.

"Thanks again for seeing me." I take my seat across from Natalie with a latte in hand, gently dropping the worn leather backpack I found at Whimsy and Wu last week beside me. After carting Marjorie around in a nondescript brown shopping bag for the last few weeks, I decided we needed an upgrade.

"Sure." Natalie studies me warily with her arms folded over her chest. "You said you found a letter for me? From Marjorie?"

"Yes," I answer, and once again, her trepidation is visible in the lines that have formed on her face. "I apologize for not reaching out sooner. She left messages for you and a few others, but I didn't come across them until recently."

Marjorie sits in the booth beside Natalie, causing her to shiver and reach for her coat.

"She looks lovely," Marjorie says. And she does. Natalie

has waist-length honey blond hair that's been tied in a loose braid, and she wears a long flowy skirt with an oversized sweater. She looks to be in her late forties. Faint crow's feet flank her blue eyes, signs that she's loved and cried and laughed well over the years.

"I'll admit, I'm still in a bit of shock." Natalie drapes the leopard print jacket over her lap. Clearly, Natalie also has great taste. "You obviously knew Marjorie also, and well, she wasn't exactly what I would call sentimental. Actually, she was quite mean most of the time."

Marjorie's jaw tenses. "I deserve that."

My gaze flicks to hers, and I wonder if this was a good idea. Marjorie is adamant about Natalie being her unfinished business, but I worry this encounter could cause more harm than good. Marjorie has her faults and we haven't always seen eye to eye, but there's more to her than the hypercritical sasspot I found in my kitchen that first night. There's a tenderness, a kindness, a loyalty that runs deep.

"She is…*was* certainly very opinionated," I say with a grin.

"That woman judged me mercilessly." Natalie takes a sip of her drink. "My hair, my clothes, you name it, she had thoughts about it and was determined to inform me of every single one."

"That sounds like her," I admit.

Now, Marjorie watches her former caretaker quietly, seemingly all out of unsolicited insights.

"I was a single mom." Natalie pauses, picking at the ends of her braid. "Between my patient load and my son Milo, I was lucky to get a shower most days, let alone be able to do anything with my hair. I used to put it in a bun and call it a day, but God, Marjorie hated it. Never hesitated to tell me."

Shame veils Marjorie's face like a shadow.

"And my scrubs," Natalie continues. "I often couldn't afford new scrubs, so I got a lot of mine at thrift stores. They were always clean, but a little worse for the wear."

"I didn't know she was a mother," Marjorie says, a regretful expression on her face. "I didn't know any of this, because I never bothered to ask."

"She speaks highly of you." I clear my throat. "Spoke, I mean. In the letter."

Natalie stares at me, her brows furrowed in disbelief.

"So, where is this letter?" she asks. "Can I see it?"

I dig in my bag for the folded sheets of paper I ripped from the lined notebook where I keep my notes for the show.

"Actually, she left specific instructions for me to read it to you," I say, unfolding the page. "I found a few different messages meant for people she knew with orders that I must read them to each recipient only once and that I'm not to share the written copies with anyone."

Natalie tilts her head. "That's…strange."

"Um, yeah," I agree, pretending I'm just as puzzled by this information as she is and I didn't just pull that vague explanation out of my ass. "But you know Marjorie."

"Probably didn't want there to be any physical evidence that she had a heart," Natalie says with a snort. "Marjorie always played things close to the vest. She never did trust easily. You must have been special for her to leave you with such a task."

My chest floods with warmth because I know how far Marjorie and I have come. We began as thorns in each other's sides, but somehow an unlikely friendship blossomed—one I never could have seen coming, but one I never want to see leave.

"I don't take her faith in me lightly," I say, and Marjorie gives me a nod of encouragement.

"Well, if those were her wishes, then we should honor them, weird as they may be." Natalie folds her hands on the table. "Go ahead. I'm listening."

My gaze darts to Marjorie before falling to the fake letter in front of me.

"Dear Natalie," I begin, waiting for Marjorie to tell me what to say next.

"You're probably surprised to hear from me," Marjorie says. "I know I wasn't exactly kind to you back when you took care of me. And I want to tell you how sorry I am. You didn't deserve that. I was an angry, bitter woman, grappling with the fact that I was dying. Friends didn't come because I didn't have any, and my husband…well, he was my biggest regret. I spent my life surrounding myself with important, influential people, but at the end of the day, it didn't matter. I still died alone, except for you."

I chance a glance up at Natalie whose eyes are glossy with unshed tears, and I'm thankful I'm not actually reading anything because what words are on the page before me have started to blur.

"You were the only friend I had." Marjorie's voice breaks. "You stayed late when you didn't have to. Watched television with me, painted my nails, and made me countless cups of tea. You took time away from your family to be with me even when I treated you so horribly. You showed me grace when I deserved none. I don't remember what I paid you, but I know it wasn't nearly enough for everything you did for me."

"Oh, Marjorie," Natalie whispers softly, reaching for a napkin from the dispenser to dry her eyes.

I swallow around the lump in my throat, but don't dare

look up at Marjorie because I know if I do I'll completely lose what little composure I still have.

"The painting you made for my last birthday, the one with the pink flowers…" Marjorie's gaze is fixed on Natalie, her eyes filled with what can only be described as love. "It was the most precious gift I ever received."

Natalie chokes out an emotion-filled laugh. "I thought she hated it. I believe her exact words were 'Florals, how quaint.'"

"I'll never forget the look of pride on your face when you gave it to me and how quickly your smile faded with my callous remarks. You knew how much I loved art, and you shared your talents with me. Your work was so much more than quaint, Natalie. It was beautiful, just like you," Marjorie says through a sob. "I'm sorry I never told you that. That I never told you how special you are. And I'm so grateful my last days were spent with someone as kind and wonderful as you. All my love, Marjorie."

I dry my cheeks with the sleeve of my sweater, then fold the pages containing my old notes and tuck them in my bag. When my eyes meet Marjorie's again I give her a subtle nod, the one thing I can do to let her know how damn proud I am of her.

Natalie blows her nose into her napkin. "I saw the way her husband was with her. Conrad, I believe, was his name. Awful man. He barely said two words to Marjorie in the months I cared for her. One day I even saw him kissing some woman wearing a tacky flamingo-printed dress. He was messing around on his sick wife. Then to see that none of her friends came…it was heartbreaking. And you…you were her friend, right? But you didn't visit the entire time I was there. Why?"

"I wasn't aware she was sick. If I had…I would have been

by her side too. But I'm so thankful she had you, Natalie. You were a lifeline for her." My heart fills with gratitude for this woman I don't know but share an unusual kinship with. It's clear we both feel a sense of protectiveness for Marjorie.

Natalie drags her hand over her mouth and releases a shaky breath. "I wish I could tell you Marjorie's story is rare, but in my line of work there have been others. I've sat at countless bedsides where I'm the only person the patient sees for weeks or even months at a time."

"Marjorie was right," I say. "You're a special person."

"My own mom passed away when I was in my early twenties. She was in hospice for several weeks, and I don't think she was alone once. Between me and my dad and her three brothers and her best friends…someone was always there. And that's how it should be." Natalie clasps her hands together on the table. "I remember her nurse saying something to my dad before she left one day about how lucky she was because she had patients who didn't have anyone. That's when I knew what I wanted to do with the rest of my life. I couldn't help everyone, but I could at least make sure my patients never had to die alone."

My chest tightens. "Your patients are lucky to have you." When my mom passed, it was sudden, so there was no nurse, no family holding vigil at her bedside. There was only the hard pavement and hurried EMT workers and hospital staff who looked at my dad and me with sad eyes.

"Thank you," Natalie says. "For finding me. For reading me that letter."

I give her a faint smile. "It's what Marjorie wanted."

Marjorie speaks. "Ask what she's doing now, about her son."

I do, and Natalie replies, "I'm still in home health. I still love it, even though some days it hurts my heart. Milo is heading off to the University of Georgia." She pulls her phone from her bag and opens it to show me a photo of her with a young man who has Natalie's eyes and blond hair. "That's him."

Marjorie catches a glimpse of the picture and presses a hand to her chest.

"I bet you're proud," I say.

"I am," she replies. "So proud, but it's always been me and him. Us against the world. I'm going to miss him terribly. But I'm engaged now to the most wonderful man, so I suppose I'll just have to busy myself with planning the wedding."

I catch a glimpse of the dainty diamond ring on her finger and grin. "Congratulations."

"I hope he deserves her or so help me God I will find a way to haunt him for the rest of his life," Marjorie mutters.

"Well, I suppose I should let you get on with your day," I say.

"Thanks again for reaching out," Natalie replies. "It means a lot."

"And thank you for taking such good care of my friend when I couldn't." My words fall short of the gratitude I feel for her, but I silently hope the world shows her the grace she's always given others. I slide out of the booth, shrugging on my coat and grabbing my coffee, but Marjorie lingers for a moment as though trying to memorize her face.

We say our goodbyes and head out, climbing back inside my SUV as the rain pelts against the windows. Marjorie and I exchange nervous glances. Is this it? Are we seconds away from her going into the light? I'm a jumbled mess of emotions. Pride, joy, and despair mix to form a potent cocktail inside my veins, causing every nerve in my body to feel electrified.

"Do you see anything?" I ask, my voice barely above a whisper as though I'm afraid that if there *is* a light, I might accidentally scare it off.

She shakes her head. "No. Nothing."

We wait in silence for a minute, then another, but the only light we see is a street lamp overhead, flickering on as dusk sets in.

"It didn't work." Marjorie stares straight ahead, her expression stoic. Water trails down the windshield, leaving tear tracks in its wake.

"You don't know that," I say. "Give it more time."

She faces me now. "It didn't work," she repeats.

My throat is dry, and I take what feels like my first breath since we've been back in this car. I'm overcome with…relief followed by a sharp stab of shame.

Crossing over is what Marjorie wants—what she *needs*. She deserves to live out her afterlife in paradise or wherever it is we go when we die. She deserves more than just being stuck with me. But I can't deny how much I've grown to care for her. How much I'll miss her.

"I'm sorry," I say, though that's not entirely true. While part of me is sad that Natalie didn't hold the key to Marjorie's eternity, there's an even bigger part that's glad I get to keep her with me a while longer.

She nods and presses her lips together before forcing a smile. "It's all right."

"But—"

"I'm fine," she insists, cutting me off. "I'm not as sad as I thought I would be."

I blink. "Really? But…why?"

She drops her head against the seat and turns toward me. "Don't get me wrong, I'm still disappointed, but I'm just glad I got to thank her for everything she did. To tell her how sorry I am for how I treated her. She's a special woman."

"Yeah, she is," I agree.

"I'll keep thinking," she says, her brows furrowed in determination. "There has to be something. Some loose end I'm missing."

Thunder rolls in the distance, flashes of lightning flickering across the gray sky.

"We should go." She gestures forward. "Sounds like a storm is coming."

"Right," I say, pausing a moment before starting the ignition. "I really am sorry." That she didn't see the light, and that part of me doesn't want her to.

"Don't be. I'm not." Her melancholy tone betrays the resolve of her words, but I don't argue. Instead, I try to take her mind off it.

"You know what we need?" I ask as I back out of the parking spot. "A girls' night."

"I'm fine, Kathryn. You don't need to babysit me. Why don't you go spend some time with Jude?"

I scoff. "Because I wanna hang out with you, that's why."

She opens her mouth to argue, but I hold out one hand, keeping the other on the wheel as I turn onto the highway.

"I'm not one of those women who starts dating someone and suddenly forgets she has a life," I say. "Besides, an entire season of some ridiculous new dating show dropped on Netflix today, and it's just begging for our astute critiques."

A faint smile tugs at the corners of her mouth. "Well, if you insist."

"I do."

"You should probably stop for snacks," she suggests.

"I wish you could have some. I still think it's a crime that you've never eaten a Twizzler."

She wrinkles her nose. "Those things don't even resemble real food."

"Okay, fine. I'll get some Twizzlers for me, and I'll even pick up some light bulbs for you to pop as a little treat."

She laughs and rolls her eyes. "I can hardly wait."

"Maybe we can do some more experiments," I say. "Or you can run through your closet for me. I'm always trying on outfits for you. It's only fair I get a fashion show every once in a while."

"A fashion show?" She clears her throat but it does nothing to tamp down the elation in her voice. "I suppose that could be fun."

I grin, happy I've managed to redirect her attention, at least for now.

"To girls' night," I say, grabbing my coffee from the console and holding it up.

She looks at me like I've gone mad. "What are you doing?"

"Cheers me."

"But I don't have a glass."

"Just use your fist."

She glances at me sideways but humors me, nonetheless, touching her fist to my cardboard cup. "To girls' night."

"That's the spirit." I nod and take a swig of my coffee, nearly choking when I discover it's now ice-cold.

chapter thirty

The week passes, bringing us no closer to figuring out what Marjorie's unfinished business is. I do my best to keep her distracted, but when I trudge into the kitchen in the mornings, I find her sitting at the dining table staring out the window with sad, vacant eyes. My chest tightens with guilt for having to leave her with nothing but her thoughts to keep her company while I sleep. I even bring her to work with me for a couple days in my trusty backpack because I feel terrible leaving her alone.

By the time Friday arrives, I'm actually grateful to get her out of the house and take her on a *Purrfect Match* date even though the last place I want to be is with any guy other than Jude. She lights up every time I take her out, and it's easy to visualize a younger Marjorie sitting at the bar of a ridiculously overpriced restaurant, sipping a gin martini. It makes me want to ditch these dates altogether and go somewhere, just Marjorie and me. We could order an obscene amount of appetizers and drink too many cocktails and laugh till our cheeks hurt. The more I learn about Marjorie's life on earth, the more I realize how little of that she had, and I just want to do everything I can to make up for it with what time we have left.

"When will you be back from your breakfast with Jude?" Marjorie asks as I shrug on my coat around 10 a.m. Saturday morning.

"We're going to Whimsy and Wu after we leave Dawn's Diner, so probably around one, one thirty. Gives me just enough time to swing back to change and pick you up before our date with…Stewart."

She wrinkles her nose. "*Stewart?* Heavens, is he eighty-five and living on a yacht off the coast of Florida?"

"Technically, he goes by Stewie," I say. "And he's thirty-three."

"That's supposed to be better somehow?"

I shrug. "Good thing we never have to see him again after tonight."

"That's true," she replies. "Well, I don't want you to keep Jude waiting. You go on, and we can discuss…Stewie…later."

"Okay," I say, grabbing my purse and starting for the door.

"And Kathryn?" She calls out my name before my hand reaches the knob.

"Yeah?" I stop and turn back toward her.

"You know you don't have to keep doing these dates on my account, right?"

"Of course," I answer, but I also realize she's one of the main reasons I haven't put a stop to them yet. I'm completely in on this thing with Jude, and enough time has passed that I can pull out of the whole ordeal without raising suspicion at work.

She eyes me as though she doesn't quite believe me, but she nods anyway.

"Please, don't misunderstand. I've had a ball, but it

seems silly to keep up this *Purrfect Match* charade when you could be spending time with the man you actually want to be with."

"You're right," I say. "Maybe I should talk to Jude, see how he feels about it."

"I think that's a wonderful idea." Her head tilts to one side and she releases a satisfied sigh. "This is a big step, and well, I'm really proud of you."

"Are you going soft on me?" I tease. But I'm proud of myself too. A few weeks ago I couldn't make it beyond a third date. I was settling for guys I barely liked, but now I have someone I'm crazy about.

"Perhaps I am."

"Not to be weird, but this whole being dead thing is kinda working for you."

"That is actually *quite* weird."

I grin. "I'll be back soon."

She sends me off with a wave, and I make the short drive to Dawn's Diner to meet Jude, enjoying the way the sunshine streams through the trees. There's a slight breeze, which sends leaves drifting onto the pavement like confetti falling from the sky.

Am I really going to tell Jude I'm ready to call off the *Purrfect Match* segment? Obviously, I haven't been seeing anyone else—not really. The dates I've been on for the segment have been nothing more than platonic. But ending them makes our relationship feel more real. More official. Just thinking about it causes my pulse to race. It would mark the beginning of something more serious, eventually fessing up to Becca and Eddie and meeting his family. Jude already knows everyone I hold dear—well, almost. Everyone but Marjorie, but maybe I could eventually tell him about her. I spend the rest of the ride talking myself through how to approach the situation.

Hey, wanna be my boyfriend, and oh, by the way, care to meet my dead friend?

I should probably take this one step at a time.

When I arrive, he rises to greet me from a table just inside the door.

"Hey, beautiful." He pulls me into his arms and gives me a brief but tender kiss.

"Hi," I say before taking a seat across from him.

"I already ordered one of those cinnamon roll towers you like, and our coffees should be here soon."

I beam over at him. "You get me."

"That I do." He passes me one of the laminated menus and smiles, but it doesn't reach his eyes.

"You okay?"

He clears his throat. "Um, yeah. Actually, there's something I wanted to talk to you about."

My heart lurches, and I nod. Anything I have to say can wait. "Okay. What's up?"

He picks at the edge of his menu where the plastic has begun to peel and draws in a breath.

"Oh shit, are you breaking up with me?" My stomach begins to churn, and my limbs go stiff. Did he realize this whole thing was a bad idea? That *I* was a bad idea? Can he even break up with me if we aren't *technically* together?

"What? No." His hand shoots across the table to take mine. "Nothing like that."

My shoulders loosen. "Then what's going on?"

"I don't want you going on any more of those *Purrfect Match* dates," he blurts.

I bring my other hand to my mouth, attempting to stifle a

laugh. But I'm unsuccessful and end up giggling damn near hysterically.

Jude blinks, his mouth frozen into a crooked line. "Why are you laughing?"

"*That's* what you were so nervous about?"

"Well, yeah. I didn't want you to think I was trying to be controlling or possessive or—"

"Jude, I was going to tell you the same thing," I say, squeezing his fingers.

"You were?"

"Yeah, I was."

He releases a long, slow breath. "So, what does that mean for the one you have tonight?"

I twist my lips to the corner of my mouth as I pretend to consider. "Actually, I think I feel a stomach bug coming on."

His brown eyes flash with concern, causing those little lines on his forehead to form.

"Oh no, do you need to go home?" he asks.

I cock my head and fix him with a *read-the-room* glare.

"Oh," he says. "*Ooooooh.* So, does this mean you might be free to go to a concert at the Ryman tonight with your... boyfriend?"

"Boyfriend, huh?" That word, coupled with the fact that he's the one saying it, is enough to make me grin so hard my cheeks hurt.

He smiles back at me, stroking my knuckles with his thumb. "Yeah. Is that...okay?"

I tap a finger to my chin. "Well, the Ryman *is* my favorite venue."

"So *that's* the only reason you want to go?"

"It doesn't hurt that my favorite boyfriend is the one taking me."

"As long as I'm your favorite," he says with a wink. "I would spend the afternoon with you till then, but I have an appointment to get my oil changed at three."

"No worries," I say, relieved I get to go home and squeal about this with Marjorie. "I'll meet you there."

"Dinner first?"

"Are you trying to woo me again?"

"That depends," he says, leaning forward. "Is it working?"

"Most definitely." My heart thumps against my ribcage. "You'll still have time to go to Whimsy and Wu today, though, right? I want to introduce you to Dennis."

Dennis is my only non-ghost friend who knows about *everything,* including the stupid lie I told about Delilah the day I brought Marjorie's urn to work.

"Yeah, but haven't I met him before?"

I grin. "Not as my boyfriend, you haven't."

chapter thirty-one

"OKAY, WHAT GIVES?" BECCA ASKS ME MONDAY MORNING after we wrap the show.

"Sorry?" I slip off my headphones.

"You've been on seven dates and only felt *friend vibes* with every single one?" She pins me with an accusatory glare, and Jude tugs at the collar of his shirt.

Eddie rolls his lips together, and I swear, if there was a microwave in the room, he'd be making himself a bag of popcorn.

"That's not true," I argue. "I felt nothing but disgust toward Todd Summers."

Becca rolls her eyes. "You know what I mean."

I do, but I'm stalling.

"I thought you wanted this, Kat," she continues, leaning toward me with her elbows on her knees. "Look, I know we got off on a rough start with Todd, but the rest of these guys seemed pretty cool. You mean to tell me you haven't liked *any* of them?"

Jude clears his throat and stands. "I'm gonna go get another coffee."

"Not so fast." Becca holds out her palm like a stop sign. "Because I have a feeling *you* have something to do with this."

He swallows and lowers back down to his chair. "What are you talking about?"

Eddie lifts his water bottle to his mouth and takes a drink, his eyes bouncing between us like balls being volleyed over a net.

Becca points at Jude. "You've been getting into her head. You were against this thing from the beginning."

Jude's cheeks flush.

"Becca—" I begin.

"Uh-uh. Don't defend him," she counters. "He's had some axe to grind about this whole thing from day one."

"*Becca*," I say more loudly this time. "This has nothing to do with him." Of course it does, but now isn't the time to tell Becca and Eddie about it.

She shifts her focus to me. "Then what is it?"

"I met someone." I suck in a deep breath. *Here goes nothing.*

"What?" The fire drains from her expression, and Eddie's mouth drops open.

"When?" he asks.

"It was recent," I answer. "But...I really like this guy."

"Are you serious?" Becca asks. "Why didn't you say anything?"

Because if I do, you and Eddie might shit a brick.

"I didn't want to end the *Purrfect Match* segment without a good reason," I say instead. "I know how much work you and Eddie put into this, and I needed to make sure what I have with this guy is...real."

The heat from Jude's gaze burns into the side of my face.

Becca blinks. "So, wait, does this mean…did you break your streak?"

My lips twitch into a grin. "I did." I broke it like an iPhone screen, shattering it beyond recognition.

Becca squeals and leaps onto me like a grasshopper, enveloping me in a hug.

"You have to tell me everything," she says, her frustration now forgotten. "Who is he? How did you meet? When do *I* get to meet him?"

I chuckle. "Slow down, tiger. Things are still new. I promise I'll tell you all about him soon, but I just…I need a little more time."

Becca groans. "Ugh. So cryptic."

Eddie's face softens. "This is great news, Kat. Congratulations."

"Must be a special guy to have wooed *the* Kat Simon," Jude adds, and my lips quirk.

"Thanks. He *is* pretty great," I say. "And I'm sorry to back out of the segment, but if it's any consolation, this whole process was instrumental in my connection with this guy. It helped me see just how much I was getting in my own way."

Becca presses her hands to her chest. "I'm happy for you, babe. You deserve it. But if this mystery guy does anything to hurt you, I'll chop off his hands and turn them into drumstick holders."

Jude coughs and takes a swig from the remnants of his coffee to mask his concern.

Eddie nods and folds his arms over his broad chest. "Once you feel ready to bring him around, I want to meet him. Gotta make sure he's good enough for our girl."

"Kat wouldn't be seeing the guy if he sucked," Jude says, scratching the back of his neck.

"We'll be the judge of that," Becca insists, tipping her chin upward.

"Right." Jude straightens the hem of his shirt and rises to his feet. "Well, I'm going to go grab some more coffee, and then I've got a meeting with the interns, so I'll see you guys later."

"Later." Eddie gives him a mock salute, and Becca and I wave.

Jude places a hand on my shoulder and gives it a gentle squeeze that sends electricity rippling through my body.

"And congrats, Kat," he says. "Whoever he is, he's a lucky man."

"Damn straight," Becca replies, beginning to gather her things as he exits the studio. "Okay, I've got a hair appointment, so I've got to run too, but seriously, I need details soon, okay?"

"Soon," I echo. "Promise."

She leans down to give me a hug before heading out the door.

I release a slow breath through my nose as I snap my laptop shut, catching Eddie looking at me with a fond expression.

"You seem different," he says. "Self-assured. Content."

"I am," I admit. "I feel…good."

"Jude was right about one thing. This guy must be special, because I haven't seen you like this in…well, a really long time."

I smile. "He is. Special, I mean."

"Well, I can't wait to meet him," he says. "But don't wait too long. I'm not gonna be here forever."

I roll my eyes playfully. "You're retiring, Eddie. Not dying. Geez."

He laughs. "I know, I know. I just want to make sure you're taken care of before I leave."

"That's not ominous or anything." This show feels like home, and that's because of Eddie. It's difficult to imagine this place without him. It's even harder to imagine my life without his laugh and the way his eyes crinkle when he smiles. "Have there been any updates? Do you know what's going to happen to the show?"

He shakes his head. "Not yet. There's still a lot of meetings to be had and things to be decided, but you'll be the first to know once I hear anything. I hope to have news after the first of the year."

"How are you feeling about it all?"

"Sad," he admits. "Radio has been my entire life. It's hard to imagine my world without it and not seeing you knuckleheads every damn day. But I'm also…relieved. I'm just ready to slow down, enjoy the spoils of my labor instead of constantly hustling."

"And you've earned that," I say.

He sighs. "I have but not knowing what's going to become of the show…it's been weighing on me."

"Why? You've worked so hard for this, Eddie."

"Because *Eddie in the Morning* is more than just me—it's *us*. It's the culmination of everyone on the program—everyone that's ever *been* on it," he answers. "Shows like ours are rare. We're family, and we make our listeners *feel* like family. If we lose that, they lose it too."

My heart drops. I hate even considering it.

"But you can't stick around because you think it's best for everyone else," I say. "It's time to do what's best for you."

"Yeah. You're right." His throat works to swallow. "Doesn't make it any easier, though."

"I know."

He rises and strides over to me, propping his large frame against the desk.

"Listen, try not to worry too much about this, okay? We've got the holidays coming up, and a lot can happen in a couple months. And if we are nearing the end…well, then we're gonna go out with a bang."

My throat tightens, but I nod. "Hell yeah, we are." Even if we find out the show will continue in Eddie's absence, it won't be the same. Our chemistry, our friendships…they're what makes what we have so special. No matter what happens, we'll never have this again, and I intend to savor every last minute.

"Speaking of the holidays, Thanksgiving is in a couple weeks, and Tai won't let me have a moment's peace until you tell me you'll be there."

I give him a faint smile. "Of course I will. I've been dreaming about her sweet potato pie since last year."

"Good deal." He holds out his fist for me to bump. "All right. I'm out. I'll see you tomorrow."

"See ya," I call as he walks out the door.

I pack up my stuff to head to my meeting with our producer Cassie, pausing to check my phone. I grin when I find a text waiting for me from Jude.

Billy's at 2?

I smile down at the screen and tap out my reply.

You bet.

chapter thirty-two

JUDE WALKS ME TO MY CAR AT BILLY'S, OUR FINGERS intertwined. "So, I have something I want to run by you."

"What's up?" I ask as we reach my SUV, resting my back against the driver's side door.

The sun is beginning to set, sending shades of deep purple and cotton candy pink streaking across the sky.

Jude takes a breath and shoves his hands in his pockets.

"They're doing some work on my condo this weekend to fix a big leak on the first floor and are gonna have to shut the water off in the whole building," he explains. "I was planning to stay with my buddy Austin, but now his brother's coming into town, and he'll need his spare room. The landlord will put me up in a hotel, so I don't want you to feel pressured at all if this isn't something you're ready for, but I was thinking...maybe I could—"

"Of course you can stay with me," I say.

His eyes light up. "Really? Are you sure?"

I grin up at him, pulling him closer with the sides of his open jacket. "I can't think of anything I'd like more."

"Good." He slides his arms around my waist. "Because I

have to admit, the idea of waking up next to you sounds pretty great."

"I'm sorry." I furrow my brows in feigned confusion. "Waking up? Are you implying we'll actually be sleeping?"

He leans down and captures my mouth with his in a slow, tender kiss.

"You're right," he says with a wolfish grin. "I'll sleep when I'm dead."

Ha. That's not how it works, buddy.

My limbs go cold, and my heart nearly stops.

Dead.

As in, Marjorie, who is *actually* dead and my cat, who he *thinks* is dead, all of whom are at my house, barring some unimaginable scenario I'm wholly unprepared for.

Oh no. No, no, no, no. What did I just agree to?

"I can't wait," he says, his voice a low rumble that would send heat shooting straight to my core if I wasn't freaking the hell out.

"Yeah," I squeak. And *I* can't wait to figure out how I'm going to manage this without blowing my cover. "Me either."

My phone rings from my back pocket, and I've never been more grateful to receive a call in my life. Dennis's name flashes across the screen.

"I've got to run home before I head to the gym, so I'll let you get that." Jude presses a gentle kiss to my lips before backing away in the direction of his car. "I'll check in later."

"Yeah, okay." I force a smile as I slide into my SUV and accept the call. "Hey—"

I don't even finish my sentence before Dennis cuts me off.

"I need you to come to the store as soon as you can. It's an emergency."

My stomach drops. "Are you all right? What's going on?"

"I'm fine," he answers, "but you've got to get here and bring Marjorie."

"What? Why?" What kind of emergency requires the help of a ghost?

There's a beat of silence before he speaks again. "I think I know what her unfinished business is."

I gasp, my sleepover predicament momentarily forgotten.

"Well, what is it?" I press. "What did you find?"

"I can't tell you over the phone. You need to see it."

It? What can *it* possibly be? And if whatever Dennis has is Marjorie's ticket to the afterlife, does that mean I'm about to lose her? I shudder, unable to wrap my mind around the possibility.

"Okay, okay," I concede, starting the ignition. "I'm headed to get Marjorie now, and I'll be there soon."

"Hurry," he says. "Oh, and bring me a tea from Dawn's Diner, will you?"

I scoff. "I thought this was an emergency."

"It is, but I also need caffeine. You're rubbing off on me."

I roll my eyes. "Fine. But this better be good."

I can practically hear his smug grin through the phone.

"Trust me. It is."

chapter thirty-three

IT'S ALMOST SIX WHEN I ARRIVE AT WHIMSY AND WU, Marjorie's urn in one hand, a jasmine tea for Dennis in the other.

We step inside and Dennis immediately flips the sign on the door to "Closed" before shutting it behind us.

"You're an angel on earth." He extends his hand toward the to-go cup, but I snatch it back before he can wrap his fingers around it.

"Not so fast. What's this all about?" I ask.

"No tea until we get answers," Marjorie agrees, making the light fixture in the center of the store flicker for good measure.

Dennis holds his hands up in surrender. "Okay. Business first." He gestures for me to follow him to the counter where he opens the register, lifts out the till, and retrieves a manilla envelope. "This. I think *this* contains Marjorie's unfinished business."

He holds it out to me, but when I reach for it, he pulls an Uno Reverse on me and yanks it away.

"Tea, please," he says, opening his palm, and the light flickers again.

Marjorie glowers at him. "He's being awfully mysterious with his vague answers and secret envelopes."

I roll my eyes and give him the drink.

"You're eating this up, aren't you?" I ask as he passes me the mailer.

"Are you kidding? This is the most excitement I've had since Dawn's Diner started offering dairy-free ice cream in their sundaes over the summer."

I shoot him a *be-so-serious* glare.

"What?" he cries. "I'm lactose intolerant, okay? Let me live."

"Oh, for Pete's sake," Marjorie mutters. "While learning about Dennis's dietary preferences is *endlessly* fascinating, I'd really like to know what he thinks is so important."

"Right, sorry," I say, sliding my finger beneath the open flap and pulling out a piece of paper large enough to have once been attached to a legal pad. It's whisper thin and creased, worn as though it's been opened thousands of times before being folded again.

"A customer bought a painting from me yesterday. It was this pretty pink floral piece," Dennis explains. "It came from the box Marjorie's urn was in from that storage unit."

I gasp. *Natalie's painting.*

Marjorie's face goes sickly pale, which is saying something considering she's...well, *dead.*

"Anyway, the lady went to hang it up today, and *that*" — he tips his cup toward the note in my hand— "fell out. She read it and felt it must be of value to someone, so she returned it to me in case I knew who it belonged to. And I'm glad she did, because I'm pretty sure it's from Marjorie's former *lover.*" His eyes are alight with curiosity. "It's quite romantic."

I scrunch my nose. "Conrad?" I don't know the guy, but I'm fairly certain he doesn't have a romantic bone in his body.

"Not unless Conrad's code name was John," he says with a chuckle. "Oooh, maybe they were role-playing."

"Do you know what this is?" I ask Marjorie. She stares at the page as though it's grown teeth and might attack at any given moment.

"Kathryn, I'm ready to go." Marjorie's jaw is set, her tone icy.

My eyebrows shoot to my hairline. "I'm sorry. What?"

"Now," she insists, already starting toward the door. "Let's go."

Why is she acting like the tornado siren went off and she must seek shelter immediately? "Um, no. I don't know where you think you're going, but it's not like you can leave without me."

"Marjorie, it's okay," Dennis calls. "We don't kink shame around here."

She pivots on her heel with a frustrated groan. "He read my letter?" she snaps as the lights begin to flicker wildly, and everything inside the store begins to vibrate. "He had *no* right."

"Oh my God." Dennis yelps, catching a lamp before it falls off the counter. "Are we having an earthquake?"

"Marjorie, stop," I shout. "What are you doing?"

An owl figurine slides off a nearby table and shatters.

"This is *her*?" Dennis's words come out shaky. "Margie! I thought we were cool."

The chandelier swings overhead, and he dives under the counter.

"I thought she'd be happy," he yells over the rattle of glass knickknacks and ceramic dishes. "Isn't this what she wanted?"

"*Marjorie*," I repeat, the force of my own voice surprising even me.

Everything stops, and we're plunged into darkness, the only sound left is that of my heart pounding and Dennis's shallow breaths.

"What the hell was that?" he asks.

"I'm sorry," Marjorie says through gritted teeth. "But I would really like to leave."

"And *I* wish I could conjure up a natural disaster anytime I'm pissed off," I fire back. "But we can't always get what we want, can we?"

There's a low hum as the power returns, each lamp turning on one by one. Marjorie refuses to meet my gaze, a frown carved into her face.

Dennis rises, clutching his tea, his eyes darting around the room. "Is it over?"

"It better be," I say, scowling at Marjorie before shifting my focus back to him. "Are you okay?"

"Yeah, are you?" he asks.

I nod as I begin to survey for damage. "Dennis, I'm so sorry. Anything that's broken…I'll pay for it."

"Oh please," Marjorie says. "The only thing that got broken was that hideous owl. Don't be so dramatic."

I glare at her. "I realize you don't have all your senses, but did you not see this entire place *shake*?"

Dennis's mouth falls open. "*What* did she say?"

"Well, it's not my fault this place is as old as the hills," she insists. "A strong puff of wind could take the whole thing down."

"Now you're blaming it on the building?" I counter, and Dennis's nostrils flare.

"Is she *ghostlighting* us right now?"

"Ghostlighting?" Marjorie and I ask in unison.

"You know," he replies. "Gaslighting…but for ghosts."

I snort and sputter a laugh, and before I know it, Dennis and I are both cackling until no sound comes out of our mouths.

Even Marjorie finally cracks a smile. "Tell Dennis I'm sorry. I…I didn't mean to cause such a ruckus and break his statue. My emotions got the better of me."

I relay the message before placing the letter on the counter and helping him sweep up the remnants of the broken owl.

"In your defense, it *was* pretty ugly," he says directly to Marjorie. "But no more temper tantrums in my store."

"I'll be on my best behavior," she promises.

"So, are you going to tell me what this is all about?" I ask, reaching for the weathered note.

Her gaze falls on the page in my hands as I gently open it to see the faded lines filled with a broken cursive. At the top of the left-hand side are the words *My Dearest Marjorie*.

When she doesn't answer, I try once more. "Who's this from, Marjorie?" Sure, I could just read it myself, but I won't. Not without her consent. I can tell from her outburst that she feels her privacy has been violated. Whatever is written in this letter is clearly meaningful to her.

Dennis's gaze follows mine to where Marjorie is standing next to me, and his face softens, his head tilted in concern.

"This John guy…" He trails off. "You really loved him, didn't you?"

Marjorie's skin flushes, and her green eyes swim behind a

wall of tears. Her voice is quiet when she finally answers. "Yes. I did."

I give Dennis a subtle nod, since he can't hear her.

He brings his hand to his mouth before dropping it to his chest. "I'm sorry, Marjorie."

I've witnessed many of her intense emotions over the course of the last few weeks, but none like this. Her fingers graze over the strand of pearls around her neck as a tear trickles down her cheek. She doesn't bother to wipe it away or hide it. Instead, she looks at me head-on, her expression a mix of longing and resigned sadness.

My throat tightens. "What happened? Did he hurt you? Did he break your heart?"

If he did, and he's still alive out there somewhere, I'll kill him. And if he isn't, well, I'll figure out how to bring him back so I can kill him again.

"No," she answers, her voice soft. "I broke his. I ruined everything."

chapter thirty-four

Marjorie and I sit on the couch with Delilah curled into a ball between us, the letter from John open on my lap.

"Toward the end, I went through the keepsake box hidden in my nightstand," Marjorie explains. "I don't know why I bothered hiding it when Conrad never cared about me enough to be tempted to look through my things anyway." She frowns, staring straight ahead. "There wasn't much in there. A few mementos from when I was a girl, photos of Frances and me during our first year at Vanderbilt. I didn't exactly have a lot in my life I wished to remember."

"But John," I say. "You wanted to remember him."

"I couldn't forget him even if I wanted to." Her smile is faint, regretful. "And I would never want to because being with him…it was the happiest time of my life." She lets out a bittersweet laugh. "But even in the face of death, I was afraid, or maybe I was embarrassed. I just didn't want anyone to find out how much I loved him, so I hid the letter in the back of the painting Natalie did for me, where I thought no one would find it. I knew of all my belongings, it was likely to end up in a trash heap somewhere, because while it was beautiful and priceless to me, Conrad would overlook it."

After we came home from Whimsy and Wu, I read the letter Dennis had found, and Marjorie began telling me the story of her first love, John Abernathy. They met when his family moved to Nashville from a small town in East Tennessee in the fall of 1966—their junior year at Hillsboro High school. She was a cheerleader and president of the class, while he ran track and was a member of the Future Farmers of America. Her family was wealthy, while his had a small hobby farm they used to supplement their income and still, they barely scraped by.

"My parents didn't approve," she continues. "But they tolerated it at first, thinking it was just a silly little fling. Then weeks together turned into months, and months became a year, and that's when they realized what John and I had was more than some teenage romance."

"Why did you listen to them?" I ask softly. It's something I can't relate to because by the time I was that age, my own mother was gone, and my father had long since checked out. My grandmother had been supportive of my choices, save for that time I came home with blue hair after a slumber party. "You knew how you felt. Why did you need their blessing?"

Her eyes meet mine, tears clouding her vision. "It wasn't their blessing I needed. It was their approval. Not just of my love life or my choices, but of *me*."

The pain I feel is reflected on her face. I never earned my father's love or acceptance, and it's a wound that will never *not* feel fresh. "So, you just…ended things with him? Just like that?"

"No," she answers. "Not at first. I told my mother and father before graduation that I did, but we continued to see each other in secret all the way through my second semester at Vanderbilt. Living on campus made it easy to lie and hide my whereabouts." She pauses, drawing in a breath. "Then my parents set me up with Conrad who was a senior at Belmont University just after Christmas that year."

"What happened after that?"

"I basically lived a double life," she says. "I went on my dates with Conrad as expected and then I would meet up with John."

That's kind of how I felt going on my *Purrfect Match* dates all while seeing Jude.

"Did John know?" I ask.

"I couldn't bring myself to tell him," she admits. "The only person who knew was Frances. At least until my father found out."

"How?"

"A coworker of his recognized me, apparently," she replies. "We were at Centennial Park one afternoon in May. He told my dad the next day at work that he saw me out with my boyfriend. Except he knew it wasn't him because he was playing golf with the Lockwoods that day, and Conrad had been with them. So, my father showed up at my dorm after work that evening to confront me, and John was there." She sniffs, her eyes misty. "I confessed everything. John left, and I was forbidden from seeing him ever again."

My heart aches for this man I don't know. "What did John do?"

"He wouldn't even see or speak to me, and I couldn't blame him," she says. "Not only had I spent months deceiving him, but he had to listen to my father go on a tirade about why he'd never be worthy of me. In fact, I was certain John would never talk to me again." Her chin drops to her chest as she smooths an invisible wrinkle in her skirt. "I continued to see Conrad because my father threatened to cut me off if I didn't. Which would mean no more Vanderbilt…no more life as I knew it. He said he would disown me."

"But why?" I ask. "I don't understand."

"Because the Lockwoods had come into a lot of money," she explains. "And my father was scheming for investors in his company. Mr. Lockwood agreed on the condition that Conrad and I would marry, and he'd be given a place at Garnet Media after he graduated."

My mouth falls open. "So…an arranged marriage? Your father signed your life away for some quick cash?"

Her shoulders slump forward. "I didn't realize that's what was happening at the time. My parents convinced me it was the right thing to do. That Conrad and I were right for each other. And I guess I…I started to believe it. I looked at my mother and father's relationship, and I thought it was normal —that one didn't marry for love but for security and power. And even if I did believe love was a good enough reason to be with someone, I knew John deserved better. Better than me or what I could give him."

"Marjorie," I whisper around the lump in my throat.

"Conrad asked me to marry him that July at my family's annual Independence Day party while I was home for summer break. The governor was there and the mayor. There was endless champagne and fireworks. It was a lovely proposal minus the fact that I didn't love the man who was proposing."

I rub my fingers over my forehead. "But Conrad…he was awful to you, wasn't he?"

"Back then he was somewhat tolerable," she answers. "At least before we got engaged. After that, his true colors began to show."

So he manipulated her, made her think he was something he wasn't. Much like Frances, he used her. "I'm so sorry."

"No," she says, her voice sharp. "Don't feel sorry for me, Kathryn. I could have backed out. I could have said no, but I didn't. I *chose* this path."

"Because you didn't know any better," I argue. "You did what you thought was right. What was safe."

"Yes, well," she says. "Look where it got me. Perhaps my money and influence kept me sheltered from some of the troubles I would have otherwise endured, but emotionally I haven't been *safe* a day in my life. Not since John. He was the one person I could be my true self with."

"So, what happened next?" I ask. "How did John find out you were getting married?"

"He saw the announcement in the paper. Back then those were a much bigger deal," she explains. "He mailed me a letter but made up some girl's name for the return address because he knew if my parents saw *his* name, they'd burn the message before I ever received it."

I pick up the page lying on my lap. "And that's what this is."

She gives me a solemn nod. "Yes. He begged me not to go through with it. He said he understood why I'd done what I did and that he forgave me." Fresh tears brim her eyes. "He told me I was the love of his life and asked me to run away with him. Said we could start over somewhere new—just the two of us."

"And what did you say? Did you write him back?" Even though I know this story doesn't end with her and John finding their happy ever after, I still find myself on the edge of my seat as I await her answer.

She shakes her head, her lips set in a firm line. "I never said a word, and Conrad and I married the following June."

"And you just never saw him again?" I ask.

"Once," she says. "About five years later, I was at the farmers market, and I saw him. He didn't see me, though. He had a booth selling fresh produce and homemade jams. There was a woman with him, and she was pregnant. They had on wedding bands and were laughing as they worked. He even stopped long enough to give her a quick kiss, and I just…I remember the way he looked at her."

"You didn't want to say hi? Nothing?"

She shrugs. "He looked…happy."

"That doesn't mean he wouldn't have been happy to see you," I say.

"Yes, well," she begins, swallowing hard. "It didn't much matter by then, and I'd done enough damage. I hurt him deeply. The best thing I could do for John was let him go."

But what if it wasn't? What if John always held a candle for Marjorie? "I think Dennis is right. John might be your unfinished business."

"No. There's no way," she replies, her tone brooking no room for argument. "He moved on, got married. He was content."

I narrow my eyes at her. "You of all people know that being married to someone doesn't mean they're happy, and hell, even if he *was*, that doesn't mean there isn't something left unfinished between the two of you."

She refuses to meet my gaze, and I lean closer.

"What if you're supposed to tell him how you felt?" I ask. "How you clearly *still* feel?"

Her face turns stony. "I don't think so."

"But—"

"I don't want to talk about this anymore."

"Marjorie," I plead, but she gives a resolute shake of her head.

"If you care about me at all, Kathryn, you'll drop this." Her voice is pained, her heart split open before me. "Please."

"All right." I hold up my hands, giving in for the moment. But this isn't over. This is far from over.

chapter thirty-five

Marjorie shuts down every attempt I make to bring up John over the next two days. Her entire mood has shifted since she told me about him, leaving the energy in the house feeling charged and unsettled. I have to do something.

Late Wednesday afternoon, I stop by Whimsy and Wu to ask Dennis for advice.

"Poor Marjorie," he says with a sad sigh. "John was the one who got away."

"What if they *both* were?" I ask. "What if you're right and this *is* her unfinished business?"

He taps a finger on the lid of the tea I brought him. "It sounds like she's adamant about not wanting to pursue this, though. I don't think this is something you can force."

I hesitate, taking a sip of my coffee. "But maybe I can give her a gentle...*push*?"

He narrows his eyes. "I see that going over about as well as you calling up the *Ghostbusters*."

"What am I supposed to do, then?" I lift my shoulders and drop them with a sigh. She needs help, even if she refuses to accept it. "If getting closure with John is what she has to do to cross over—"

"Then don't you think she has to *want* to do it?" he counters. "Look, you know getting in other people's business is my favorite pastime, but this feels…different. Delicate. Besides, have you considered what will happen if you *do* decide to stick your nose where it doesn't belong? You saw what she did the other night. She's likely to cause some hundreds-year-old volcano to erupt and kill us all."

"She would not," I argue. "A small cyclone, maybe."

He fixes his stare on me. "If you play with fire, you're gonna get burned."

I wince. "So, I suppose now isn't the time to tell you I already started googling John Abernathy."

"I'll take things you *definitely* shouldn't be doing for five hundred."

"I have to do *something*, Dennis," I say. "If this is what's keeping her here, I have to try."

"Well, please make sure Marjorie knows I had nothing to do with this. I don't think my store could survive another one of her outbursts." He leans forward with his elbows on the counter. "Did you find anything?"

I shake my head. "Not yet. He'd be in his midseventies now, so it's a toss-up with social media."

"Unless he's anything like my dad. I swear, if he doesn't put it on social media, it didn't happen. Which is fine if you're going to dinner or a concert, less so when you're going in for a routine colonoscopy." He takes a long pull of his tea and clicks his tongue with a satisfied *ahh*. "Let's just say my cousins feel a lot closer to him now."

I scrunch my nose. "Ew." My phone pings from my back pocket, and I pull it out to find an incoming text from Jude.

"Must be the boyfriend," Dennis says. "Your face went all doe-eyed and squishy."

I nod, heat rising to my cheeks as I read the message.

At the store. Do you have cinnamon and nutmeg? If not, I'll grab some to bring Friday so I can make you coffee all weekend long. 😉

I gasp, my hand flying to my mouth. "Oh no."

This weekend. Our first overnight. I've been so preoccupied by the whole John thing that it completely slipped my mind. What the hell am I gonna do about Marjorie and Delilah? I can't just be like *Surprise, my cat isn't actually dead, but I do have a houseguest that is.* I'm going to tell him, of course. But it has to be done the right way. At the right time.

Whenever that is.

I set my coffee on the counter with a thud and push my fingers through my hair. "No, no, no. Shit." *Think, Kat. Use your brain.*

"You okay?" Dennis asks, interrupting my thoughts. "What's got you in a tizzy?"

Oh, you know, the usual. My dead friend, my not-dead cat, and the fact that I've been lying to Jude about them both.

Dennis. Marjorie and Delilah could stay with Dennis.

"Um, actually, I need a favor," I say, bringing my eyes up to his.

"I'm not getting involved in this John thing. I mean it. Though, I do demand updates as you get them."

"It's actually not about that," I explain. "It's about Jude."

He lifts his brows. "I'm listening."

"He's spending the weekend with me."

He blinks, his mouth opening, then closing before he speaks again. "And how exactly is *that* gonna work? Even if you didn't have Marjorie hanging around, you have a very much alive cat that he thinks is dead."

I let out a nervous laugh, my lips stretched in a hopeful, possibly deranged smile. "Yeah, that's what I want to talk to you about."

"No," he says. "*Hell* no. Absolutely not."

"Please," I beg. "Just this once. I'm going to tell him. Soon."

"Why not tell him now?"

"I…I need a little more time," I say, my voice pleading. "It's not like I'm telling him I snore or that my freckles come from one of those little freckle pens. I've been lying to him for weeks. I have to handle this carefully."

"And you can *handle* it without me."

"Please," I implore, palms locked together in front of me. "Please, please, *please*. I'll do anything."

He draws a long breath in through his nose. "Kat."

Would begging help? I'm about five seconds from dropping to my knees. "Dennis, I wouldn't ask if it wasn't important. This could be a big step in our relationship."

His expression softens. "Okay, fine. I'll do it, but if Marjorie freaks Thomas out, you're paying his therapy bills."

"She won't," I promise. "I'll make sure of it." Obviously, I have no way of ensuring this, but I'm hoping Dennis doesn't call me on that.

"And there's something else," he says. "Thomas and I are visiting his family for Thanksgiving in Virginia this year. I *was* going to have to return early so I could be open Black Friday and Small Business Saturday."

"I'll cover for you," I insist, picking up what he's laying down. "We're off from the station all week, anyway. It's perfect."

He stretches his hand out to shake mine. "Then you have yourself a deal."

Now all that's left to do is break the news to Marjorie.

chapter thirty-six

I ARRIVE HOME TO FIND MARJORIE SEATED ON THE CHAIR IN the living room with Delilah curled up on the arm while an infomercial for bento lunch boxes plays on the television in the background.

"Have you seen these before?" she asks, not bothering to look my way as I plop onto the couch. "They're compartmentalized carriers for your meals."

"Yeah," I answer. "They're pretty cool."

"You should call and order one," she says, continuing to stare straight ahead. "What a clever design. You can keep all of your fruits and vegetables separated from your cheese and crackers." Her voice drops to a low mutter. "Or in your case, your gummy bears and Twizzlers."

I roll my lips inward and release them with a pop. "Busy day, huh?"

"Is there something I was supposed to be doing?" she counters. "Did you leave me a honey-do list I wasn't aware of?"

My jaw tightens. "No, but there is that small matter of your unfinished business."

"Yes, well, I haven't thought of anything new."

I gesture toward the TV. "You didn't even change the channel."

We learned she has this ability by accident one night when she got annoyed with me for not putting *The Bachelor* on fast enough for her liking.

She shrugs. "Didn't need to. I watched the news and a couple of soap operas and some talk show hosted by a lovely woman named Kelly, and then this came on."

I hit the remote, making the screen go black. "I'm cutting you off. Too much television rots your brain."

"Does that old adage still apply when you're dead?"

"Better safe than sorry," I tease, curling one leg beneath me. "Actually, there's something I need to talk to you about."

"Kathryn, if this is about John, I already told you—"

"It's not," I say quickly. "It's about this weekend."

Her brows are pinched with curiosity. "What are we doing this weekend?"

"*We* aren't," I answer. "Not together, anyway."

She tilts her head toward me.

"Jude is having some work done at his condo, so he's going to come stay here."

"Oh. What about me? Where will I go?" she questions. "I can make myself scarce, I suppose, but what will you do with the cat? Are you going to tell him?"

"Not yet. I think I need a little more time," I reply. "But, um, I stopped by to see Dennis on my way home and asked if you and Delilah can spend a couple days at his place, and he said yes. Isn't that nice?"

She blinks at me, her mouth hanging open. "Absolutely not."

"Please," I say, dropping my head against the cushion. "It's just for the weekend."

"This is absurd." She rises and begins to pace as Delilah lifts her head with a *meow*. "Do you hear what she's doing to us, cat? Shipping us off to a babysitter so she can shack up in her love nest with her boyfriend."

"It's not like that," I argue, though I know it very much is.

"Oh, it's not?"

"Okay, it's exactly like that," I reply, pushing to my feet. "But come on. I deserve a *little* privacy, don't I?"

She grits her teeth. "First it's a couple of days, then it'll be weeks and months, and the next thing I know, you'll have pawned me off on Dennis."

"Marjorie—" I begin, but she doesn't let me get a word in.

"Or worse, I'll be shoved away in some godforsaken storage unit with the roaches," she says, her volume rising. "*No*. I won't allow it."

"Marjorie, listen to me," I shout to get her attention before softening my tone. "Is that what you're afraid of? That I'm going to abandon you?"

She stops midstep and faces me, her expression stony. "Isn't it? It's what everyone else has done."

The desperation in her voice makes my heart ache because I've felt the same way. "I'm not like everyone else. You should know that by now. Give me a little credit here."

Her hands clasp in front of her, and she drops her gaze.

"Look, I know what it feels like to be left, okay?" I say. "And I'm *never* gonna do that to you. Not ever."

She folds her arms over her chest. "Because you feel obligated."

"Because I care about you. Because you're my friend." I move closer, my eyes locked on her. "I just need to buy myself a bit more time before I tell Jude about Delilah…and about you."

She lifts her head. "You're going to tell him about me?"

"How can I not?" I ask. "You're a big part of my life now. An *important* part."

A faint smile tugs at the corners of her mouth. "Oh. Well, you and Jude *do* deserve some time to yourselves, and I suppose a change of scenery for a couple of days wouldn't hurt. And I like Dennis."

"You've got to be good, though," I warn. "His husband doesn't know about you yet, and he might freak out if you start causing earthquakes and flickering the lights."

Mischief sparkles in her eyes. "Ooh, that could be fun."

"Don't even think about it."

"It's already been thought of."

I did ask for this, didn't I? "Please don't make me regret this."

chapter thirty-seven

She's *definitely* going to make me regret this. Dennis starts sending me the play-by-play only an hour after I drop Marjorie and Delilah off Thursday evening.

Sooooo I probably should have told Thomas that the friend of yours who'd be staying with us was dead. He's saging the house right now.

Wow, Marjorie really loves her reality TV. She's changed the station three times already. Thomas just wants to watch his murder mystery shows.

BTW is sage toxic to cats? He's still saging. I swear to God. It smells like a witch's underpants in here.

Ugh. Delilah has declared Thomas her favorite, and now he wants a damn cat. Thanks a lot.

I begin to wonder if I should have waited to drop them off at the last minute because the updates continue even as I finish cleaning the following afternoon, removing every possible trace of Delilah while waiting for Jude to arrive.

Should have reconsidered bring-your-ghost-to-work day. This hussy has already knocked a flamingo figurine off a shelf.

She knows I called her a hussy because she just threw a pen across the room.

I WOULDN'T CALL HER A HUSSY IF SHE'D STOP BEING SUCH A 💩

THIS B MADE ME DROP MY PHONE

The texts continue throughout Friday evening, while Jude and I make tacos and listen to nineties music.

Margie wants to know if you and Jude have gotten freaky yet. 👀

The guilt I felt asking Dennis for this giant favor goes straight out the window.

"What are you laughing about?" Jude asks after dinner as he returns to the couch with topped-off tumblers of bourbon.

I slide my phone onto the coffee table as he sits beside me, handing me one of the drinks.

"Just Dennis," I answer. "He, um, has some houseguests this weekend, and they're kinda driving him crazy."

He takes a pull of his bourbon. "Uh-oh. Does he need a rescue?"

"No," I say quickly. "No, he's okay."

"Good," he replies, pulling my legs onto his lap. "Because I don't really want to give you up."

"Me either." I smile at him over the rim of my glass, my limbs warm and soft like fresh-baked bread, drunk off the liquor and Jude's proximity. "I'm glad you're here. This is… nice."

"It is." He rubs his hand over my foot and gives it a squeeze. "It feels right."

I hum my agreement and settle back against the cushion. It *does* feel right—having him here in my space, doing normal things together. It makes it easy to imagine more days like this.

"So, what are your plans for next week?" he asks. "For Thanksgiving break."

"I'm going over to Eddie's," I say. "Then I'll be spending the rest of the week working at Dennis's shop while he's out of town."

"That's sweet of you."

"Well, he's a good friend. My best friend, besides Becca. And I do kinda owe him."

"For what?"

"Oh, um." I should just tell him about Delilah. About Marjorie. Why keep dragging it out? The longer this goes on, the harder it's going to be to fess up. I need to just rip the Band-Aid off. That's it. I'm gonna do it. I'm *doing* it. "The thing is…" I swallow and shake my head slightly. "He's always doing favors for me. He's great like that, and it's just my turn to return the gesture."

I mentally kick myself. So much for ripping the Band-Aid off. All I've managed to do is slap on another one.

"What about you?" I ask, attempting to shift the focus away from myself. "You spending the holiday with your folks?"

He nods. "Yeah, I have family stuff Thursday and Friday, but I'm going to this Friendsgiving dinner that my old college roommate is hosting that Saturday, and I was thinking you might want to come with me?"

My breath hitches in my throat. "You want me to meet your friends?" It's a step I want to take, one I'm ready for, but what if the people in his life don't like me? There's something comforting about us staying in our own little bubble for a while longer—something safe.

"Of course, I do. You're important to me, Kat," he says. "I want you to meet the people in my life because…" He trails off, his brown-eyed gaze holding mine. "Because I want them to become people in *our* lives."

My heart hammers against my rib cage. "Yeah?"

He glides his fingers up my shin. "Yeah."

I reach forward and take his glass, setting both our drinks aside before straddling his lap.

"I'd like that," I say, slipping my arms around his neck.

He tucks a strand of hair behind my ear. "And I want to know the people in your life too."

I swallow, my mouth going dry. "I want that too."

Quit being stupid and just *tell him*. He needs to know the truth. He *deserves* to know.

But what if he doesn't understand? What if he freaks out and I lose him? No—I can't do it yet. I need more time. It's not like I'm *never* planning to tell him. I will…eventually.

He runs his hands down my back before sliding them over my thighs. "You know, since we're talking about things we want…there is something else I'd like."

I lift my brows and grin. "Oh, there is?"

"Mm-hmm," he says.

I tilt my head, pretending to have no idea what he could be referring to. "And what might that be?"

He cups my face, his thumb grazing over my bottom lip. "Well, first, I'd like to kiss every inch of your body."

"Yeah?" Heat pools in my belly as he leans closer, pressing a kiss beneath my ear. "And then what?"

He drags his lips down my neck, eliciting a breathy sigh from me.

"And then I want to spend all night memorizing every little noise you make when you're turned on," he whispers against my collarbone between kisses. "And every sound you make when you—"

My phone buzzes loudly against the coffee table, causing him to pull back so he can look at me.

"Do you need to get that?" he asks.

"No," I blurt before reaching back to shut the damn thing off. Whatever havoc Marjorie is wreaking on Dennis can wait till tomorrow.

His lips are back on my skin in an instant, sending tiny bolts of electricity shooting through me.

I return the favor, placing kisses along the stubble of his jaw. "Now, where were we?"

chapter thirty-eight

JUDE MAKES GOOD ON HIS PROMISE TO KISS EVERY INCH OF MY body, becoming well acquainted with every moan and sigh, as well as sounds I didn't know I was capable of. We sleep late, his golden legs tangled with mine until he slips out of bed to brew a pot of coffee. Notes of toasted pecan, nutmeg, and cinnamon pry me from the sheets around 10:30 a.m.

"Good morning." Jude's voice is low and raspy as he slides one hand around my waist, offering me a steaming mug with the other.

I take a sip and beam up at him. "It *is* a good morning."

"How's the coffee?" he asks.

"Perfect," I answer, setting my drink aside. "How about some breakfast? I was thinking cinnamon rolls."

He arches his brows. "You're gonna cook for me?"

"Through Pillsbury, all things are possible." I toss a grin over my shoulder as I pad to the fridge to pull out the can of pastries and a bottle of heavy cream.

He leans against the bar with an appreciative smile on his face while I set the oven to preheat.

"You know," he says as I retrieve a baking dish from the cupboard next to the oven. "I could get used to this."

"Eating pastries from a tube?" I tease, lifting the tiny tab and peeling the paper back. When it doesn't open, I give it a good whack on the counter, causing it to pop. "Because I'll have you know, I'm something of a tubed pastry connoisseur."

"Is that so?" he asks, watching as I spray oil on the dish, plopping the cinnamon rolls in, one by one.

"Biscuits, rolls, pizza crusts, cookie dough—you name it, I can bake it and probably not even burn it." I dust my hands off before unscrewing the top on the cream and pouring the liquid into the open space between the rolls. "Did you know that if you cover the dish with cream, it turns each roll into an ooey gooey piece of heaven?"

He chuckles. "Are you sure? Because it looks like you just poured milk on refrigerated cinnamon rolls."

"O ye of little faith," I say. "Just trust me."

His phone trills from the counter, reminding me I haven't turned mine on yet, and he grabs it, squinting down at the screen.

"Sorry, do you mind if I take this?" he asks. "It's my mom."

I wave him off. "Yeah, of course. Take your time."

He answers the call, and I retrieve my own phone from the living room, powering it on as I head back into the kitchen.

"Oh, you did? Last night?" Jude says into the phone. "Sorry, I guess I didn't hear the text come through. I'm not home this weekend." A couple of beats pass, and he clears his throat. "No, I'm not out of town. Just…staying somewhere else. Anyway, what's up?"

My stomach clenches. He didn't tell his mother his whereabouts—no mention of me or a girlfriend or even a *friend* friend. *Is that weird?*

I shake my head, attempting to clear the thoughts from my mind. *No, it's not weird.* Last night he said he wants me to meet the people in his life. So what if he didn't mention me to his mom? That doesn't mean he feels I'm not *worth* mentioning...does it?

My phone vibrates in my hand as text after text comes through. I glance down to find six unread messages from Dennis and one from Becca that I attempt to read while still paying attention to what Jude is—or isn't—saying.

His back is to me when he clears his throat and lowers his voice. "Oh, um, that's good. Sure, you can tell her hi from me, I guess."

A giant black hole forms in my chest. The *her* he's referring to has to be his ex, Lauren. She and his mom still work together, and I suspect they're close from what he told me previously. *But why is he sending her greetings through his mother?*

I bite my lip. *Don't go there.* It's not like he seemed enthusiastic about it.

I return my focus to the series of texts from Dennis.

You owe me three light bulbs. I'm putting them on your tab.

Marjorie keeps blowing out my candle. She either really hates lavender or she's just trying to get on my last nerve.

Remember when I said you were living my dream? I take it back. I take it all back.

Aaaand now Thomas wants a ghost. I can't believe I'm saying this, but I'd rather have a cat.

I knew cats were nocturnal but ghosts??? Marj keeps turning the TV on. It's 1 a.m.!!! I have to work tomorrow.

Your invisible friend stole my husband. Thomas is now in the living room watching some stupid reality show while I'm in bed alone. He doesn't even like reality TV yet he's in there cackling like the damn Wicked Witch of the West.

I'm glad to hear Marjorie has made herself right at home. I press my lips together, stifling a laugh as the oven beeps, signaling it's ready for the cinnamon rolls. I pop them in and set the timer.

Jude catches my eye and winks, the phone still pressed to his ear. "Are you serious? Mom, that's amazing. Congratulations."

I smile back at him, propping myself against the counter while I read Becca's message.

How much more time before I get to meet this guy?????

I lift my gaze and watch Jude leisurely pace around the kitchen as he talks, lifting his mug to his mouth to take a sip. Part of me wants to shout it from the rooftops and tell her now. But another larger part is afraid. What if she thinks Jude and I are a bad idea? Or worse, what if his mom does?

My grandmother's words, the advice I gave Marjorie when she was worried we wouldn't find Natalie, come to mind.

Let's not borrow trouble.

I type out my one-word response as Jude ends the call.

Soon.

I hope.

"Sorry about that," he says, sliding his phone back onto the counter.

"No worries." Actually, I'm doing nothing *but* worrying right now, but I reach for my coffee and take a swig in a vague attempt to appear calm and collected. "Everything okay?"

"Yeah," he answers. "Great, actually. My mom wanted to tell me she's been nominated for a Franklin Albrecht, which is apparently some kind of prestigious award for surgeons. Anyway, this is the first time anyone from her hospital has even been considered, so it's a huge deal."

"That's incredible. You must be proud."

"Definitely. She's worked hard, and she deserves the recognition."

"Tell her I said congratulations. I mean, if you want to. Unless she doesn't know about me, then definitely don't say anything because that would be weird. Like, who is this strange woman congratulating me? Yikes." A nervous laugh bubbles out of me, and I scratch the back of my neck.

"Wait, what are you talking about?" Jude's eyes go soft as he reaches for me. "My mom knows about you."

She does? "Oh. I just…I didn't know. It sounded like she asked where you were, and you didn't…tell her."

"So, that's what this is about," he says with a nod, his tone sympathetic.

"Sorry…I couldn't help but overhear."

He takes my mug and sets both our coffees on the counter before folding me into his arms.

"Kat, the only reason I didn't say where I'm staying is because my parents are *really* old-fashioned. Not telling them that bit of information just helps me avoid an unpleasant conversation about something that is frankly none of their business."

"But what about your ex? Surely you stayed with each other." Though it turns my stomach to even *think* about it now.

"We practically lived together for about six months," he says. "But *my mother* didn't know that."

My nerves begin to settle. I suppose that makes sense. If my mom was still alive, would I tell her things like this? My dad was never around to tell anything to anyway, so he doesn't count. I might've told my grandmother, although, who am I kidding? She would have already discovered Jude's favorite treats, then made him two batches from scratch and brought them over. *Geez, I need to step it up.*

He reaches out and cups my face. "But she *does* know about you."

See, you were just making a mountain out of a molehill. Crisis averted.

Except the black hole in my chest is still there, growing and stretching toward my heart.

"And I'd like to introduce you to her one day soon." He presses his lips to my forehead. "If you're up for it, of course."

"That'd be great," I say, though doubt still gnaws at the edges of my mind, reminding me how much his mom *loved* his ex. Can I really compete with that?

He leans down and kisses my cheek, his voice a low, seductive rumble in my ear. "You know what else I'd like?"

God, how did I sit next to this man at work all these years without melting into a puddle?

"What?" I ask, my hands gliding up his chest.

"To take you back to bed right now and find more of those magical places that make you squirm," he whispers against my collarbone.

I swat at him playfully. "The cinnamon rolls will be done soon. Aren't you hungry?"

"Oh, I'm famished," he says with a wolfish grin before nipping at the soft skin of my neck, his stubble tickling me. "Starving."

I reply with a shriek of laughter, and the darkness retreats.

chapter thirty-nine

I'M GLAD TO HAVE MARJORIE AND DELILAH HOME WHERE they belong, but no one is happier than Dennis.

"That woman is a menace," he hisses when I go to pick them up from his place Sunday afternoon.

"She is not," Thomas argues. Much like Dennis, he's stylish, but less eccentric. I'm pretty sure I've never seen him in anything but black.

Marjorie gives me a satisfied smirk as a picture frame in the foyer crashes to the floor.

"I love you, Marjorie, I do." Dennis hands me the backpack containing Marjorie's urn, which I sling over my shoulder. "But can you kindly leave without doing any more *redecorating?*"

Thomas dismisses him with a wave of his hand. "It was a weird photo anyway."

Dennis gasps. "Of my parents."

"From Glamour Shots circa 1995," Thomas says, running his fingers through his wisps of light brown hair.

A painting tilts on the wall beside me, but I steady it before it can fall. I shoot Marjorie a look before thanking

Dennis and Thomas *profusely* and showing my gratitude in the best way possible—by leaving.

"My visit was actually quite pleasant." Once we're back at home, Marjorie smiles and takes a seat on the couch. "It's a shame your friends can't see me because I think we'd get on famously."

Delilah jumps onto the back of the sofa and stretches before curling herself into a tiny ball.

"Dennis told me you both made quite the impression on Thomas," I say as I sit beside her with the coffee I picked up from Dawn's Diner on the way home.

"He's a delightful young man," she replies. "Dennis too. Though I'll admit, it's fun to try to get under his skin."

"Fun for who exactly?" I tease.

"Tomayto, tomahto." Her eyes sparkle with mischief, and she appears to be in much better spirits than last week. "So, aren't you going to tell me about your weekend with Jude?"

"Oh, you know. It was low-key." I figure it's better than telling her we had sex on this very couch earlier this morning.

She scrunches her nose. "Low-key?"

"That's disappointing to you?" I ask with a chuckle.

"Well, yes," she says, as I take a sip of my coffee. "I was expecting tales of romance and adventurous sexcapades."

I sputter, nearly choking on my drink. "*Marjorie!*"

"What?" She rests her palm against her chest, feigning innocence as though she didn't just use a word straight off a *Cosmopolitan* cover to describe my sex life. "Don't tell me you spent all weekend together and you didn't *do it*."

I bring a pillow over my face to hide my burning cheeks.

She scoffs. "You think I'm so repressed I don't know anything about sex?"

"No," I answer before considering it further. "Maybe."

"Not that Conrad and I had a love life worth writing home about," she says with a dry laugh. "But I did spend many an evening curled up with a good bodice ripper."

I drop the pillow and cock my head. It's hard to imagine her holding a cup of tea and a book with a bare-chested man on the cover. "You're full of surprises, aren't you?"

"So?" she presses. "How was it? Was he good in bed? He looks like he'd be good in—"

"Oh my God," I shout. "Are you picturing him naked?"

"I may be dead, but I'll have you know, my imagination works just fine," she quips.

My mouth falls open.

"Don't be ridiculous," she says, swatting at me. "Of course I'm not, but I may be forced to resort to such extreme measures if you don't give me some details, missy."

"Okay, okay," I relent before diving in and telling her about my time with Jude, leaving out some of the more salacious details.

She listens with rapt attention, and when I mention Jude not telling his mother where he was, she helps me feel better.

"I don't find that strange at all. Take it from someone who spent most of her life not telling her parents anything. You know how much I had to hide John." Her eyes fall to her lap as she fiddles with the hem of her skirt. "There were even aspects of my relationship with Conrad I didn't feel comfortable voicing."

"I'm sorry."

She meets my frown with a shrug. "It's certainly not the path I would have chosen if I'd been a parent. I would rather my child feel they could come to me with anything versus worrying about all the ways I'd judge them."

I blink, my face softening.

"Don't give me that look," she chides. "I know I can be a bit…*opinionated*, but—"

"No," I say quickly. "That's not why I was looking at you. I was just thinking…you would have been a good mom." The kind of mom I wish I had—a little overbearing at times, opinionated, but with a heart of gold.

"Oh. Thank you, Kathryn." Her cheeks turn rosy, and she gives me a tight smile. "That's kind of you to say." Her gaze turns longing, as though she's watching a movie being projected somewhere off in the distance, and that's when it hits me.

"You wanted to be a parent, didn't you?"

Her shoulders droop, the question almost seeming to knock her off-balance.

"Yes," she answers, barely above a whisper.

"Did Conrad?"

She nods. "But not because he wanted a child to love. He wanted someone else to control, an heir."

"Is that why you didn't…" My voice is buried beneath the heaviness in the room.

Another nod. "I couldn't stop the way I was treated growing up, but I could prevent someone else from ever having to experience it."

My stomach sinks. Marjorie sacrificed her dream to save her potential child from enduring the life she had. From feeling unloved, unaccepted. "Do you think you would have had kids if you'd ended up with John?"

Her lips twist to the corner of her mouth. "Perhaps. But it does no good to wonder about such things. To think about the what-ifs."

Sure never stopped me. "Right. Sorry."

We sit in silence for a moment before she speaks again.

"Can I ask you something?"

"More burning questions about my sex life?" I joke.

"No, nothing like that," she says with a faint smile, her eyes searching mine. "I was just wondering…where are your parents?"

The air leaves my lungs all at once. It's a question I haven't been asked in a while that has an answer I typically do everything I can to avoid. Telling people my mother passed away when I was young is the easy part and is generally met with sad eyes and an *I'm sorry to hear that*. Explaining what happened with my father is far more difficult.

"In all the time I've been with you, you've never mentioned them," she continues. "I know you said you lived with your grandmother at one point when you were a teenager, but…what happened to your mother and father?"

Twenty-two years has done little to ease the ache in my chest.

"My mom died when I was thirteen," I finally answer, the words thick with grief. "Car accident."

The only sound in the room is that of Delilah's soft purrs as she sleeps.

Marjorie's brows pull downward. "I'm so sorry, Kathryn."

I take in a shaky breath. "And I didn't realize it at the time, but it was the day I lost my father too." The day he left is etched permanently in my mind like a scar that never quite healed. Of course, when he left me with my grandmother that summer when I was fourteen, I thought it was temporary. I had no idea it would be the last time I saw him.

"What do you mean?" She studies me, searching for an answer I don't know how to give.

I pull the pillow back onto my lap, hugging it to my chest. "He didn't…cope well when my mother passed away. She was his world, and with her gone, he didn't know how to…do life anymore?" I didn't exactly know how to carry on either, and the one person I should have been able to count on wasn't there. He was there physically in the days after my mom died, but he was a shell of the man he'd once been. All of the life had been drained out of him, leaving an emptiness in his eyes that never went away.

Her expression is pained as she studies me. "But…surely he continued to care for you, right? You're his daughter."

The black hole inside me that had made its presence known over the weekend returns with a vengeance.

"I think I reminded him too much of my mom," I say. "Or maybe I didn't remind him *enough* of her. Either way, he couldn't be around me anymore, and I had to go live with my grandmother."

Marjorie's jaw clenches. "And since then? Have you seen him? Heard from him?"

My shoulders slump forward, the darkness inside me spreading. "No, it was too hard for him. He couldn't—"

"Why are you making excuses for him?"

"Because he's my father."

"And that's precisely why you shouldn't justify his behavior." She sits forward, her elbows on her knees. "He's your *father*."

"Don't you think I know that?" I fire back, my nose burning as tears pierce the corners of my eyes. "Don't you think I've questioned why I wasn't worth sticking around for every day of my life?"

Her chin quivers. "Kathryn, I'm sorry. I didn't mean to—"

"No, I'm sorry," I cut her off with a heavy sigh. "I didn't mean to snap at you. I just…"

She places her hand on the cushion between us. "Just what?"

It's not something I've ever said out loud. But now, sitting here with Marjorie, the truth refuses to be ignored. My heart thumps, pulsing in my ears. "If my own father didn't think I was good enough, if the one person who was supposed to love me no matter what couldn't stay…how can I expect anyone else to?"

Marjorie scoots closer and reaches out as though she's about to hug me when she remembers she can't.

"Sweetheart," she begins. "You have to know your father's actions have *nothing* to do with you. It wasn't because of you or anything you did."

"Of course it was."

"It wasn't," she insists.

I dig my fingers into the plush pillow, my knuckles turning white. "My dad left because I wasn't enough of a reason for him to stay, and the same goes for Nick." Everyone has the potential to leave—even those who are supposed to stay. If my own father can bail on me, anyone can. Anyone *will*.

She shakes her head. "That wasn't true then, and it isn't true now."

"I wasn't enough. What if I'm *still* not enough?"

"Not enough? You are *everything*." Her voice breaks as a tear escapes past her lashes. "And it's *their* fault for not being able to see that. For not understanding how special you are."

My head spins, but my arms hang from my body like anvils anchoring me in place.

"Kathryn, listen to me. You cannot hold yourself prisoner for the actions of others," she says. "You'll spend your life waiting to be set free of the shame and guilt, but the only person with the key to that cage is you."

I knead my fist into my chest, attempting to dull the ache in my heart.

"I don't want to talk about this anymore." The weight of loss sits heavy on my chest, making it hard to move or breathe or think.

"But—"

"Just drop it, okay? Please."

She opens her mouth to try again, but I beat her to the punch.

"Unless you're ready to talk about John Abernathy," I add, knowing this will put us at a stalemate. It's a cheap shot, but it's the only one I've got.

She says nothing for a moment, her sad stare fixed on me.

"All right," she says finally. "I'll let it go."

"Thank you." I suck in a deep breath, trying to slow my racing pulse before reaching for the remote and turning on the television. "You want to watch a movie or something?"

Her eyes are practically drilling holes in the side of my head, but I don't turn to face her. I can't. Because if I do, if I look at Marjorie with her pitying gaze, I'll break.

I wordlessly change the channels until she speaks again.

"Actually, I'm going to sit in the kitchen for a bit," she says. "Think more about my unfinished business. There has to be something I haven't considered yet. If you'll excuse me."

"Marjorie, wait." I try to stop her but she's already halfway to the next room with Delilah following behind her.

I set my coffee down and press the heels of my palms against my eye sockets so hard I see stars. She wants to figure out what's keeping her here. I can't blame her for wanting to see what's waiting for her on the other side. But once she goes into the light, I'll lose her for good, and she'll become the only thing I'm able to keep within my grasp—a memory.

chapter forty

THANKSGIVING WEEK PASSES IN A HAZE OF SLEEPING LATE, binge-watching some reality baking competition with Marjorie, and eating leftover sweet potato pie for breakfast. The tension from the previous weekend dissipates, and she comes with me to Whimsy and Wu while I take care of the store in Dennis's absence. I think she likes the change of scenery, and I enjoy the company. My holiday weeks are typically spent solo with the exception of going to Eddie's the day of, but having Marjorie around makes me feel like I'm spending the break with family.

"So, I know I told you I've been giving more thought to my unfinished business," Marjorie says, studying a watercolor painting of a small country cottage hugged by strands of ivy.

"Yeah? Did you think of something?" It's late Saturday afternoon, and I'm cleaning up the shop about fifteen minutes before closing so I can quickly take Marjorie home and get ready for Friendsgiving with Jude.

"I haven't," she admits, a far-off look in her eyes. "And the more I ruminate on it, the less clear it becomes. It has to be something big…meaningful. Otherwise, why keep me here in limbo?"

"What if you're thinking *too* big? What if this was all an elaborate scheme to contact you about your car's extended warranty?" I tease, trying to lighten the mood.

"Then I'd very much like to speak to a manager," she mutters.

I lean against the doorframe leading into the next room, my hands wrapped around the wooden handle of a broom.

"I know you don't want to hear this," I begin, "but I think you have to consider the possibility that whatever is holding you here has something to do with John Abernathy."

She sighs and rolls her eyes. "Not this again."

"Yes, this again," I say, stepping closer to her. "Why are you being so stubborn?"

"Because, Kathryn," she replies. "I don't wish to go back down that road any more than I already have."

"Why?" I ask, setting the broom aside.

She huffs. "I've told you, it does no good to wonder about the what-ifs."

"Maybe it isn't about that," I insist. "Maybe it's about getting closure."

"He moved on," she cries as she moves away from me, weaving around the displays. "He got married and built a life that didn't include me. How much more closure can I possibly get?"

"Oh, I don't know," I say, hot on her heels. "Maybe tell him you got his letter and that you loved him too?"

She whirls on me. "What good does that do, exactly? Bringing up things that don't matter anymore."

"So, I suppose you tucked that letter into the back of your painting because it *didn't matter*," I retort, curving my fingers into air quotes. "You were thinking of him in your last days, and I'm sorry, but I have to believe that means something."

"It *means* I was a dying woman reminiscing about happier times," she counters. "That's all!"

"*That's all?*" I grip the sides of my skull, my fingers digging into my scalp. "Do you hear yourself? John was one of your happiest memories. So much so that you wanted to relive them before you died." I pause and release a slow exhale. "If you still remember him after all these years, what makes you think he doesn't still remember you?"

She shakes her head. "The only thing contacting John would accomplish is bringing up unpleasant memories for him."

"I read that letter, Marjorie," I say. "Maybe the way your relationship ended wasn't the best, but it wasn't *all* bad. He loved you."

"I don't want to cause him any more pain than I already have."

"How can you be certain it would hurt him if you're not even willing to *try* and reach him?" I ask. "The answer is, you can't. Not for sure."

"You're like a dog with a bone," she hisses. "Why won't you let this go?"

"Because I promised I'd help you figure out what's keeping you here, for God's sake," I shout. "I'm doing this *for you.*"

Wooden floorboards creak behind me, and my breath catches as I spin around. I was so focused on my argument with Marjorie that I didn't hear the bell above the door chime.

"Um...hi?" A gray-haired woman who appears to be in her seventies regards me with the caution of a hostage negotiator arriving at a crime scene.

"Hello." I plaster on my best customer-service smile. "Welcome in."

"Smile less, you look straight out of a horror movie," Marjorie warns.

I ignore her. "Can I help you find something today?"

The customer's eyes flick over the room as she straightens the scarf around her neck. "Miss, um, who were you talking to?"

"Oh, just now?" I ask, feigning ignorance. "No one."

The woman blinks as she takes a step back toward the door.

"I was running lines," I blurt. "I'm, um, in the community theater."

Her brows draw together. "We have a community theater here?"

I nod. "Mm-hmm."

Her shoulders begin to relax. "I did a bit of acting back in my college days. It was such a joy. How do I sign up?"

I clear my throat. "You can't. It's, uh, very exclusive."

Marjorie stifles a laugh as the woman frowns.

The woman narrows her gaze. "An exclusive community theater?"

"Yep. Took me months to get in," I lie.

"Right," she says, her tone skeptical. "Actually, I just realized I'm late for…it doesn't matter. I'll pop in next week when Dennis is back."

"Drive safe," I call as the woman all but sprints back outside, the door clanging shut behind her.

"How can you stand there like you didn't just shatter that poor woman's dreams of stardom?" Marjorie jokes, calling a temporary truce as she breezes past me. "Have you no soul?"

I snort. "I had to think of *something* that wouldn't make me the subject of the town's rumor mill."

She chuckles, a smirk spreading over her face. "Somehow, I don't think you'll avoid that."

"Oh whatever," I say, waving her off, glancing at the clock on the wall that reads 5 p.m. "You ready to get out of here? Maybe you can help me figure out what to wear to this dinner tonight?"

"Only if you promise to skip the leopard print."

"I make no promises," I sing as I venture behind the counter to pack up my things. As I do, I catch Marjorie staring at that painting again, and I can't help but wonder if it makes her think of the life she could have had with John—simple, perhaps, but beautiful all the same.

My chest aches as I take in her wistful expression. I understand she doesn't want to reopen old wounds for John, but she can't know how he'll feel without asking. That's why I'm going to find John and talk to him myself. If he doesn't want to hear from Marjorie, she'll never have to know. But if he does…she'll finally be able to give his letter the response it deserved.

chapter forty-one

Marjorie convinces me I should go to Jude's prepared with an overnight bag, which turns out to be a wise decision because Friendsgiving extends well past midnight when we all get carried away playing Cards Against Humanity. By the time we head back to his place, our hands entwined over the center console of his car, my insecurities feel miles away. Jude's friends are a lot like him, kind and laid-back, and it's easy to picture more gatherings just like this one.

On Sunday, I'm having a hard time prying myself from Jude's arms, and he asks me to stay the night. Of course, I can't tell him I have to get home to check on my (not) dead cat and my (actual) dead ghost friend, so I call in reinforcements in the form of Dennis and Thomas who made it home early that afternoon. After a few days away, they were both dying for a Marjorie and Delilah fix, so they were more than happy to use the spare key I keep in the potted plant outside to check on them.

Jude and I get up for work Monday morning, our first day back since Thanksgiving break, and admittedly, it's nice to get an extra hour of sleep. I also love getting ready with Jude—

having coffee together and brushing our teeth side by side. It just feels…*right.*

We plan to drive in our separate cars so as not to raise suspicion since it's not unusual for us to arrive at work at the same time. But that plan is thwarted when we walk outside with our tumblers of coffee to find my tire is flat.

I curse, throwing my overnight bag onto the backseat of my SUV and slamming the door. "This is just perfect."

Jude places a hand on my arm. "It's gonna be okay. I can call you an Uber."

"If Eddie or Becca sees me pull up in an Uber they'll know something's up," I say. "We don't even have Uber out in Jingo. They've heard me talk about it enough to remember that."

"Right." He tilts his head to the side, hand swiping over the stubble on his chin. "I can fix it, but we'll both be late."

"That's definitely not what we want."

"Look, let's just ride together," he suggests, but I shake my head.

"They might see us. I know we need to tell them, but this isn't the way. Especially not right before we go on-air."

"We'll be out of the car so quick, I doubt anyone will notice," he says. "There's so many cars in the lot. I don't think anyone will be looking for yours."

Right. It's sound logic. Nobody will be paying *that* close of attention. No one will even notice.

"Come on." He takes my hand, tugging me toward his car. "We don't want to be late. I'll fix it this afternoon, okay? We can act like we're grabbing lunch after the show if anyone sees us leaving, and we can plan to tell Eddie and Becca on our terms. It'll be fine."

I groan but allow him to lead me away. When we pull into

the lot at the studio, I sink down in the passenger's seat, keeping watch.

"Looks like the coast is clear," he says once he parks and cuts the ignition.

My fingers are already on the lever to open the door as I blow out a breath. "Let's go."

I stay a few paces ahead as we walk inside, my eyes darting around to make sure we haven't been spotted. We approach the door, and I can almost taste the relief, until I enter to find Becca standing by the elevator with her mouth hanging open.

Just be normal. "Hey." I wave and hope her shocked expression has nothing to do with me.

"What's this?" she asks as Jude stumbles in behind me.

When in doubt, play dumb. "What's what?"

She arches one perfectly-plucked brow. "You two came in together. I saw you pull in."

Jude's face remains neutral as he takes a sip of his coffee.

"Oh, that?" I gulp. "I had a flat this morning."

She nods, and for a second, I think I'm going to pull this off.

"This morning, you say? That's weird, considering it would take an extra two hours for him to drive to Jingo and back to bring you in. What did you do? Call him at 3 a.m.?"

"Um…I…uh…" My brain buffers, trying to come up with a reasonable response.

She snatches my tumbler from my grasp and unscrews the lid before taking a giant whiff. "This smells like Jude coffee."

Jude narrows his eyes. "And what does Jude coffee smell like?"

"I don't know. Like Starbucks and HomeGoods had a

baby," she says. "How did I not see this? Jude is your mystery guy? Seriously? *Jude?*"

He throws up his hands. "Really?"

"I didn't mean it like that," she insists, shoving the coffee back toward me. "Just that you're not exactly an *enigma* here. We already know what a dork you are."

He scoffs and rolls his eyes. "Thanks, Becca."

She grins. "Don't mention it."

"Please don't be mad," I say, placing a hand on her shoulder. "Becca, I promise we were going to tell you and Eddie. We just didn't want to do it like this."

Her face softens. "I'm not mad. A little disappointed maybe, but I'm not upset."

Jude squeezes my arm. "I'm gonna head on up and give you two a minute."

I nod my thanks as he steps into the elevator.

"I swear, I was going to tell you," I say. "I was just… nervous. Because what if this wasn't what I thought it was? I didn't want to make this a whole thing if it wasn't going to last."

"I get that," she replies with a sympathetic smile. "But you know I wouldn't have said anything to Eddie. I would've kept your secret."

Guilt needles at me because this particular secret is only the tip of the iceberg, and I'm barreling toward it like the Titanic. "You would have, but I was just…scared. I felt like I needed time to see what we have before bringing other opinions into the mix. I'm really sorry you had to find out like this."

She shrugs. "It's okay. I can see why you kept it close to the vest, but now we have some serious catching up to do."

"I promise, I'll tell you everything," I say as she loops her arm through mine and guides me forward, jamming the button to take us upstairs. "What do you want to know first?"

"How long has this been happening?"

"Honestly? We kissed the week after my first *Purrfect Match* dates."

She gasps. "You little shit. And let me guess, you continued the ruse for a couple weeks just so we wouldn't figure it out?"

I grimace. "Guilty as charged."

"So, it's serious, huh?" she asks, her lips curving upward as we step onto the elevator.

"Yeah," I admit.

"Wow." The doors slide closed, and she chuckles. "Jude? Are you sure?"

"Shut up." I swat her arm.

"Sorry," she says with a laugh. "He's just…you know… *Jude*."

I shoot her a look and her laughter fades. "What's that supposed to mean?"

"I'm sorry, it's kinda like I found out you're dating my brother. I wanna know the details, but I also *really* don't."

"Then I'll keep all my updates PG."

She gags, waving her hands wildly. "Ew. As far as I'm concerned, he has Ken parts, okay?"

I snort. "I can confirm he most *definitely* does not."

She plugs her ears with a loud *la, la, la* as the doors open onto our floor. "I can't hear you."

I smile as we stroll down the hallway.

"So, when are you gonna tell Eddie?" she asks.

"I might as well do it today," I answer. "I think I'll feel better with it out in the open."

She giggles, and my brows furrow.

"What?"

"I'm just imagining the dad chat Eddie's going to give Jude," she says with a satisfied smirk. "I hope we have popcorn in the break room."

I swat her again, but I can't hide my smile. It feels good to have one less secret to keep. Soon, I'll tell Jude about Delilah and Marjorie, then hopefully Becca and Eddie. My chest is already lighter just thinking about having everything out in the open, once and for all.

chapter forty-two

"Jude…wow…really?" Eddie leans back in his office chair later that morning after the show wraps.

"Is that a good *wow*?" I ask, nervously clicking a pen I swiped from the mug on his desk.

"It's definitely not a bad one," he answers as he sits forward, folding his hands on the wooden top. "I guess I still have a bit of lingering anxiety after what happened with Lexi back when she lost her shit on Tanner from management on-air."

"With a name like that, he had it coming," I quip.

"True," he says with a sigh. "But I do feel I'd be remiss if I didn't warn you about the potential risks of getting involved with someone you work with."

My thumb continues to bounce against the end of the pen. "Trust me, I know."

"If things end badly, it can affect the whole vibe of the program. Hell, even if you're on great terms, it can still be rough," he adds. "Look, I know the future of the show beyond next fall is up in the air, but in a perfect world, I'd like to see it carry on after I retire. If things were to go south…it just took us a long time to get the chemistry right. I'd hate to see you guys lose that."

The pen-clicking intensifies. "You're right, and it *is* something we've thought about. That's why we wanted to give it some time."

He reaches across, swiping the pen from my grasp.

"Sorry," I mumble.

"I'm guessing it must be pretty serious if you're this nervous to tell me about it," he says.

I tuck my hands under my thighs to keep from moving. "It feels serious. I can see a future here, you know?" More than that, I *want* one.

"Jude's a great guy. I think the world of him. He's been a godsend for me, for this station, and it looks like he's been one for you too." Eddie tilts his head, his gaze fixed on me. "You seem happier lately, and I take it a lot of that has to do with Jude."

"Yeah. It does," I say with a smile. "He's good to me."

"He better be. I'll kill him if he isn't."

I chuckle. "What happened to him being a *godsend*?"

He shrugs. "If he hurts you, I'll put a stamp on his ass and return to sender."

"You're gonna give him a dad talk, aren't you?"

He gives me a *do-you-even-have-to-ask* glare. "Obviously."

"You have to be nice."

"I'm always nice."

I narrow my eyes. "Nick told me otherwise." I distinctly recall coming home from the New Year's Eve party that year and Nick being convinced Eddie hated him, which was fair.

"Me?" Eddie presses a palm to his broad chest. "I would never."

"You would, and it's one of the things I love about you." I grin. "I appreciate you always looking out."

His face softens. "I love you like one of my own, kid. I've been betting on you since you were an intern, and I'm not gonna stop now."

"Thanks, Dad," I say with a playful wink. "Don't be too hard on him, though."

He gives me a dismissive wave. "I didn't even bring my gun with me today, so he'll be fine."

"Eddie!"

"I'll just make sure he remembers I have one," he teases.

"You're terrible," I say, though I'm laughing right along with him. He wouldn't *actually* hurt a fly—not really—and it's another one of the things I love about him. But what he *can* do is talk a big game. And since I don't have my actual dad in my life to do fatherly things like put the fear of God in the men I date, I'm thankful he's willing to step in.

There's a knock on the already-open door, and Jude pokes his head in, a folder tucked under one arm.

"Well, if it isn't the man of the hour," Eddie says, beaming.

Jude gives him a tentative smile in return. "Um, I was up in marketing, and they asked me to bring this to you."

"Come on in and have a seat." Eddie gestures toward the chair beside me. "Kat was just heading out, and I'd like to have a chat with you."

I point my finger at Eddie as I rise to my feet. "You better behave."

Jude casts a nervous glance in my direction as we pass each other.

"Am I in trouble?" Jude jokes as he sits, though there's a hint of concern in his voice.

"I don't know. What did you do?" Eddie's mouth flattens into a hard line.

I stifle a grin as I reach the doorway.

"Kat?" Eddie calls out, and I turn. "Close the door on your way out."

"Of course." The last thing I see is the look of pure amusement on Eddie's face flanked by a flicker of panic on Jude's.

chapter forty-three

Jude fixes my tire at his place later that afternoon, then we brew a pot of coffee before I head back to Jingo.

We're on his sofa, my legs tented over his, mug cradled in my hands.

"So, I was thinking," Jude says.

I raise my brows. "Sounds dangerous. What about?"

"Well, Delilah's been gone a few weeks now. I know it's been hard on you being in that quiet house," he begins.

It takes every ounce of self-control I possess to stop myself from reacting. Between Delilah, who is still very much alive, and Marjorie, my home is anything but quiet.

"I was wondering if you've considered getting another cat. A kitten, maybe," he continues. "We could even go together to pick one out. I looked at some shelters online and found a few that have litters ready to be adopted."

Uh-oh. Delilah's life has been disrupted enough by having Marjorie around. The last thing she'll want is a new brother or sister. I just need to put on my big girl panties and let the proverbial not-dead cat out of the bag.

I suck in a breath. "Actually, Jude, there's something I need to tell you."

His eyes are locked on mine as one hand rubs along the arch of my foot. "Okay."

This is it—the moment of truth. I'll start from the beginning, explain how I ended up with Marjorie's urn, how she wanted to go to work with me that day, and that I panicked when they asked about it. He'll understand.

"I'm not quite ready to get a new pet," I say instead.

No, you idiot! You're supposed to tell him the truth. But I can't make the words leave my mouth. What if he doesn't believe me or worse still, what if he does and is totally horrified? I have to be more intentional about this. Perhaps I can even have Dennis present to back me up.

"This just isn't the right time," I add. Whether it's to him, regarding the idea of getting a new cat, or to myself about telling Jude the truth, I'm not sure.

"Hey, it's okay," Jude assures me. "I get it. I'm not going to pressure you one way or another, but if you get to the point when you *are* ready to adopt another cat, I'd love to be part of it. I could see myself being a cat dad."

My heart is in my throat. He wants to do this with me. He wants to make plans for the future—*our* future.

"You'll be a great one."

I'll tell him the truth. Soon. I just have to do it right. For now, I need to get off the subject of cats.

"You know, things at work went better than I thought they would, considering we didn't plan on telling anyone today."

He snorts. "Speak for yourself. I got an hour-long lecture from Eddie about my intentions with you and" —he pauses, taking a sip of his drink— "did you know he has a gun?" I sputter a laugh, and his mouth drops open. "It's not funny."

"Come on, it's a little funny," I tease. "He's just looking out for me."

His fingers trace the side of my shin, giving me a playful grin. "It's bad enough I'll have to watch out for Becca. Now I'll have Eddie on my ass too. Nobody is on team Jude."

"Oh stop. I'm sure your folks will put me through the ringer when the time comes." It's something I've thought about a lot over the past several days. Meeting Jude's parents is inevitable, and I *want* to meet them—I do. But knowing how much affection his mother still holds for his ex makes me feel like there are some giant shoes I'll be expected to fill.

"No way, and even if they *do*, neither of my parents are packing." He gives me a playful wink.

"Maybe not," I begin, "but I'm pretty sure your mom probably has enough medical knowledge to kill me and make it look like an accident."

His phone pings on the coffee table, the screen lighting as the word *Mom* flashes, along with a photo of her and Jude. She has blond hair that's peppered with streaks of white and Jude's golden skin.

"And she appears to have your place bugged," I say, bringing my mug to my lips.

Jude chuckles as he reaches for the device and answers the call. "Hey, Mom. What's up?" There's a brief silence on his end before he speaks again. "Yeah, I'm home. Just having coffee with Kat."

Relief scatters through my chest like confetti. She really *does* know about me.

His brow furrows, and my brain darts to the worst-case scenario as he listens to whatever she's saying. Perhaps she's telling him how much she wishes he would get back with

Lauren or that she's decided she would rather be eaten by sharks than be forced into a room with me.

Jude sits forward with a smile on his mouth. "Mom, that's incredible news. Oh wow. I'm so proud of you."

Whew. So, whatever she's saying probably has nothing to do with sharks or his ex, both of which feel equally deadly in my world.

"Of course, I'll be there," he says. "Next Saturday? You bet." Another beat of silence. "And I'm sure Kat would love to come."

Surprise knocks my head back and I mouth *me? Really?*

He nods, listening to whatever his mom is saying. "We wouldn't miss it. Okay. I'll tell her. All right. Love you too. Bye."

"That sounded…good?" I say as he leans back and places his phone face down on the arm of the couch.

He's practically beaming. "Very. Remember when I told you my mom was nominated for the Franklin Albrecht?"

I nod.

"She just found out she won."

"That's *amazing*," I reply. "Tell her congratulations for me."

"Actually, you'll get to tell her yourself," he says, squeezing my leg. "They're presenting the award to her at some big gala a week from Saturday. She wants me to be there and asked if you'd be able to come too."

"She did?" I attempt to disguise the shock in my voice, and I must do a decent job because Jude doesn't seem to notice.

"Do you mind?" he asks. "I know we were planning on going to that holiday market in East Nashville."

"What? No, that's great. I'm honored she wants me there."

But the words come out laced with trepidation. Does she really want me there? Was this a pity invite because I happened to be here when she called? Or maybe she wants to dump pig's blood on me in front of everyone like they did in *Carrie*?

My face must reflect the unhinged thoughts swirling around my brain because when I come back to earth, Jude is staring at me.

"Kat," he says, narrowing his eyes. "What's going on in that head of yours?"

"Nothing," I insist. "I'm excited. Really."

"Then why do you sound like I invited you to a root canal?"

"I don't," I argue, but I *so* do.

"Out with it."

"It's nothing," I lie. "It's dumb. Really." That part's true.

"So you admit, it *is* something." He rests one arm over the back of the couch, pivoting to face me. "Come on. Tell me. What's wrong?"

I sigh, flopping my head against the overstuffed edge. "I'm afraid your mom won't like me, okay?"

He gives me an empathetic smile. "That's what this is about? She's gonna love you. Stop worrying."

I roll my eyes. "Oh yay, I'm healed. Can you cure depression next?"

He laughs, then reaches for my hands, pulling me up and guiding me onto his lap. "I know it's not that simple, but I mean it, she's gonna love you."

"But what if she doesn't?" I hate how small and pathetic the question comes out, as though it's peeking through trembling fingers.

He presses a kiss to my forehead, a gesture that almost

instantaneously quiets my racing mind. Thoughts of his mom, of his ex, fade to a low hum.

"She will." He says it with such certainty I almost believe it's true. "My dad too. They both want to meet the woman I'm crazy about."

The world slows, and Jude's living room dims until only we remain. "You're crazy about me, huh?"

"Completely." He takes a strand of my hair between his fingers. "It's always been you, Kat. Long before either of us were ready to admit there was something between us, I felt it."

Thousands of shared smiles and inside jokes and years of fiercely having each other's backs converge, bringing us to this moment. My breath catches, and I hold his gaze, wanting to forever remember the way he's looking at me.

"I'm in love with you. Like, ridiculously, hopelessly in love." He touches me like I'm a secret worth keeping, a story worthy of being told. Is this what it feels like to be treasured?

"I'm in love with you too." Except love almost doesn't feel big enough to hold all the moments that led us here.

He takes my face in his hands and kisses me with a tenderness that lights up all my darkest corners, leaving no shadows, no doubts behind. For this moment, I am his, and he is mine, and that is impossibly enough.

chapter forty-four

"This is exciting." Marjorie is practically bubbling over as we climb out of the car, my backpack slung over my shoulder. "I haven't been shopping in so long."

"Thanks for coming with me." I pull my coat tighter around me as we start toward Bev's Boutique, a formal dress shop on the outskirts of Jingo, Saturday morning. "I'm kinda freaking out. This dress has to be perfect."

The peace I felt Monday has melted away, leaving my insecurities raw and bleeding. I'm one week from meeting Jude's parents, and I'm spiraling.

"Don't worry about a thing," she says. "We're going to find the perfect gown, and you're going to wow Jude's family at the gala next weekend."

I wish I shared her conviction, but I'm too busy imagining all the ways this can go wrong as we step through the entrance of the nondescript pale brick building with a simple black-and-white sign out front.

"What on earth is this place?" Marjorie asks, her nose wrinkling in disgust.

While the exterior of the shop is plain, the inside is reminiscent of a Lisa Frank daydream, full of bright colors, sequins, and glitter. The walls are hot pink with a zebra-printed accent wall and floors that look like they've been constructed out of disco balls. An assortment of white and cream wedding gowns line the right side of the store, while the rest boasts dresses in every imaginable hue.

"Hello," a southern soprano calls, though I can't make out where the voice is coming from. "I'll be right with ya."

Marjorie rounds one of the circular racks closest to the wall, her forehead creased in concentration. "Well, these are certainly…*something*."

My gaze travels to the dresses showcased on the wall. One is traffic-cone orange, and another is red velvet, trimmed in white feathers like some sexy Mrs. Claus. Neither exactly feels like the vibe I'm going for to win the approval of Jude's mother.

"Hi there, hon," a voice says from behind me, and Marjorie gasps. "I'm Bev."

I turn to find a woman who looks to be in her fifties with skin so fair it's nearly translucent, wearing a red sequined dress. Her lips have been painted to match, and her brows have been drawn on in thick black rectangles. The shoulder-length bob atop her head is slightly askew, which she notices in one of the full-length mirrors.

"What can I help you with today, doll?" she asks, straightening her wig.

"I'm not sure we're the ones who need help," Marjorie mutters.

I shoot her a glare before plastering on a smile.

"I'm attending a gala with my boyfriend and his parents next Saturday," I answer, tugging at the sleeve of my sweater. "It'll be my first time meeting them."

"Oh my stars," she drawls. "Not to worry, darlin'. Auntie Bev will fix you right up."

I'm doing a *lot* of worrying for someone who keeps being told not to worry.

"Auntie Bev needs to fix her eyebrows," Marjorie whispers, but I pretend I don't hear her. She died in 2016 while the rest of us were busy framing our eyes in a pomade that looked like oil paint. We are not the same.

"Now, tell me a little about what colors you might like." Bev sweeps through the store with an elegance I don't quite expect, plucking dresses from hangers in a rainbow blur. "I'll pull a few that I think will look good on you. Ones you might not pick for yourself, but I also want to know if you have anything special in mind."

"Darker shades, maybe?" I say. "And definitely floor-length."

"Of course," Bev replies with Marjorie on her heels, scrutinizing every gown she selects. "You'll probably want a sleeve or maybe a nice shawl." She shivers when Marjorie gets too close. "Goodness, it's a bit chilly in here, isn't it? I'll turn the heat up before you start trying these on."

I follow Bev, each rack of dresses more overwhelming than the last, but I don't bother to pick any myself. Instead, I'm relying on Bev to seal my fate.

"All right, follow me, sugar," Bev says, her stiletto heels clicking across the floor. "I'm gonna put you in a fitting room so you can get started, but I'll keep checking in and bringing more for you to try on. How does that sound?"

"Sure, that's great. Thank you." She leads me down a short hallway with smaller rooms that shoot off to the sides, filled with more glittering garments.

"I wonder if that's where the good dresses are," Marjorie comments, walking beside me.

"By the way, baby doll, I didn't catch your name," Bev says.

"Oh, it's Kat," I answer.

"Well, here we are, Kat," she says, stopping in front of an open arched doorway with three generous-sized fitting rooms and one pedestal surrounded by mirrors. I imagine many a bride has stood in that very spot, saying yes to the dress while their mothers dabbed their eyes with a tissue, telling them they've never looked more beautiful. It's an image I haven't given much thought to before, but it sends a pang of longing through my heart.

Bev slides open the curtain of the center room, hanging the dresses neatly inside as I set my backpack on the floor.

"Now, if you need anything, you just give me a holler, sweet pea," Bev says. "You might have to shout. It's hard to hear much once that heat gets going."

I nod my thanks as she disappears back into the store. Despite Marjorie's concern over the dresses Bev chose, she waits expectantly with her hands clasped in front of her.

"Go ahead and try on the first one," Marjorie urges. "I'll be out here."

"Right," I say, sliding the curtain closed. A couple of moments later, I emerge in a black dress with a sleek silhouette that hugs my hips, a low-cut neckline, and bell sleeves.

Marjorie rears her head back in disgust. "You look like the mother from *The Addams Family*."

"Morticia?" I whisper.

She dismisses me as though she's swatting a fly. "Next."

This time, I select a Christmas green one that hangs off my shoulders slightly.

Marjorie purses her lips as I step out of the dressing room and onto the pedestal. "I don't hate it."

"But you don't love it."

She cocks her head, considering. "The color is a bit too bold. It almost drowns you out. I should see you before I see the dress."

"Back to the drawing board, then," I say with a sigh, heading back in and snapping the curtain shut. We repeat this about seventeen times with Bev popping in midway to drop off more gowns. There are some pretty ones (and one cow-printed one that has Marjorie and me giggling), but none of them feel *right*. Finally, on dress number eighteen, I slump onto the pedestal in a heap of blush tulle.

"It's no use," I mutter, stretching out my legs. "I'm destined to meet Jude's parents looking like a farm animal." At least when his mom references the awful cow that stole her son, I'll be easily identifiable.

"What's wrong with the one you have on?" she asks, gesturing toward the strapless dress draping my body. "It looks lovely on you."

"But lovely isn't good enough," I whine, burying my face in my hands. "It has to be perfect."

"Kathryn, few people understand the importance of a good outfit more than me, but don't you think you're putting a lot of pressure on yourself? That dress looks great and so did at least seven others."

I huff and lift my face to hers. "And they'd be just fine if I wasn't meeting Jude's parents, or more specifically, his mother. It has to be *flawless*."

"What's really going on here?" she asks. "Much to my surprise, there are dozens of nice dresses in this shop. Bev may not be able to draw arches into her eyebrows, but I cannot deny she has good taste. You can't find *one* you like?"

"I'm afraid Jude's mom is going to hate me," I blurt. "And whatever I wear to this gala is going to set the tone for our entire relationship. What if she thinks I'm too bold, too mousy, too slutty? What if she thinks I'm not good enough for Jude?"

"This dress isn't going to amount to a hill of beans," she says, her green eyes warm as she gazes down at me. "I'd be willing to bet Jude's mother won't even remember it, but she *will* remember you."

"The woman who doesn't deserve her son." I don't recall much about Lauren besides the fact that she's gorgeous, supermodel tall, and a freaking *doctor*—the exact kind of person any mother would want for their child. She's every-thing I'm not.

Marjorie props her hands on her hips. "First of all, she's out of her mind if she thinks that. Any mother should feel honored you'd given their son the time of day. And second of all, so what if she *does* think that? Jude worships the ground you walk on."

"But she's his mother," I argue. "Of course, her opinion matters."

"He's a grown man. He shouldn't be looking to his parents to decide who he can or cannot be with."

I lift my shoulders in a resigned shrug. "You did." I wince the second the sentence leaves my mouth. "I'm sorry, Marjorie. I didn't mean that." But I guess I *did*. Marjorie gave up on John because of *her* parents. It didn't matter how much she loved him, she still made the choice to leave.

The corners of her mouth turn downward, her fingers grazing the pearls around her neck.

"You did mean it. And you're right. But it's also the biggest regret of my life," she says finally. "Worrying about what other people thought of me, instead of what *I* thought of me."

Logically, I know she's right. I can't control what anyone else thinks, and even if his mom *does* hate me, there's no dress that's going to change that. But that doesn't make me worry any less.

She crouches beside me. "I missed out on something that could have been beautiful because I listened to everyone else when I should have been listening to what was in here." Her hand hovers in the space above my heart, covering me with an icy chill.

"But what if his mom doesn't like me and her opinion makes Jude feel differently? What if he decides he doesn't want to be with me?" And there it is—the crux of the issue. What if, once again, I get left alone?

"Then *he* is an idiot," she says, leaning closer. "Take it from me, you don't want to spend your life tied to a man without an ounce of sense in his head."

I gather the poofy pink skirt by the fistfuls, the tulle imprinting on my palms.

"Do you remember what you said about me the day we got my earrings back from Conrad?" she asks. "You said I was a hurricane. Well, you, my dear, are the sun. You bring light to everything and everyone you touch. And if Jude or his mother or anyone else doesn't see that, then let them sit in the dark."

Tears cloud my vision. "You mean that?"

"Sweet girl," she says with a maternal tenderness that makes my chest ache. "Do you understand how dismal and dull my existence was before I found you?" She tilts her head and gives me a warm smile. "Of all the people in this world who could have seen me, I'm so thankful it was you."

The knowledge that our time together could be coming to an end looms over me like a dark cloud. Now that Marjorie's in my life, it's hard to imagine being without her. But I'm aware we're on borrowed time, and once I find John Abernathy and connect him with Marjorie, it's likely the light will appear, and she'll be on her way to her next destination.

I sniffle. "Thanks, Marjorie. Me too."

"Oh honey, don't you fret." Bev appears with a merlot-colored frock dangling from her arm, concern etched on her face as she assumes my emotional distress has been caused by a fashion emergency. "Aunt Bev is gonna find you the perfect dress for your gala. In fact, I might have it here in my hands."

Marjorie and I rise to our feet, and I wipe away the dampness on my cheeks.

"This color is gonna look spectacular on you," Bev says, handing me the long velvet gown. "And the low back and the high slit gives it a little something sexy without being overdone. It's got a nice sleeve on it too."

I thank her, and she exits the room to give me some privacy, promising to return in a couple of minutes.

"Go on," Marjorie encourages. "Let's see it."

I fold myself behind the curtain, slipping the dress on, the luxurious fabric hugging my skin. When I step back out of the dressing room, Marjorie lays a hand against her chest.

"Get on the pedestal," she says as she moves around me.

I step up and smooth my hands over the soft material, taking in the way the dress dips with my body, while Marjorie inspects the dress from every angle. Finally, she stands to the side, admiring me with glossy eyes.

"Well, what do you think?" I ask.

She removes a handkerchief from her pocket and dabs beneath her lashes. "You look absolutely stunning, Kathryn. How do you feel?"

I turn, checking out the back, and I see why Bev suggested it. It fits like it was made for me. I gather my hair in my hands, twisting it on top of my head, mimicking an elegant updo.

"Pretty," I answer. "It's comfortable too."

"I think Bev's right," Marjorie says. "This is the one." She makes another circle around me, slower this time, before settling in front of me with her tissue clutched between her fingers. "I've never seen anyone look more beautiful."

"Really?" The emotion I feel is reflected back at me on Marjorie's face, and it's another moment when I'd give anything to hug her.

"Really," she answers. "You're going to be the most beautiful woman at that gala."

We exchange smiles as Bev comes bustling back into the room, her sequins swishing as she walks.

"Now, that's what I like to see, pumpkin," she says. "What do you think? Do you like it?"

"I love it," I reply, and she claps, shaking her hips in a happy dance.

"Oh, I'm so glad. Does that mean it's a yes?" Bev asks, and I nod.

"Give me a twirl," Marjorie says, and I oblige.

It may not be a wedding dress, and Marjorie isn't my mother, but somehow, this feels like the next best thing.

chapter forty-five

"YOU WON'T GIVE ME A HINT?" JUDE ASKS, CUTTING INTO the last of his biscuits and gravy. It's the day of the gala, and we're having brunch at a cozy spot in Nashville before I head home for the afternoon. "Not even one?"

"Nope." I spear a bite of my red velvet waffle with my fork. "I want to watch your eyes bug out of your head like a cartoon when you see me."

He lets out a low whistle. "Wow, must be some dress. Am I gonna require medical attention? Will I need mouth-to-mouth?"

"I hope so," I tease, waggling my brows.

"You saw my tux," he pouts. "I show you mine, you show me yours. That's how this works."

I lean forward, dropping my voice to a whisper. "I recall showing you a *lot* this morning."

"What can I say? I'm greedy." He gives me a devilish grin. "By the way, I'm gonna pick you up around six, so we can make it to the gala by seven. Though, I still think you should have brought your stuff to get ready at my place, just because I don't want to wait forty-five extra minutes to see you in your dress."

It would have made sense, considering I stayed with him last night, but I have my reasons for wanting to go back to my house. I need to take care of Delilah, though Jude doesn't know that, but I also promised Marjorie I would be there so she could see me off. I'm not sure who's more excited about our plans—me or her.

"I know, but I have a friend helping me," I say. "We've both been really looking forward to it."

"Oh, cool. Becca?" he asks, and I shake my head. "Dennis?"

"No, she's someone you haven't met yet. Anyway, we're making a whole girls' day out of it."

Marjorie and I spent the week trying out different hair-styles and makeup options, until we landed on the perfect look to go with my gown. We're planning to put on *Pretty Woman,* and then we have a playlist of all our favorites to listen to while I get dressed, including everyone from Otis Redding to Taylor Swift.

"That sounds fun."

My mouth feels thick, as though I swallowed a spoonful of the powdered sugar sprinkled on top of my waffle. It's time for me to confide in Jude. I'm meeting his parents this week-end, and it just feels...*right.* Tomorrow morning, I'm telling him everything—about Delilah, Marjorie, and her unfinished business. I already warned Dennis I may need his help, and he assured me he'll do whatever it takes. The longer this lie carries on, the harder it will be to tell Jude the truth, so it's time for me to face the music.

"She's kind of a new friend," I say. "We only met in October, but we've gotten pretty close over the last couple months. Actually, I'd love to introduce you to her soon."

"That'd be great. How'd you guys meet?"

"Um, she was at Whimsy and Wu," I answer, because it's not a *total* lie. She *was* there, in the urn I bought for ten dollars that has now become priceless.

He grins. "Ah, you two must be a match made in heaven."

"I wasn't so sure at first," I admit. "We're at, um, different *life stages*, so I didn't know if we'd have much in common." I mean, we *are* at totally different life stages. I'm alive and she's…well…not.

"Is she married with kids or something?"

I twist my lips to the side. "No kids, and her husband is… out of the picture. She's just quite a bit older than me, but it turns out she's the kind of friend I didn't know I needed. She's special."

He gives an amused nod. "It's funny you mention that. An article came up in my feed yesterday about the benefits of multigenerational friendships. I was going to pitch it as a topic for the show next week."

"Really?" I ask, though I doubt it was referring to the types of multigenerational friends who also happened to be dead. *I wonder if there's an article about cross-dimensional friends…*

"It made me think of Eddie and how he is with you, me, and Becca," he continues. "Yeah, he mentors us profession-ally, but he also gives good life advice because he's lived more of it. He's been through it all. And we're able to offer him a different perspective on stuff that he sometimes can't see. Like a few years ago, when he got into that huge argu-ment with Jay."

Eddie had been adamant that all his kids attend college, but Jay, his youngest, was equally intent on *not* going. Jay knew from an early age he wanted to get into sports podcasting. His dad felt the only way to do that was to go to school for broadcasting, but Jay found a different path, interning for other podcasts and learning from every sports journalist he could convince to speak to him. Now, he has his own sports news show that lives in the top ten in that category across multiple platforms.

"We're all kind of limited by our own experiences," I say. "And Eddie finally realized there can be more than one right way to do something. He just needed a little push."

A push, like the one I'm working on to reconnect Marjorie with John Abernathy. This week, I've sent out, in total, messages to seventeen possible matches for family members of John's via social media. Only six have replied so far, all dead ends.

"We all need one on occasion," he says, reaching across the table for my hand. I think of how Marjorie picked up on Jude's feelings for me the first time she saw us together. If it hadn't been for her, I might not have gone to Billy's with him that day. Without her, we might not even be together.

"Jude?" A woman's voice slices through the moment, causing him to pull his hand back, blinking in surprise.

"Lauren, wow. Hi. How's it going?" Jude's jaw ticks with the effort it takes to swallow.

My gaze travels up and up and up this woman, who is at least seventy percent legs with the shiniest, most beautiful blond hair I've ever seen. Her nose turns up slightly at the end as she flashes a blinding white smile at me before turning her attention back to Jude.

"Things are going well," she replies, and she even sounds like a Disney princess. I imagine tiny birds help her get ready for work at the hospital where she saves lives every day. "It's good to see you. It's been forever."

"Yeah, um, yeah it has." Jude shifts slightly.

I'm staring at him, but his eyes are squarely on her. He seems tense, and the air is so thick, I can almost reach out and touch it.

"I didn't mean to interrupt," Lauren says, casting a brief glance at me. "I'm just meeting some girlfriends." She points to a table toward the back of the restaurant where three equally stunning creatures are waiting for her. "I saw you and had to say hello. You look great."

Jude runs his hand over the back of his neck. "Oh, uh, thanks. You too."

I clear my throat, in an effort to remind him I'm still here. Or maybe it's to remind *myself* I'm still here.

Jude gives a slight shake of his head. "Sorry. Lauren, this is my girlfriend, Kat."

"Right, your mom mentioned you were seeing someone," she says before facing me. "Nice to meet you, Kat."

"You too," I respond with a polite nod.

"So, I'll see you tonight, right?" Lauren asks Jude. "At the gala?"

Wait. Lauren's going? My heart hammers against my ribcage like it's trying to escape.

"I'll be there," he answers. "We both will."

"Oh good," she says, and to her credit, she doesn't seem totally put off by the fact. "Isn't it wonderful? Susan worked so hard for this. She deserves it."

"Yeah, she does." Jude finally sounds like himself again. "I'm proud of her."

Lauren clasps her hands together in front of her, and even her fingers are perfect.

"Me too," she says. "Well, I suppose I'll see you two later."

"Absolutely. Can't wait." I force the most pleasant smile I can manage, just hoping it doesn't make me look like a rabid raccoon caught on a doorbell camera.

Jude gives her a polite wave as she saunters off to join her friends. He massages his temple, avoiding my eyes for a moment.

I glide my tongue over my teeth. "So, um, *that* was strange."

"I'm sorry she ambushed us like that," he says, pinching the bridge of his nose.

I jut my chin forward and cock my head. "Ambushed us? All she did was say hello, but you got all weird like you were about to face an interrogation or something."

"I wasn't trying to be weird. She just took me by surprise is all."

"You seemed kind of…on edge." He also appeared to forget I existed there for a moment, the sting of that brief sense of rejection causing heat to climb up my cheeks. "Were you…embarrassed of me?"

Panic flares in his eyes. "What? No. Of course not. I was just…the whole thing caught me off guard, and I didn't want you to be uncomfortable. I guess I just freaked out a little."

"Did you know she was going tonight?"

"No. Not for sure, anyway."

I fold my arms over my chest, shielding myself. "But you knew it was a possibility?"

He rakes a hand through his hair but says nothing. "I knew you were worried about meeting my folks, and I didn't want to add to your stress."

"That seems like something worth mentioning." How could he just not tell me?

"Please don't be mad," he pleads. "I have no control over who's going to this thing and—"

"I'm not. She's important to your mom, and I get that," I counter. "But I'm frustrated that you didn't at least give me a heads-up."

"I thought that might make you feel more nervous about tonight."

This makes me feel nervous because it makes me wonder if he was keeping it from me. But what reason would he have to do that? I try to pump the brakes on my thoughts before they can spiral even further, but it's too late. What if there are still some sort of unresolved feelings between them—if not on her part, on his?

He pushes his plate out of the way and reaches for my hand. "Kat, I'm sorry. I didn't mean to upset you. I'd never do that intentionally. You know that, right?"

Yes. No. I don't know. There's still that small voice lingering in the back of my mind, telling me I won't be enough to make him stay. That there isn't anyone exempt from leaving, no matter how good their intentions.

"I do," I finally say. "I know. Sorry."

"Don't apologize. I could have handled that better. I should have." He squeezes my fingers. "And I will from now on."

"It's okay," I say, even though I don't *feel* okay. The black hole that lives inside my chest grows wider. "Seriously," I add in an effort to convince both of us.

He gives me a relieved smile. "Tonight is going to be amazing, I promise. My parents are going to love you, and I'm going to *love* seeing you in your dress." He drops his voice low, so only I can hear. "And then I'll enjoy taking it off you when we get back to my place."

His words ignite a spark in my belly, casting a soft glow over the darkness within me.

I smile. "I like the sound of that. Speaking of, I should probably get going soon. I have a full day of pampering ahead." It's the truth, but I also want to get out of here, away from perfect Lauren and her perfect friends, away from the nagging sensation that I am and always will be inadequate.

"Okay. I'll grab the check when the server comes back, and we'll head out."

I do my best to shove my feelings down and attempt to shift my focus to the afternoon. A few hours with Marjorie will have me in a better headspace and tonight *will* be great.

This is fine. I'm fine. Everything's fine.

chapter forty-six

"Do you think I have anything to be worried about?" I ask, beginning to pick at my cuticle. "With Lauren, I mean?"

"Stop that," Marjorie scolds from beside me on the couch with Delilah napping between us. "You're going to ruin your nails after all the effort you went through to paint them."

It *was* quite a feat. Between my endless coffee refills, having to pee eight times, and the cat fuzz I managed to somehow embed in the polish on my thumb during the first half of the movie, it had been a seemingly impossible task.

"They're dry," I insist, gently pressing my fingertip against the oxblood paint on my index finger, causing it to dent slightly. "Okay, they're *almost* dry."

The credits are rolling on the television in my living room, but we stopped paying attention thirty minutes ago. Marjorie sensed my mood was off when I came home from brunch with Jude despite my best efforts to forget what happened with Lauren. An hour and a half and a full pot of coffee later, she weaseled it out of me.

"Jude loves you," she says, finally answering my question.

"I don't believe he'd do anything that would jeopardize your relationship."

I worry my lip between my teeth. "You should have seen him, though. He seemed…I don't know…nervous."

"Wouldn't you be?" she asks. "It's an awkward situation, introducing your new love to an ex."

"What if she still wants him?" It's a question that's been nagging at me. She acted nice enough at the restaurant, but isn't that exactly how a boyfriend thief would act in public unless they were just a diabolical mean girl?

"It doesn't matter what she wants because Jude wants *you*." She gives me an empathetic smile. "You're overthinking this."

"No shit."

She shoots me a *watch-your-language* glare. "And you need to stop before you sabotage what I'm positive will be a beautiful night for the two of you."

I plop my head against the cushion. "You're right." But there's a lingering doubt that crawls inside me, pulling up a chair with every intention of staying a while.

"I know I am," she says, leaning closer to me. "Look, keep an eye out for any devious behavior from Lauren tonight, and if you notice something, mention it to Jude."

I nod, releasing a slow exhale. "Yeah. Okay. I can do that."

"I'm sure it's nothing, and tomorrow you'll come home and tell me all about your magical night." The conviction in her voice is a life raft that's been tossed out to bring me to shore, saving me from drowning in my sea of uncertainty. I surrender to the waves and let her pull me in. "Now, there's no time to waste. You've got to get ready."

She starts to rise, but I hold out a hand, stopping her. "Before I do, there's something I want to tell you."

Her brows furrow as she settles next to me. "Oh? Is everything all right?"

"Yeah," I answer quickly. "It's a good thing. I just want you to know I'm telling Jude tomorrow—about you, Delilah, everything."

Her eyes widen. "You…are you sure?"

"I am. It's time to come clean, and I want him to meet you," I say. "As much as he can, anyway."

Her face brightens. "I'd love that. How do you think he'll take it?"

"I'm not sure," I admit. "But I did enlist Dennis to help me prove it, in case he thinks I've hit my head or something."

"That's probably wise. Perhaps some smelling salts would be advisable in case he passes out like you did that first time." Marjorie smirks. "So dramatic."

"Hey, your hand literally went through my hand, okay? I think my reaction was more than reasonable," I tease. "Anyway, let's get ready."

This time Marjorie is the one to stop me. "Actually, Kathryn, there's one thing I want to discuss with you. About John Abernathy."

I hold my breath, nodding.

"I've given some more thought to the possibility of reaching him, and I want you to know I'm not ruling it out anymore."

I blink, gobsmacked. "You're not?"

"No," she says. "I'm not. I'm not totally on board yet, but I'm willing to give it further consideration."

"What made you change your mind?"

She shrugs, a thoughtful expression on her face. "It's

seeing you so happy with Jude, I suppose. Not that I think John and I are going to ride off into the sunset together. I know that's not possible. But I do think there could be some benefit to telling him the truth about what happened back then. And as much as I don't want to admit it, I think you could be right. He might be my unfinished business."

Her epiphany is bittersweet. I'm happy she's giving it more thought, that she's seen the potential value in reconnecting with John, though I know once she does, I may lose her forever. But I swallow those emotions and put on a happy face for her.

"Well then, it sounds like we have a lot to celebrate this afternoon." I grab my phone, connecting it to the bluetooth speakers in the house before hitting play on the playlist I've made called "Marjorie & Me." The beat of an old Whitney Houston track begins to play. I jump to my feet and shimmy my hips.

"What on earth are you doing?" she asks.

"What's it look like I'm doing?" I twirl around, my arms waving wildly like one of those dancing wind socks.

"Do you really want me to answer that?" Marjorie narrows her eyes, and Delilah lifts her head, regarding me through slits.

"Oh, come on. Humor me." I cast an imaginary fishing line out to her, and she huffs, but to my surprise, she allows herself to be reeled in.

She bunny hops toward me, and we dissolve into peals of laughter as we dance together. For a moment, we are suspended in time, just two girls having fun.

chapter forty-seven

ONCE I'M THOROUGHLY SCRUBBED AND EXFOLIATED, I WRAP myself in a fluffy robe so I can get ready.

"A little to the right," Marjorie instructs as I hover another bobby pin over the elegant updo I've crafted with her help. "For heaven's sake. Your *other* right."

Marjorie acts as my eyes behind me, guiding where each pin should go as I study my reflection in the bathroom mirror.

"Here?" I ask, and she nods before I slide the thin strip of metal in.

She clasps her hands together in front of her as her lips turn up. "It's perfect, Kathryn. Now, don't forget the hairspray."

I grab the bottle from the counter, shielding my face as I aim the nozzle, releasing enough mist to form a light fog inside the small space.

"Spectacular," Marjorie says, and I have to agree. My chocolate hair has been swept off my neck, leaving my bangs and a few loose tendrils framing my face.

My phone rings from where it sits on top of my cosmetics

bag, and I smile when I see Jude's name flash across the screen.

"It's him," Marjorie chirps. "I'll bet he's about to leave. But there's still so much to be done, including your makeup, so hurry. No dillydallying."

"Relax. I've got plenty of time," I say as I answer the call on speaker. "Hey, babe. You heading out?"

He responds with a huff. "There's been a slight hiccup."

Marjorie's eyes widen with alarm, but I try to keep my cool.

"What's going on?"

"My mom just informed me the hospital paid for a limo to pick my parents up," he explains. "And now she wants me to ride with them. Our wires got crossed somewhere along the way, and I guess she assumed you'd already be here."

I groan inwardly. "What time will the car be at your place? Maybe I can make it to you by then."

"How?" Marjorie hisses. "You will *not* be doing your makeup while driving, missy. That's a safety hazard."

"Six thirty," he answers. "But it's already a quarter after five."

"Damn. There's no way. I'd be cutting it too close. I haven't even done my makeup yet." I pull my bottom lip through my teeth and bite down. Jude's mom may or may not end up liking me, but at the end of the day, that doesn't matter. What *does* matter is he has a mother who loves him and wants to share something special with him. I'd give anything to have moments like this with my own mom, and I'm not about to let him lose precious time with her. "Why don't you ride with your parents, and I'll meet you there?"

Marjorie raises her brows.

"Are you sure?" she and Jude ask in unison.

"Listen to me," I reply. "This is an important night for your mother. You should take the limo with her and your dad. Tonight is about your mom. It's not a big deal for me to drive to the gala on my own so you can spend a little more time celebrating her," I insist. "Seriously. Don't even worry about it."

There's a brief pause before he speaks again. "Have I told you that I love you?"

I chuckle. "You might have mentioned it a time or two."

"Thank you," he says. "For being so understanding. For just…being you."

A grin spreads over my face. "Now, I better go so I can finish getting ready, but I'll see you in just a bit, okay?"

We say goodbye, and I end the call as Marjorie regards me with soft eyes.

"What?" I ask.

"Nothing," she answers. "I'm just proud of the way you handled that. I know you're insecure about what his mother will think of you, and you could have easily allowed your imagination to run wild over this, but you didn't."

"You told me it's going to be a magical night, and I'm just choosing to believe you," I say with a shrug. "Besides, I don't want him missing out on special moments with his mom for me. Jude and I will have plenty of time together."

"That you will." She gives me a resolute nod. "All right. We're down to the wire. You better hop to it."

I grip the counter and blow out a breath, trying to settle my growing nerves. What if this *was* his mother's way of making it so I couldn't arrive with them? What if—

"None of that," Marjorie interrupts, as if reading my mind. "Tonight is going to be perfect."

chapter forty-eight

"You look beautiful, Kathryn." Marjorie's gaze is fixed on me as I do one last twirl in front of the mirror a few moments later. The merlot-colored gown hugs my curves, creating a sleek silhouette. Marjorie's diamonds dangle from my ears, my lips painted a deep oxblood. "Absolutely stunning. Jude will be speechless."

"You think so?" I take in a shaky breath through my nose, already imagining the moment he'll see me. We'll lock eyes from across the crowded room, and the rest of the world will fade into the background, leaving only us. He'll introduce me to his family, we'll hit it off, and we'll be there to witness his mother receive her award.

"Of course, he will," she insists. "Look at you. You're radiant." Her eyes fall to the clock on my bedside table. "And you're about to be late if you don't get going."

"Right," I say, spinning on my heel to grab my purse and overnight bag from the bed beside Delilah's sleeping form.

"Do you have everything?" she asks. "Keys, lipstick, phone, a small compact?"

"Yep. It's all in here." I hold up the black beaded clutch in my hand and start for the foyer, my heels clicking against the hardwoods.

Marjorie practically floats beside me. "I went to many a gala in my day, and they were always such elegant affairs. You'll have a wonderful time."

My mouth goes dry as I pause in the doorway. "I will, right?"

"You have nothing to worry about," she promises. "Now go and have fun. I'll expect a full report tomorrow."

I nod. *Tomorrow.* After I've told Jude the truth about Delilah and Marjorie. Maybe he'll even come home with me, and we can tell her about it together. Jude won't be able to hear Marjorie, but I can be the go-between, and I'm sure she'll pop a light bulb or two.

"Go on, now," Marjorie urges with a smile, gently shooing me away. "Watch your step going down the walkway. You don't want to twist an ankle in those shoes."

"Okay, okay," I reply with a chuckle, opening the door. "I'm leaving."

"Drive safe," she says. "Don't worry about a thing. Delilah and I will be just fine."

I grin. "You're calling her by name now? You're practically besties."

She narrows her eyes and points toward where my SUV is parked, and I hold up my hands.

"All right. I'm going." I lock up and head down the path to my car, tossing my purse and backpack inside. Marjorie watches, waving from the window as I start the ignition and back out onto the street.

My fingers drum along the steering wheel to the beat of an old Mariah Carey Christmas song on the radio, and I spend the forty-minute drive to the hotel where the gala is being held imagining Jude and I dancing the night away, surrounded by twinkle lights and rich greenery.

Is there dancing at these kinds of things? It seems like there should be dancing.

I picture us dining with his folks at a table covered with crisp linens, drinking holiday-themed cocktails while laughing at his dad's jokes, then cheering his mother on when she takes the stage. If all goes well, this could be the beginning of a wonderful relationship between Jude's mom and me. Before long, we'll be getting pedicures together and having lunch after spending the morning antiquing.

My stomach flips as I pull up to The Hermitage Hotel, parking in a neighboring lot. People in fancy attire are exiting Ubers and strolling along the sidewalk. My breath forms small clouds as I head toward the building decorated with lights and slim Christmas trees. A sleek black limo pulls up in front of the building as I near the edge of the property, and my heart lurches when I spot Jude climbing out of it, smoothing the lapels of his tux.

I stop in my tracks, drinking him in. He's so handsome, he could easily be the lead in a rom-com or a prince or someone equally dapper and debonair. I'm about to call out to him and wave when he turns back toward the car and extends his hand. I'm expecting to see his mother, but the warmth drains from my face when Lauren steps out in a shimmering navy gown. Her blond hair cascades over her shoulders in loose waves as she stumbles slightly, only to be caught by Jude's waiting arms.

I squeeze my eyes shut and open them again, hoping the scene unfolding in front of me is the product of a lucid nightmare and not my reality.

Lauren waits at Jude's side as he helps his mother from

the car. She's wearing a lovely black dress and a grin that tells me she's clearly thrilled to have the two of them together again, at last. My hand presses against my chest in a weak attempt to soothe the all-encompassing ache spreading through my body.

This is what his mother wanted all along. *This* is the reason for the last-minute change in plans, asking Jude to ride with the family. She orchestrated the entire thing, and Jude played right into her hands—and straight into Lauren's arms. This, after I brushed off what happened this morning when she stopped by our table at brunch. When Lauren said she'd see Jude at the gala later, did she already know this was coming? Her nice-girl persona was all an act to disarm me, to make me think she wasn't trying to sink her claws into him. Have they been talking behind my back all this time?

Jude smiles down at Lauren, and it's all I can do not to scream. How could he just forget me like this? Why wouldn't he at least send me a text to warn me Lauren was riding with him? The answer steals my breath as though a bucket of cold water had been dumped over my head. *Because he didn't want me to know.*

My vision blurs as I back away—from the building, the limo, and from Jude and Lauren in her perfect dress. Every hope I had shatters when she says something in his ear, and they laugh together like old lovers. I dig my fingers into my clutch so hard I snap a thread, sending beads falling to the pavement.

"Watch out," a man says when I accidentally bump into him.

"Sorry," I choke out before spinning on my heels and sprinting back toward the parking lot.

How? How could he do this to me? I trusted him. I loved him.

Love him…

Cold sweat beads along my hairline, and I shove my bangs off my face. My mind whirls, the world turning at a dizzying speed.

How did I let myself believe this would go any other way? I was never going to be good enough for him because I've never been good enough for anyone.

The air that had felt alive with magic moments before is suffocating me now, and my temperature is rising, despite the cold. I don't look over my shoulder. I can't. I've seen enough.

There will be no glass slippers left in my wake, only a few glittering beads and the pieces of my broken heart. I fumble for my keys with shaking hands, dropping the heap of metal on the ground in front of the driver's side of my SUV.

"Dammit," I cry, snatching them up and hitting the fob. My breaths come sharp and fast as I wrench the door open and slip inside, tossing my purse onto the seat beside me, the contents spilling out everywhere. My overnight bag taunts me from the floorboard, and I grab it, hurling it into the back with a thud.

My cheeks burn as I throw my car into gear, desperate to get away from downtown and the holiday lights, out of this stupid dress. I don't chance a glance at The Hermitage until it's in my rearview. The limo is gone, along with the dreams I held for me and Jude and his family. But they were never real, never more than childish, naive fantasies. All I want is to get home to Marjorie. She'll know what to do.

chapter forty-nine

MY MIND GOES NUMB ON THE WAY HOME, MY THOUGHTS congealing in a haze of darkness that matches the inky black sky. I barely remember how I got here when I pull into the drive moments later and head inside.

"Kathryn? What are you doing here?" Marjorie asks when I burst through my front door. "Are you okay? Have you fallen ill? Why aren't you at the gala? Where's Jude?"

I can't answer her barrage of questions because this godforsaken dress is squeezing all the oxygen from my lungs like a corset made of iron. The door slams shut behind me as I kick off my shoes, already reaching around my body to locate the zipper. All sense of modesty flies out the window when I have the thing wrenched halfway down my chest as I storm to my bedroom.

"What's going on?" Marjorie averts her gaze as I strip the gown the rest of the way off and take a big gulp of air, yanking my dresser drawer so hard I nearly pull it off the track.

"He was with *her*," I manage around the white-hot pain burning my throat, tugging on a sweatshirt and sweatpants.

"Who?" she asks. "His mother?"

"Lauren," I wail.

"What? Why was she there?"

My eyes burn as I kick the dress into the closet. "I don't know, but she rode in the limo with Jude and his mom."

She gasps. "What? No…That can't be."

"It can, and she did," I say as I shuffle over to the bed and crawl under the covers.

"I don't understand. What happened?" She frowns as I pull the comforter up to my chin and describe the whole scene like it was straight out of a horror movie.

Marjorie gives a slight shake of her head. "But Jude…he wouldn't do this. He couldn't. His mother…It has to have been her doing. Or *that awful girl*. I'm sure she manipulated the situation."

I snort. "Well, Jude didn't exactly seem to be bothered by it, so I can only blame them so much."

She opens her mouth, then closes it again before asking, "Has he tried to call you? Text you? Anything?"

"I…I don't know." I sigh. "Everything in my purse fell out, and I think my phone slid under the seat. But what difference does it make? There's no mistaking what I saw."

"Why didn't you go talk to him?" she demands. "Ask him what on earth he's doing?"

I let out a sardonic laugh. "And be humiliated there in front of perfect Lauren and his mother? In front of everyone on the sidewalk? It's bad enough he just *forgot* to tell me his ex-girlfriend was riding with them."

"Maybe he didn't know."

"Well, he had to once he got in the car," I counter. "He *knew* I felt insecure, especially after what happened this morning. And you mean to tell me he couldn't send me a text?

Something to give me a heads-up? He was hiding it, Marjorie."

"That part *is* damning." Her lips settle into a rigid line. "I just…I can't believe this. How could he betray you in such a way?"

"Pretty easily, it turns out." I can't get the image of him smiling at her out of my mind, like they were sharing some sort of secret. "How am I ever supposed to look at him again? How can I sit beside him at work?" I burrow deeper beneath the covers, wishing I could disappear.

Marjorie sits on the edge of my bed, her hand hovered over my side as though she wants to comfort me but remembers she can't. I would give anything to be able to sink into her arms, but I hug one of the pillows instead as she watches with pitying eyes. There's a small meow from the floor before Delilah jumps onto the mattress, curling up beside me.

"I don't know what to say," Marjorie says finally. "I'm so sorry. You didn't deserve this."

"The worst part is, I'd started to convince myself this could be real. That what Jude and I have…what we *had*…was real." I squeeze the fluffy cotton, but it does nothing to dull the throbbing in my chest. "I almost thought I could be good enough to make him stay."

She releases a soft breath, placing her palm against her heart. "What do you mean? You *are* good enough. You *are* worth staying for, and if Jude doesn't see that—"

"It's not just Jude," I sob. "It was Nick. It was my father. I'm always one flaw, one wrong move away from losing everyone I care about."

"That's not true, Kathryn. You have Dennis, Becca, and Eddie," she says. "And you have me."

"Until you're gone too."

Memories I kept locked in a drawer come flying out, swarming like angry bees: Sitting in the funeral home alone after my grandmother died of a heart attack and picking out her urn, when I still haven't picked out a couch for my shitty apartment. The smell of antiseptic and hospital cafeteria food while my dad talks to a doctor about my mom after her car accident. Overhearing words like *blunt force head trauma* and *ventilator* and being too young to know what they mean, but old enough to understand they aren't good. Pouring my dad a bowl of Cheerios every day before I get on the school bus, only to come home and find them untouched.

"Don't you get it? Everyone leaves. *Everyone.*"

Whether they intend to leave or not, they always do. They either go willingly or life rips them from me. My mom and grandmother left me in an instant, but my father left me one day at a time, until the morning he dropped me off at my grandmother's the summer I turned fourteen. He told me to take my things upstairs, then I heard hushed voices, followed by the bang of the old screen door. I ran to the window, just in time to see his old pickup truck pull out of the dirt drive. Then, years later, Nick disappeared from my life in much the same way my father did. Conversations became shorter, goodnight kisses forgotten. And just like that, love faded to dust.

"Sweetheart," Marjorie begins, her voice breaking. "I know it all feels…impossible right now, but I have to believe there's a reason, some sort of explanation for all this."

My words get lodged in my throat, and all I can manage is a strangled sob.

There *is* an explanation—a simple one, really. I am not enough. And for those who love me in spite of that fact, *love* will never be enough to bind them to me. Life will ultimately steal them away.

"It's all right, sweet girl," she says softly. "Let it out. I'm here."

She repeats it like a mantra as I shrink into myself, growing smaller and smaller. The world becomes fuzzy, the edges of my vision going dark, until all that's left is her voice.

"I'll always be with you. You can count on that."

chapter fifty

"Wake up…Kathryn, darling. You need to get up. Jude's here."

"Huh?" Jude's name makes me sit up straight. I rub behind my ear, where Marjorie's diamond has been digging into my skull like a small boulder, while Delilah squints at me, annoyed I've ruined a perfectly good nap.

A loud knock echoes through the house, and Marjorie's tone is more urgent now.

"The door. Jude is at the door."

Jude. My Jude who isn't really mine. Not anymore.

I'm on my feet in an instant, starting for the foyer, the feel of the cold hardwoods against my skin jarring me back to life.

Jude's shouts are muffled by the walls. "Kat, open up. Come on. I know you're in there."

"Shit," I whisper, scrubbing my hands over my face. "How long was I asleep?"

"I don't know," Marjorie answers. "Couldn't have been more than a few minutes."

When I got home earlier, I hadn't been concerned with grabbing my things or calling Jude to let him know I wouldn't be coming. Hearing his voice would have done nothing but poured salt into an already gaping wound. I was too devastated to speak to him then.

But now…now I'm not just hurt. I'm *pissed*.

I fling open the door to find him pushing his fingers through his hair. He's even more handsome up close, and the sight of him standing there, his forehead pinched with worry, is enough to take my rage down a notch or two. Then I want to yell at myself for being so quick to fold.

He covers his mouth with his hand, raking it down his jaw. "You're okay," he says before releasing a shuddering breath and stepping inside. "Jesus Christ, I called you a hundred times. Are you sick?"

He steps inside, and I shut the door but don't stray far. "No."

"I'm going to give you two a moment. Try to keep calm. Give him a chance to explain," Marjorie urges before disappearing back down the hall.

"Are you hurt?" he asks, eyes searching my body for some sign of obvious injury.

I fold my arms over my chest. "Depends on your definition."

"What does that mean?" His brows furrow as he shakes his head. "What's wrong?"

I try to keep my expression stoic but fail miserably when my nose begins to burn, and my bottom lip starts to quiver.

Dammit.

"Honey, what is it?" he asks, placing his hands on my arms. "What happened?"

"You did," I manage, though my words shake. "And I let myself believe that meant something. That *I* meant something to you."

He blinks as his head jerks back. "You do, Kat. You're everything to me."

There's a high-pitched ringing in my ears, like an alarm that won't turn off. My pulse pounds so hard, I feel the vein in my neck throb.

"I saw you," I cry. "I was walking up to the hotel, and your limo pulled up."

His arms fall limply to his sides, then he closes his eyes on a sigh.

"That's right. I saw you with Lauren." The scene plays out in my mind again, and I wince. The moment he took her hand, the smile they shared, tattooed on my brain. "Getting out of the limo together."

He scrubs his hands over his face. "Whoa. Hold on a second."

"Your mother did that on purpose, didn't she?" I ask, not pausing long enough for him to answer. "Was Lauren in on it too? God, you *knew* I felt weird about her and the dynamic between her and your mom. And you *especially* knew how freaked out I was after the way you acted this morning at brunch. Then you didn't even bother to send me a text to warn me they'd concocted some sort of scheme to get you and Lauren back together?"

"Wait. What?" He holds out a hand to stop me from going any further. "You've got this wrong. It isn't what you think."

"Did Lauren ride with you?" I counter.

"Yes, but—"

"Then it's *exactly* what I think," I snap.

"No," he says with a light chuckle. "It's really not."

His laughter makes heat rise up my chest. "I saw you take her hand and help her out of the limo. I saw you smiling together, like you were both in on some inside joke."

"Will you listen to me for a second?" Jude's volume rises. "Yes, Lauren rode with us, but so did four other people."

My thoughts come screeching to a halt. "What?"

Jude nods. "Yeah. My mom wanted everyone important to her to ride together, so she asked my aunt, her head nurse, her assistant, the chief of surgery, and Lauren."

It doesn't matter. Just because all those other people were there doesn't mean this wasn't a ploy of his mother's to put the two of them back together.

"Then why didn't you tell me when you realized she would be going with you?" I fire back.

He grits his teeth and swallows hard.

"You were hiding it," I say somberly, not as an accusation but as a sad fact. "You didn't want me to know."

He throws up his hands. "You're right. I wasn't going to tell you, at least not until later."

"And why not?"

"Because of *this*," he shouts, gesturing between the two of us. "Because I know you're insecure, and I get that, but I also know you have no reason to be."

"How can you say that?" I choke out. "How can you—"

"Delilah! Cat! No!" Marjorie's shrill voice interrupts me, followed by a loud meow as Delilah appears at our feet. Jude's gaze falls to where she's now weaving figure eights between his legs.

Oh no. No, no, no, no, no. This isn't happening.

Marjorie appears at my side, wringing her hands. "I'm so sorry, Kathryn. I tried to stop her."

"Did you…did you get a…" He crouches down to get a closer look, running his fingers along her back. "You got a new cat?"

"I…uh…no. I didn't," I sputter.

I grip my hair, tugging at the scalp. "It wasn't supposed to happen this way. I had this whole thing planned out."

"What thing?" he asks, tilting his head. "What are you talking about?"

My reply comes out strangled. "I never wanted you to find out like this."

"Find out what?" His eyes widen with awareness, falling to the cat peering up at him. "This…this is Delilah?"

I suck in a breath. "Jude, let me explain."

He stands, pressing the heels of his hands to his forehead. "What the hell, Kat? You told me she was *dead*."

Tomorrow. I was going to tell him tomorrow before everything went so wrong. How did it go so wrong?

My palms sweat, my body beginning to tremble. Why didn't I just tell him the truth?

"Jude, please…" I reach for him, but he pulls away.

Away, away, away.

Away from me.

Spots cloud my vision.

"Listen to her. She lied for me," Marjorie says, her voice pleading directly in his ear, but of course, he can't hear her. "This whole thing started because of me."

I look at her through glassy eyes. *It's not your fault. It was never your fault.*

"Who does this?" Jude backs away as though he can't stand to be near me. "Who lies about their cat being dead?"

Me. I did. And it was a stupid, *stupid* lie. One that never needed to go this far. It didn't have to end this way. Why didn't I tell him the truth when I had the chance? Before this lie could grow wings and fly away from me, making it impossible to catch.

My shoulders slump forward, and I bring my arms around

myself. Because deep down, I feared this reaction, no matter when I told him the truth, and I didn't want to give him a reason. A reason to leave. But I was always going to. It's what I do.

"I'm so sorry," I rasp. "I didn't mean to—"

"To lie to me for the last two months?" he shoots back, aiming right for my heart. "To accuse me of what—cheating on you? Not giving me a chance to explain? For making me miss seeing my mother get her award because I was sick with worry about you?"

"Jude, please," I beg. For him to listen, to stay, to not stop loving me. "There's a reason—"

"I don't care," he says, moving toward the door. "I don't want to hear it. This is messed up."

I start after him, but he hisses, "Don't. Just…don't."

"Sweetheart, I'm so sorry." Marjorie is next to me in an instant, her voice the only thing keeping me from floating away.

Numbness spreads through me as I watch him walk out of my house, out of my life. My feet are anchored in place as the web of lies I spun unravels, leaving broken threads pooled around me.

chapter fifty-one

"THIS IS ALL MY FAULT." I'M CURLED UP IN BED WITH Marjorie and Delilah at my side, the only light in the room coming from the silvery slices of moon peeking around the curtains. I swipe at my cheeks, releasing a shaky sigh. My initial panic has settled into dazed acceptance as I stare blankly ahead. "I ruined everything."

"Now, hold on a second. Jude isn't completely blameless here," she insists, her gaze fixed on me. "He still should have made you aware of what was happening."

"But *I* should have trusted him. I should have known he wouldn't do something to hurt me." My voice trembles. "He's never going to speak to me again."

"He will," she promises. "Give him time."

"I don't think that's going to help. I really screwed up." Not only did I accuse him of lying to me, but I did so after deceiving him for months about Delilah. "I never should have doubted him. If I hadn't assumed the worst, I could have still told him the truth tomorrow, and maybe we wouldn't be in this mess." Maybe he would have received the news about

Delilah better if I'd told him as planned, especially once he understood why I lied to him in the first place.

"I understand why you did, though," she says gently. "That's no disrespect to Jude. But Kathryn, our experiences shape us, for better or worse. You've been through so much. The losses you've suffered…they'd make it hard for anyone to trust."

I give an emphatic shake of my head. "That's no excuse."

Her eyes are trained on me with a tenderness I don't deserve. "I'm not saying it's an excuse, but it *is* a reason to give yourself a little grace."

But I can't. I *can't* give myself grace when I've single-handedly pushed away one of the most patient, loving people I've ever known because of my own insecurities. The moment Jude mentioned his mom's connection to Lauren that afternoon at Billy's, the day we shared our first kiss, a seed had been planted in my brain. In the weeks since, I allowed my worries to get the better of me until they grew gnarled, tangled roots. It didn't matter how amazing Jude was, because all I could see when I looked at him were the shadows of everything I'd lost before.

"He missed his mother's big night because of me. I accused him of *cheating*." I drop my gaze to Delilah who is snuggled beside me and run my fingers through her fur. "Why didn't I just go talk to him at the hotel? Give him a chance to explain?" My heart aches when I close my eyes, picturing the moment I saw Jude and Lauren together. The culmination of my worst fears.

"Because you were hurting. Because you've been hurt so badly before." Marjorie leans closer. "It's hard to believe there are people who won't abandon you when that's what you know."

My chin drops to my chest and I avert my gaze, too ashamed for even Marjorie to see me like this. Every weakness and flaw I own is on full display, my past traumas flashing like bright neon lights while I desperately search for the plug to pull, banishing them back into the darkness inside me where they belong.

"Sweetheart, look at me," she urges, lying beside me.

When I finally do, she continues. "We're a lot alike, you and me. We both let other people's actions decide how we're going to exist in the world. It took meeting you for me to finally realize that not everyone has ulterior motives or something to gain. That not everyone will walk away if I'm not perfect, if I'm just...*me*." She pauses, giving me a sad smile. "Before you came into my life...my *afterlife*, I thought relationships were transactional, that if I wasn't benefiting someone, I was no longer valuable. But you saw my worth when I had nothing to offer."

Her face is hidden by the wall of tears that forms in my eyes. It's easy to love Marjorie. Yes, she drives me crazy sometimes. But she's *my* kind of crazy. She's my favorite person to talk to and have a girls' day with. She just *gets* me in a way no one else does.

"You've given me more than you can ever possibly know," I say.

She nods, moisture clinging to her lashes. "So have you. That's why it hurts to see you being so hard on yourself."

"I don't deserve anyone's pity." The darkness that lives inside me grows, spreading like a virus, until every cell of joy has been driven from my body.

"You don't have my pity, darling. You have my understanding," she says. "Because people like us don't break overnight. We're too strong for that. It happens one crack at a time until we're so fractured we don't recognize ourselves anymore."

"I think I'm too broken to be fixed," I whisper.

"You don't need to be fixed, Kathryn. You need to be *loved*, cracks and all." She places her hand beside mine on the mattress between us. "But you have to let people love you, which means you allow them to see you. Not just the good, the pretty, or the easy parts, but every broken piece that makes up the beautiful mosaic you are."

"What if it's too late?" I attempt to swallow the lump in my throat. "For me and Jude? What if he doesn't want to hear anything I have to say?"

"Then he isn't the right person for you," she answers. "And I know how painful that is to hear. I do. But if that's how this all shakes out, then you move forward without him."

I tug the comforter tighter around me, warm despite the chill that comes from lying in such close proximity to Marjorie.

"Then what?" I ask. "Then what do I do?"

Her emerald gaze is rueful, haunted. "You let this serve as a lesson that you can't hide from the past or the things that make you who you are. If you don't make peace with them here on earth, they'll follow you to the grave."

Her words land heavy, like stones, weighing me down. She knows firsthand because she's still here, tethered to this world because of some unfinished business.

"You're exhausted," she says softly. "You should try to rest."

She's right. I'm physically and emotionally wrung out. My muscles are weak from years of carrying this baggage, and I don't want to carry it alone anymore.

"Will you stay with me?" I ask. "Until I fall asleep."

Her voice is the lighthouse in the middle of my storm.
"I'll be right here. Always."

chapter fifty-two

As promised, Marjorie is still beside me the next morning as the sun bathes my room in a golden glow. My head pounds, the events of the night before rushing back, colliding in my mind like bumper cars.

Marjorie is perched on the side of the bed, watching me closely. "How are you feeling?"

"Hungover," I answer, because I'm at the age where an emotional breakdown renders the same results as a tequila binge.

"You need to drink some water," she says as I slowly sit up and massage my temple.

"There's water in coffee."

She narrows her eyes in disapproval. "A glass of water, Kathryn. *Before* you have your coffee."

I groan and rise to my feet with Marjorie trailing behind as I pad into the kitchen where Delilah is already waiting by her food bowl.

"I'm coming," I assure her, pulling a small glass down from the cabinet and filling it with water from the fridge. I take a gulp to soothe my parched throat before setting it on the bar.

Delilah chirps and weaves around me as I move to the pantry to get her food before dumping it into her bowl.

"You should check your phone," Marjorie urges. "Just in case Jude sent you a message."

My stomach twists. "I doubt it." But there's enough hope left inside me that I slide on the slippers I keep by the front door and head outside to gather my things from the car. I don't hesitate before checking the device, my chest aching when I see the only missed calls and messages I have are from Jude *before* he arrived at my house yesterday evening. I listen to the three frantic voicemails he left while en route to me as I trudge back inside, guilt clawing at me with every step.

"Anything?" Marjorie's eyes are hopeful as I stumble back into the kitchen and dump my things on the counter.

"Nothing since last night when he was on the way here." My shoulders sag. "I should call him or at least send him a text. Tell him how sorry I am and try to explain."

"I think the best thing you can do right now is give him space," she says. "He needs time to cool off."

I nod. The thought of hearing his voice makes me ache with longing, but I can't. Not yet.

Pushing him to talk to me isn't going to do any good. He's angry and hurt and for good reason. I want to apologize again and begin to untangle this web, but I have to do it when he's in a place to hear it.

Her lips curve into a faint smile. "Just not *too* much space." A shadow passes over her face, and I know she's thinking of John Abernathy. The space she gave him stretched into a lifetime because telling him the truth became harder than letting him go. But I can't let that happen with Jude. *I won't.*

"Yeah, you're right." But what if Jude never wants to see or speak to me again? I swallow the thought and begin readying the coffee, adding a pinch of cinnamon and nutmeg to the grounds before setting it to brew. I close my eyes as it starts to percolate and imagine him sliding his arms around me, his morning scruff tickling my neck.

My phone pings and I lunge for it, my heart sinking when I see a text from Dennis instead of Jude.

Hope everything's going okay. ✌ I'm ready to help you explain things to Jude however I can. Just say the word and I'll be there.

"It's Dennis," I say. "He was going to be here when I told Jude about you today."

"Yes, I remember." She sighs. "I suppose you should let him know that won't be happening after all."

I start to text back but stop, my thumbs hovering over the screen.

"What is it?" Marjorie asks.

I chew the inside of my cheek for a moment as I stare down at the message. "Maybe I won't be telling Jude today, but there *are* still people who deserve to know."

Her eyes widen. "Becca and Eddie?"

"I can't keep lying to them," I reply. "I don't *want* to."

Marjorie steps closer to me, mouth turned down. "I can't help but feel responsible for this. You never would have lied about Delilah if I hadn't insisted on going to work with you."

"If it hadn't been Delilah, it would have been something else," I say. "I was too afraid to tell them the truth about you because I didn't think they'd believe me." My brain was always ready with a host of reasons why the people in my life would leave, and this definitely fit the bill.

She steeples her fingers. "Do you think they will now?"

"Honestly? I don't know," I admit with a shrug. "They might not. But it doesn't matter because it's the truth. *You* are part of my truth, and I'm sharing that no matter what."

"You're certain about this?" she asks, narrowing her eyes.

"Nope," I reply. "Not even a little. But I think I have to do this. You said last night that I can't keep hiding, that I have to let people see me." I exhale and drop my shoulders back. "Who better to start with than Becca and Eddie?"

"This is a big step, though," she says. "I just want you to be sure."

"I am." The response comes out with more conviction than I feel. "They're two of my closest friends, and if I can't be honest with them, who *can* I be honest with? They've been by my side this long…I just have to trust they'll stay there."

"All right. Then you have my full support."

I open a new text, adding Becca and Eddie as recipients before typing out a message, asking them over for dinner because I have something important to discuss. It doesn't take long for them to agree because they know I wouldn't make such a last-minute request without a significant reason. I also let Dennis know about the change in plans, and he's ready to assist however he can.

"They'll be here at six." I blow out a breath and shake out my hands, already questioning my decision. There's no turning back now. But I *know* this is the right thing to do, and it's what I should have done weeks ago.

She nods. "What do you need from me?"

"Just be yourself," I say. "And be *loud.*"

Her brows lift, and her mouth quirks. "That, I can do."

chapter fifty-three

I introduce Becca and Eddie to Dennis, then start from the beginning, the words tumbling out of me with the speed of a race car lurching ahead once the checkered flag has been waved. With every new piece of information I give them, I find myself talking faster and faster, the relief of finally telling the truth fueling me like gasoline. I tell them about finding the urn, how I met Marjorie, how she came with me on every *Purrfect Match* date. I barely touch my food as I explain why I told them the urn belonged to Delilah—because the truth was far stranger than fiction.

"You…see dead people?" Eddie leans forward and folds his arms over my dining table, pushing the remnants of his pizza out of the way after dinner. He looks to his right at Becca, an entire conversation spoken in a single glance.

"Just *one* dead person," I answer. "Marjorie."

"I know how it sounds," Dennis says from beside me. "When Kat first told me, I'll admit, I was…concerned. My mind jumped to the worst possible scenarios. A brain tumor. A complete mental breakdown. I consider myself a spiritual person, but this seemed…impossible." He goes on to tell them the story of that first night, the way I was able to recite the obituary he found word for word because she was speaking it in my ear. Things I knew, but had no reason to know about this deceased stranger.

Becca stares at me, unblinking, while Marjorie sits at the head of the table, waiting for her signal.

"So," Becca begins, her brows angled inward. "Delilah's...alive?"

I nod and turn to Marjorie. "Would you mind letting her out?"

Marjorie rises from her seat, Becca and Eddie follow my gaze to where she's standing.

"Of course," she replies. A few seconds later, we hear the click of my bedroom door opening, and Delilah slinks into the room. She stops in the middle of the floor, one leg extended toward the sky as she cleans herself.

"Holy shit," Becca mutters.

"We can show you more proof." The lights flicker above our heads. A bulb pops, causing Becca to yelp and practically leap onto Eddie's lap as Delilah skitters away. "I didn't tell you to do it yet," I hiss at Marjorie through gritted teeth.

She smirks as she returns to my side. "Just warming up."

"Can you hear her too?" Eddie asks Dennis, who shakes his head.

"No, but she did stay with my husband and me the weekend before Thanksgiving, and that was...*interesting*." He pushes his glasses up the bridge of his nose. "Let's just say, Marjorie has very particular taste in decor and a deep-seated hatred for birds. I may not be able to hear her, but she finds ways to voice her...*displeasure*."

A tiny canvas painting of sparrows beside us jumps off the wall and lands on Becca's plate. She's on her feet in an instant with a shriek, sprinting across the room, ducking behind the bar in the attached kitchen.

"Really?" I chide Marjorie. "It's gonna have pizza sauce on it."

She holds up her hands. "Sorry."

I sigh. *No, she's not.*

Eddie studies the portrait, then lifts his eyes to mine. "This is...this is real. You're being haunted by this woman. I don't know a lot about this stuff, but I think you might need an exorcist."

Marjorie, Dennis, and I burst out laughing, but Eddie and Becca are unamused.

I chuckle. "Trust me when I say, no one is in danger with Marjorie."

"Except your light bulbs and your glassware if she hates it," Dennis adds. "And any furniture or decorations she finds especially offensive."

Becca stands slowly but makes no effort to move, continuing to use the bar as her own personal shield.

"Hold out your hand," I tell Eddie before lifting my gaze to Marjorie. "Touch him."

He pulls back before she has the chance. "Now, hold on a minute."

I reach across the table, palm up. "Trust me, okay? Just... please. Trust me."

His jaw ticks but he places his hand on mine, then Marjorie rests hers gently atop Eddie's.

"What the..." His mouth gapes open as he flexes his fingers against hers. "That's her?"

I nod.

"Crazy, right?" Dennis asks.

"The air right here…it's cold," he says. "Like ice, but it also feels kind of like when your foot falls asleep."

"He has such strong hands," Marjorie purrs. "Tell him I said so."

"Absolutely not," I mumble before shifting my attention to Becca. "Come here. I want to show you something." I gesture toward her chair. "Marjorie will be on her best behavior," I add, giving her a stern glare.

She heaves a dramatic sigh. "If I must."

Becca steps back toward us, hugging the perimeter of the room until she finally settles back in her seat.

"I did some digging today," I say, as I pry my phone from my back pocket, unlocking it. "I was able to hunt down some old photos of Marjorie online." I turn the device toward Becca and Eddie. "This is her."

The photo is from *Nfocus* magazine, a local publication dedicated to Nashville's high-society social scene. It was taken at a Nashville Culture Club banquet in the spring of 2012. Despite it clearly being Marjorie—hair perfectly styled, signature pearl necklace, and matching two-piece skirt set— the woman in the photo hardly resembles the one I've come to love. Her eyes are lifeless, so different from the vibrancy I've seen in them during our time together.

I swipe, showing them a couple more photos I dug up in the *Nfocus* archives, including one of her and Conrad.

"That's her husband?" Eddie asks, and another bulb flickers.

"*That* is a long story," I answer.

"She's pretty," Becca remarks, head tilted. "But she looks so…sad."

Marjorie reclaims her seat at the head of the table and gives me a faint smile.

"I was," she replies as I say, "She was."

"She was here the night I came to check on you after I thought Delilah died, wasn't she?" Becca asks. "No wonder you were acting so strange."

I drag my bottom lip between my teeth and scrunch my nose. "I'm sorry. You have no idea how much I wanted to tell you the truth, but I was so scared of what you'd think."

"Did you tell Jude yesterday?" Eddie asks, rubbing his thumb over his chin. "Did it not go well?"

My mouth goes dry. "No. I didn't...I tried to last night, but..."

His expression turns troubled as he drums his fingers along the table.

I feel like I'm in the shower and the hot water has been suddenly cut off. "Why? Did he say something?"

"He called early this morning. Said he needed some time to clear his head." The words come out pained, as though it physically hurts him to have to say them to me.

I press my tongue to the roof of my mouth, trying not to cry. "Oh."

He clears his throat. "I thought you knew. I assumed that's what you wanted to tell us. That you and Jude broke up."

"You broke up?" Becca cries.

"Yes...no...I don't know," I answer.

Marjorie gives me a sympathetic nod. "Tell them the rest."

And I do. I relive my weakest moments over the last few weeks. I tell them my fears about his mother and Lauren, and I explain what happened last night with painstaking detail.

Becca frowns. "You never got to tell him about Marjorie."

"No," I admit. "I didn't know how to tell *any* of you. It started as this off-the-cuff lie I told to explain why I brought that urn to work, and then it just spiraled out of control. The longer it went on, the more nervous I got about coming clean."

"I can't believe he wouldn't even *listen* to you," Becca says. "He could have at least had the decency to hear you out."

Eddie's mouth twists. "Think about it from his perspective, though. The cat he thought was dead all this time comes waltzing in after Kat essentially accused him of lying." He lifts his shoulders and sighs. "I hate it as much as you do, but I get where he's coming from."

"He missed his mom's big night because of me," I say. "This is exactly why he and Lauren broke up. She didn't show up for things that were important to him. And then I went and did the same thing." Worse, actually, because I made him miss it too.

Becca scowls. "He has to talk to you eventually." She's going to take my side no matter what, and I love her for it.

"I hope so," I say, but that hope is dwindling now that I know he won't be at work this week. "I just...I'm sorry I didn't tell you the truth sooner. I should have. I should've trusted your friendship, but I..."

"You were afraid." Eddie reaches over the table, covering my hand with his. "You've always been scared to let people in, and I understand why."

Warmth spreads through me. "You do?"

"Of course, I do," he says. "You've been hurt. Badly. Every time I think about what your father did to you..." He trails off and squeezes my fingers. "You deserved better, and I've always wanted to give you better. I wanted to show you what it was like to have people who truly look out for you. But Kat, at some point, you've got to start trusting that not everyone is going to run off on you." His gaze holds mine. "Wild dogs couldn't keep me away from you, kid."

"Me either," Becca agrees. "Yes, the whole Marjorie thing *does* freak me out a little, but I'm never going to be freaked out enough to leave you. You could start seeing dead people all the time, and I still wouldn't go anywhere. I'd have a lot of questions, but I'd be right by your side asking them."

I chuckle, the tension in my muscles from last night slowly beginning to release.

"Jude will come around," Eddie assures me.

"Handsome *and* wise," Marjorie murmurs.

Dennis puts a hand on my shoulder. "He just needs to get over the initial shock. That man loves you. He'll listen. It might just take him a few days."

I swallow. "But I have to be prepared that he might not want to hear what I have to say. And even if he does, he might not accept it." I drop my gaze to my lap. "He might not accept *me*."

"And he'd be a damn fool," Marjorie says.

I don't know about that, but I can't pretend to be something I'm not. I can't hide pieces of myself anymore.

"For the record, it would be his loss." Becca gives me an empathetic smile.

"So, what's your plan?" Dennis asks. "How are you going to get him to talk to you?"

"I've tried to call him, but so far, no answer." My heart aches when I think about the number of times I've listened to the outgoing message on his voicemail today. "But I'll keep trying until he picks up."

"He will," Eddie promises.

"In the meantime, I think there's someone else I owe an explanation," I say. "And a really big apology."

Becca, Eddie, and Dennis exchange curious glances. Marjorie tilts her head. "Who?"

chapter fifty-four

THE STUDIO FEELS WRONG WITHOUT JUDE MONDAY MORNING, our radio family fractured because of me. I stare ahead as the outro plays and slide off my headphones.

Becca slips hers down so they loop around her neck. "You okay?"

"Nope," I answer. "Not at all."

I've barely slept or even eaten since Jude left my house, the faint blue circles framing my eyes a reminder of the harm I've inflicted on him and myself. There was one benefit to last night's insomnia—it gave me plenty of time to continue my research on John Abernathy. While Marjorie thought I was doom scrolling, I was scouring the internet for more hints and sending out a few more messages. If I can't help myself, maybe I can at least help Marjorie.

"Still no luck with Jude?" Eddie asks.

I shake my head. "Nothing. He hasn't answered any of my calls or texts."

"He will," Becca says, reaching across the round table for my hand. "Jude is one of the most understanding, patient people in the world."

"I'm afraid I might have broken us beyond repair," I admit. My belief that no one would stick around becoming its own self-fulfilling prophecy is still something I'm grappling with—the fact that Jude never really had to leave on his own because I was too busy pushing him away. "I really hurt him."

The pain on his face Saturday night still haunts me—first, when I thought he was capable of hiding something so awful from me, and then when he realized *I'd* been the one lying to him since the beginning of our relationship.

"All you can do is keep reaching out, keep trying," Eddie says. "Just give him some time."

"Have you tried to get in touch with him?" My voice wobbles. "Just to…check on him? Make sure he's all right?"

Eddie's eyes turn downward. "I did. He didn't answer my call, either. I left him a message, but I haven't heard back."

I give him a faint smile. "Thanks for trying."

"We're a family," he says, lifting his shoulders. "That's what families do. They show up for each other."

My laptop dings with a notification, and my heart lurches, settling once I see it's not from Jude. It is, however, from a young woman named Lana Abernathy. I scan the screen, reading her message.

Kat,

Wow! I know who you are. I'm a huge fan of Eddie in the Morning. *I think the man you're searching for may be my grandfather. I asked my mom, Heather, and she said he would have attended Hillsboro High around the same time as your friend. I'm attaching her number. She said she'd be happy to answer any questions you might have.*

"What just happened?" Becca asks, rolling her chair closer to mine. "Your face got all weird."

I tug on a strand of my hair, picking at the ends.

"Remember when I told you guys about Marjorie? How we've been trying to figure out what her unfinished business is?"

"Yeah," Eddie replies. "Did you find something?"

I explain what I know about John Abernathy in broad strokes in an effort to respect Marjorie's privacy, and I tell them about my search and the reply from Lana.

Becca's head tilts. "But she doesn't want you to talk to him?"

"She's afraid he won't want to hear from her," I answer. "The way we left it last was that she was considering it." I shrink back into my chair. "Which is good because I've been looking since before Thanksgiving."

Eddie narrows his eyes. "After she asked you not to?"

"I know," I say with a sigh. "I know how it sounds, but she needs this, Eddie. If she doesn't figure out what's keeping her here, she'll be stuck with me forever. No one else can see her. She can't talk to anyone else. That's no way to exist."

"So, what's your plan?" Becca asks. "How do you make this happen if she's not even sure she wants you to reach out to him?"

I wince. "I do it first, ask for forgiveness later."

Eddie gives a slight shake of his head as he chuckles. "I would *not* be trying to piss off a ghost."

"All I have to do is confirm that John wants to connect with her," I say. "Then she'll see it was a good idea."

Becca raises her brows. "And what if he doesn't?"

"Then I let it drop and pray she never brings it up because I don't want to break her heart like that." I release a slow breath. "She still loves him, even after all these years. I may not be able to fix what I did to Jude, but I might be able to fix this. And if I *can*, I owe that to Marjorie."

"You really love her," Becca says.

I worry my lip between my teeth. "Is that crazy?"

"I won't pretend that you having a ghost bestie doesn't freak me out a little, but I also think she's been weirdly good for you. She helped you get out of your own way," she says, then hesitates. "It's because of her you started dating Jude."

"Which I still managed to screw up," I remind her.

"But you *tried*," she says. "You put yourself out there. Maybe you didn't handle it perfectly, but you've been more *you* since Marjorie came along than you've been in a long damn time."

"I don't mean to bring up bad things, but have you given any thought to what happens if she *does* go into the light?" Eddie asks. "How that will affect you?"

My throat tightens. "I've been trying not to think about that because it doesn't matter. It's not about me. It's about doing what's right for my friend."

I can't picture her walking into the glow of eternity without my palms sweating and my heart racing, but it's a bridge I'll cross once I come to it. Or rather, I'll watch her cross it without me.

"So, are you going to call this Heather woman?" Eddie questions. "See if she's connected to John?"

"Yes, but I have something I need to take care of first." I push myself up from my seat. "Do you mind if I head out early? I've got to run to the florist and then I'm…" I can't even finish the sentence.

Becca leans forward, elbows on her knees. "You're really going through with it?"

I scoop my bag off the floor. "I have to. I owe her an apology."

Eddie nods. "Go on. If you need anything, you call, all right?"

"I will," I promise.

Becca rises to her feet. "Are you sure you don't want me to go with you?"

"No," I say, stepping closer to the door, squaring my shoulders with a self-assurance I don't feel. "This is something I need to do on my own."

chapter fifty-five

MY TEETH ARE CHATTERING WITH NERVOUS ENERGY BY THE time I arrive at Vanderbilt Hospital. I can barely see around the sizable arrangement of white roses and blue hyacinths I picked up on the way. The glass vase slides against my palms, and I hug it to my chest, whacking myself in the cheek with a thorn.

It takes several minutes of being passed around from floor to floor, receptionist to receptionist, before finally making it to the cardiac wing and Dr. Keller's nurse's station where a nice lady seats me inside Jude's mom's office. I'm regretting the extra coffee I drank before coming here because not only did it make me more anxious, but now I also have to pee.

I sink into one of the leather chairs, glancing around the room lined with shelves of textbooks and medical journals. Photos of her and her husband and Jude decorate the mahogany desk along with an anatomical heart paperweight. Seeing Jude's face makes my own heart feel as heavy as the brass one beside it. There's a diamond-shaped crystal perched on a wooden stand, and my chest squeezes when I read the words etched beneath her name: Franklin Albrecht Award recipient. Sun pours into the room through the floor-to-ceiling window and slices through it, casting prisms along the walls to taunt me.

I'm so lost in my own thoughts, wondering if I should even be here right now, that I almost jump when the door opens, and Jude's mom appears. Her hair is pulled into a bun, wire-rimmed glasses are perched on her nose, and she's wearing a white coat with her name embroidered below her left shoulder.

"Kat, it's so good to finally meet you. Gosh, I feel like I know you already," she says with a warm smile, and I stand with the flowers clutched awkwardly in my grasp. "What's all this?"

"Dr. Keller, hi," I reply, holding the blooms out to her. "These are for you."

"For me?" Her brown gaze widens as she takes them from me, and a pang of sadness stabs at me. It's instantly clear where Jude gets his kind eyes. She breathes in the petals and sighs. "They're gorgeous. Thank you. You didn't have to do this."

"I wanted to say congratulations and that I…" I swallow, wishing I was still holding the arrangement so I'd at least have something to do with my hands. "I'm sorry about Saturday night. About Jude missing the ceremony. It was all my fault, and I just…I'm so sorry."

Her face softens, and she nods toward the chair I'd been sitting in. "Sit. Let's have a chat."

She places the flowers on the desk, and instead of taking the seat behind it, she opts for the one beside me. Up close, she's nothing like the villain I imagined her to be. For a moment, I'm a kid again, terrified of the monsters lurking in my room, only to find out the creatures were nothing more than shadows created by my treasured stuffed animals. It's funny how different things appear in the light of day.

"Dr. Keller," I begin, but she cuts me off gently.

"Please, call me Susan."

"Right. Susan." My mouth is so parched, I consider slurping the water from the vase. "I wanted to apologize for what happened this weekend."

"What *did* happen, Kat?" she asks. "Jude was so worried when you didn't show. We all were, but the only thing he told me when he made it back for the end of the gala was there'd been a misunderstanding. He seemed upset, but I didn't want to push."

Of course, Jude had protected me, even when I didn't deserve it.

"A misunderstanding is a very generous way for him to put it," I say, my cheeks flaming with shame. "I was feeling insecure, which caused me to jump to *massive* conclusions, and I would give anything if I could take it back."

She crosses her legs, her petite frame facing me. "Do you mind telling me what was bothering you? I mean, if it's not too personal."

If she didn't hate me before, I'm certain she will once I'm finished. I drop my gaze, unable to look at her as I tell her about the vivid picture my mind painted of her and Lauren scheming and how that had been my brain's way of explaining why Jude would leave me—why I'd never be good enough. I share how my anxieties reached a fever pitch when I witnessed them getting out of the limo together and the assumptions I made that led to Jude missing her big moment.

"I'd give anything to have time like that with my own mother," I say, "and I'll never forgive myself for taking that away from you and Jude."

When I finally bring my eyes up to hers, I expect her to be annoyed, angry, or even disappointed. But what I find is understanding.

"I get the feeling you've been left before, haven't you?" she asks, and it's like she's peering into my soul, seeing parts of me I can't even reach.

"Yes." The word comes out strangled.

"Me too," she confesses. "My sister."

"Did…did she die?" I ask before I can catch myself. "I'm sorry. My mom…she died, so that's why I—"

"It's all right," she says, shaking her head. "And no, she didn't." Her pink lips turn downward. "Our parents weren't exactly the most warm and fuzzy people. Love wasn't guaranteed. It was what we earned through our accomplishments," she explains. "Beth and I were…we were best friends. Growing up in our household, we both needed a lifeline, and from the second I was born, she was mine, and I was hers. She's the oldest, which meant our parents were extra hard on her, and she…she didn't handle it well. She struggled and started getting into trouble when we were teenagers. I just wanted to help, to keep the peace, so I did everything I could to be the perfect daughter. I figured if I was good enough for the both of us, they'd give her a break."

"But they didn't?" I ask.

"If anything, it got worse. They didn't understand why Beth couldn't be more like me when even *I* wasn't anything like the version they knew." She releases a weighted breath. "Eventually, it reached a point where Beth couldn't take it anymore and she left, right after she graduated, without so much as a goodbye. She thought she was leaving our parents. And she did, but…"

"She left you too," I finish for her.

"Yes, she did. And it broke me. We didn't speak for seven years," she confesses. "At first, she didn't try to contact me because apparently, I played the role of perfect daughter so well, she thought that's who I was…who I *wanted* to be. When, in actuality, it was just how I survived. I did what I thought I had to do to protect her, and well, I also wanted to be loved."

I feel like my chest is made of glass, leaving my heart on full display. Jude's mom could tell I've been abandoned because she had been too. "But you and Beth…you're back in touch now?"

She pauses a moment. "We reconnected eventually, and our relationship is *much* better, but it was bumpy for a while. It took several years of therapy for me to finally understand that her leaving had nothing to do with me and everything to do with her doing what she had to in order to take care of herself."

Her words sink into my brain like rocks tossed into a pond. I picture my father's pickup truck pulling away from my grandmother's house, disappearing in a cloud of dirt and retreating taillights. It's so easy to see from the outside looking in that there was nothing Susan could have done differently to make her stay. Just as there was nothing I could do to make my father come back for me.

"That one incident really affected me moving forward," she continues. "In fact, not long after my husband and I got together, we went through a pretty major rough patch because of it."

"Really?" I ask. It's hard to imagine, based on Jude's idyllic description of their marriage.

"We were inseparable, but it wasn't just because we were madly in love." She leans closer, hands folded on her lap. "I thought if he was always within arm's reach, I could keep him from leaving me the way my sister did."

I blink. "So, what happened?"

"I became suspicious of everyone he came in contact with. I feared other people would see what he hadn't yet—that I wasn't good enough for him—and it would all be over," she admits. "I almost lost him. He felt I was suffocating him and didn't trust him. But it wasn't *him* I didn't trust, it was *me*."

My mouth goes dry. It's like she's inside my head.

She gives a bittersweet laugh. "I lost all sense of who I was because I was constantly changing like one of those old mood rings, shifting my colors to match whoever had me in their possession—my husband, my family and friends, even my teachers."

It's what I'd done too, up until I started seeing Jude. And even then, I had a hard time showing my flaws or doing anything to shatter the facade that I was anything less than perfect for him.

"How did you fix it?" I ask, desperate for any sort of guidance that might help me set things right.

"By no longer trying to fix anything," she answers. "Now, it wasn't always that simple. Old habits die unbearably hard, but it comes down to letting go of the need to be loved, the desire to be perfect. You have to give yourself permission to just *be*."

But what if everyone leaves? What if my worst fears come true and I lose everyone I care about? The panic in my eyes must be obvious because Susan reaches over and places her hand on my arm.

"You'd be surprised what happens when you give people a chance to truly see you—when you let them love you," she says.

There's a knock at the door, and a woman in pale blue scrubs pokes her head in the room. "Dr. Keller, you're needed for a consult."

"I'll be right there, Crystal." The nurse disappears as Susan rises to her feet, and I stand too. "I'm so sorry to cut this short."

"Thank you for taking the time to see me," I say. "And I just…I'm really sorry for what happened."

"I forgive you, Kat." She grips my shoulders. "Don't beat yourself up, all right? It was a mistake, and we *all* make them."

"Thank you," I say as I step toward the door with her on my heels.

"By the way, are you around for the holidays?" she asks. "I have some vacation days coming up, and I'd love to spend some time getting to know you."

I realize Jude hasn't told her he isn't speaking to me, but I also know it's not my place to tell her. Maybe it's not even my place to have come here at all, but I needed to make things right. Regardless of what happens with me and Jude, I owed Susan an apology.

"Oh, um, yeah, I'll be around."

"Good. I'll set something up with Jude. He can't keep you to himself forever." She squeezes my arm before setting off down the fluorescent-lit hallway.

I pull my coat tighter around me with trembling hands. I can only hope I'll have the opportunity to get to know Susan. But there's a possibility that won't happen. In fact, there's a strong possibility Jude won't be keeping me in his life at all.

chapter fifty-six

I PRESS THE CALL BUTTON ON THE ELEVATOR AND WAIT FOR the doors to slide open before stepping on. I'm so in my own head, I don't see the person already on it when I push the square for the ground floor.

"Kat? Is that you?"

I glance up to find a familiar face smiling at me. "Lauren, hi."

"You okay?" she asks. "You looked lost in thought."

"Sorry," I say as the elevator begins its slow descent. "I was a bit distracted. How are you?"

"Great, because I am officially off for two whole days." She shakes her blond hair free from its ponytail, running her fingers through the shiny strands. Even in scrubs, she's stunning. "Were you visiting Susan?"

I clear my throat. "Yeah. I wanted to drop by and congratulate her."

"That's sweet of you. I hated that you couldn't make it Saturday night," she says. "I know Jude missed you. He said you got sick? Are you feeling better?"

My fingers move over the back of my neck to soothe the

tension growing there. He didn't blow my cover with Lauren, either.

"Yeah, much," I answer before changing the subject. "So, do you have big plans for your days off?"

"I'm supposed to go to this happy hour thing with my boyfriend's work friends."

Boyfriend. Lauren is pretty, smart, and driven. By all accounts, she's a catch. Of course, she isn't still pining over an ex, even one as amazing as Jude.

"That sounds fun," I reply.

"I actually think I'm gonna cancel. I'm zonked." She pats the leather laptop bag looped over her arm. "Besides, I have about a million emails to catch up on and charts to update."

I can't help but think about the reason Jude said things didn't work out with Lauren. She didn't show up for him. I'm pulled to give her a friendly bit of unsolicited advice. I open my mouth but close it again, unsure if I'm really in any position to be doling out words of wisdom. But Lauren is a nice person, and sometimes we all need a nudge in the right direction.

"Aw, come on," I urge. "You should go. A break wouldn't hurt, right?"

She shrugs as the doors open, letting another passenger on. "Time is just so limited, you know? I feel like things have to be *really* important for me to justify taking a break."

"I get that," I concede with a nod. "And yeah, maybe it's not the most important thing you could be doing, but I bet it would mean a lot to him if you went. Work is always going to be there. But the people we care about...they won't be." Images flash through my mind like grainy home movies. Pictures of my mom, dad, grandmother, Jude, and Marjorie. "Our time together isn't guaranteed."

She studies me for a moment, brows pinched, before finally nodding. "You know what? You're absolutely right. I *should* go."

"That's the spirit."

"Thanks for the reminder. I actually have a bad habit of letting work kind of take over my life," she replies. "Susan is always telling me I need to relax more."

"She's a wise woman."

"She's great, isn't she? She's the mom I never had."

My chest constricts, my breath catching in my throat as the elevator slows to a stop and opens on the ground floor.

The mom I never had. With those five words, I suddenly understand why Susan kept such a close bond with Lauren. It had nothing to do with Jude or her desire for them to get back together. She loves Lauren and saw, for one reason or another, she didn't have a relationship, or at least not a *good* one, with her own mother. Susan understands complicated family ties and what it feels like to be abandoned. I may not know Jude's mom well, but I learned enough from our conversation today to know she's compassionate and caring. She wouldn't just cast someone aside without a damn good reason.

"We all have habits we need to break," I say as we step out onto the tiled floor of the lobby.

"I'm glad I ran into you today." She beams over at me as we stride toward the automatic doors together.

"Me too," I reply with a genuine smile. "Have a beer for me tonight."

"I will," she says before dropping her voice low. "I might even have two."

I feign shock. "Scandalous."

She laughs and tosses a wave over her shoulder as she heads out into the parking lot. "Bye, Kat."

"See ya," I call back, stepping out into the sun. I shiver as the icy December wind kisses my cheeks and scurry to my SUV, hitting the fob.

Once inside, I pull my phone from my purse and dial Heather, the woman I hope might be John Abernathy's daughter. She answers on the second ring.

"Heather, hi. This is Kat Simon. I'm—"

"Yes, I'm so glad you called," she says quickly. "I'm actually with my father now, and he'd like to speak with you."

My mouth feels full of gravel. "Really?"

"He was hoping you might be able to come by?" she continues. "He's at The Blake nursing facility in Green Hills. Listen, I know you're probably busy this afternoon, but dad is dying to meet with you."

"I could come now," I suggest far too eagerly. "I'm only about fifteen minutes from the area now."

"Oh, that's perfect," she says. "I'll text you the address."

"Thanks." I end the call, dropping the phone onto my lap as I take a deep breath.

The corners of my eyes sting, and I grip the steering wheel hard. If this goes the way I think it will, the way I *want* it to for Marjorie's sake, I'm going to lose her. She'll disappear into the light and I'll never see her again, never hear her say *Oh, for heaven's sake* or call my cat a vile beast. I'll never have a friend like her ever again in this world or the next because she's one of a kind.

I plug the address into the maps app on my phone and drop my head against the seat, preparing myself for what I'm about to do. This isn't about me. This is about Marjorie.

chapter fifty-seven

I'm not sure what I was expecting to find when I walk into The Blake, but it isn't this. The second I step through the door, I'm met with the scent of freshly baked chocolate chip cookies, which I spot immediately under a covered glass platter on the reception desk. Senior citizens and staff dressed in scrubs shuffle through the lobby toward a room with French doors where jazz music is playing. They're laughing and talking amongst themselves like they're headed to a cocktail hour or brunch with friends.

"Hello there." A young woman wearing a bright pink pantsuit greets me with a smile, hands folded on the desk. "Can I help you?"

"Hi, I'm Kat Simon," I reply. "I'm here to see John Abernathy in room 407. I believe he's expecting me."

She runs a finger down the notepad in front of her. "Ah, yep. Heather had to leave, but she let me know you'd be coming." She points toward the clipboard in front of me. "Just sign in there, and I'll send you on up."

I do as she asks, and she gives me directions to John's room, which I find with ease. My heart races as I stand outside with my hand poised to knock, knowing that once I open the door, there's no turning back. There's a very real chance Marjorie will be going into the light within a matter of days.

With a shaky breath, I rap my knuckles against the door.

"Come in," a raspy baritone calls back, and I enter. The space is larger than I imagined, holding enough space for his bed, which is covered in knitted blankets, an oak dresser, a love seat in front of the window, and a dinette. A television is mounted to the wall, and there's a mini fridge in the corner adorned with colorful magnets. Framed photos and crayon artwork decorate the white walls. The homey touches make it feel more like a studio apartment than a room in a nursing facility.

"Mr. Abernathy," I say, stepping closer when he rises to his feet in front of the small couch. "Don't get up on my account." I quickly make my way over and take his outstretched hand, dotted with age spots.

He's tall, thin, and his hair is white, but despite all that, it's easy to visualize the man he once was—rugged but handsome all the same.

"Please, call me John." He gives me a grin that I imagine won a lot of hearts back in his day, including Marjorie's. "And I was raised that when a lady enters the room, you get up."

"I'm Kat, by the way," I reply with a smile.

"Come on and have a seat." He gestures to the sofa. "Make yourself at home."

We sit, and I place my bag on the floor beside me.

"Thank you for seeing me," I say, and he dismisses the thought with a wave of his hand. "I was surprised when I found out a famous radio personality was looking for me." He leans back, threading his fingers together and resting them on his chest. "My grandkids are going to think I'm some kind of superstar."

I chuckle. "I assure you, I'm no celebrity."

He tilts his head. "I beg to differ. Heather and I listened to your show when she was here earlier. She pulled the podcast up on her phone. That Eddie fellow is a hoot."

"I appreciate that. I'll tell him you said so," I say, glancing around the room at the numerous framed photographs. "Are all of these your family?"

He nods. "I've got three children, seven grandchildren, and two great grandchildren."

"Wow. That's amazing." My eyes land on a picture hung on the wall over his shoulder of him and a woman, whom I assume is his wife, standing in the sand with a gorgeous sunset behind them. She's wearing a floral sundress and is folded against John in his denim button-down and khakis. Her fluffy bangs and tight perm make me think it must've been taken sometime in the late eighties or early nineties. They're flanked by two teenage girls and a young boy.

John's gaze follows mine, and he turns back to me with a wistful smile. "That picture is from the weekend of my fortieth birthday. We took the entire family down to St. Augustine. It was our youngest's first time seeing the ocean. Clayton. He was seven then, I believe." He pauses and sighs. "Somehow feels like yesterday and a hundred years ago. Clay's forty-two now, which is hard to believe. That was actually our last vacation as a family before my Colleen left me."

She died? "Oh. I'm so sorry."

"Goodness, I just realized how morose that sounded," he says, scratching the back of his neck. "She didn't die. She divorced me."

"Oh, well, that's…um, good?" I stifle an awkward laugh. "I mean, that she didn't die, not that she divorced you."

"Trust me, it was good that she left. We're still great friends, but as a couple, we were like oil and water. We married young after we found out Colleen was pregnant with Heather and tied the knot because we felt it was the right thing to do at the time," he explains. "Don't get me wrong. There was love between us. I loved Colleen to death. Always will. But we made better friends than we did lovers."

"I bet that was tough, even if it was the right move for both of you. Especially with having kids."

"It was, especially at first. Co-parenting—I believe that's what you young folks call it now—wasn't easy. Back then, we just called it parenting. But it was hard after I moved out. We tried the whole custody agreement thing, but we both wanted to be with the kids full time. So, I furnished our basement and turned it into a little apartment for me. I didn't need much, and this let me keep up the farm and be there with the kids while they were growing up."

I hesitate. "Did that ever get…weird?"

"Less than you would imagine," he answers. "We each had our own space, and we got to do things together as a family. It probably wouldn't work for most, but it did for us."

I want to ask so many questions, none of which are appropriate, so I settle for one that is. "You're close with your family?"

"Very," he replies.

"Do your kids visit often?"

"Every week. Each one of them has a day they've claimed as theirs," he says. "Colleen and her husband, Steve, come around a few times a month. Even after all these years, she's still my very best friend. And the grandkids come a lot too and bring the great grandbabies."

As I study the memories plastered to the walls, it's clear John is well-loved, his life well-lived.

"I could tell you stories about my family all day once you get me going, but what I really want to talk about is why you're here." John leans forward, studying me closely. "Heather told me you know Marjorie Lockwood."

"I do." I clear my throat. "I have to be honest with you, John. She doesn't know I'm here."

His brows knit together.

"She's afraid you might not want to hear from her because of the way things ended between the two of you," I say.

He hums in response, his thumb stroking his chin. "I'm not sure I can."

Was Marjorie right? Did I just go and dredge up a painful old memory for this man?

"Oh?" I squeak out. Maybe once he understands the reason she needs to connect with him, he'll agree. "Do you mind if I ask why?"

He fixes his piercing blue eyes on me. "Because the Marjorie Lockwood I knew died nine years ago."

chapter fifty-eight

John looks at me, wide-eyed, with his hand over his mouth after I finish explaining exactly how I know Marjorie, how we came across his letter that she kept, and everything she told me about him. I don't leave out a single detail, probably oversharing about my own life in the process. But I tell him enough that by the time I'm done, he's staring through me like he's seen a ghost.

"John?" I finally say after a couple moments of silence.

He blinks and shakes his head slightly. "Sorry, I…I can't believe it. How is this even possible?"

"I have no idea," I reply with a shrug. "I'm not a medium or anything. This isn't normal for me. I'm not sure I'll ever understand why I'm the only one who can see or hear her."

He leans forward, hand pressed to his chest. "I just…I thought I'd never speak to her again."

My lips tug downward. "I wish you *could* speak to her directly. You'll still have to use me as the go-between."

"But I can connect with her? You can tell me what she says? How she looks?" He rattles off the questions, his eyes dazed.

"I see and hear her as clearly as I do you," I answer.

"You really think I'm what's keeping her here?" His voice is soft and hopeful.

"It makes sense." I give him a sad smile. "I think you were the great love of her life, John. Her biggest regret was letting you go."

He pushes up from the love seat and moves to the dresser, opens the top drawer, and lifts out a long wooden box. His fingers run along the lid before he removes it and returns to the sofa.

"I tried to keep up with her over the years," he says, placing the box between us. On top is a copy of Marjorie's obituary, the very same one Dennis and I found the first night I met her. He lifts the worn clipping, revealing several others beneath it, all cutouts from various local newspapers and magazines. "I never contacted her or crossed any lines. She chose Conrad, and I never would have disrespected their marriage, but I just wanted to know she was okay. That she was happy."

I lift my eyes to his. "You never stopped loving her, did you?"

He doesn't answer, but his eyes are soft as he gives me a wistful smile. "Marjorie isn't the kind of woman you get over. She seeps into your bones until loving her becomes a part of you."

My throat grows thick. It's a romantic sentiment, but it's also true. It's hard to imagine life before Marjorie, and I know it won't be the same once she's gone. *I* won't be the same once she's gone.

"I almost went to her funeral," he confesses. "Well, technically, I was there but I never made it inside. It was at the big church over on Woodmont Boulevard. I sat outside in my truck and listened to the bells ring."

"Why didn't you go in?" I ask.

"I'd said goodbye to her a long time ago," he answers with a shrug. "By the time she died, we were virtually strangers. I didn't feel it was my place."

I tilt my head, studying him. He's longing personified, and for a moment, I can picture him outside the church, mourning the life he never got to have. "But you still showed up. Why?"

His eyes are covered in misty clouds. "I just couldn't stay away."

My nose stings, the corners of my eyes prickling as I touch his arm. "I don't think either of you could. You were on her mind in her final days." I think about the folded letter, the paper worn thin from the hundreds, maybe thousands, of times she touched it over the years. She may not have sought him out the way he did her, but she never completely let him go.

I can't help but wonder if this is how my story with Jude will end too. Will I live a whole life without him, forever yearning for the brief moment in time we shared? Will we become strangers who exist only within the confines of memories tucked away in keepsake boxes? I push the thought away, unable to let myself go there. I'm not ready to give up. Not yet.

"Will you bring her to me?" he asks, barely above a whisper. "So we can have the goodbye we deserved?"

My breath and my words shake, but the answer comes quickly, without hesitation. "I would be honored."

chapter fifty-nine

My stomach churns the whole way home that afternoon. Marjorie said only a couple of days ago that she was willing to consider the idea of speaking to John, but she didn't actually agree. I'm not sure how she's going to take the news that I went to him without her blessing.

"There you are." Marjorie is waiting for me when I step through the door. "How'd it go today? Any word from Jude?"

I shake my head. "Nothing." I even tried to call him from the parking lot of The Blake and was sent directly to voicemail.

She frowns, walking with me to the kitchen where I begin setting up some coffee to brew. "Did you end up going to the hospital to see his mother?"

"I did," I answer, pulling a mug down from the cabinet as Delilah slinks around the corner, inspecting her empty food dish with disdain. "It went better than I could have ever hoped."

"Good," she says. "She forgave you?"

I nod. "And she understood. She's kind of...been there before. She didn't hate me. In fact, she wants us to get to know each other. Of course, I'm not sure if that's going to happen because Jude may never talk to me again. He could be using his time away to find another job somewhere far away from here." *Far away from me.*

"You and Jude still have plenty of story left to tell," she assures me. "I'm certain of it. Just give him time."

"I hope he doesn't get upset that I visited his mom."

"I don't see how he could," she says. "You did the right thing. It's not like you were there begging her to get him to talk to you. You were apologizing, for heaven's sake. It takes a lot of courage to admit you were wrong, to take account-ability."

I scrape my teeth over my bottom lip as I watch the coffee begin to drip. Unable to wait, I swap the pot for my cup until it fills, then switch it back.

She looks down her nose at me. "You really are addicted, you know."

I ignore her remark and blow out a breath. "Marjorie, I need to talk to you."

"That sounds serious," she says, her brows drawing together. "Is everything all right?"

I gesture toward the living room and she follows me, taking a seat beside me on the couch. Delilah joins us in a graceful leap, settling atop the back cushion. I moisten my lips, staring into the steaming depths of my drink.

Marjorie watches me through slits. "You're acting strange, Kathryn. What's going on?"

There's no point in beating around the bush. No sense in delaying the inevitable like I did with Jude about Delilah. I'm telling the truth even when it's hard.

"I went to see John Abernathy today," I blurt out.

Her eyes widen, then her face hardens. "You did *what*?" I

open my mouth to speak again, but she cuts me off. "Why would you do that? I told you I'd give it more thought, but that wasn't permission to do it behind my back."

I hold my hands up in surrender. "I know, and I'm sorry."

"If you were that sorry, you wouldn't have done it," she argues.

"You know what? You're right," I say with a shrug. "I'm not sorry at all because it needed to happen, whether you want to admit it or not."

"How did you even do it that fast?" she asks. "How did…" She gasps, her hand rising to her chest. "You've been looking for him this whole time, haven't you?"

I bite the inside of my cheek, stalling. "Yes."

She rises to her feet, her finger jabbing in my direction. "You had no right, Kathryn. No ri—"

"He never got over you," I shout, which stops her in her tracks. "He has a box with all these clippings…pictures of you from those *Nfocus* magazines and the newspaper. He was at your funeral, Marjorie. He didn't go inside, but he was there."

Her eyes turn glossy as she sinks back onto the sofa. "He…he was?"

"He didn't think he had any right to be, but he *was*. He was there." My face softens. "He loves you. He never stopped loving you." Her jaw tightens as she gazes straight ahead, and I lean closer. "This is it—what we've been working toward. You're finally going to be able to go into the light. And maybe I shouldn't have done it without your permission, but I did it because I care about you. Because you deserve closure. You deserve to tell him goodbye the way you always wanted to."

Seconds tick by, then a minute, maybe two. I begin to worry I've messed things up between us, and it's more than I can take.

"Please," I urge. "Don't hate me. Say…something. *Anything.*"

Finally, she meets my gaze. "I could never hate you. I'm perturbed with you, yes, but I could never *hate* you." She sighs. "Because you're right. This *is* what we've been working toward, but I was so scared of John rejecting me that I didn't want to try."

"I know," I say, placing my hand on the cushion between us.

She swallows, her voice trembling as she asks, "He really wants to see me?"

I nod.

The doubt in her eyes is replaced with fierce determination. "How soon can we go?"

chapter sixty

"So, you're going today?" Becca asks after we wrap the show the next morning.

"As soon as we leave here," I answer. Marjorie came to work with me so we can head straight to The Blake to visit John. Her urn rests on the desk between me and Jude's vacant spot, a constant reminder of what I allowed to die between us. Not only did I allow it, I caused it.

Eddie leans back in his chair. "How's she feeling about it?"

"Excited," I say. "Nervous, but mostly happy to see him again."

"Eddie's such a kind man. So caring and gentle. I'll miss him once I go into the light." Marjorie is practically swooning. "And oh! That voice of his. It makes me shiver."

I stifle a laugh.

"What?" Eddie asks.

"Trust me," I say. "You don't want to know."

Once the initial shock of me admitting I went to see John wore off, Marjorie seemed…happy. The happiest she's been since she appeared in my kitchen. Going into the light was no longer just a hypothetical but a very real possibility. I listened last night as she chattered on and on about what she hopes the other side will be like. Turns out, her idea of paradise includes evenings spent dancing to crooner music, sipping tea at sunset, and an endless supply of coq au vin, chocolate mousse, and champagne. She wants to wade into crystal clear water on sandy beaches, then wrap herself in the finest silk. I smiled and asked questions at the appropriate moments but found my focus drifting not to what Marjorie will gain, but what I stand to lose.

"The whole thing sounds like a movie. Him going to her funeral and waiting outside?" Becca sighs and presses her hand to her heart. "That's the most romantic thing I've ever heard."

Marjorie beams. "It is special, isn't it?"

"Tell her I said good luck," Becca says.

"You know she can hear you," I remind her.

"Right. Sorry. I keep forgetting," she replies before glancing around the room as though Marjorie might materialize in the flesh. "I hope this reunion is everything you dreamed."

"Thank her for me," Marjorie says, and I do.

"Eddie, have you heard anything from Jude?" I ask, and he shakes his head.

"I sent a text last night to check on him, but he must be taking this time off pretty seriously."

I chip at the polish on my nails leftover from Saturday. "Do you think he might quit?"

He hedges, and I know it's because he's afraid to give me his honest answer. The thought must have crossed his mind too. "I'm not sure where his head is at the moment, but let's not jump to any unnecessary conclusions. Maybe he really just needed a break."

My eyes are drawn to his empty chair. "I hope you're right."

Marjorie watches me, her sunny expression turning cloudy.

"Give it a little more time. He's Jude. He'll come around." Becca starts gathering things and rises to her feet. "Okay, I've got a meeting with Cassie. Need anything else from me before I go, Eddie?"

"Nope," he replies. "We're all set."

Becca slings her bag over her shoulder. "I'll see you guys in the morning. Let us know how it goes this afternoon, yeah?"

I force a smile. "Of course."

She exits the room, the door shutting with a thud behind her. I start to stand, but Eddie holds out a hand to stop me.

"Do you mind hanging back a sec?" he asks with that tone of voice that tells me I'm not going to like whatever it is he's about to say. Maybe he *did* talk to Jude but wanted to tell me privately.

"Oh dear," Marjorie says, watching the way his face turns stoic. "I don't like that look."

I settle back into my chair. "What's up?"

He rounds the table and takes a seat beside me. "I had a meeting with upper management on Friday. I was going to tell you about it yesterday, but given how torn up you've been about Jude, I didn't want to make things worse. I just don't want you to be blindsided when the news comes out."

My stomach drops like it used to when my mom took me

to Opryland as a kid and I'd get on the tallest roller coaster, almost losing my lunch when we descended a hill so steep we were nearly standing.

"What news?" I ask as Marjorie steps closer to me.

"This has to stay between us," he says. "And Marjorie, of course."

I nod. "I know."

He takes a breath as though bracing himself. "The show is going to die with me, kid. They're not sure what they're going to do yet, if they'll put on another syndicated show or go to a music-only format, but as it stands, when I retire, so will *Eddie in the Morning*."

His words land like a punch, knocking the wind out of me, and an icy chill grazes my shoulder. When I glance up, I realize Marjorie has placed her hand there.

He drops his head back against the chair. "I'm so sorry, Kat. I never wanted this to happen. I've even wondered if maybe I should put off retirement for another year or—"

"No." I cut him off quickly, shaking my head. "You deserve this time. Your family deserves this."

Head tilted, he studies me. "Will you be all right?"

I swallow down the emotions pushing their way to the surface.

"You will," Marjorie promises, sensing my hesitation.

"Listen," I say, bending forward, resting my elbows on my knees. "Don't worry about me. I won't lie and say I'm not sad, but I'll be okay."

He eyes me with a worried expression.

"I mean it. As long as I still have you and Becca and…" I drop my gaze, unable to finish the sentence. "I just…I don't want to lose you, Eddie. You're like a dad to me, and it scares me when I think about not seeing you every day. I don't want us to grow apart or—"

"Hey." He leans forward and places his hand over mine. "That's not going to happen. You will never lose me, Kat. Not ever. We're still going to see each other all the time." He gets to his feet and pulls me up. "Come here." He folds me in his arms, one hand cupping the back of my head.

"I don't say it enough, but I love you, Eddie," I whisper.

"I love you too, kid." We hold each other for a moment before he speaks again. "I'm always gonna be here for you."

"I know," I say as I pull away and wipe at the dampness on my cheeks.

He grips my shoulders. "Are you good?"

"Yeah," I answer. "I'm good."

"Good luck today, Marjorie," he says a bit louder.

"Tell him thank you." She flashes me a mischievous grin. "And that I wish I knew what it felt like to have those strong arms of his wrapped around me."

I burst out laughing, grateful to her for lightening the mood.

"What?" Eddie asks. "What did that feisty woman say?"

She props a hand on her hip, flipping her hair. "You, sir, have no idea how feisty I can be."

I roll my lips inward to keep from giggling. "Marjorie has a bit of a...*crush* on you."

His brows shoot up. "Is that so?"

I click my tongue. "Yeeeah."

He hums and nods as he starts toward the door, a hint of swagger in his step. "I'm so hot even the dead ladies want what I got. I'm telling my wife she has some competition." He stops and turns around. "Margie, girl, feel free to look me up on the other side whenever I get there. I'd love to meet you."

She cocks her head. "Tell him I'll be the one wearing the pearl necklace."

I slap a hand over my mouth at the double entendre I'm sure she has no understanding of. "Um, nope. I won't be doing that."

"What'd she say?" Eddie asks, and I grin.

"That she's looking forward to it."

chapter sixty-one

We arrive at The Blake about an hour later. I cut the ignition but don't move to get out of the car, content to stretch out our remaining moments together.

"So," I begin, "this is it. Moment of truth."

She irons out invisible wrinkles on her skirt with her hands.

"Do you feel ready?" I ask, and she nods, though she still resembles a deer in headlights.

"This feels right," she says. "Like it's what I'm supposed to do."

I swallow. "Good. That's good." And it is. She's likely about to begin her journey to her final destination. Like I told her yesterday, this is what we've been working toward, what we've hoped for. But it also feels like everything is happening on fast-forward, and I'm just not ready to let her go.

She touches her necklace, twisting the pearls between her fingers.

"You know, something just occurred to me," I begin. "Ever since you learned you could change your clothes, I don't think I've seen you in the same thing twice. But you never take off your pearls. Why?"

She gives me a rueful smile. "John gave them to me for my birthday after we graduated from high school. He couldn't afford the real deal, but he found some that looked as close as he could get. He wanted me to have something nice, a token of his love."

My chest squeezes. "Marjorie…"

"The first time I took them off was the day I married Conrad because it felt like a betrayal…to John…to Conrad… maybe to myself," she admits. "I wore them less over the years because I didn't want the string to break, but I made sure I had them when I died."

"When we first met, I had no idea you'd end up being such a mush," I tease gently.

"Women like us are full of surprises, Kathryn," she says, and my heart melts into a puddle on the floorboard.

"I don't know if I'm nearly as strong as you, but if I can turn out to be even half the woman you are…I'll be doing just fine." We both grin, then sit in comfortable silence for a moment before I take a deep breath. "Ready to go get your man?"

"I am." She says it with the certainty of a bride preparing to walk down the aisle, knowing who waits for her at the end of it.

I sling the backpack containing her urn over my shoulder and head inside, stopping to sign in at the desk.

"This place is lovely." Marjorie glances around, and I wonder if she wishes she'd lived out her final days in a place like this, somewhere she wouldn't have spent so much time alone.

She takes it all in as I lead her to the elevator where we

get on and ride up to John's floor. We step out and within a matter of seconds are right outside his door. I knock and John's voice beckons us inside.

He rises to greet us, the lines on his face seeming to disappear as though Marjorie's presence alone is enough to make the years fall away.

"It's good to see you again, Kat," he says, but his gaze is glued with such intensity to the space beside me where Marjorie stands, I wonder if he can see her.

Marjorie is frozen in place, bottom lip trembling. "I never thought the day would come when we'd be in the same room again."

"She's right there, isn't she?" he asks, and I nod.

"I can feel her." There's a longing in his eyes as he reaches out, Marjorie meeting his hand with hers, and he gasps. "It's so…cold."

"That's how it is when she's close," I say as Marjorie's fingers graze his.

His breath catches. "Is she…is she touching me?"

"Yes," I confirm, and he closes his eyes. I wait, barely breathing, not wanting to make a sound and interrupt this moment they've both waited so long for.

Finally, he lowers his hand to his side. "Come, take a seat. We have so much to catch up on."

We follow John farther into the room where he takes a seat on the small sofa, and I gesture toward the vacant spot beside him.

"Go sit with him," I tell Marjorie, while I perch at the end of the bed.

She studies the photos on the wall, much like I did yesterday, and her gaze snags on the family photo from St. Augustine before returning to John.

"Why does he live here?" she asks. "He must be ill if he's in a place like this."

I relay her question to John, and he sighs.

"Congestive heart failure," he answers, pushing up the sleeve of his sweater to reveal a swollen arm. "About a year ago, it got to a point where I couldn't go up the stairs without being short of breath. Sometimes it gets a bit…scary. I don't get around so well these days."

"I thought he had a good relationship with his family," she says. "Why wouldn't they take care of him?"

"Did you consider staying with your family?" I ask.

He shakes his head. "When I made the choice to move into this place, it stirred up a hornet's nest with my kids. All of them wanted to take turns having me live with them and carting me around. But I didn't want that for them. I cared for my mother when she got sick, and I don't regret a second, but it's hard being a caregiver. It takes so much out of you, and they've got lives and children of their own. I'm lucky enough to have the means to live in a place like this. It's a gift to us all, really. We get to enjoy our time together when they visit, which they do often. They won't end up burned out, and *I* won't end up crazy because they're constantly hovering over me like a bunch of mother hens."

"And I imagine you have everything you need here," I add.

He nods. "There's always something going on—a craft night or dance party. I can choose to be social or not. All my meals are prepared for me, bland as they may be since I can't have much salt." A beat passes before he speaks again. "But I know neither of you are here to discuss the exotic cuisine The Blake has to offer."

We're not, but Marjorie clings to his every word, savoring

each syllable like it's the most beautiful thing she's ever heard. I pull the faded letter he wrote all those years ago from my purse, unfolding it carefully before handing it to him.

"We brought this to show you." She wanted him to see how worn it was from decades of wishing on stars, yearning for the life she didn't choose.

He takes it, his fingers ghosting over the page. "I remember this like it was yesterday. For weeks, I waited for a response, but it never came."

Her voice shakes. "Please tell him how sorry I am. How much I regret what I did. I thought about it…I thought about *him* every single day of my life."

I do, and he smiles, giving a slight shake of his head. "I'm just glad she's here now."

She blinks, mouth opening and closing. "You should be angry. You should be furious at me for hurting you the way I did."

"She thinks you should be upset with her," I say.

"Would it make her feel better if I yelled?" he asks. "Perhaps I can make steam come out of my ears if I try hard enough."

Marjorie is incredulous. "He's teasing me."

"You can talk directly to her," I say. "She's listening."

He chuckles softly. "I've had a lifetime to be sad, to wonder what I could have done to change the way things turned out, but the truth is, if you hadn't made that choice, I might not have my family." He pauses a beat, releasing a breath. "Besides, the what-ifs won't give us the years back that we missed. The way I see it, I can hold a grudge or I can hold on to you with what time we have left."

"I never stopped loving you," she says, and I tell him so.

"I couldn't have stopped if I tried, and believe me, I did."

His eyes turn misty as he stares ahead at the space she occupies. "But you're in my blood. You're carved inside my bones. Marjorie, you're the great love of my life, and I refuse to believe our story is over."

My vision blurs, and Marjorie stifles a sob as she touches his cheek.

His hand hovers over hers. "The fact that we're here together is a miracle. And when my time comes, I'll fight heaven and hell to get back to you. My heart will always return to you because it's always belonged to you."

"Always," Marjorie promises, sliding her fingertips beneath her lashes. "There's so much to say, so many things I want to know, things I want to tell him."

He smiles when I repeat her message. "Don't worry, darling. We'll have all of eternity to catch up."

"Yes," she chokes out. "Yes, we will."

John lifts his gaze to me. "Kat, would you mind giving us just a moment?"

I swallow hard. "Of course. Take your time. I'll be right outside."

The door shuts behind me, and I lean against the wall to the left of the frame as I give him privacy to say his goodbyes, the ones he's held on to all these years, keeping them locked away inside a box. Today, he finally gets to set them free—to set Marjorie free.

With every second that passes, my heart grows heavier with the knowledge that I'm going to lose her, but then I picture my mother, my grandmother, even my father, and I remember there's no word we're more privileged to say than goodbye.

chapter sixty-two

WE BARELY MAKE IT ONTO THE ELEVATOR BEFORE THE question pops out of my mouth. "Do you see anything yet?"

She shakes her head, hands wringing together. "No. Nothing."

I nod and give my best attempt at an encouraging smile as we make our descent. "Don't worry. I'm sure the light is coming."

My eyes don't leave her as we ride in silence to the lobby, then trudge toward the exit. Her gaze is fixed ahead as we step outside, a cold blast of air greeting us.

"Will you stop staring holes in my head, Kathryn?" she asks. "You're making me nervous."

I wince, holding up my hand as a physical blinder. "Sorry. I can't help it. *I'm* nervous."

She glares at me before returning her focus to the pavement. I try to peek at her through my fingers, which she doesn't miss. "*Kathryn.*"

"*I'm sorry,*" I say again as we approach my SUV and climb inside. I deposit the backpack gently onto the backseat before starting the ignition. The heat blasts through the vents, and I rub my hands together. "Should we sit here for a minute?"

"Well, I don't think we have to be stationary for the light to appear," she snaps.

"Maybe, but I also don't want to be driving down the road and you get sucked out of the car," I cry.

"Don't be so dramatic. It's a light," she argues. "There will be no *sucking*. Also, don't say *suck*. It's not ladylike."

I cross my arms over my chest. "You just said it twice."

She drops her head against the seat and sighs. "I'm sorry. I'm just stressed. Who knew this whole crossing over thing was such a big deal?"

"Um, probably everyone?" I say, and she shoots me a look. We sit in a silent stalemate for a moment before I decide to pivot to something more practical. "What would you like me to do with your urn when you…go?"

"What?" she asks, mouth dropping open.

"In all this time of trying to get you into the light, we never talked about what I should do once you actually go," I answer. "Your urn, your mother's diamonds…what would you like me to do with them?" She brings the back of her hand to her lips as though she's considering, so I continue. "I can scatter your ashes anywhere you want or find you a proper burial space. And your earrings…maybe you'd like them to go to Natalie."

She's quiet so long that I start to wonder if the light came and took her, leaving a Marjorie-sized hologram in my passenger seat.

"Marjorie?"

"I want you to keep the diamonds." She turns to me, her voice soft. "And if it's not too much trouble, I want you to keep me."

My chest constricts, and my nose stings. "Of course, it's no trouble. I would be honored to keep you. But are you sure you don't want someone else to have the earrings?"

"You are the closest thing I have to family, Kathryn. Those diamonds belong to you," she says.

I force down the lump in my throat to prevent myself from becoming a blubbering mess. The last thing I want during Marjorie's final moments is for her to have to worry about comforting me. I can fall apart later. Right now, I have to be strong for her.

"Thank you," I manage.

She gives me a faint smile. "I'll miss you, you know."

There are a million things I want to say. I could start with how my life is better, that *I'm* better, for knowing her. I could tell her that she's the strongest woman I've ever met or that no one makes me laugh the way she does. But all I manage are four measly words that will never do justice to the pain that is losing Marjorie Lockwood.

"I'll miss you too."

A moment passes with nothing but the sound of the car running and the low beat of a Christmas pop song. I start to wonder if we should have waited in John's room or if I could have done something to make this better. I could've written a eulogy, lit a candle, made a Going Into the Light playlist—*something* to make it more special. I was so worried about getting her to this point that I never actually considered how I would send her off to her final destination.

"I don't think it's coming," she whispers.

"It will," I insist. "It has to."

"I'm telling you, it's not."

"How do you know?" I ask. "Maybe if we give it a little more ti—"

"It's not coming," she shouts, punctuating every word, and I flinch. "I…I'm sorry. I don't mean to be cross."

"It's all right," I say. "I know this can't be easy."

"I'd like to go home now." She turns her gaze out the window as a slight rain begins to fall. "Please."

My heart sinks as the realization she's already come to seeps into my veins. What we've prepared for, what we've hoped for, isn't happening. *The light isn't coming.*

What if it *never* comes?

I nod, placing my hand on the gearshift. "Of course."

chapter sixty-three

If Marjorie notices me casting glances at her every five seconds out of the corner of my eye on the drive home, she doesn't mention it. In fact, neither of us speaks a word. She stares out the window as the rain traces beaded patterns on the glass, while I try to come up with something to say that might possibly help her feel better. John may not have been her unfinished business, but we *will* get to the bottom of this. There has to be something we've missed, a stone left unturned, and I'm going to find it.

We head inside, and I place my backpack on the counter while Marjorie goes into the living room and sits on the couch. Delilah is at her side almost instantly as though she can sense her sadness. I pour myself a glass of water before joining them.

"Would you like to watch a movie?" Marjorie asks, like it's just an ordinary afternoon.

I blink. "I'm sorry?"

"Or a reality program, if you'd prefer," she adds with a nonchalant shrug. "I think there's still a couple seasons of *The Bachelor* we haven't watched."

I hesitate. *Excuse me?* The Bachelor? *She can't be serious.* "I…no. Marjorie, we need to talk."

"I'm fine, Kathryn," she insists, and it actually sounds like she is, which only makes me more concerned about her emotional state. It's like that eerie calm before a storm hits—the kind that can wipe an entire town off the map. "Really. I'm all right."

"What?" I shake my head. "Listen, today was tough, but I want you to know we're going to solve this thing. I told you, we're in this together, and nothing has changed."

"*Everything* has changed," she says. "*I've* changed."

I shake my head. "I don't understand. We can't give up. We have to keep trying."

She pivots toward me, feet crossed at the ankles, and gives me a soft smile. "I don't want to."

"You don't mean that," I reply. "I know you're sad and disappointed, but we're not done, okay? You have to believe that. I promise I can help you. I—"

She holds out a hand to stop me. "Kathryn, what I'm trying to tell you is, I don't want you to, but it's not because I'm heartbroken."

"You're…not?" I expected many reactions from Marjorie: anger, confusion, devastation. But radical acceptance?

"No, dear," she answers. "Seeing John today was…it was perfect. I need you to know I will cherish that moment forever." She leans closer. "And I have you to thank for it."

"But this doesn't have to be the end of the search. We'll figure it out." My skin prickles with nervous energy. Just this afternoon, I was an anxious mess over the mere thought of Marjorie going into the light, but now I can't bear the idea that she won't. That she'll never get the peace she deserves.

"You're not hearing me." There's a patience, a clarity in

her voice I haven't heard before. "I don't want to continue the search because I don't want to go into the light."

I shove my fingers through my hair. "What are you even talking about? Of course, you want to go into the light. This is everything we've worked toward, and we can still get you there."

"I don't want to," she says, more firmly this time.

My frustration rises along with my voice. "Why? Tell me *why*. Give me one good reason."

"Because I don't want to leave you," she cries. "*That's* why."

My breath catches. "What?"

She fixes her gaze on me. "You and Jude still aren't speaking and you're losing your job at the end of next year when Eddie retires. You need me, Kathryn."

My eyes sting, but I press my tongue onto the roof of my mouth to stop myself from crying. "Marjorie, I'm going to be okay."

"You need me," she says again. "And you know what? If living out eternity here is what I need to do to stay with you, to be here for you, then I'll do it. I'll do it a million times over if it means making sure you're taken care of."

My throat burns with the effort it takes to tamp down my emotions. "No. You can't do that."

"And why not?" she asks.

"Let's pretend for a moment I would even *consider* letting you give up your eternity for me," I begin. "But what happens in fifty, sixty years when *I* die? When no one else can see or hear you?"

"Then I'll survive. I did it for nine years, and I'll do it again."

"But you don't have to do that anymore," I argue. "Don't you see? We can figure this out."

"No," she says. "We can't. Because I want to stay here. With you. You've lost so much in the past." Her green eyes are filled with tears and conviction. "You deserve to have someone that stays by your side, and I can be that for you. I *want* to. I never want you to feel alone again."

"No," I say with an emphatic shake of my head. "You can't do this. I'm not letting you sacrifice your afterlife for me."

"I've made my choice, and I choose you."

"But what about John?" I ask, bordering on frantic now. "You were supposed to get to the other side and wait for him so the two of you can finally be together. Don't you want that?"

She gives me a bittersweet smile. "I love you, Kathryn. You're my family. My very best friend. And if I get to pick between going to the other side—heaven or paradise, whatever it is—I will *always* choose you."

Her words crash over me like a wave, cool water soothing the angry scars lingering inside me. Marjorie would give up forever for me. She's willing to forgo the happy ever after she's longed for, the one we've *fought* for, the one she *deserves*, all because she loves me.

"I love you too." My voice comes out broken, but my heart is whole. "And that's why I can't let you do this. I *won't*."

She opens her mouth to speak, but I cut her off.

"No," I say. "Marjorie, you've given me enough love to last a lifetime. You changed my life. You led me to Jude, and I'll never be able to thank you enough for that. I know we're not together anymore, but you showed me I could find love.

You did that. You showed me I'm *worthy* of it, flaws and all." A tear slips down her cheek, and I scoot closer. "You don't need to worry about me. I'll be okay because I'll have your voice in my ear cheering me on and judging me for wearing leopard print."

She laughs through her tears. "Maybe it *is* a neutral."

My lips quirk. "I knew you'd come around eventually." I take a deep breath and swallow hard. "Look, no matter what happens, I'll always have this—these crazy, beautiful, unbelievable two months I wouldn't trade for anything. You've loved me so well. Now let me do the same for you. Please."

Before either of us can speak, a glowing bright light pierces the windows from every direction, making us gasp and jump to our feet as Delilah bolts under the sofa. It's not blinding or stark or painful like looking at the sun. It's soft and casts dancing ripples of shimmering gold over everything.

Oh my God. Without thinking, I reach for Marjorie and find that this time, there is no more cold. Only solid warmth. Our eyes widen before her arms wrap around me, enveloping me in the scent of Chanel No. 5, and we hold each other as she rocks us gently back and forth.

I hug her even tighter. "I can feel you."

"Oh, Kathryn," she cries. "I've wanted to do this for so long."

"I can't believe it's here," I choke out. "It's actually here."

"I...I don't understand." she says, uncertain. "I'm not ready. I don't want to leave you."

"You have to," I whisper.

"Why?" she asks. "Why now?"

I lean back, gripping her shoulders. "I don't know. But what I *do* know is you did it."

The light swirls around us, capturing us in a glimmering

bubble. It's so dazzling, it outshines our need for answers and spotlights the only thing that matters—each other.

"*We* did, darling," she says into my ear. "We did it. You and me. Always."

"Always," I echo.

"If I'd been lucky enough to have a daughter, I would have wanted her to be just like you." She pulls back, taking my face in her hands, which I cover with my own, wanting to embroider this moment on my heart forever. "Promise me you'll be okay."

I nod. "I will. Because of you."

She wipes my damp cheeks with her thumbs, then turns her head toward the kitchen, where I follow her gaze.

"Do you hear that?" she asks.

"No, what is it?"

"Music," she replies with a dreamy smile before it fades into an expression that can only be described as wonder as the light shifts, paving a glittering path toward my counters where a golden circle spins, hovering, waiting.

She hesitates, caught somewhere between this moment and what comes next.

"You have to go," I say, taking her hands in mine.

She folds me in her embrace again. "My sweet girl."

I cling to her a few more seconds, committing her touch to memory. "When my time comes, I promise I'll find you."

Her smile is radiant as she looks at me once more. "We'll have a girls' night." We laugh, then she places a tender kiss on my cheek. "Until then."

"Until then," I echo as she begins walking toward the light. The closer she gets, the brighter it burns, the circle twirling faster and faster.

She stops just shy of the glistening orb and turns back toward me. "Goodbye, Kathryn."

"Goodbye, Marjorie."

In the span of a breath, she steps forward, fading from view as the light expands until I'm suspended in a sea of brilliant gold. It's warm, like a perfect day in May, and I feel light as air, vast as the universe. There's no sadness, no worries weighing me down. There is only love. Love so bright it eclipses all else.

And in a blink, it's gone.

Marjorie is gone.

chapter sixty-four

The house is plunged into a peaceful silence, the kind that happens after a good snowfall—when the world is so quiet, you're almost afraid to step outside and disturb the stillness. My own shaky breath is the only sound I hear until Delilah creeps out from under the couch, wide-eyed. She jumps back onto the sofa and sniffs, glancing around the room, searching for Marjorie. Once she realizes her ghostly friend is nowhere to be found, she leaps onto the ground and prances down the hall like we didn't just witness something impossible.

I move slowly toward the kitchen, where Marjorie disappeared into the light, but there's nothing there. The only evidence I have that it happened at all is deafening silence. Her absence feels like sinking into a dark winter after months of basking in the sun. It's gloomy and cold and all wrong.

What happened that made the light come? Was it some sort of delayed reaction from Marjorie's time with John or was there something else? My mind is a jumbled mess of golden puzzle pieces, but none of them seem to fit. There's only one person I can think of to help me sort through them.

In a matter of seconds, I've grabbed my coat and purse, and I'm in the car. I back out of the driveway, my gaze snagging on a lipstick rolling around on the floorboard. I must've missed it when I picked up the contents of my spilled bag. The top has twisted open, leaving the wine color exposed. My heart jumps into my throat as I imagine the last time I put it on, right before Marjorie sent me off to meet Jude. And now, they're both gone from my life.

When I arrive at my destination, I barely manage to cut the engine before flinging the door to my SUV open. There's a single car in the lot, and it belongs to the one person I need to see. The bell chimes as I enter, and Dennis looks up from the book he's reading, perched behind the register.

His smile falters when he takes in my face. "She's gone, isn't she?"

I nod, choking back a sob.

He's on his feet in an instant, striding across the room until I'm wrapped in his arms. "Oh, Kat. I'm sorry," he says, his hand rubbing soothing circles into my back. "I'm so sorry. When did she go?"

"Just a few minutes ago," I manage. "It was so quiet, and I just...I can't be in that house without her yet."

"Was it after you took her to visit John?" he asks, leaning back to look into my eyes.

"Not right after," I answer. "It was a while later, which is what's so strange. We both thought for sure the light wasn't coming since it didn't while she was with John."

"It does seem like it would be pretty instantaneous. At least, that's what the books I've read always say," he replies. "So, *how did* it happen?"

"We drove home, and we were just sitting on the couch talking when this warm, golden glow appeared."

"Hmm." His forehead creases. "Hang on. Let me lock up so we won't be interrupted, then I want you to tell me everything you remember." He quickly flips the sign to closed and turns the deadbolt, then leads me into the next room toward a set of wicker peacock chairs.

I pour out every detail I can recall about the day, starting with our visit to John. I tell him about the silent drive back before wringing the words of my conversation with Marjorie from my brain like a sponge. Dennis doesn't speak, allowing me to get out every single thought.

"She looked at me one last time, and then she was… gone," I say finally.

He draws his lips together and nods, rubbing his thumb and forefinger over his chin. "I don't think John was her unfinished business."

"Well, yeah," I say. "But what *was* it?"

He leans forward with a sad smile. "I think it was you."

"*Me?*" I blink, the weight of his statement knocking me back. "What? How? That doesn't make sense. We didn't even know each other when she was alive."

"I don't think it was ever about that," he says with a slight shake of his head. "Do you remember what I told you the night you called me to come over when you found Marjorie?"

I nod. "That there was some sort of unfinished business keeping her here."

"And I also said it was possible there was a lesson she needed to learn. Something she didn't figure out while she was alive."

I tilt my head, brows furrowed. "Okay, but what was the lesson?"

"Kat, Marjorie was ready to give up eternity to stay with you. You know I adore the woman but based on what I know about her when she was alive, she was never exactly the *giving* type. Not unless it was a tax write-off or she got something in return." He blows out a breath and shrugs. "I don't mean to speak ill of the dead here, but I think even Marjorie would probably agree that most of her relationships were… transactional."

Transactional. The word unlocks a memory from Saturday night when I was in bed, crying about Jude, and the mess I'd made of everything. Marjorie was at my side comforting me. *"Before you came into my life…my* afterlife, *I thought relationships were transactional, that if I wasn't benefiting someone, I was no longer valuable,"* she said. *"But you saw my worth when I had nothing to offer."*

"You taught Marjorie how to truly love someone," Dennis continues, his voice soft. "Without condition or expectation."

"But…John," I say. "She loved him."

"She did, but when you took her to John, she was still looking for something. She wanted his forgiveness so she could cross over. With you it was different. She didn't want anything from you. All she wanted was to love you."

My throat tightens around the realization. *She* saw *my* worth when I had nothing to offer. Marjorie was willing to give up everything to stay here, for no other reason than she loved me.

"She would have done anything just to make sure you never felt alone again." Dennis reaches for my hand. "But you cared enough to set her free because you know that nothing, not even death, can take away the love you have for each other."

I nod, squeezing his fingers. "No, it can't."

My chest aches with the force of how much I already miss her. Even in her absence, I feel her everywhere because she's woven in the tapestry that makes me. Just like everyone I love, and even those I've lost. Some threads are shorter than others but that doesn't make them any less beautiful or meaningful. They're still a part of me, and my life wouldn't be the same without them. *I* wouldn't be the same without them.

"Thank you, Dennis," I say. "For everything. For always being there for me and all you did for Marjorie. She thought a lot of you and Thomas."

He smiles. "That woman was a damn earthquake, and I have a feeling we'll be experiencing the aftershocks of her existence for a long time to come."

The corners of my lips tug upward. "Yeah. I think we will."

chapter sixty-five

"You're sure about this?" Eddie asks, folding his arms over his chest Wednesday morning after we wrap the morning broadcast.

I nod. "I need to do it, Eddie. I know I'm asking a lot, but if I hope to get Jude back, I *have* to do this."

"I don't know, Kat. You'll be putting yourself out there in a major way," Becca says, shaking her head. "Not just with Jude, but with *everyone*. Telling millions of listeners about your friendship with a *ghost* could have some serious consequences. People might think you're…I don't know…*not well*. That you're fabricating it all for clicks. You're having a hard enough time as it is. I just don't want you to end up feeling worse."

"I know," I reply. "And I get your concerns. I spent all night thinking about every possible terrifying outcome, but I need you to trust that I know what I'm doing."

I barely slept, tossing and turning for hours while the idea took shape in my mind. Marjorie is and always will be part of me. Our story is one of my favorites. It's one I'll revisit over and over again until the ink on the pages begins to fade, the

"

paper wearing thin. But the thing about good stories is they deserve to be told. And mine isn't over yet. If anything, it's just beginning. Being loved by Marjorie gave me permission to be imperfect, to mess up and be loved anyway. If it weren't for her, I never would have gotten a chance to be with Jude, because I never would have allowed myself to believe one existed in the first place. He *did* love me, and I let my insecurities tear us apart. Then Marjorie helped me understand that you don't have to be perfect to be loved. But you *do* have to be willing to show up, flaws and all.

Becca glances at Eddie, who leans forward, resting his elbows on the table.

"I'm inclined to say yes," he begins, "but let's say this whole thing goes south. What if Jude still doesn't…" He trails off, but the implication is clear. What if Jude still doesn't want to be with me?

It's a very real possibility I've imagined a million times over. There may be too much water under the bridge. I might have hurt him too deeply. But even knowing that, I *still* want to do this. I need to take accountability, to show him my whole heart instead of perfectly curated glimpses. To let him know I may never be the perfect partner, but I promise to put in the work to be the one he deserves.

"Then I'll respect his decision and move on," I answer. "I can't pretend it won't crush me because it will. But I owe it to him and to myself to be authentic. If Marjorie taught me anything, it's that I have to let people see me, to allow them to know *all* of me—not just the pretty parts or the ones that are easy to love."

"And that's a beautiful sentiment," Becca says, her eyes softening, "but I'm not sure she meant you should do that with thousands of people."

She's just worried about me, and honestly, *I'm* a little worried about me. But I also know this is the right thing to do.

I sigh. "Look, you both know how much I love this job, and I'm grateful for our listeners. But at the end of the day, their judgments aren't going to dictate the way I live. I don't know them. I'm not going to them for advice. They can like me or not, believe me or not. But if I'm not comfortable enough to be myself around people who *aren't* in my life, whose thoughts of me *don't* matter, how can I ever get comfortable being myself around those who *do* matter?" I pause, taking in their thoughtful expressions. "And I know something this out of the box probably needs to be run by upper management—"

"Don't worry about that." Eddie cuts me off with a wave of his hand. "I'll deal with them."

I smile. "Does that mean I can do it?"

"I just needed to know you're gonna be okay no matter what happens," he replies, "and I feel confident you will be."

I look at Becca, whose face is unreadable. "What do you think?"

"That I'm still a little worried, and that I'm overprotective because I love you so much," she says. "But you know I'm going to support you no matter what."

I reach across the table and squeeze her arm. "Thank you."

"So, how's this going to go, exactly?" Eddie asks.

"I'm going to start with a little background about my life…about what I've lost," I answer, taking a deep breath. "Then I'll explain how I came across Marjorie, how she helped me. I'll talk about my time with Jude, though I won't mention him by name because our listeners don't need to know that part. But *he'll* know. And I'm going to ask for forgiveness and hope maybe he'll be willing to at least have a conversation with me."

Eddie nods. "Okay. We'll push most of tomorrow's schedule to Friday. Get your thoughts together tonight and email me a rough outline so I can split it up between each scheduled break."

"And we'll back you up on Marjorie too," Becca says. "We know she's real."

"You don't have to—"

Becca holds out a hand. "Don't be ridiculous."

"Maybe your friend Dennis would be willing to call in as well?" Eddie offers. "We can all vouch for how real Marjorie was."

Was. The word stings more than I care to admit. It's impossible to think of her in past tense when I still feel her everywhere.

"Would you mind trying to get in touch with Jude?" I ask Eddie. "Try to get him to listen tomorrow?"

"Of course, I will," he says. "But I can't promise he'll respond."

"I know," I reply. "All we can do is try."

We finalize our plan and Becca heads out for a meeting, leaving me and Eddie alone.

"You're sure this is okay?" I ask. "I mean, with the higher-ups? I don't want to cause any bad blood between you and them."

He barks out a laugh. "They already did that when they decided to cancel this show."

"Yeah, but we *do* still have several months left, and I don't want them pulling any shit on you during your last year."

"They won't," he assures me. "And even if they're crazy enough to try something, I've got dirt on most of them, so it'll be in their best interest to let it slide. Besides, maybe something like this is just what we need to show them how much listeners want this show, even without me. It's vulnerable and messy and relatable. It's *life*."

I take a deep breath and blow it out. "All right, then. I guess we're doing this." I rise from my seat, gathering my things. "Seriously, Eddie. Thank you."

"Don't mention it," he says as I start for the door. "And Kat?"

"Yeah?" I ask, turning back to face him.

"I'm proud of you, kid."

I can't help the smile that spreads over my face. "I'm proud of me too."

chapter sixty-six

Becca's gaze snags on me when I step into the studio Thursday morning, looking more than a little green and without my usual tumbler of coffee.

"You okay?" she asks as I take my seat and fire up my laptop.

"On a scale of one to ten, I'm sitting firmly at a negative fourteen," I answer, wiping at the beads of sweat dampening my hairline. "I'm so nervous I couldn't even drink my coffee."

"You can still back out," Eddie assures me. "If you're not sure—"

"I am," I reply. "But I'm also freaking the hell out." My hands are shaky, and there's a knot in my stomach the size of Dolly Parton's left boob, but nothing worth doing is easy, right? At least that's what they say. Though right now, I'm seriously wondering who *they* are and if *they* should be trusted. "Did you get in touch with Jude?"

Eddie shakes his head. "Nope. I texted him last night and again this morning."

The elastic ball of nerves in my belly rolls on a few more rubber bands, as if it wasn't already tight enough.

Becca slides out of her chair with her water bottle. "I'm going to the kitchen for a refill. Anyone need anything?"

"I'm good," Eddie replies, but all I manage is a grimace.

"I think there's some ginger ale in there," Becca offers. "At least let me get you some water, Kat. You look like you're about to pass out."

I bury my head in my hands, my fingers threading through my hair. "Water, please. Thank you." If I die of anxiety or humiliation, at least I'll go out hydrated.

The door shuts with a gentle thud as Becca leaves the room, and I attempt to calm myself with deep, steady breaths.

A beat passes before Eddie finally speaks. "You've got this, kid."

I lift my eyes to his and give him a grateful smile. "I know." It doesn't feel like it right now, but I do. I touch one of the diamonds that adorns my ears, the jewelry a little fancy for my oversized sweatshirt and leggings. Marjorie may not be here physically to help me through this, but I need her to be a part of it somehow.

Becca returns with the water and a packet of crackers in case I feel like I can stomach something during one of our breaks. As the seconds tick down, I check my phone one more time just in case Jude sent a text. There isn't one from him, but there is a message from Dennis.

I'm all set up for you guys to call me. You're gonna kill it today! ♥ Proud of you and I know Marj is too. She's probably raising absolute hell up there trying to get them to tune in.

The visual makes me chuckle, releasing some of the tension mounting in my muscles as the countdown to our morning broadcast goes from minutes to seconds. I squeeze my eyes shut and slip on my headphones as our prerecorded intro plays.

"You're listening to Eddie in the Morning *with Eddie, Becca, Kat, and Jude."*

The music fades, and Eddie's voice fills my ears. "It's Thursday—or as we like to call it around here—pre-Friday. As you all know, Jude has the week off, but we have a special show planned for this morning. We're deviating from our usual Thursday content for something a little different. Our very own Kat Simon has been dealing with some personal struggles recently, and she's ready to share her story. I promise this is something you won't want to miss." He gives me an encouraging nod. "Kat, the floor is yours."

"Well, I want to start by telling you all about a dear friend of mine. Her name is Marjorie." I swallow, wishing I'd taken a sip of the water Becca brought me. "But for you to fully understand the impact she had on my life, I need to tell you a bit more about me."

Becca holds my gaze in quiet support as I start from the beginning with losing my mom, dad, and grandmother, and the way each of those losses shaped the woman I became. I skip forward to dating Nick, our sad if not anticlimactic end, and how it shook what little confidence I had left.

When I get to the part where Marjorie's ghost first appeared, I can't help but chuckle as I describe our encounter and her initial disdain for Delilah.

"Tattooed miscreant?" Eddie asks with a bark of laughter.

"Yep," I answer. "That's what she called me. And if memory serves, she referred to my cat as a vile beast."

The words roll off my tongue as I tell the story of us— everything from our failed attempts to figure out what her unfinished business was, to her coaching me on my *Purrfect Match* dates. Dennis, Eddie, and Becca back me up with their own stories about Marjorie, but saying it all out loud reminds me again how unreal it all sounds, and I start to wonder if I've made a big mistake.

We reach our final break, and our producer Cassie pokes her head in the room. "You guys, the phones are going *nuts*."

"Shit," I mutter. This was a big swing, and I missed, live on the air.

She quickly shakes her head. "No, people are *loving* this. When you were talking about your past, folks were calling to share their own experiences, to say they understood where you were coming from."

I blink. "Wait, really?"

She nods. "And when you got into the part about Marjorie? They lost their minds. Turns out, a lot of listeners either have their own paranormal experiences, or they're at least curious about it. I think we may have to turn this thing into a two-parter. Maybe we can continue tomorrow and allow people to call in?"

I look at Eddie, who lifts his brows. "I think that's a spectacular idea."

"But what will upper management think of that?" I ask.

Eddie just grins. "I'll be sure to ask them after we get the ratings for the week."

The counter lets us know we have ten seconds left before the break ends. Cassie steps out just before the "On-Air" light blinks on, and I steel myself for what comes next.

When we come back, I begin to talk about my relationship with Jude. I don't mention him by name, and I leave out any details that would allow the supersleuths out there to identify him. I relive our relationship with fresh eyes, my insecurities on full display as I recall every beautiful minute. It's then I remember why I'm here, why I'm doing this. It's my last ditch effort, my Hail Mary pass, and all I can do is hope he'll receive it with open arms or at least an open mind.

"And to this special person, I'm so sorry," I begin, imagining Jude listening in his living room with a cup of coffee in his hands. "You're one of the best things that ever happened to me, except for maybe Marjorie, because in her own way, she brought me to you. She took off my blinders and helped me see what had been standing right in front of me all along." I draw in a breath, my fingers finding the diamond on my ear. "I messed up, and not in a small way. Maybe I don't deserve your forgiveness, but I'm asking for it because I love you. Because these last few days have been hell, and I can't imagine my tomorrows without you. And I'm asking for a chance to make this up to you." My voice breaks. "I can't promise I'll be perfect, but I *can* promise I'll be honest, that I'll communicate with you, and I'll do every ounce of work it takes to be the partner you deserve. If you're listening, and I hope you are, please…can we just…can we talk?"

I emotionally blackout as Eddie takes over, telling the listeners about our plan for tomorrow's show before our outro plays.

"Holy shit," Becca cries as she leaps from her seat, but her voice is muffled because my headphones are still on.

With trembling hands, I slide them off as she pulls me from my chair and throws her arms around me.

"You were amazing," she says and Eddie gets up to join us, wrapping us both in a hug.

He beams. "Now *that* was some damn good radio, kids." My gaze falls to Jude's vacant spot beside me, and I say a silent prayer that even if what I did today wasn't enough to get him to come back to me, that it would at least be enough to get him to come back to the show.

Cassie bursts through the door with a squeal. "The phones are still going crazy. Social media is blowing up."

Interns and other staff bound into the room, buzzing with excitement. Their voices narrow to a low hum, my mind focused on only one thing: Jude. While they talk amongst themselves, I reach for my phone, fingers clasped around it so tight, my knuckles turn white, and I do the only thing left for me to do.

I wait.

chapter sixty-seven

I wait for almost forty minutes, but the only things that come through are seven texts from Dennis asking if I've talked to Jude yet and hundreds of social media notifications. Eddie was called into a meeting with upper management, and now I have a crushing sense of dread that not only did I *not* get Jude back, but I've also gotten my boss in major trouble.

Becca stays with me in the break room after everyone returns to work, her eyes lighting up every time my phone pings, only for us both to be disappointed when it isn't Jude. It buzzes again, but I can't bring myself to look anymore. Right now, I need to wallow.

"At least I tried, right?" I say, powering off my phone.

"Wait." Becca's hand darts out, grasping my wrist. "What if he calls?"

"If he was gonna call, he would've done it already." I tuck the device in my purse. "And all of these messages popping up are doing nothing but reminding me that he's *not* calling or texting or sending a smoke signal. There'll be nary a carrier pigeon sent."

"I'm so sorry, Kat." Becca's shoulders sag. "I can't believe he hasn't reached out."

"Look, I need you to promise me that if Jude comes back, you won't blame him for this," I say. "This is still my fault."

She cocks her head and narrows her eyes. "I don't give a shit. He could at least talk to you."

"I don't even know if he listened to the show," I admit. "He never texted Eddie back."

Her gaze drops to the mug in front of her, the tip of her nail tapping against the rim. "He was listening."

Three simple words send me reeling, my mouth dropping open. "What?"

She sighs. "I called him. When I went to get your water earlier, I called, fully prepared to leave a voicemail telling him how pissed I was at him, but he picked up."

"Oh my God." I nearly leap from my seat with the sheer force of the words. "What did you say? What did *he* say?"

"It was a short conversation. There wasn't a lot of time." She holds out her hands as though she can physically stop me from spiraling. "I said if he ever cared about you at all, he needed to listen to the show this morning, and he promised he would."

Her words knock the wind out of me. "He did?"

"Yes," she answers softly.

Knowing he tuned in and *still* chose radio silence feels like a knife twisting into an open wound. "Why didn't you tell me?"

She pins me with a stare that says *you-know-exactly-why*. "I was afraid you'd panic, that it would make you even more nervous."

I fold my arms on the table, nudging my own empty cup out of the way. "It would have."

"I'm sorry. I was so sure he'd pull his head out of his ass after hearing what you had to say," she explains. "I just knew he'd call or speed into this parking lot on two wheels to get to you. I never imagined for a second he'd ignore you."

Ignoring me is exactly what he's doing, but hearing it put so plainly makes my stomach hurt.

I nod, releasing a slow breath. "I know. It's okay. You were only trying to help."

"Apparently, there's no fixing stupid," she grumbles.

"How'd he sound?" I ask.

"What do you mean?"

"Did he seem…happy?"

She raises her brows. "Honestly? He sounded like shit."

I frown. "Well, I hope, if nothing else, maybe he heard everything and will at least understand why I did what I did. Maybe he won't think I'm just an awful person." I sigh and rise to my feet. "Regardless, it's out of my hands."

"Where are you going?" she asks.

"I need to get out of here," I answer. "Clear my head." Get away from reminders of Jude and all the ways I messed this up.

She stands too, gathering both our mugs to place them in the dishwasher. "You want me to come with you? We could go to Billy's."

I wince. "I'm probably going to be avoiding Billy's for a while."

"Or somewhere else," she adds. "I can get out of band practice, and we can do something."

"There's a stop I need to make on the way home today," I say, gathering my things. "How about tomorrow?"

"Deal," she replies with a soft smile. "We can have a girls' night."

I return her smile with one of my own. "That sounds like exactly what I need."

chapter sixty-eight

The lobby of The Blake is bustling as usual when I arrive and sign in next to the covered dish of oatmeal raisin cookies. The receptionist, whose name I now know to be Darlene, greets me as I sign in. I toss a wave over my shoulder as I head toward the elevator before making the familiar journey up to John's room.

"Come in," he calls out when I knock on the door. His eyes widen and he breaks into a broad grin, rising from the love seat as I step inside. "Kat, what a surprise."

"I hope you don't mind me dropping by like this," I say, meeting him halfway. "I probably should have called first to make sure it was okay."

"Nonsense," he replies with a chuckle. "I'm happy to see you. Now, have a seat." He guides me to the couch, his hand on the small of my back. "I listened to your program this morning."

"You did?" I ask.

He nods. "Heather was in yesterday afternoon, and she showed me how to pull up your show. I've always been an early riser, probably from years of working on a farm. I usually watch the news, but your show is far more interesting."

"Oh wow," I say. "So you…you heard."

"I did," he answers. "It was a moving tribute to Marjorie. You know I wasn't inside the church the day of her funeral, but I have no doubt you captured her spirit better than anyone else ever could."

My throat tightens. "You really think so?"

"Absolutely. You may not have known Marjorie long, but you knew the *real* her. Not just the woman she wanted everyone to think she was. You got past all her pomp and circumstance, the mask she spent a lifetime wearing." A far-off look clouds his eyes. "Kat, you tore down all her defenses and let her just be a girl again. Those stories you told today… *that* was the Marjorie I knew. Vibrant, funny…God, she made me laugh more than anyone. And she had a big heart. She loved fiercely, but it wasn't something most people knew about her. You and I, we were the lucky ones."

I manage a smile, though my lips quiver. "Yeah, we were."

We sit quietly for a moment before he reaches out and squeezes my shoulder. "So, what brings you by today?"

"Well," I begin, my voice wobbling. "I was wondering if…maybe it'd be okay if I came to visit every once in a while? I know we don't really know each other yet, but I'd like to change that." I tuck my hair behind my ear. "You're the only other person who really understands what it's like to lose Marjorie, and I don't know…I think that could help us keep her spirit alive in some small way. Maybe it's silly, but I think she'd like it if we kept in touch."

"It's not silly at all," he says, his eyes creasing as the corners of his mouth draw upward. "I'd love that."

"Yeah?"

"I'd be honored, young lady," he replies. "Now, tell me, what happened after the show today? With the guy?"

"Jude." I drop my gaze and manage a slight shake of my head. "He didn't call."

"Oh." His chin drops to his chest. "Oh dear. I'm so sorry."

"It's okay," I say, though it's hard to imagine a time I'll truly feel okay again. "Maybe it's better this way. I mean, if you and Marjorie hadn't broken up all those years ago, you wouldn't have ended up with your beautiful family. Maybe there's some reason we can't be together." I'm not sure I believe it, but I have to tell myself something to keep from completely breaking down.

"Hmm…perhaps. But not even death could stop Marjorie from finding us, and if this Jude fellow is supposed to be in your life, he'll show up."

His words should fill me with hope, but all I feel is empty. What if the split I caused in our path together is so great, even time can't fix it?

He leans forward with an encouraging smile. "Take it from an old man, Kat. A love that's meant for you will always find its way back."

chapter sixty-nine

I leave John's with a promise of bringing him lunch next week from somewhere that isn't The Blake's cafeteria. Low sodium, of course. I power on my phone as I get in my SUV, just in case Jude has finally reached out, but all I find are more social media notifications. When I start the car, the holiday music playing on the radio feels like a personal attack on my dreary mood, so I shut it off, choosing silence over violence toward "Rudolph the Red-Nosed Reindeer." No one's expecting me at home but Delilah, so I take the scenic route to put off returning to an empty house just a little while longer.

It'll take time to get used to being alone again when the walls still hold the echoes of Marjorie's laughter. But I've been on my own before, and I'll do it again. I may not be okay right now, but I will be. One day, I will be.

My chest grows heavy as I turn onto my street, knowing Marjorie won't be at home waiting for me. She won't be bombarding me with questions about my day or asking about Eddie or waiting to watch the next season of *The Bachelor*.

She won't be wondering why Jude is parked in my driveway.

Jude is parked in my driveway. Not only that, but he's standing on my front porch, hands tucked in his pockets. My stomach churns. What's he doing here? Is it possible he could forgive me, or is he just here to tell me in person that it's really over between us? That's respectful, kind, and a very Jude thing to do.

Or maybe my emotions are playing tricks on me, and Jude is just a mirage that'll disappear the second I blink. But he doesn't, so I roll to a stop, cut the ignition, and get out of the car. His eyes are framed with faded purple half-moons, indicating that the past few days have been as hard on him as they've been on me. He smiles as I approach, making my heart flutter.

"Hi," I say, though the inflection on the end of the word makes it sound more like a question. "What are you…what are you doing here?"

"I listened this morning," he answers as I climb the stairs.

"Becca told me, but you didn't call or—"

"It felt like more of an in person conversation," he replies. "In hindsight, I probably should have let you know I was coming instead of just showing up."

"No," I say quickly. "I'm glad you did, but how long have you been out here?"

It's a mild December day, but it's still chilly.

"About an hour. I've been staying a few hours away at this little mountain cabin in East Tennessee for a few days." He pushes a hand through his hair. "I was supposed to be there through Saturday, but I don't care. I packed up and left before the show was even over because I had to see you."

My breath catches. "You…you did?"

"Yeah, I did." The hurt and disappointment that had been in his eyes the last time I saw him is gone, and he gives me a sad smile. "Kat, I owe you an apology."

I shake my head and start to argue, but he cuts me off.

"I should've listened and given you a chance to explain," he says, stepping closer. "My mom called while I was driving. She heard the show this morning, and she…she told me you went to visit her. It meant a lot to her, and it means a lot to me too."

"I had to tell her how sorry I was." My chin drops. "I wanted to tell you too."

He reaches out and tilts my face upward. "I know. I didn't handle any of this as well as I could have—as I *should* have. But when I came here the night of the gala and found out you thought I was even the slightest bit capable of doing those things to you…it gutted me."

"I'm so sorry," I say. "It was never about you. It was about me not feeling good enough to keep you." My eyes search his. "I was so busy waiting for the other shoe to drop that I didn't realize I was the one causing it to fall."

"Kat, I need you to understand something. I've wanted to be with you for so long. I'm not about to try and mess this up, all right? I'm not going anywhere."

"Really?" I ask softly. "I haven't missed my chance?"

"Definitely not." He cups my cheek. "I want this. I want *you*."

I squeeze my eyes shut and sigh, grateful for a fresh start. "I can't promise there won't be days I need a reminder, but I *do* promise I'll work on keeping my insecurities in check. Then when those moments come up and I'm doubting myself, I'll talk to you."

"And I'll be there to tell you how much I love you, how

much better my life is with you in it." He places his hands on either side of my face, and my soul relaxes as his words wash over me. I collect them all, bottling up every syllable to hold onto during the hard days when that familiar fear creeps in.

"I love you too," I whisper, sliding my arms around his waist. "I'm so sorry, Jude. For everything. For lying to you about Delilah and not telling you about Marjorie. I should've known I could confide in you."

He tucks a strand of hair behind my ear. "It's okay. I get why you didn't, but I'm sorry I never got to meet her. Well, as much as I could have, anyway."

"She really liked you," I say with a grin.

He opens his mouth, then closes it as it dawns on him that while *he* may not have known about Marjorie, *she* definitely knew about him. "She was at Billy's that day, wasn't she?"

I nod. "And in the studio. All those flickering lights? That was her."

"Wait." His forehead creases. "Oh God. Was she here when we…" He gestures between the two of us with wide eyes.

"Oh no," I answer. "She and Delilah had a slumber party with Dennis that weekend so we could have some alone time." The look of relief on his face is short-lived when I add, "She definitely had questions, though."

He nearly chokes. "I'm sorry, what *kinds* of questions?"

"She wanted to hear about our sexcapades," I reply with a shrug.

"Our *what*?"

I laugh. "Her words, not mine."

"And what exactly did you tell her?" he asks with an amused grin.

"I'm sorry, but that information is protected under the law of Girl Code," I tease.

He shakes his head and smiles down at me. "I missed the hell out of you."

"I missed you too," I say, rising on my toes, bringing my lips to his. I want to kiss him until the hurt I caused him disappears, but I'll save that for later. For now, I kiss him like I intend to do this every day for a *very* long time. Because I do. "How about you come in and I can tell you *all* about the legend that is Marjorie Lockwood?"

He takes my hands in his. "I'd love that."

My phone dings from my bag as I unlock the door and push it open. "That's probably Becca or Dennis checking on me."

We step inside, and Delilah is already there waiting to greet us.

"Delilah," Jude sings, crouching down to allow her to sniff his hand. She meows her blessing, allowing him to scratch her head. "I'm glad you're not dead."

The cat flicks her tail and darts away, almost colliding with the wall.

"Too soon?" he asks with a laugh as he rises to his feet and squeezes my shoulder. "How about I make us some coffee?"

"Oh my God. Please." I'm practically salivating at the thought as I dig around in my purse for my phone. "I can't quite get the nutmeg to cinnamon ratio right. You do it so much better than me."

He pecks me on the cheek before heading toward the kitchen. "One pot of Jude coffee coming right up."

My fingers finally clamp around the device, and I pull it out to find the message I received is from Eddie.

Be at the studio early tomorrow so we can chat. Got some GREAT news, kid.

I smile to myself before tapping out my reply.

Me too. Jude's here. 😄

He responds immediately with a string of happy emojis, and I stuff my phone back in my bag, dropping it in the foyer.

I move down the hall toward my room, pushing the slightly ajar door all the way open. Delilah has already claimed her spot on the bed, watching me intently. A lump rises in my throat when I think about the many times Marjorie and I argued here over what I should wear. I can almost hear her voice, her laughter, her words of wisdom. But the loudest of all is her love.

"You coming?" Jude calls.

"Be right there." The floorboards creak as I step inside and kick off my shoes before padding over to the dresser. I remove Marjorie's diamonds, holding them in the palm of my hand for a moment, my thumb ghosting over the smooth stones. I press a kiss to each one and tuck them in my wooden jewelry box for safe keeping. Marjorie may be gone, but she left me with something far greater than her jewels. It isn't tangible, but I feel it everywhere.

Her light lingers in this house.

And it lives within me.

epilogue

Seven years later…

"Oh my God, Kat. Did you do this?" Dennis gapes in amazement at the perfectly frosted birthday cake on the counter. "It's gorgeous."

And it is. It's a pink and purple leopard print confection because apparently the love for leopard is inherited.

Becca barks out a laugh as she opens the fridge to grab another beer. "The fact that it looks like that should be the first indicator that she *didn't* make it."

I'd be insulted if she wasn't right. "No, Heather did."

"Of course, she did," Dennis says. "That woman is a saint."

Over the last few years, Jude and I have gotten to know John's family—especially his daughter Heather. We grew closer as her father's health worsened and spent a lot of time together during his final days. After he passed, our friendship continued to blossom, and now she's like an honorary aunt to our little girl.

"Has anyone seen Deli—" I start to ask as a flash of orange bolts past with a streak of gray close on its heels. "Never mind."

"I see Delilah and Casey are still besties," Dennis teases. Casey, an orange tabby named after radio legend Casey Kasem, is the newest addition to our family.

"Hey, she only hissed at him once yesterday," I say, placing my coffee mug in the dishwasher. "I think he's wearing her down."

"By the way, I'm sad Jett couldn't make it today, Becca. She's the only person I know who might be cooler than me," Dennis says with a chuckle as he follows me and Becca onto the back deck. Jett is Becca's girlfriend who happened to be the bass player in her former band. Their story was all too familiar—close friends who realized they wanted more.

Becca sighs. "She hated to miss it. Her new band is finishing up their tour. She doesn't get back for another couple weeks."

I breathe in the chilly October air. The sun is setting, casting a warm glow over everything, and there's a soft breeze rustling through the trees. Our backyard has been transformed into an outdoor movie theater, complete with a blow-up projector screen, picnic blankets, and sleeping bags.

Jude is sitting on one of the Adirondack chairs with a drink in hand, chatting with Imani and Kamal, the newest cast members of the morning show. He glances up and winks at me. I step closer to him, and he reaches for me, kissing my hand. We've been married five years now, but he still makes my heart race.

"Hey Kat, I was thinking maybe we could do a holiday

auction this year." Imani grins as I approach, sweeping her long braids off her shoulder. "Or what about a gift wrapping fundraiser? We could turn it into a whole party. I bet we could get the brewery that helped us with the school supply drive last year to host."

"I love it," I say. "You want to take point?"

Her dark skin shimmers gold in the sun. "Absolutely."

After Eddie retired, *Eddie in the Morning* became *Morning Coffee*. Eddie still joins us in-studio once in a while, just for fun, and it's nice to see him get to sit back and enjoy the magic that all started with him. It still feels weird sitting in his spot sometimes and even weirder being in charge. A week into the gig, I nearly psyched myself out of a job because I felt like I wasn't good enough, that I'd never match up to Eddie's legacy. But Jude was there to remind me I didn't have to be Eddie. I just had to be me and follow my heart. And that meant making sure the heart and family vibe of the program stayed intact.

"Oh no." Eddie's voice booms from the yard. "The monsters are going to eat me!"

He's being chased in circles by a four-year-old girl with a mess of curls and a birthday tiara.

"Run, baby girl, run," Eddie's wife, Tai, also known as Nana T, calls.

"Whose side are you on, anyway?" Eddie shouts back, out of breath.

"The cute one," Tai says with a shrug. She's standing in a huddle with Heather, Dennis's husband Thomas, and Jude's parents, laughing while my daughter growls like the monster she's pretending to be.

Eddie plays his part, acting petrified. "Help," he cries. "They're gonna get me!"

"She's having a ball, isn't she?" Jude's mom beams at me as I step farther out into the yard. Not only did she welcome me with open arms, but she's also helped fill the hole left in my heart from losing my mother. She's the best mother-in-law, and an even better grandma.

I shield my eyes, using my hands like a visor. "Marjorie, honey, you're gonna make Papa Eddie pass out."

Eddie slows to a stop, panting as he braces himself with his hands on his knees. "I'll have…you know…I'm the picture…of health," he wheezes.

Marjorie squeals as she bounds toward me in her leopard print romper, bare feet against the grass, blond hair flowing wildly behind her. She barrels into me with the force of a small bull, and I scoop her into my arms.

"Are you ready for cake?" I ask, kissing her cheek.

"Yeah," she answers. "But I need Ginger Bear." Ginger Bear is her favorite toy, the one she snuggles every night as she falls asleep. His fur is a reddish brown, hence the name, and he has a patch of hair missing on his left paw from that time when Casey Kasem briefly thought Ginger Bear was his mother.

"Oh, you do, huh?" I say, starting back toward the house. "Will Ginger Bear be eating cake too?"

She nods, and I nuzzle her hair. "And where is he?"

"In my room." Her tiny voice is enough to make my heart ache.

"All right. Let's find him." I climb the steps, stopping next to Jude, who rises to tickle her.

"What are you doing, birthday girl?" he asks as she squirms and giggles.

"We've got to go get Ginger Bear," I tell him. "Do you

mind bringing everyone in for cake before we start the movie?"

"Of course." He gives me a quick kiss before I head inside, easing Marjorie to the floor. I follow her to her room where she leaps onto the bed, right next to her treasured bear. She grabs him and flops back with a grin. Her hazel eyes are heavy, and I run my fingers through her soft hair. She yawns, and I can already tell she'll be asleep within the hour.

"Have you had a good birthday today?" I ask, tugging her onto my lap.

"Mm-hmm."

"What's been the best part?"

She scrunches her little face in thought, and I'm certain she'll name the dollhouse Uncle Dennis got her, one of the many plushies she unwrapped, or the cheese pizza she ate.

"All of it," she says instead.

I melt, hugging her close. "I love you, sweet girl."

"I love you, Mommy."

It's moments like these when I wish Marjorie could be here to witness the beautiful life Jude and I have built and our spirited girl who will one day learn all about her namesake. I wish she could see how far I've come since that day she blew into my life like the hurricane she was. The lights flicker on the nightstand, and I smile to myself.

Maybe she already knows.

acknowledgments

Some ideas strike like a lightning bolt, demanding to be written immediately. Others form one sentence at a time, simmering until the moment is right. From the day I dreamed up Marjorie, I was excited to bring her to life, but after some soul-crushing losses, I fell into a pretty dark place. I seriously questioned if I was meant to be an author, if I had what it takes. I considered never writing this book. Then the sassy, loud, often demanding, always fabulous Marjorie Lockwood came along. After nearly four months together, I realized she wasn't only here for Kat. She was here for me. It was through this story that I found my voice again and along with it, a renewed sense of purpose as a storyteller. Marjorie helped me rediscover the magic that is writing, and I will forever be in her debt.

Like Kat, I have a wonderful support system of friends I could never do this without. At the top of that list is my critique partner and dear friend, Jen Davis, and trusted alpha reader and wonderful friend Kate Oscarson who both cheer me on and help ask the hard questions that help make my work shine. They've both been with me from the very first page of my career, and I hope we'll be together through the final chapter. Thank you to Kayla Kleffman who is the ultimate hype girl and friend. I'm forever thankful you popped into my DMs that day.

I could not have written this book or done life without Reah Kelly, who had the audacity to MOVE while I was finishing this book. (I know. So rude.) The two years we lived down the road from each other are some of my favorites, but there is no distance great enough to separate us. Reah, even when I die, I promise to haunt your ass like Marjorie because you aren't getting rid of me. I love you and I miss you.

Speaking of people I can't live without, I want to thank Sydney English, Tiffany Billingsly, and Abbey Ziemba who are not only three of the best and sweetest friends a girl could ask for, but who are always on my team. If you've ever met me at an event, you've probably met Sydney. She helps me keep my head on straight and makes me laugh more than just about anyone. Abbey and Tiffany are always there, happy to troubleshoot, talk plots, or cheer me on when the imposter syndrome gets too loud. I love y'all.

Thank you to The Bridge Coven Book Club who are as fabulous as they sound. My life is better, and *I* am better, because of all of you. Thank you to my family and my precious friends who are like family, Nicole Hazel, Kia Clay, Heather Weibye, and Danielle Hoegy.

I am endlessly grateful to my amazing editor and friend Chris Wheary, my cover designer Sam Pallencia of Ink and Laurel, my assistant Vanessa Valdez, and Jenny Bailey with Pen Pal PR. Thank you to my amazing street team, The Hostile Kitties. (If you've been around long enough to get that reference, please know I love you, and I couldn't do this without you.) I want to thank my favorite indie bookstores: Reading Rock Books, A Novel Romance, Bound Books, and Parnassus, and the fabulous booksellers who have championed me, especially Angela Redden, Natalie Sanford, and

Katie Garaby. Special thanks to Thomas Wallace who is not only a brilliant bookseller but one of my favorite people.

None of my books would exist without my high school English teacher, Ms Ross. Teachers are changing lives. Let's pay them more, shall we?

Big thanks go to Cassie Young with *The Bert Show* (which I love and listen to every morning) for answering my many questions about life in radio. And a giant thank you to Abigail who shared her taxidermied dog story with me and gave me her blessing to use it. Sometimes reality truly is stranger thank fiction.

To the author friends who get me, who have lifted me up, and are absolutely vital in this crazy, beautiful, magical career. Jen Davis (again and always), Abby Jimenez, Sarah Smith, Lauren H. Mae, Tarah Dewitt, Lauren Thoman, Leah Brunner, Andrea Nourse, Melissa Collings, Sophie Sinclair, Sarah Estep, Mia Heintzelman, Eve Kasey, SL Astor, Noreen Mughees, and Julie Olivia.

Thank you to my husband who helped me plot this book over wine and pasta, who has been there for every heartbreak, and cheered on every small victory. I'm so lucky to be yours.

And most of all, thank YOU, the beautiful human with this book in your hands. You are the reason I get to live my dream of telling stories, and I am so grateful you exist.

meet melissa grace

Melissa Grace is the author of the *Midnight in Dallas* romcom series, and her freelance work has been featured in publications like *Medium, Thought Catalog,* and *The Mighty*. She resides just outside of Nashville, Tennessee with her husband and many fur children. When she's not writing, she can often be found reading or curled up in her bed with snacks like a trash panda, avoiding simple tasks because of her anxiety.

Find Melissa on social media @heymelissagrace on Instagram, Threads, Facebook, and TikTok.